To

Monica,

A Chieftain's Wife

I hope you'll enjoy
Book 4 as much as
the first 3 in my series.

Thanks for making such
amazingly beautiful
dreamcatchers. You are
very gifted!
Best Wishes,
Leigh Ann Edwards
20

A Chieftain's Wife

An Irish Witch Series, Book 4

Leigh Ann Edwards

TULE
PUBLISHING

DEDICATION

I would like to dedicate this book – A Chieftain's Wife to the three males from my original family.

To my dad, Frank Edwards, I am really very grateful I had such a hard-working steadfast father. It was reassuring to know he was always someone I could depend on as a child and as I grew older.

To my little brother, Grant Edwards, who we lost at age eleven. His gentleness, endearing smile and beautiful dark brown eyes are forever treasured in my heart. Grant's love for animals, nature and life in general, were inspiring to me even though I was the eldest sibling. I miss him still and will "always" wonder what might have been.

To my brother Kerry, I've mentioned it before, but your wit and humor are gifts I appreciate very much. You have lightened the losses and many difficult times we have shared through the years. Although it's only you and me who remain from our childhood family, I'm really so glad we have each other and we can still share the many memories.

ACKNOWLEDGMENTS

I'd like to sincerely thank Meghan Farrell, Managing Editor, Lindsey Stover, Marketing and Editorial Manager, Michelle Morris, Editorial Assistant, and Sarah McDonagh, Marketing and Publicity Assistant. These four ladies at Tule Publishing are all remarkably efficient, skilled, personable, and helpful in all they do. They have assisted me in so many ways during this journey in seeing my series published and marketed. I am greatly indebted to each of them for ensuring Alainn and Killian's story continues.

Thanks to Sinclair Sawhney for her content editing. Her great ideas and insightful suggestions are always appreciated. Thanks so much to the diligent copy editors as well for your hard work in assisting me in some of the areas in which I struggle.

I would once more like to acknowledge Ravven who continues to come up with beautiful and captivating cover designs for The Irish Witch Series. I am truly in awe of her creative gifts.

I would like to say a heartfelt thanks to my wonderful family for always supporting me when I'm sure it seems my head, and probably sometimes my heart, are in sixteenth century Ireland more than with them. I am grateful they understand how passionate I am about my writing and my series.

Thanks to my great friends for your unending encouragement and the various ways you continue to assist me in realizing my dream.

I would like to say a huge thank you to the amazing readers who have been so good at reaching out to let me know how much they are enjoying my series. It is always such a delight and a confidence boost to hear there are others who love my books and want to keep reading more. Their interest and investment in the lives of Alainn and Killian makes me even happier to be able to continue creating my stories.

Chapter One

Ireland 1536

A S THE OCEAN breeze rustled her skirts and caressed her long unbound hair, Alainn O'Brien inhaled the salty sea air. She and her husband, Killian, had been living at his castle, Castle O'Donnel, for over two months now. During this time together they had finally begun to experience wondrous peace and contentment.

She attempted to simply embrace this long awaited happiness… and yet there was an undeniably ominous feeling that steadily grew within her, and threatened to disrupt their newfound joy. She had decided she wouldn't dwell upon it. Instead, she had chosen to revel in this time of serenity, unwilling to consider what uncertainties or upheaval the future might hold for her and her only love.

As she gazed out upon the beauty of the wild Irish Sea, her heart fluttered, for today she would see her man again. They had been parted for well over two weeks now; he was off at a gathering of the clans and she'd missed him much. In all the years they had known each other, even long before they'd declared their love for one another, they had never been apart for that long.

Since their arrival at Castle O'Donnel, named for Killian's mother's clan, Alainn had attempted to calm all her unusual magical abilities; she had pushed each one of them deep, deep down inside her, hopeful she would truly be capable of leading an uncomplicated life… a normal life. Yet she was loath to admit, she suspected she was only temporarily suppressing the feeling that this time of tranquility would not last. She couldn't say exactly what was bringing about this uneasiness, but something within her caused her to believe the winds of change would soon be upon them. She shook her head to dispel the disparaging thoughts and walked toward the seashore to sit for a time and soak her tired feet within the cool water.

She sat, staring out at the sea, feeling the frothy waves lapping rhythmically upon her feet, and the spray of the churning water against the rocks softly falling upon her face. She watched as a large seal lazily sunned itself on a nearby rock. When he noticed her, he slapped his flippers together jubilantly and barked out an invitation to join him.

"Not today, young friend," She smiled. "Although you know how I take much delight in swimming with you and your kind, the white crests on the waves this day keep me safely bound to the land," she said as she lovingly rubbed her belly. He nodded to her as though understanding her every word and he soon resumed his sedentary position upon the rocks.

She observed many brightly colored puffins awkwardly walking upon the shore and playfully diving beneath the water. Several vocal seagulls squawked loudly to one another as they glided gracefully against the wind. A jaunty heron scooped up a fish and dropped it so near to Alainn, she jumped, startled as the water splashed her.

"If you're thinkin' to share your meal with me, sure I'm grateful, but I prefer my fish well cooked, Mr. Heron." The tall gangly bird blinked knowingly at her and gobbled down its catch before setting off once more.

As always, during times when her mind went to dismal subjects, she calmed herself with her great affinity for nature, her deep connection to animals, and most especially loving thoughts of her husband, young and valiant, Killian O'Brien. Now that they were married and shared a bond and an intimacy she'd never even dreamed two people could know, she thought these past weeks were unbearably lonely without him.

She felt the sturdy kick within her, and a warm smile crossed her lips. Their son would be born in just over two moons. She placed her hand to her swollen belly once more and chuckled to herself. Killian would surely see a noticeable change in her for the child now grew at a rapid rate, and her belly had grown considerably also.

After she'd placidly sat for a time, she placed her hand to the small of her back as she stood, and brushed the sand from her skirts. Her waist remained small for she carried the child low and entirely frontward. When she glanced down she laughed again. She thought she looked as though she'd swallowed a wee boulder so round was her belly. And her boy-child would grow inside her for nearly two more months; surely she'd be enormous by then.

The southern sun still held lovely warmth, though the September wind that blew in from the sea brought a promise of cooler days. She pulled the woolen shawl around her shoulders and sighed. As she glanced at the sun's position, she deducted it was time she made her way back to the castle. She placed her slippers upon her feet and reluctantly turned and left the water behind her. All the years Killian had lived at Castle O'Brien, which boasted a location near the mighty River Shannon, he had spoken of how glorious it was to live near the sea, and now she knew firsthand it was truth. She adored living here.

These past weeks that he'd been away, she'd scarcely missed a day strolling along the seashore. She'd longed to explore the many intriguing caves nearby, but Killian would not be in favor of her walking near the slippery, sea-swept rocky surfaces given her advancing term, for he was fiercely protective of her and their unborn child.

She had nearly lost the child over three moons earlier and it had caused much consternation and fear for both of them. There had been an attempt on her life. She had been struck with a dart that contained a potent poison and, in truth, she had very nearly died. She absent-mindedly caressed the protective amulet that hung from the silver chain around her neck. It had been charmed by her mother, Mara, soon after Alainn was born and more recently by her grandfather, a gifted druid.

Killian had sometimes questioned the power within the amulet after she'd been purposely attacked and poisoned, and why it hadn't prevented the mishap entirely. As with any strain of magic, there was seldom a concise answer. Perhaps the amulet had partially protected her and had been the very reason she had lived through the ordeal. Even with all the many supernatural powers and intuitive abilities she possessed, she was often left with many unanswered questions and not a few doubts.

Although Alainn was hesitant to admit it, she believed it was because of her unusual magical abilities she had drawn the attention of any number of evil beings and untoward creatures and, regrettably, she probably always would. An unwelcome shiver ran up and down her spine for even a magically charmed amulet would surely not be capable of protecting her against those types of dark enemies and that level of evil.

Once again, she pushed the unpleasant memories and fearful thoughts from her mind and lingered only on their present happiness. She steadied her uneasiness by allowing hers thoughts to drift back to her beloved, Killian.

He had sent a messenger a week earlier, alerting her to his late return and though he was not to be expected home for at least another two days, he would be here by sunset today. Often times her unusual abilities were not welcomed for she had been an apt seer all her life. There had been many instances in her seven and ten years when she would have gladly traded that ability, but not this day. Today she had awoken knowing she would be in her husband's arms this night and she'd spent the entire day anticipating that with great pleasure. She'd alerted Cookson, their head cook who had come with them from Castle O'Brien, that Killian would be home for the evening meal and she hoped it would give him ample time to prepare a glorious feast. He had assured her it would.

As Alainn pleasantly meandered through the verdant glens that clearly resembled a patchwork quilt of varying shades of green, interrupted only by the numerous for-mations of winding stone walls, she stopped briefly and leaned against one of the uneven moss-covered stone struc-tures. She listened to the soothing sound of the plentiful waterfalls tumbling down the rock face of the nearby hills.

She hesitantly glanced toward the location of the adja-cent raised ground that formed a large perfect circle, a fairy ring. The local folk were most fearful and suspicious of these fairy forts. They were adamant they remain undisturbed and often were hesitant to go anywhere near them.

Alainn could distinctly hear the lovely familiar music and the many soft voices of the fairies and other mystical crea-tures that dwelled within. They were whispering softly to her, beckoning her to come spend time with them… and a part of her ached to do so. But, as she'd done so many times in the past weeks, she resisted. She was attempting to quiet her own magical abilities entirely, as well as terminate her association with all things supernatural. She turned away from the enchanting call of the fairies, lifted her skirts, and hurried on past the fairy ring, once more ignoring the deep desire to enter the magical realm.

As Alainn continued on homeward, she could see the familiar, distant grey outline of Castle O'Donnel. It was an undeniably grand structure. Castle O'Brien, where she had lived most of her life, had been built by the Normans and was a tall imposing castle, but not nearly as large as Castle O'Donnel, for it was magnificently massive and sprawled widely over a considerable area. There were many adjoining structures that had been erected in different eras by various kings and chieftains. The parapets were enormous and the giant turrets seemed to reach up to the clouds. She had spent many a day searching through the nearly endless chambers, alcoves and corridors within the castle's walls. It had taken some time, but she believed she had surveyed nearly every inch of the castle she was proud to now call her home.

Alainn passed the grove of apple trees and noticed there were several still heavy with ripened fruit. An apple dessert would be a delicious addition to the banquet, and she would be most pleased to make the dish herself for it was Killian's favorite. When she'd first arrived, the servants had been disbelieving that a woman of noble station would be compelled to spend time in the kitchen and even lend a hand when it was needed, but she dearly missed being in a kitchen where she had spent much of her life.

Alainn thought it unlikely the servants here knew much of her past history. For although she was the granddaughter of Niall O'Rorke one of Ireland's most important and influential chieftains, that had only recently been discovered. She had lived most of her life believing she was a farrier's daughter, a servant of lowly birth. She had been a healer, a respected and revered herbalist, but a servant to Chieftain Hugh O'Brien and his kin. Killian was Hugh's nephew and she and Killian had fallen in love even though their love was greatly forbidden. They had secretly married much to the fury of Killian's uncle, but that, too, was long since in the past and as always Alainn tried to keep her disagreeable thoughts of Hugh O'Brien far distanced from her mind. She seldom allowed herself to recall the many unpleasant memories involving the ill-favored man.

She missed his wife, Lady Siobhan, though, and their son Rory O'Brien, her cousin. Lady Siobhan was a daughter to Niall O'Rorke and Rory, his grandson. Rory had been a friend throughout her life and both he and Killian had never treated her as a girl of low station, but as an equal, long before it had proven to be true.

As she filled her frock's apron with the juicy red apples, she heard a horse approaching and she smiled up at Mac-

Kenzie MacCarther. He was a huge burly man, a Scot who had lived in Ireland for over two decades and Captain of the Guard of Killian's large army. He was also a valued friend to Killian and Alainn. He had once been in the employ of Hugh O'Brien, but had a falling out with the man and now served as his nephew's captain.

"Lady O'Brien, you should not be reaching so high in your delicate condition, nor carrying such a heavy load, it can no be good for the wee bairn you carry."

"Mac, I swear if you address me as Lady O'Brien one more time I'll pitch the entire lot of these apples at you, and I've a good arm! You have known me all my life and my title is not a requirement when you speak to me."

The large Scot smiled down at her from his position atop the huge steed.

"Aye, that may well be, but you are a lady now, Alainn. And your husband wouldna be so verra pleased to see you carrying that load."

"Sure you're correct about that. He's undoubtedly protective of me, and he's clearly enlisted you in keeping watch over me as much as the castle and his land in his stead."

"Aye, well the lad loves ye well, lass. And he'd not be liable to loosen his grip on ye, even if you didn't carry his bairn."

Alainn beamed at Mac's statement and, as she placed her hand to her belly, the unborn child issued a hearty blow. She smiled as she saw the apples tumble from their nest in her frock. The bulky man dismounted and grabbed several handfuls of the ripe fruit placing them in his saddle pouch.

"I'd offer you a ride back to the castle on my horse, but I know you've not ridden in these past months."

"Aye, since the dreadful fright we had when we nearly lost the babe, I've not been on a horse. And I do so miss it. But, soon enough, when our son is born, I'll be back upon a horse, and the child soon after, for sure he'll be as able a horseman as his father one day."

"Aye, well, his mother's no slouch in that area either. I have a clear picture of you as a child, ridin' bareback across the glens with your lovely golden hair flyin' out behind you. In truth, you were probably too young to be out alone on a grown horse, but you've always been a spirited lass and not one to be held back or told what to do."

"I know I must have seemed most difficult at times, though it was truly not my intention."

"Och, 'tis not a crime to be spirited, lass, though I can't say I'd be declaring that so readily if you were my daughter or my wife!" He chuckled. "And would you like me to take these apples to young Cookson, then?"

"No, they can be taken to the kitchen, Mac, but you may tell Cookson I'll be makin' a sweet dessert myself for my husband's dinner."

"This day?" the captain quizzed doubtfully.

"Aye, this day, Mac!" A bright smile crossed her full rosy lips. "Even as we speak, Killian is on his journey homeward, in only hours he'll be back here with me!"

The man was one of few who knew of the young woman's many supernatural abilities for he had witnessed them firsthand, on more than one occasion.

"Aye, well, I'll tell the tower guards to be on watch for his return. I'll alert you to his arrival, then."

"There's no need, Mac, I'll know as soon as he's near. My heart will know." She smiled as she spoke and she was pleased to hear his thoughts in believing he'd never known a couple so entirely in love as Killian O'Brien and his young bride.

⌘

AS ALAINN CONTINUED walking she heard a familiar voice within her mind. She grinned as she listened telepathically to the soldier and druid, Danhoul Calhoun. He was a young man who was claimed many unusual abilities, many likened to her own. He had assisted Killian in protecting her back at Castle O'Brien. Her grandfather had once suggested Danhoul might come live at his castle so that he would be close by should he be needed again. It had been determined that Killian and Danhoul were to be Alainn's guardians and protectors. However, Danhoul had reasoned she and Killian needed this time alone to begin their new life together. He had since returned to his life as a bonnacht in the Irish army.

On occasion Danhoul's voice would come to her and she always welcomed his telepathic thoughts for he seemed to understand her perhaps more than anyone else. He evidently was aware she was keeping her magical abilities at bay so it had been some time since he had sent his thoughts to her.

"*Are you well, Alainn?*" Danhoul asked straightaway.

"*Aye, I feel well enough. Sure I tire more easily than I might if I wasn't carrying a large, strong babe within me, but I am well.*"

Something in his tone had made Alainn wary.

"*What is it Danhoul? What causes you to be fretful?*"

"*Nothin' really... nothin' I can actually put my finger on, but maybe that's what troubles me the most!*" he admitted.

"*Have you had a foreboding premonition, then?*" she queried.

"*No... well, aye, I have foreseen a small battle involving your husband and his kin.*"

"*You what... where... when... is Killian well? Has he been harmed?*"

She could detect the regretful tone in his words that came to her and he attempted to quell her fears.

"*No, truly all is well with your husband! I simply thought I would put your mind at ease lest you had a fearful presentiment of your own regarding the event.*" He assured her.

"*Perhaps I should not have distanced my abilities as I have. How will I be capable of alerting those dear to me of oncoming peril if I do not allow myself to use my gifts? Yet my magical powers have caused much discord as well. Sure, it is a conundrum for me, Danhoul. It has been an encumbrance to me for so long, for I know not what to do.*"

Morag, the old healer who raised me, always insisted I keep my powers hidden lest I be persecuted because of them. Yet, Mara, the woman I have discovered is my mother was of opposing beliefs in that regard. Now, my paternal grandfather who is a powerful druid believes I should become much accomplished in the use of my magic. But I want my wee child to know a life of normalcy. Sure, I know not what to do. Might you advise me, Danhoul!

His voice came to her again and she welcomed his thoughts on the perplexing topic.

"Nay, 'tis not a simple decision, and often our abilities are not actually within our control. I believe they were gifted to us for a purpose and that perhaps your grandfather is correct, it would be wise to both develop and harness them. Yet, I do understand with the use of these powers comes great responsibility and often dire consequences, as well."

She nodded her head to the emptiness beside her as though her were actually there conversing with her. Her eyes narrowed and her brow creased with concern.

"I continue to have the reoccurring vision regarding Killian, and my cousins Rory and Riley's death; it frightens me to the core each time. I fear for all of them every time they are away, that it may actually come to pass. It is why I have insisted they must never travel together or be together at one location at any time!"

"Aye, and I am aware that Riley doesn't take kindly to your suggestions!"

"No, he does not welcome my abilities, nor have faith in

their accuracy. He never has."

As the wind grew stronger against her face, Alainn turned her head and lifted her nose to the air. There was something amiss, most certainly an ill omen blowing on the breeze and she shivered to calm the dread she felt.

"Aye, I feel it as well!" He did not try to keep his growing concern from her any longer.

"Do you sense what it is, Danhoul? Is it a restless spirit or a being associated with the dark demon that once pursued me?"

"Sure, I can't say for certain but, at the moment, I believe it may actually be a person simply intent on causing much havoc. I will see what I can find out by way of my powers and you, Lady O'Brien, must do what you can to ensure you and the wee babe continue to remain well. So wipe those unpleasant thoughts from your mind and put a broad smile on your face for when your husband arrives this night."

That certainly brought a bright smile to her face when Danhoul confirmed her premonition of Killian's early arrival.

"You know he'll be distressed if he senses a hint of melancholia or learns you're fretting about anything at all, so be happy, elegant and noble Lady O'Brien!"

She turned up her nose at his insistence at referring to her by her title and she laughed out loud.

"Aye, my guardian, wise druid master and brave bonnacht!" She giggled.

"Oh, be off with you, Alainn!" He jested at her sarcasm and she heard his laughter, too, as she turned and headed

down the stone path that led to the massive castle.

⌘

WHEN SHE WAS a safe distance away, Danhoul allowed himself to appear in physical form. He lowered his head, kicked at the ground, and cussed out loud. His abilities were telling him he would be needed here most assuredly, that Alainn and Killian would soon be plagued with many troubling times and harrowing unpleasantness. Something or someone appeared to be blocking him from being able to determine where the vexation was coming from.

Chapter Two

A S ALAINN CUT in to one of the pans of apple desserts she'd left cooling near the open window, she sampled a warm juicy sliver.

"Oh, Cookson, 'tis lovely and sweet. You simply must try some!"

The husky young man, whom at the moment was up to his elbows in bread dough smiled warmly at her spirited and cheerful enthusiasm.

"I've no doubt it's sweet; you've managed to use half my honey supply to make your husband's favorite dish. And I'll taste some in a moment, but you may have noticed, I've no free hand just now."

She smiled back at the man before her who had been a lifelong friend. Cookson, whose actual name was Joseph, came from a family who had been kind and generous to Alainn her entire life. His parents, Seamus and Margaret Kilkenny were extremely important to Alainn, and Cookson's sister, Molly, was her dearest friend. In truth, the Kilkennys were the closest Alainn had to an actual family before she'd been wed to Killian.

Alainn sliced another hearty serving of the sticky dessert and shoved it in the mouth of the unsuspecting young man. He nearly choked for he'd clearly not anticipated it and Alainn laughed at the man's reaction.

"Jesus, Mary and Joseph, you might warn a man if you're goin' to literally force him to sample yer cookin'!" He finally managed when he'd choked down the food.

Her friend possessed a boisterous, contagious laugh and Alainn giggled happily. She wiped her very sticky hands on her frock and then attempted to push the many wisps of long blonde hair from her face which only proved to cause her lengthy hair to stick to her face unbecomingly.

They heard a displeased sound behind them and Alainn turned to look into the face of Maire O'Donnel. She was the wife of Killian's mother's cousin, Cormac O'Donnel, another important chieftain of the O'Donnel clan. Alainn had only met the woman twice before, and neither meeting had been entirely favorable. Now the woman appeared filled with disdain at the sight she beheld, and she clucked her tongue in a disapproving manner meant to belittle Alainn.

"Lady O'Brien, your behavior is hardly fittin' of a chieftain's wife; you do your husband no favor by acting so entirely unladylike, fraternizing with the servants, or acting brazenly with another man. And look at your messy frock, girl, it is improper to appear so uncaring of your own appearance. Most women of your station don't typically care to be seen once they reach this point in their term. Sure it would be more proper and acceptable to be kept concealed within your chambers."

Alainn wanted to scold the woman, but she glanced at the meek woman who stood beside the chieftain's wife. Eireen Flannery was a kind, gentle woman, and one who disliked conflict or discord. She and her husband, Fergus, the castle's steward, had lived in Castle O'Donnel most of their lives. And in all the years since Killian's mother had died and his father had been missing and presumed dead, the man had aptly run the castle while waiting for Killian to follow in his father's footsteps and take over as chieftain.

Eireen was clearly awaiting Alainn's reaction to the other woman's unkind words, for she had learned Alainn O' Brien was not only undisputedly spirited, but not one to hold her tongue no matter what the situation.

Alainn glanced back at Cookson for he, too, was obviously expecting his friend to deal severely with the unpleasant woman. Alainn smiled warmly and set them both at ease. She had decided she would not let this woman darken her day or spoil her jubilant mood.

"Maire, 'tis so very good to see you. Have you missed your man as much as I've missed mine? Have you come in need of company?"

The sweetness Alainn was showing clearly took the other woman aback, especially after her own insensitive and critical words.

"I am much accustomed to being without the company

of my husband and you might do the same. A chieftain's duties oft take him away for long periods and with the English so near and ever present, it is likely soon they'll seldom be here with us, unless it is to defend their castles."

"Have you had further word of the English approaching?" The seriousness in Alainn's tone and the concern in her startling blue eyes were evident.

"Aye, a messenger brought word this day. I have been informed both your husband and mine were in battle only days ago with a band of English near Dublin."

Alainn was well pleased Danhoul had warned her of the battle Killian had taken part in and she trusted Danhoul entirely when he said Killian was unharmed, and yet her heart sank at the possibility of the outcome being less fortunate.

"Were there losses?" Alainn felt her heart constrict as she dared to ask the question.

"No losses on our side, only minor wounds, I am told!"

Alainn breathed a heavy sigh of relief and slowly lowered herself to the stool as she absent-mindedly wiped her sticky hands on her apron again.

"You appear tired, milady! Allow me to escort you to your bedchamber for a time. You should rest; your long walk to the seaside had surely tired you this day." Eireen suggested.

Alainn sensed the caring woman wanted to berate the older woman standing beside her for both insulting her chieftain's wife and causing her to be fret regarding her husband. Eireen gently touched Alainn's shoulder in concern. Alainn pulled herself from her thoughts and smiled at the empathetic woman.

"No, I am well enough, Eireen, but I thank you for your genuine concern."

"You walk to the sea yourself, and at this stage of your term? Sure that can't be good for the babe; you're liable to lose the child if you behave so recklessly. I tell you once again you should take to your chamber straightaway and remain there until the child is born for 'tis vulgar to openly display your condition and draw attention so boldly to the fact you share your husband's bed!" Maire blurted.

Alainn could still her tongue no longer and she glared at the woman as she spoke.

"I will not lose my babe, and I will most certainly not lie in wait liken to an invalid because I carry a child. I am well and in sturdy health, and not ashamed I carry a child. I relish being with child; I adore carrying Killian's babe. I will not be made to feel shameful because my belly grows or because I have shared a bed with my husband. I suspect most people are either learned or perceptive enough to know what causes a swelling belly and I'll not be hidden away for fear people might reach that very conclusion. And I will spend time in the kitchen, with my dear friend, Cookson and *whomever* else I please, *whenever* I please for I do not in any manner need to answer to *you*, Maire O'Donnel!"

The woman was clearly startled at the younger woman's outburst, but retorted in an equally confrontational tone.

"And if your behavior causes discord for your husband and reflects badly on him as a chieftain, would you not then feel shame, Lady O'Brien? Have you no absolutely notion how to conduct yourself as a chieftain's wife?"

Alainn proudly held her chin high in defiance as she replied. She wrinkled her nose and glowered at the troublesome woman.

"Perhaps you might inform me then, Maire, write me out a lengthy list of rules to abide by so that I might act accordingly."

The woman narrowed her cold eyes at Alainn, but did not speak, therefore Alainn continued on with her ranting.

"And sure my behavior will in no way affect my husband's good name. Killian's merit and reputation have already been firmly established. He is respected and his word is seldom questioned even by men who have been chieftains much longer than he. He has an apt understanding of our country's politics and an uncommon ability to rally men. Perhaps his knowledge of strategy in battle, together with the fact he can best any man with his sword or sway them with his authority and eloquence, has ensured his swift appointment to the council of the clans. He is the youngest chieftain ever to be sworn to council."

"Aye, my husband is proud to be in allegiance with yours and 'tis true your man seems to have made a name for himself in an uncommonly short time. Though being members of the council does tend to keep men away from their homes and families. I can attest to that fact."

That would be a definite drawback having Killian away from her so much, but she knew it was necessary to keep peace in the country and hopefully to keep the English at bay.

"Would you care for some apple dessert, Maire? It appears I have made enough for half the county." Alainn hoped to make peace with the woman after snapping at her for Killian did think it was important to be on the good side of his kin.

"Not this day, Lady O'Brien, perhaps another, for I must be off, my coachman waits."

⌘

ALAINN SAT SOAKING in the large round tub that Killian had recently employed the castle's carpenter to make for them. He knew of her love of bathing even though many believed it was not proper to wash any part of one's body other than the hands and face. Many were of the belief warm water might allow evil into a body as well. Alainn thought that was a ridiculous notion. She adored the sensation of feeling clean and smelling fresh. As she soaped her protruding belly with the rose-scented soap she'd created just this week, she inhaled the lovely scent and tried unsuccessfully to keep her thoughts from Maire O'Donnel.

She believed the woman was entirely incorrect regarding her views on women with child. How could it be improper to allow people to see her simply because she carried her husband's child? It was not considered sinful to share a physical relationship with her husband, it was how it was meant to be, the way the lord intended it. In truth, Alainn thought it was possibly the greatest gift ever given to a man and woman.

Even women as apparently staunchly Catholic as Maire couldn't truly think it was sinful to be out and about simply because a woman carried a child. The woman had six grown children of her own so it was evident she shared her husband's bed, or did at one time at the very least. But perhaps part of what the woman had said might have rung a hint of truth, for Alainn often wondered if she possessed the ability to be a proper wife to a chieftain. She knew precious little about living life as a noble, and practically nothing about what truly might be required of her, what might assist Killian in his dealings as a man of importance.

As she rinsed her lengthy hair, she tried to push the dismal thoughts from her mind. Alainn had vowed she would not let the unpleasant woman or her spiteful words dampen her joyful mood, but she'd fallen short of her good intentions as they nagged at her long after the woman had gone. Between the meeting with Maire and the worrisome conversation she'd had with Danhoul, she was beginning to feel most maudlin. She heard a soft knock on the door and she placed a wrap around her body and called out.

"Come in, Eireen!"

"Milady, do you need assistance with dressing this day? I might secure the fastenings for you, if you need?"

"I am capable for now, Eireen, but stay and speak with me awhile; keep me company if you've time." Alainn called out as she stepped behind the partition in her chambers. Alainn had turned down Killian's offer to employ a hand-maid, for she did not desire assistance with menial matters of a personal nature, but Alainn recognized Eireen's caring, motherly nature and knew she hoped to dispel some of this afternoon's displeasure.

"Aye, I've time if you wish it, milady!"

"You know you can call me by my given name, Eireen. I feel old and matronly when people refer to me as milady. Sure you're not more than a dozen years older than I am and I consider you my friend."

"Oh, milady, it would not be proper of me to speak to you in such a manner, and my husband would disapprove entirely."

Alainn did not actually dislike the woman's husband. It could not be disputed that he was a diligent and loyal servant to Killian and had always been completely respectful of Alainn, but she was not always pleased with how he treated his wife. She was considerably younger than the man and was his second wife. The couple had no children, and apparently his first wife had died in child bed. However, the child of that union had lived and was now a grown woman and married to Killian's carpenter. Alainn had never met the young woman for the man lived miles from the castle in a wooded area necessary for his trade.

Alainn knew through her abilities as a seer that Eireen and her husband's daughter did not see eye to eye on much. And because Alainn liked Eireen so well Alainn had already formed an unfavorable opinion of her stepdaughter, Ciara, without ever having met her.

Alainn donned her chemise and then pulled her pale green gown over her ever-growing body. She had employed the tailor to create a handful of new gowns for her, for the ones she'd worn only weeks earlier were no longer capable of being fastened. As she glanced down at the lovely soft gown, she saw the movements clearly visible even through the fabric. She smiled at the sight and was certain she could almost make out the outline of a wee foot. She rubbed the location and was rewarded with a swift response. How she adored the wee babe within her, her darling son, and she couldn't wait to look upon him and to hold him in her arms, to rock him and sing to him. How could she possibly feel shame at the treasure she carried within her or how he'd been created?

"Are you quite well, milady? You've been unusually quiet this afternoon. Don't allow that spiteful gossipmonger of a woman and her unfeeling comments color your elation in carryin' a child. It is the greatest of bestowments to carry your man's child and I would give much to have a child of my own. It was apparently not meant to be for me. I have conceived many times, but only carried for but a few weeks and then lost each one. It was a grievous loss to me each time, and now I am not likely to carry another for 'tis only on the rarest of occasions does my husband ever care to share my bed any longer."

Alainn stepped out from behind the partition and caught the notable sadness in the other woman's eyes and in her tone. She looked empathetically at the woman.

"Forgive me, milady, I have truly misspoken, I should not be relating such intimate information with another, I don't know what's come over me. I do not share such talk with anyone much less my chieftain's wife! I have felt at ease with you from the time you came to this castle, but I cannot say why that information just slipped so readily from my mouth."

Alainn smiled and sat upon the settee. She turned her back to the other woman so that she might fasten the lacings to her gown.

"I am pleased to have you speak to me so candidly, Eireen. It is a great relief to have a woman to speak with. My mother lives far from here and we have never had a close relationship. Although my cousin's wife, Mary, and I have become fast friends, she is off in Scotland visiting her kin. She was dreadfully homesick for her family and her land, though in her most recent letter she says she will return to

Ireland soon. So, you may feel free to speak of whatever topics you desire for it is a great pleasure to have a female friend to converse with."

"I do feel as though we are friends, milady!"

"We are friends, Eireen."

The other woman gently fastened the lacing of the gown and then helped brush out Alainn's full lengthy golden tresses.

"Would you like me to plait it for you, milady?"

"Aye, I would appreciate it, for when it is damp and placed within a plait when I remove the plait this night it will appear to have many curls. I have always greatly desired to have curly hair."

"Oh, not a word of it, milady! You have the loveliest hair I've ever seen; my husband has even made mention of your hair, and he never notices anything of that sort. It is the shiniest, softest hair I have ever seen and so full and radiant. And you may not have curls but it is abundant with lovely waves."

"Aye, that's what Killian says. He adores my hair. He says when it falls upon his chest when we make…"

She stopped mid-sentence and her cheeks blushed a warm pink, the other woman questioned.

"What were you about to say, milady?"

"It was something not meant for ears other than my own. I was thinkin' aloud I suppose. I have missed being with my husband in an intimate fashion and I am eagerly awaitin' this night!"

The woman's eyes grew wide and round as she spoke. "You and your husband continue to be partake in such activities so late in your term? Oh, milady, that was horridly improper and disrespectful of me to ask such a personal question, and sure it is none of my concern. I just, I've never… Is it even possible when you have blossomed so much and so quickly?"

Alainn smiled at the other woman's discomfort and embarrassment.

"Aye, we do. Well, we did only weeks ago, sure my belly has grown, but my husband is a most imaginative man and a gifted lover, sure we'll find a way."

"Oh, milady!" The woman tittered at Alainn's bold talk. She placed her hand over her mouth but couldn't conceal her smile. Then she added a comment that Alainn would not have expected from the usually quiet, reserved woman. "Perhaps your husband might offer mine a wee bit of advice."

Chapter Three

KILLIAN RODE ALONG side his cousin, Riley, and Riley's grandfather, Niall O'Rorke. The day had been long on horseback for they'd started out before dawn and now dusk was approaching. Niall appeared visibly weary and earlier Killian had encouraged both the men who accompanied him and the guards who rode with them, to take a room at an inn along the way. He'd assured them he would be safe enough traveling the remaining leg of the journey alone, but they would hear none of it. They knew he was eager to get home and rather than have him travel alone or with a guard, they pushed on as well.

Niall assured them he could rest for days once he made it to his own castle, and that his granddaughter would soon prepare an elixir to ease the tired ache within his bones, and so they had continued on. But now by the look of exhaustion on the old man's weathered face, Killian felt he should have stopped as well, and spent another night without Alainn. The very thought made him feel empty inside, for this time apart from her had seemed insufferably long.

He'd found the council meetings tedious and often

proved little for sometimes it was liken to dealing with unreasonable children, listening to the bickering and disputes between the clans. And the arguing had led to more than a few fistfights and the drawing of swords had been commonplace. How were the clans ever to come to any agreement in how to deal with the English if they couldn't even put away their differences of opinion for the good of Ireland? Some of the chieftains were so damned long-winded he'd wanted to shout in frustration. And the entertainment had been hardly necessary and much of it unappreciated, though he thought he was clearly outnumbered in that opinion for the majority of the chieftains were a raucous lot. He glanced at Niall once more and slowed his horse.

"Are you well, Niall? You look sorely tired and you must accept my apology in forcin' the long journey this day."

"Ah, Killian, I'm most weary, 'tis true enough, but you hardly forced me. Though in light of the recent battle with the damnable English, I'd not have wanted you to travel without kin or clan, sure I could have chosen to stay at an inn as you suggested. I well know how eager you are to get home to my granddaughter, especially in her increasing term."

"Aye, you know me well, Niall. Though my wife would hardly thank me for getting' home a day earlier if it causes her grandfather any ill effects, I'd suggest!"

"Oh, cousin, you can do no wrong in Alainn's eyes, you know that by now, and I think it would have taken more than the armies of our clans combined to keep you away from your wife another night."

Killian smiled at his cousin, Riley, and nodded his head. In truth he could scarcely contain the urge to gallop the few remaining miles to his castle. The elderly man glanced at him and smiled.

"Oh, be off with you then, lad! Go on to her, let your steed run wild, for he's clearly not been worn out by this day's journey. We'll stop by soon enough to speak our greetings to Alainn, but you go now."

He smiled at the older man and was thankful for his druid ability of hearing his thoughts. He nodded to Riley, who smiled back, but shook his head at how his cousin appeared unable to get to Alainn fast enough.

"Go on then, you haven't been able to keep up a decent or stimulating conversation in the past few hours at any rate, so go and give your woman a warm embrace for me as well, if you can still manage to get your arms around her."

"Cousin, if you say one unkind comment to my wife regardin' her lovely growin' belly, I swear I'll kick your arse or blacken both your eyes! Riley O'Brien, you would think you'd never seen a woman with child, the way you carry on about her lovely wee belly."

"Because she has a slender frame, I'm only concerned she'll not be able to walk soon enough if she gets any larger, and I've not seen her in these two weeks."

"Not a word!" Killian sternly warned and then he could

wait no longer, he turned his immense grey stallion home-ward and galloped off at an uncommon speed.

ALAINN STOOD ON the castle steps looking out at the sunset. It was beautiful and brilliant and the pink and crimson tones blended with the splashes of orange and gold in lovely contrast shining through the billowing cloud filled sky. She was so excited she felt as though she could leap with joy, if she could actually leap, that was. She could sense Killian drawing nearer to her and she closed her eyes to envision how near he was. She squealed in delight and the guard who stood nearest the drawbridge looked at her as though she was entirely daft.

"You may begin to lower the drawbridge, Ian. My husband will be here by the time it is lowered in place!"

"I've had no signal from the guards in the watch tower or on the other side, Milady!"

"Tis true enough, but trust me, for it is as I have said. I am a seer, Ian, a druid seer, granddaughter to Niall O' Rorke, a great chieftain, but also a noted druid priest."

"Aye, milady!"

Though the man looked as though he wasn't completely convinced, he gave the signal to the man at the levers and the large timbers and weighty chains holding the sprawling drawbridge, began to creak and groan under the enormous weight.

The evening wind had grown cooler and Alainn pulled her shawl around her shoulders as she glanced up at the rustling leaves on the surrounding trees. Many had begun to change color and soon autumn would be upon them. It would be early this year, she obsereved, but had little time to dwell on that for she heard the thundering of a horse's hooves upon the bridge. She squinted in the dusk to make out the outline of Storm, Killian's huge steed. It was an unusually large horse, over seventeen hands, but Killian O'Brien needed a large horse for he was a man of grand proportions. He was taller than nearly all men and he towered over her when they stood together. He was muscular and brawny and entirely strong and stalwart.

By now she could see Killian and she immediately began to move up and down on her toes. As a child, and even now as an adult, whenever she was excited beyond control, she would begin her "wee dance" as Killian had always referred to it Killian and her cousins Riley and Rory O'Brien had often taunted her about the unique habit. At present the guard beside her was looking at her like she'd lost her mind entirely. What a sight she must be so clearly laden with child, and squealing like a young child herself and now bouncing up and down. The man surely thought Killian O'Brien had wed an impulsive wee girl who was perhaps not quite right in the head.

She started down the many stone steps and made it to the bottom the same time Killian pulled the horse to a halt.

He leapt off the horse with grace and agility not expected from a man with such physical grandness. He dropped the reins and ran to her, scooping her up into his arms. She squealed again in complete delight.

"Oh, Killian!" She gushed as she threw her arms around his neck.

She inhaled his familiar masculine scent and felt his warm full lips upon hers. The kiss was lengthy and heated by the time it was through. When they finally managed to break from the kiss, he looked down at her with such intense happiness she placed her hands on his stubbled cheeks and her lips on his once more. This time she grew dizzy with how passionate the kiss was. And the guard who stood not far from them surely thought his chieftain might have his way with his wife there on the steps of the castle.

"Oh, Lainna, my darlin' Lainna! I have missed you so. I hope never ever to be parted from you for such an insufferable amount of time. My God, it is has felt like an eternity!"

"Aye, Killian! I think it has been an eternity. How I have missed you holding me. This night I intend to spend every moment in these arms." She caressed his muscular arms with alluring promise as he looked down into her eyes.

"Aye, well, we can't get to our bedchamber fast enough by my estimation, Lainna! But, let me look at you a moment!"

"And, once you do, you might soon change your mind about headin' to our bed!"

"Not ever, my Lainna. You are an enchantment, a vision of loveliness and so beautifully radiant now that you are with child. I have missed you much and missed bein' with you so, I want to love you as soon as possible. But, how is our son, then, is he well, are the two of you well? My messenger brought me your letters and I cherished them. Sorry, I am that I had to be away so long, my love."

"I know your presence at the council is necessary, Killian; I would never question that. I have known for very long you would be an important man, a respected chieftain and it is already so. I am proud of you, husband!"

He beamed at her and even in the limited daylight his deep green eyes charmed her as no actual magic ever could. He finally released her from his arms and set her to standing on the ground beside him. He knelt down before her and placed his hands to her belly.

"Ah, he's grown much, Alainn, and how strong his kicks are now! Sure, that must be uncomfortable for you, for you've a slight build, and he's clearly a sturdy wee babe."

"Like his father; and I don't find his movements uncomfortable, Killian. I adore them; I revel in them. I love him so, and I love you, Killian. I am more blessed than any woman in all of Ireland."

He placed a soft kiss on her belly and Alainn happily sensed Killian was almost driven to tears at the complete joy and love he felt for her and their unborn child. He stood once more, gathered her in his arms and held her tight and before a moment had passed their eyes locked and soon after their lips followed suit, which was how Riley O'Brien and Niall O'Rorke found them moments later as their horses came across the bridge.

"My God, Killian, have you not got done with the kissin' by now, or at the very least not gotten on to somethin' a little more pleasurable!"

"You've clearly never kissed my wife!" Killian pulled himself from the kiss long enough to respond to his cousin's taunting.

Alainn smiled at Killian and turned to greet her grandfather and her cousin.

Riley O'Brien was cousin to both Killian and Alainn. Killian and Riley's fathers had been brothers and Lady Siobhan, Riley's mother, was sister to Alainn's father, Teige O'Rorke. Alainn had never met her father and only learned of her paternal connections recently. In truth, Teige O'Rorke had not been seen by his family since before Alainn was born. No one knew if the man still lived, and if he did, his whereabouts were unknown.

Alainn smiled at the two men and stepped closer to them as they dismounted. Her grandfather hugged her to him affectionately and smiled.

"You look lovely and radiant, Granddaughter, and very happy, considerably happier I am certain now that you are reunited with your husband?"

"Aye, much happier, Grandfather!"

With that she smiled up at Killian and when their eyes met, she was by his side, in his arms and sharing another kiss before she could greet her cousin.

"My God, Killian, just take her to bed then!"

"Aye, sure I plan to, Riley; never you doubt that!"

When Alainn finally left his arms and went to embrace her cousin, he seemed dumbfounded as to what to say after he'd actually viewed her.

"By God's bones, Alainn, your belly is apt to burst if it grows any larger. And Killian tells me you've nearly another two moons till your term is through and your time is here. You'll surely not be able to walk, I'd wager, and you might forget about the beddin' Killian, for I doubt you'll actually be able to accomplish it!"

Alainn stood staring intently at her cousin, her eyes wide and her mouth agape. Killian noticed and he threw his cousin a displeased look. Through the years, there had been many times that he had been forced to act as peacekeeper between these two and it was often not an easy or desirable task.

"Do you want me to deal with your untactful cousin, Alainn, or would you like to attend to him with some form of magic spell?" Killian only half jested.

Alainn glanced mischievously at Killian and then to her grandfather.

"Might I turn your grandson into a mule, Grandfather?"

"In truth, I think he is already a bit of an ass, Alainn, but if you feel you must, so be it! I'll see to it he has adequate food and a reasonably comfortable stall in the stables."

Riley knew very little of the druid ways as he had always been completely unwilling to accept druidism. He also was disbelieving of many of Alainn's supernatural abilities and, although he had witnessed some of her unusual powers, clearly, he didn't know whether what she'd just spoken of could truly be accomplished. Alainn continued on with the jesting for she had caught the look of utter uncertainty on her cousin's face. She mumbled something in the druid language that meant nothing but gibberish, but Riley didn't know that.

"Alainn, what are you doing? Don't do anythin' rash now! I did not mean to insult you, and I didn't say you're not still bonny and fine, for of course you are. From behind you cannot even tell you carry a child, for you still have a narrow, slender waist and you've not a large unattractive backside, not like those women whose arse gets as wide as an axe handle when they carry. Neither is your face swollen and unattractive nor liken to a bloated hog as are some women when they are about to birth a child. And I apologize if you thought I was rude. In truth, you're surely still the loveliest girl ever created. I was just surprised to see how much the child has grown."

He stammered and stuttered and soon Killian was laughing earnestly at Riley's frightened face and his groveling toward his cousin. The elderly man standing with them chuckled as well. Alainn finally relented and placed a quick apologetic kiss on Riley's cheek.

"Grandfather, you and Riley must come in and join us for our evening meal. Cookson has been working all day to create a wonderful feast for you. And I have made a dessert as well."

"You did, Alainn?" Killian asked, grinning widely at the thought of his wife helping out in the kitchen for he knew how much she enjoyed such activities.

"Is it actually edible?" Riley queried.

"By God, Riley, 'tis no wonder your own wife left the country to have a time apart from you. You clearly have no notion how to deal with the fairer gender." Killian shook his head as he lifted his own wife into his arms and effortlessly carried her up the many stone steps to the castle.

KILLIAN GLANCED AROUND the table and smiled widely. His wife had insisted that not only should their kin share the meal with them, but, his captain, and the captain's son Pierce, and the cook, Joseph, as well. Killian did not object for these men had been his friends the entire time he'd lived at Castle O'Brien, but he saw the disapproving look his steward, Fergus Flannery, had worn when he'd seen servants and members of the guard dining with nobility. Killian would need to speak with the man for he would not want Alainn to feel she couldn't dine with whomever she pleased.

"The meal was entirely delicious, Cookson; you have outdone yourself!" Killian praised the young man.

"And your apple dessert was most flavorful, Alainn!" Cookson smiled at his friend. "Even if you did use half my honey supply!"

"Aye, it was superb, Lainna. You knew it was my favorite, aye?"

"Aye!" She smiled back at him and they gazed at each other as though they were alone in the room.

Killian leaned over and placed a lengthy kiss on her lips and he thought they were considerably sweeter than the dessert he'd just completed. Riley cleared his throat loudly and they regretfully pulled from their embrace.

"Think of the amorous reunion you and Mary will surely have when she returns, Riley. She has been gone for nearly six weeks now. You must miss her presence terribly!" Alainn suggested.

"Aye, of course I miss my wife!" Riley stated as he gruffly cleared his throat, but did not sound even the slightest bit convincing.

Killian noted Alainn staring at Riley and believed they both were thinking their cousin's marriage was not as strong as they'd hoped it might be.

The captain and her grandfather were in deep conversation with each other regarding the English and Alainn recalled both Danhoul and Maire O'Donnel telling her of the battle Killian had been involved in. She questioned him on it, but he clearly downplayed it.

"I did not send word of the incident, Alainn, for I feared it would simply cause you undue concern. There were only a handful of them."

"How many?" she demanded to know.

"Two dozen… perhaps three dozen at most… and they only carried swords."

"And how many were you and your men?"

"Five and ten, but we are far superior with the sword, Alainn. You needn't fret so!"

She reached out to touch the amulet that hung from his neck. She had charmed the amulet for him and thus far it had proven beneficial in keeping him safe. She prayed it would continue to do so, but if the English came in the great numbers as was predicted, no amount of magic in an amulet would keep him safe, and she shivered.

"Are you cold, Lainna? Here, take my overcoat."

He took the garment from its place on the back of his chair and placed it around her shoulders tenderly, and she touched his hand and smiled at his caring gesture.

The conversation went to talks of the gathering of the clans and what, if anything, had been decided. Even the few men here seemed divided on how might be best to deal with the English and their damnable king who seemed set on once again taking away the Irish ways, and the Irish rule. Even the title of chieftain was not to be used, for they were actually to be known as earls or lords, but it was scarcely adhered to.

The Irish way of speaking, their music, customs, and even their dress were once under strict scrutiny of the English, and it appeared the Tudor king wanted this again, as well as being named sole King of Ireland. That was something few Irishmen could tolerate, to have an arrogant English ruler declared King of Ireland, when it was the English who had stripped the actual Irish kings of their titles centuries before. When the conversation became heated, Alainn was driven to change the subject to something she thought would be much more amiable. She was soon proven wrong.

"Have you recent news of Rory? It has been some time since we've had a message from him or from your mother, Riley. Do you know if all is well at Castle O'Brien? I know since he's your twin brother, the two of you remain close. Have you heard from him then, Riley?"

"He looked well enough."

Both Killian and Niall threw Riley a warning glance, but the damage had already been done.

"He looked well enough… you saw Rory?" Alainn asked in a strained, hushed voice.

Riley looked sharply toward Killian in hopes he could diffuse this unpleasant and quickly escalating situation, but Killian had closed his eyes and waited for the thunder to begin.

"Rory was with you when the council met near Dublin? Killian, you saw Rory?" her voice trembled as she spoke.

"Aye, Alainn, but……

She stood up so suddenly her heavy chair fell backwards and crashed to the stone floor. All the men at the table rose as well.

"No, sit down, the lot of you; remain as you were, I simply require a breath of air."

Alainn felt light-headed as she began to walk toward the far end of the great hall, to the large arched windows, but Killian caught her elbow.

"Alainn."

"It would be wise to allow me this time alone, Killian O'Brien!"

Surely most of the men at the table had no notion what had caused the woman's unusual reaction. Only Niall, Riley, and Killian knew why she had stormed off in a furious state. And none of them seemed inclined to offer any explanation.

Killian followed her across the immense room where she stood by the arched window and deeply inhaled the fresh evening air in attempt to calm herself. As she lowered herself to a nearby chair, Killian crouched beside her.

"You did not heed me, none of you! Not even my grandfather, but you, Killian; I believed you would!" A sob caught in her throat as she spoke.

"Rory needed to be there, Alainn. He is chieftain as well, together with our Uncle Hugh."

"But I thought it has been decided Rory would not attend, that only your uncle would attend? Riley would go with our grandfather this time. Because you have been appointed to the council of the clans your presence was necessary, but Rory was to stay at Castle O'Brien, what caused him to deviate from the plans?" she asked her voice shaking with emotion.

"We were only together during the gatherin' of the clans, not once afterward, not at the inns not even for drinks or meals! We did not journey anywhere together." He assured her.

Killian saw Riley heading toward them and he gestured for him to stay away for he thought he was on the way to calming Alainn's fears as well as her temper. His cousin, being typically boar-headed and unintuitive, approached anyway.

"Alainn, how can you tell me I cannot be with my own brother; or Killian either for he is like a brother to us? It is unnatural for us to be parted because of some damnable vision you've had? How can you possibly know it will ever come to be?"

"I know it well!" She glared at her cousin. "I have seen you dead, the three of you more times than I can count now. Do you know what it is to see the man I love dead, and you and your brother who are dear to me as well? In my visions I see all of you lying bloody and lifeless on a field during a battle with the English. I know not how to prevent it but to keep you apart, but still you refuse to heed me!"

"And are your damnable abilities so infallible that you couldn't be wrong on this? Do you think yourself so powerful that you know all?"

"This has nothin' to do with how powerful I am. I tell you now; if the three of you are together you risk the chance of being killed. If you stay apart then the vision cannot come to fruition."

"You will not prevent me from seein' my brother! Tell me, Alainn, what clan would you suggest forfeit their vote, then?"

"You and our grandfather share joint chieftainship as do Rory and your father. You and Rory can simply alternate in attending the council. Did your father not attend council as was planned?" she demanded to know.

She shuddered at even mentioning Hugh O'Brien for in the past he had caused much trepidation and heartache for Killian and herself.

"My father's health has been failing recently and his physician insisted he could not make the journey!" Riley replied in a solemn tone laced with apparent concern regarding his father. "It was then decided our Uncle Sean would go in their stead, but that also did not happen."

"And why could Sean not attend then?" Alainn demanded.

"Well, you'll know Iona is with child and she was apparently most grievously opposed to Sean leaving her for she was feeling poorly." Riley offered.

"Oh, aye, far be it for poorly Iona to be alone for such an insufferable time when she is newly with child!" She rolled her eyes indignantly and glanced from Rory to Killian and back again. "So 'tis that bitter and spoiled young woman, Iona who rules Castle O'Brien at the moment, then is it?" She sarcastically suggested.

That was when her grandfather slowly made his way across the gargantuan room most certainty moving unusually slowly due to his advancing age and his lengthy time upon a horse this day.

"Alainn"—he spoke in his stern yet gentle manner— "sure it cannot be beneficial for you or your unborn child for you to become so aggrieved."

"Aye, Grandfather, sure you speak the truth, but tell me then, do you suppose it will be beneficial to me or my unborn child if his father and his kin lie dead on an open moor outside of Dublin? Would it be beneficial to me to know I have been unable to prevent a vision I have been seeing for so many months now?"

He shook his head slowly, realizing he was not achieving the desired effect of soothing and calming his granddaughter.

Alainn looked at each of the men's faces with exasperation and then pulled her anelace from her pocket.

Chapter Four

RILEY JUMPED BACK at the sight of her weapon, unsure of her intentions and Killian stepped toward her.

"Alainn, please calm you down, let me take you to our bedchamber and settle you. There's no need for further unpleasant discussion."

She stepped away from him and walked toward Riley once more. His eyes grew wide and his hand went to the hilt of his sword.

"I'll not use my weapon upon you, Riley O'Brien, though if it were the only manner in which I could ensure my husband and your brother would live, then perhaps the cost would not be so very great in sacrificing your life!"

She walked past him and to the nearest castle wall. With her weapon she began scratching a rough drawing upon the stone. She placed three large marks upon the drawing and began to explain.

"In my reoccurring vision it is apparent the battle will take place on an open moor, but in the far off distance a city is within view. Since your council meetings are almost always held near Dublin, I feel it is a great likelihood the battle will ensue at that location." Her voice shook as she continued. With her weapon she tapped loudly upon the site of the first mark.

"This is the location where Rory shall die for he is the first to lose his life, by way of arrow through his neck and throat, his death is undisputedly bloody, but quick and mostly painless."

As she pointed to the second mark she glanced up with tears in her eyes and pain in her voice. "This is where my husband shall meet his death, a sword so near to his heart that it, too, shall be quite swift!" By her achingly sad tone, it was obvious her very own heart was breaking at conveying this information. "It shall be deemed a brave and admirable death for you will kill over a dozen of the enemy before you are overcome, Killian. I shall be certain to inform our son of your dauntless bravery while relating the reasoning why he shall never know his father!" Her tone was now lower and laced with a hauntingly sad sarcasm.

"And you, Riley O'Brien, shall be the last to die; you shall witness the death of both your brother and your cousin. You shall suffer a sword's blow to your belly. It shall leave you near a state of disembowelment, and it will be a long and excruciatingly painful death. Perhaps hours you will lie there on the cold, wet ground looking upon the dead bodies of your kin! Perhaps it is a death befitting you, Riley, since your stubbornness will surely be the death of you!

Believe me, for I have seen this vision in its brutal gore

entirely, surely more times than I can count. I know how it will happen; I am almost certain where it will happen. It is only when it will happen that eludes me. So I cannot force you to heed my words, if that is your choice. Though every one of you can be asininely stubborn, I urge you to listen to my words and abide by my wisdom for I know not how else to warn you of what is to be!"

Riley's face had grown pale at her ominous words, but he chose to retaliate in anger.

"I won't believe it!" He roared, nostrils flaring indignantly.

"Your obvious stupidity will end up costing you your life, Riley O'Brien, and that of Rory and Killian as well!" She fumed.

"Are you callin' me stupid to my face, woman. You have no right!"

"Riley, would you just shut the hell up, man!" Killian yelled loudly and his authoritative voice echoed off the walls of the enormous room.

"And you, Killian, cannot order me about!" Riley shouted. "You've been damnably irritable and cantankerous these past weeks. You might not know that about your husband, Alainn, but he becomes entirely unpleasant to be with when he does without the company of a woman in his bed."

Alainn glared at her cousin once more at choosing to refer to a topic that would further enrage her.

"You might have accepted the invitation of the many

women dancers at the gatherin', Killian. Apparently you seem no less appealing to other women, maidens or whores, now that you are a married man and so boldly choose to wear a ring to alert others. They want you still and proposition you often. By Christ, the whores offer to service you for no coin, simply for the mere pleasure of being with you in that manner!"

"Are you completely consumed with drink or is it simply your own discontented embitterment that causes you to speak in such a manner, Riley O'Brien?" Killian glared at the other man and stood threateningly to his full height beside his cousin.

Riley was a tall man as well, but Killian was taller and at the moment clearly angrier.

Alainn looked up at both of the men in disbelief of what was being discussed. "You were openly propositioned by lewd and promiscuous women, Killian? Who are these dancers of which you speak... Irish dancers?"

"Hardly, cousin, now who's bein' naïvely stupid?" Riley scoffed. "They were sultry and exotic female dancers, not typical Irish dancers by any stretch for they were naked women dancers who dance for the chieftains and the lords at the gatherings and provide entertainment and a vast array of other favors." He elaborated as his eyebrow arched in a suggestive manner.

"Riley, you can get the hell out of here until you learn to keep your mouth shut!" Killian ordered. "Niall, take your grandson home before I slit his cursed throat!"

"Riley, get you back to our castle, you're acting like a bitter child instead of a man! These are topics not broached with womenfolk present. How can it be you don't respect or understand that?" Niall O'Rorke declared.

Alainn had started up the winding stone steps, but Killian went after her.

"Alainn, we must speak on this further!"

"I am simply fetching my grandfather an elixir for the pain in his back and a balm remedy for the nagging ache in his shoulders. If I do not distance myself from our cousin immediately the dark magic I direct toward him will not be nearly as kind as what I alluded to earlier this day!"

The distant thunder had begun to rumble loudly in the sky and Killian noticed when he glanced back to where'd they feasted earlier, many of the tables and chairs in the room had begun to shake. Killian knew how valiantly Alainn had fought to stem her powers these past months but, in her dark, unpleasant mood, she seemed unable to suppress them any longer. By now the captain and the other men had long since left the room, only Riley and Niall remained behind with Killian after Alainn had gone for her remedies.

"What by God's nails were you thinking, Riley? You knew Alainn was already upset about learning we'd been with Rory, about the horrid vision she continues to see, and then you purposely aggravated her. She is in a most delicate condition. And I know well enough you are aware of how given to jealousy she can be. I should beat you soundly for upsettin' my wife!"

"Well, I don't believe her confounded visions. I won't have it dictated for me when I can be with my brother. And sure she has no reason to be thrown into a fit of jealousy, 'tis not as if you actually did anythin' with the other women. You seem entirely loyal to her and faithful as well. I don't pretend to understand it, but sure 'tis your choice, I suppose. Or maybe it is only that you simply fear her and you believe with all her many unnatural abilities she would sense if you'd been unfaithful!"

"I do not fear Alainn, but I love her greatly and I respect her, and I intend to remain true to my vows, for clearly I take them far more seriously than you have taken your own marriage vows, Riley."

Niall's brow was furrowed and his eyes appeared tired. As Alainn stood at the top of the stairs she could sense her grandfather's troubled thoughts. She knew oftentimes he felt his grandson was an undeniably trying lad and so like his father it was apparent Niall sometimes questioned having Riley becom joint chieftain of the O'Rorke clan. In truth, he'd been surprised when Riley had decided to assist him in being chieftain, but with Teige still unaccounted for after all these years, and his own advancing age and his health beginning to fail, he needed the assistance of his grandson, though hard-headed and impulsive he may well be.

Alainn saw how all three men watched as she slowly

made her way back down the massive winding stone steps. She headed straight to her grandfather.

"The elixir is to be taken before you retire for it is sure to make you tired and perhaps even dizzy, and the balm is to be rubbed upon your aching muscles several times a day. It will appear warm for a time, but that is usual. I know it will capably lessen your discomfort!"

She gently placed her hands on his stooped back and the old, white-haired man felt the warmth immediately spread across his aching back and shoulders. He knew her healing touch would be far more effective than her remedies although knowing Alainn they were surely charmed by her magic so unusually powerful as well. She placed a gentle kiss on the man's leathery cheek. She turned to go, but the elderly man caught her arm.

"I apologize for your cousin, Alainn, for Riley is an unthinking buffoon at times. And I regret that we were unable to heed your word. There was little to be done about it for each chieftain needed to be at council or they would forfeit their right to vote on most pressing issues."

"And so they chose to risk forfeiting their lives!" She spoke in a venomous whisper. "Goodnight, Grandfather!" And with that, she left the sprawling room without a farewell to her cousin or address to her husband.

After the other men had left the castle, Killian went to his steward to discuss happenings and details that the man wanted clarified. He would soon go to Alainn, but he knew her well enough to know she needed time to cool down, to sort through her temper and her thoughts, and Killian thought he perhaps needed that time as well.

Chapter Five

KILLIAN STOOD OUTSIDE the door in disbelief that Alainn, even in her deeply displeased state, would lock him out of their shared bedchamber, he became less than patient. He pounded loudly on the large wooden door and called out even louder.

"Alainn O'Brien, open this door this instant; if you think I'm spendin' another night out of my own bed and away from you simply because you're sore at me, you can think again!"

He heard her footsteps and then heard her attempting to open the door. Several moments had passed and she still wasn't able to manage it.

"Alainn, why in hell would you lock me out of my own bedchamber?" He roared.

"Are you alone out there?" She questioned as she called through the keyhole.

"Aye, I'm alone, but what by God's bones does that have to do with any of this?"

Killian watched as she magically appeared as her abilities allowed her to capably move through the thick wooden door.

"Killian O'Brien, settle you down; I did not lock the door. I don't know who was responsible for it wasn't locked with the key. In actuality, I am entirely unaware of where the key is kept!"

Killian tried the door once more and strangely enough it now opened with no resistance.

"I think it was held tightly closed by some form of magic!" Alainn deduced.

"You magically locked it?"

"No, it is as I have told you, I did not lock it by any fashion, and if I had used my magic to lock it, you would have been able to open it, for if you'll recall I have uttered a spell to make you immune to any unfavorable magic I produce."

"Aye, I recall, but who else in the castle is capable of magic?" He questioned as he moved inside the chamber.

"No person that I am aware of. Well, I do suspect the old healer, Glynnis, knows some magic, though she lets on it is only healing she does. But I can't see why she would want to keep you out of our bedchamber. It is as though someone wants to keep us apart. You thought I would lock you out of your own bedchamber?" she asked, clearly doubtful.

"Aye, well it is *our* bedchamber and you did seem mightily angry about the gathering and the dancers!"

Alainn's eyes flashed with jealousy as she spoke.

"Aye, well, 'tis true I am not pleased to know you have looked upon other women without benefit of clothing, but as long as it's only lookin' you've been doin', I suppose I can't fault you too harshly, then!"

Killian wore an obvious look of relief, until she spoke again.

"And if I thought you'd done more than look you'd not only not be sleepin' in the same chamber with me, or even under the same roof, you'd quite possibly be missin' a few parts of your body that you're surely somewhat fond of!"

"And if memory serves me correctly, you tend to be somewhat fond of them as well!"

Alainn pretended to remain perturbed at him, but she smiled nonetheless, though soon went back to pondering who might have enlisted magic to keep them apart.

"If Riley was capable of any form of magic, I would suggest it might be him, for he does seem to prefer to have us at odds."

"Aye, I've noticed that as well, and I've no notion why, unless he thinks misery loves company."

"And I've no desire to be miserable, Killian." With that she put her arms around his neck and pulled him close for a kiss as she stepped inside their bedchamber and closed the door.

"Nor I, Lainna!" he whispered as he returned the affection.

She began unfastening the ties of his tunic and he smiled at how eager she was to remove his garments. He reveled in the fact even though she carried their child she still seemed to require the joining as often as he did. He thought himself a fortunate man indeed to be wed to a woman as lovely as any goddess, and as insatiable as any woman he'd ever heard tell of. Her long golden hair was now loose and her beautiful lustrous locks hung nearly to her waist.

He looked down at the soft pink nightdress she wore and noticed the ties were already unfastened. He slipped the gown off her shoulders and gazed at her unsurpassed beauty. Her skin was creamy and flawless. Her breasts had always been full, but now that she carried their child they were voluptuous and he moaned as his bare chest brushed against her skin. She traced the lengthy scar that ran from his neck to his navel. He had been nearly killed as a boy, and Alainn had not only healed him, but ensured he'd had a reason to live, for even then, back when they were children, he believed he had fallen in love with her. Now there was only a long, thin line to remind him of that torturous day, for Alainn had healed him almost completely.

These past weeks, he had spent every night and half the day in such desperate need to be with her, he'd thought he couldn't bear it a moment longer. As his lips traced her jaw and neck and lingered on her peaked nipples, she moaned softly and pulled his head to her possessively and passionately.

"Oh, Killian, I have missed you so; I have missed this intimacy, being with you like this!"

He gently turned her and touched her soft loveliness. She caressed him as well, and his growing arousal was heightened further with her tender touch.

"You must take me now, Killian. I cannot endure bein' parted from you a second longer. Next time we will take the time to be more diligent in prolonging the arousal and the coupling. For now I need you within me for I am mad with desire for you."

Her words echoed his own thoughts and he needed no further discussion on the matter. He entered her with an urgency they both required, yet with gentleness he felt impelled to show her in her condition. As they moved together and her moans grew louder and more intense, he felt her body tremble and felt her warmth tighten around him as he moved within her. Twice more she achieved fulfillment before he finally allowed himself to reach his pinnacle as well. Then he carried her to their large bed and laid her down where he then joined her beneath the quilts.

"You are a masterful lover, Killian O'Brien! How I have missed this. The naked women dancers would be lusting after you in earnest if they'd actually had you as I have!"

He smiled at her and their gazes met in the candlelight. They continued to caress one another and soon he was in a state of arousal once more.

"Sure, I'm not opposed to bein' with you for as long or as often as you can love me, Killian."

"And there's no discomfort for you because of the babe?"

"What I am feelin' at the moment could hardly be considered discomfort!" She cooed as he continued with his touch, and he noticed her breath came in ragged gasps as he entered her and he looked down into her eyes.

Killian smiled as Alainn's body trembled almost as soon as he'd entered her. Later as his warmth spill within her, she moaned contently as they held one another and remained still joined.

"And Eireen thought it couldn't be managed?"

He looked at her with doubt in his eyes, "You speak of our intimate time with our servants?"

"No, only today we did, but not as a rule."

"Aye, well our cousin was questionin' the likelihood of it bein' a possibility as well."

"It would take more than a swollen belly to keep us apart in this manner!" Alainn whispered as she looked into his emerald eyes.

"Aye, and what a lovely wee belly it is!"

"Not so wee, but I am well pleased it does not offend you!"

"Alainn, how could I be offended by any part of your loveliness, and the fact you carry our child, that you carry my son, created as a result of our love and our lovemaking, how could any man be offended by that. It makes me proud and honored and hard!"

"Hard?" she whispered, as she caressed him once more and discovered he spoke the truth. "My God, I am married to an uncommonly grand and virile man!"

"Not so grand, I am simply a man who has been too long

parted from his love, and who has imagined this time with you in each gloriously sensual detail for weeks now."

"And you do possess such a magnificent imagination, Killian O'Brien!" she whispered happily as they kissed passionately and tenderly coupled once more.

⌘

LATER, NEITHER OF them seemed ready to sleep though they'd made love several times and were surely both completely exhausted. They'd spent a lengthy time talking as well. Killian was hesitant to speak with her of the matters that had upset her so severely earlier in the evening, but the only times they had ever experienced any difficulties in their relationship was when they had allowed subjects to be left unresolved. He was about to broach the topic when she spoke on it first.

"I am apologetic for losing my temper earlier, Killian, and for allowing my abilities to present themselves. I have attempted most consciously to keep these powers concealed, to never call upon them, Killian."

"I've never asked that of you, Alainn. As long as they are no danger to you or our child, or you don't use them around people who might think them of an evil origin, I do not have an aversion to the use of your magical powers. They are part of who you are, and I have known about them for as long as I have known you."

"I am aware of this, Killian, and I am most thankful of

your acceptance of them, but I don't need them. I am entirely content without them. When I am in a temper, it is most difficult to control them, though I assure you, I fight them even then."

"I am regretful you were driven to use them because of your temper. I would see you never angry or displeased, Alainn. I knew you would be most unhappy in learning about Rory bein' with us near Dublin when we were there, but I could see no way to avoid it. I know how you worry regardin' your vision."

They stared at one another and he saw the uncertainty in her eyes.

"'Tis because I don't know how to keep you safe, other than to keep the three of you parted. If I could dispose of the entire English army through use of my powers maybe then I could rest easy that the vision would never come true."

"Aye, well I think that would be a great feat even for you, Alainn, for apparently their army is massive. I keep hopin' the English king will simply forget this intention of takin' over and ruling all the countries around him and remain content to direct his attention to his personal life which always seems to be the talk of the entire of Europe."

Alainn gently touched the stubble on his jaw and he smiled at the tenderness within her fingertips.

"And you've not decided to become healer for Castle O'Donnel. I find it difficult to imagine you are content to keep such a tiny plot for your herbs and to prepare such few concoctions when you have lived your entire life as a healer. You once adored healing and helping people, and you'd spend most of your days in the herb garden at Castle O'Brien, or in the chamber creating remedies."

"I am content to grow the herbs only necessary to heal those close to me. Besides, Glynnis is the healer here at this castle."

"Has she been unkind to you, Alainn?"

Chapter Six

SOMETHING IN ALAINN'S tone had clearly left him with that assumption.

Alainn didn't respond, but fell quietly to her recollection of her recent distinctly memorable encounter with the healer, Glynnis.

The morning had been bright and sunny, discovering that some of her herbs were dwindling and her herb garden was only beginning to become established, Alainn thought it would be an opportune time to introduce herself to the castle's healer. She reasoned they might possibly share or trade some needed ingredients or worthwhile knowledge. Alainn had heard very little of the woman other than she was somewhat peculiar and elusive.

When Alainn had been healer at Castle O'Brien, she and Morag had shared a large open chamber within the castle walls where they prepared their many elixirs and remedies. She brought to memory the chamber and all that was inside—the large cupboard that housed the well-organized vials and remedies, the herbal concoctions specific to aid in any number of conditions. She envisioned the shelves lined with mortars and pestles of varying sizes; the large hearth with the many tied bunches of herbs hanging to dry to the state of perfection. She could clearly recall the familiar scent within the chamber and it brought a smile to her lips in appreciation of many happy years there as a healer.

Alainn stood before Glynnis's home and noted it was a typical cottage with a thatched roof. She knocked upon the door, but when no one appeared to be within, she started down the winding stone pathway to the small hut behind that evidently served as a healing chamber. It was built into the side of a hill. There seemed to be only one tiny window and the shutters were closed tight. At the moment there was smoke drifting out the partially open door. She hesitantly knocked and waited. No response. She drew nearer and called within.

"Glynnis, are you here?"

When there was no reply, she gently pushed on the open door and it creaked opened wider. Alainn's eyes met with near darkness in contrast to the bright sun. The smell within the tiny smoke-filled chamber was most pungent. Her eyes began to sting and water, and her throat tickled and sent her to coughing. Standing in the doorway, she called out once more as she glanced over at the spewing cauldron on the small hearth. She noticed the many vials and containers lying scattered about the tiny room in disarray, on shelves, tables and even tipped over upon the earthen floor.

She turned to leave for being here was beginning to make

her feel quite intrusive, when she heard a tiny mournful sound being emitted from deeper within the chambers. Even when she wasn't employing her powers of perception, Alainn always possessed a keen instinct and kinship to animals. She could now sense and hear that there an animal in distress. She made her way through the dark room, careful not to trip over the many articles scattered about the floor, and followed the noise as it took her to another doorway. The sound had grown louder and more insistent as she drew closer. She pushed open the door and this time the odor she encountered was not simply acrid, but vile and disturbing. It made her stomach lurch for it was the distinct smell of decomposition. She immediately covered her nose with her hand.

She willed her eyes to see clearer in the dark chamber, and then immediately wished she could not see what horrors that room held. There were perhaps two dozen cages filled with an array of animals in various states of tortured abuse and ill health. She drew nearer to the cages and dared to inspect further. There were rats and mice missing feet or tails, lizards with eyes gouged out; toads and frogs also legless and suffering. One cage held a large hawk missing each one of its talons, and another contained a bat void of one wing flapping about, disturbingly hitting itself against the bars of the cage.

Along the wall was a shelf that held many jars filled with liquid and what appeared to be some of the missing parts of the animals, eyes, feet, claws, tails, wings. Within the tiny hearth was another cauldron and although there was no fire beneath it at the moment, it was filled with an appalling green congealed mixture that made Alainn gag and feel as though she might actually spew. As she drew nearer to the cages, she noted none of these despairing creatures appeared to be uttering a sound. She used her powers to learn why and was further disturbed to discover their throats had been sliced and altered in such a way that ensured they were not capable of making a sound. She also spotted a pile of rotting corpses of various different animals in the corner of the room. Her stomach protested and she felt it queasily lurch yet again.

Alainn noticed against the far wall, which consisted entirely of earth, there appeared to be a nearly hidden doorway that perhaps led to a tunnel within the side of the hill. She dared to wonder what further horrors might lay beyond that door.

It was then she glanced at a cage against the wall and saw a dead cat within. It was missing its ears, tail, and a front paw. And from beneath its swollen pitiful body came a small mewing sound. A tiny kitten squirmed out when it heard Alainn cry out in horror of all the pathetic animals' suffering. Alainn opened the cage and tearfully picked up the wee ball of fur. The cat must have given birth to the kitten as she'd died. She sensed others kittens were still within her and despaired further in knowing it was too late for them.

"You poor wee baby, it's to be thankful she hasn't discovered you yet!" She cuddled it soothingly, tears falling down her cheeks as she placed it on her chest.

"You should not be here!"

Alainn started and whirled around at the voice behind her, and then stared accusingly at the woman who must be Glynnis.

Her face was grimy with ashes and soot. She had long, matted grey hair and dark wild eyes. She was dressed in a grubby black garment and in her gnarled hand she carried a candle, long, dirty pointed fingernails clasped it tightly.

"You should not be here!" She repeated in an eerie, gravelly voice.

When she spoke, Alainn noticed she had few teeth in her mouth and even they were rotted and black. Alainn thought her appearance might surely be frightening to some, but at the moment it was not fear she was experiencing.

"How dare you perform such atrocities on these innocent, defenseless creatures and worse yet leave them alive to suffer!"

"You should not be here; leave at once!"

"I am Alainn O'Brien and—"

"I know very well who you are, that is of no consequence to me. Because you have title and position does not change the fact you are not welcome here."

"I will simply not permit you to keep these animals in such a state! What is it you are doing with them?"

"That is none of your concern. This is not my chamber!"

"Then whose?" Alainn demanded to know.

The old woman appeared unwilling to reply.

"Who is it you defend, Glynnis? Is it Fergus's daughter, your granddaughter, Ciara who has caused such torment for these innocent creatures?"

The old woman remained disinclined to respond to Alainn's queries.

"This is truly immoral and unforgivable!"

"She has capably created remedies for many ills." The old woman finally spoke.

"Is it remedies she creates here, or potions for dark spells?" Alainn accused.

"Ahh, so you are aware of such practices. Much can be achieved by using certain bits and pieces from animals?"

"Aye, I have heard of such inhumane and dark practices and I am much in disagreement with them. And to leave the pitiful animals to suffer is unforgivable. Tell me where I might find your granddaughter so that I might speak with her regarding these despicable acts."

"No, that would be unwise. I warn you, you should steer clear of her. She is not one to tangle with." A hint of something close to fear crossed the old woman's eyes. "Leave now and she need never know you've been here."

"Aye, I will leave, but not before these animals are put out of their misery."

"She has given them all a potion to numb their pain and

assures me they feel nothing."

"That's utter horse shite; she's simply silenced their painful protests. I'd dearly like to get my hands on her at the moment and make certain she feels even a portion of the suffering these poor creatures have been made to endure!"

"Are you threatening my kin?" The old woman snarled lowly and drew closer to Alainn, "A woman with child should not be issuing threats or poking her nose about uninvited in other's affairs... wife of a chieftain or not!"

Alainn stepped back from the abrasive old woman.

"Go back to your castle, Lady O'Brien, mind to your noble affairs, and leave me and my granddaughter alone. We don't require another healer here. We are capable without your assistance or your interference."

"I did not ever intend to infringe on your healing or to take over any of your duties or patrons, I simply came to see if I might borrow some sage, for mine has not rooted well. And sage is well known for keeping evil from entering a location. Come to it, I doubt you would welcome sage within these walls."

"If I am made to ask you again to leave my healing chambers, Lady O'Brien, I will locate my granddaughter and you will be most sorry if you are made to deal with her."

"And are you threatening me, Glynnis?"

The old woman's cold eyes stared at her intently, but she did not reply.

Alainn turned as though to leave.

"You'll not take that animal with you. It does not belong to you."

Since Alainn had lived most of her life as a servant to a chieftain, she was reluctant to use or hold her present title over another, but at the moment she deemed it was necessary in dealing with this troublesome woman and her abhorrent granddaughter.

"In truth, everything that sits upon this land, your cottage, this chamber and all within, actually belongs to my husband, Glynnis. You might remember that in future, and sure you'd have this innocent creature end up as ill-fated as its mother then, would you? Have you no heart, no conscience, no notion of what is decent?"

"You judge most harshly, Lady O'Brien. You are foolish to believe we do not need animals to better our remedies and test them upon the creatures."

"Perhaps there is some truth to your words, but I will not condone the needless suffering of these animals. Maiming them and leaving them to unmercifully agonize will not be permitted here... not ever!"

"And what would you do about it, then, wait till your husband returns so that he might fight your battles and wield the power of his nobility?"

Alainn glared at the old crone and glanced at each of the pathetic creatures that held no hope of survival in the wild if released.

"No, Glynnis, my husband will not be needed to deal

with such matters."

She placed the tiny kitten within the pocket of her cloak and strained to come up with a way to handle her present predicament without calling upon her magical powers.

"You think I am unaware you possess unnatural abilities?" The old woman spoke, "I know you have been given the druid gift."

"Not simply druid, Glynnis, for I possess potent fairy blood as well. I am a strong witch."

The woman raised her eyebrow and narrowed her eyes, appearing doubtful on that count. Alainn longed to be free to deal with this woman and her granddaughter by way of her magic, but she wouldn't allow the woman to actually see all that she was capable of.

She sensed Pierce, the captain's son, was close by and within her mind she summoned him. She heard him enter the outside chamber straightaway and he called out to her.

"Alainn, are you in need of assistance?"

The old woman sneered as Pierce came into the room where they now stood. He coughed and gagged when he smelled the overpowering odor.

"What by God's name is that foul stench?"

Glynnis was as unwelcoming to Pierce as she'd been to Alainn. "This is my chamber and I demand you both leave at once!"

Pierce ignored the woman and his jaw dropped when he'd had a chance to survey the many disturbing sights. "Are you mad, old woman? How could you be so despicably cruel?" His hand went to his sword and he stared angrily down at the aged woman.

"It was not Glynnis, but apparently her granddaughter, who committed these atrocities. Although, the fact Glynnis knew of it and allowed it to be done perhaps makes her no less blameless."

"Ciara did this?" Pierce seemed even more in disbelief at this revelation.

"Aye! It would appear that is truth!"

He shook his head in disgust. "What's to be done with all these pathetic creatures, Alainn?"

"Their lives must be ended in a quick and painless manner, Pierce. I will send some of the guards to assist you, and to dispose properly of all the bodies." She reluctantly pointed to the disturbing pile of animal corpses so unfeelingly tossed in the corner.

He nodded his head in sober agreement. "And what's to be done with this old crone and her wicked granddaughter then?"

"Do you inquire if their lives should be ended in a quick and painless manner?" Alainn suggested only partly in jest.

"Well, I hadn't thought to be entirely that rash, but sure Killian will not take kindly to this, for you know well of his opinion of those who mistreat lesser creatures, he is liable to judge these acts severely." He stared at the old woman with disgust in his eyes and distaste in his voice. "I should see to it my father, the captain, hears of your misdeeds and he may deem the both of you should be taken to the dungeon until Killian arrives home to pass judgment on your objectionable practices. You may well have your chambers taken from you as well as your time as a healer here at Castle O'Donnel ended. You'd be wise to realize all of this belongs to Killian and to his kin. Sure, he might decide to have you punished and sent off somewhere entirely undesirable. He could insist Alainn take over the duties as healer, for always her practices at Castle O'Brien were done in a kind and capable manner with no harm befalling any innocent creature."

Alainn stared disapprovingly at the old healer. "I don't care to take over the duties as a healer, but I will see to it there is an end put to these incomprehensible acts of cruelty, and perhaps we might justly allow the animals their own revenge on the wrongdoers," she whispered more to herself than to the others.

The hawk, perhaps the least affected of the injured animals, flapped its wings in earnest agreement at that suggestion. Alainn attempted to use her abilities to see if she might mend any of the injured creatures by way of her magical healing, but she was saddened to realize they were beyond saving. Although she was capable of much through her healing, she could not manage to create new limbs or wings even by employing her magic. Even the unfortunate hawk would not survive in the wild without its talons, and this beautiful feral creature should never be made to live out its life in a restrictive cage. She closed her eyes and immediately all the wounded animals in the chamber fell into a deep and peaceful sleep.

"Keep solely to the remedies that are derived only from plants and herbs, Glynnis. Disallow your granddaughter from such barbaric and unforgivable practices and I'll not mention this to my husband. Do I have your word on this?"

The woman looked disbelievingly at the sleeping animals and hesitantly nodded her head.

"Do I have your word?" Alainn respoke.

"Aye, I'll do what I'm able, but I fear no one is truly able to control her. Consider yourself forewarned in that regard."

"Rest assured, I will have the guards keep close watch on your granddaughter for some time until I feel you have kept your word and that she can be trusted."

Alainn had summoned several guards and sent them to assist Pierce so they might follow through with the distasteful task of ending the animal's misery. She had taken the kitten to the dairy shed and was relieved to find a new mother cat who readily took in the wee orphan as one of her own.

She shuddered at the vivid memory of her meeting with Glynnis and Killian's warm hand upon her cheek brought her back to the present time. He repeated his previous inquiry.

"Has Glynnis been unkind to you?"

Not desirous of relating any of the unpleasantness of what she'd beheld and what had transpired within Glynnis's healing chambers, she downplayed it entirely.

"She is very wary of me, Killian. She does not wish for me to encroach upon her boundaries. Healers are most possessive of their gardens and their herbs, as well as their patrons. You remember how unwelcoming I was toward Thomas O'Donaugh, the physician your uncle employed at Castle O'Brien. I believe Glynnis feels the same regarding me and, besides, apparently she is apprenticing her granddaughter to one day become healer."

Chapter Seven

"CIA IS TO assist her grandmother?"

"Aye, Ciara. You know of her; well obviously you do if you refer to her by a fond name?"

"I knew her when I was younger. She is older than I and, when I was a boy, I was smitten with her I suppose."

Given what Alainn now knew about Glynnis's granddaughter, Ciara, and what cruelty she'd displayed with the helpless animals, she was not pleased in the slightest to learn Killian had once been enamored with the woman even though at the time she would have only been a girl.

"And now that you are a man?" She inquired in a displeased tone.

"She is a married woman and I am married to the loveliest woman alive, so I have no need to spend time thinkin' of other women. I haven't seen Ciara for a goodly long time, now."

Alainn contemplated this new information, and she sensed Killian seemed no more eager to discuss the woman than she was.

"And you don't believe you will miss your many duties as

healer; I know how dearly you loved creatin' potions and remedies?" Killian hastily changed the subject.

"It involves much time and endless toil to be a healer for an entire castle and village, and I shall be content to spend all my days with my son and my husband. I am most impatient to see him, Killian, to hold him and sing to him."

"Aye, I've heard you singin' to him already. You've the loveliest voice, Lainna. But, you know some women of noble breeding prefer to have servants care for their children and wet nurses feed their babes."

"I will never hear of that. I intend to nurse our son and care for him. No other woman will take that honor away from me. I will be the best mother there has ever been, Killian, I promise you that!"

"You've no need to feel you must convince me on that count, Alainn. I know well you will be."

Killian realized this was a sensitive subject for Alainn. Her own mother had sent her to be raised by another couple when Alainn was a newborn infant. Although it had been learned she had done it to ensure Alainn was allowed a normal life away from the scrutiny her mother had suffered, Alainn would never be entirely accepting of the fact she had been made to live out most of her life without her mother's love.

"So what do you do to fill your days now, Lainna, when I am away? If you have turned your back on your healing and on your magic, how do you fill your time?" He questioned trying to dispel her unhappiness.

"I do tend my wee herb garden. I walk to the seashore, swim occasionally, and spend time in the stables and the orchards. I go to the kitchen and help Cookson or talk to Pierce on occasion. I have been creating some quilts for our son."

"You've been sewing, Alainn? You always told me you were uninterested and easily bored by sewing and fine needle work!"

"Aye, 'tis true, I once felt that way, but now that I am creating articles for our son, I well like it! And I have been lonesome with you gone and Mary away as well, I am looking forward to her return for I have missed her. Therefore I also have spent considerable time preparing a chamber for our son."

"Is it the room where I slept during my childhood?" Killian questioned.

A curious expression crossed her face as she replied.

"No, I believe it is too far distanced from our own bed-chamber. I wanted to be close to you, but to our son as well. Although Maire O'Donnel tells me most men, especially chieftains, don't care to have their babes so close by for they tend to disturb their sleep, she also says men are not so inclined to care to have their wives nearby after they have produced children for they oft find them less appealing thereafter."

There was clearly some doubt and worry in Alainn's tone

and Killian knew he must set her mind at ease.

"You will never ever be unappealing in my eyes, Alainn, and why would I not want my wife and my son as close by as possible?"

"Sure, I don't know, but I promise I will attempt to ensure we don't disturb your sleep, Killian, for I realize your duties are gravely important and that you must be well rested so your mind is keen and your thoughts clear."

"Alainn, you make me sound as a tyrant! Do you truly believe I would ever make you feel as though you are unimportant to me, that my health, my sleep, or my clear thought is anywhere near as important to me as you or our unborn child?"

"No, never!" she admitted.

"Then forget these foolish notions and show me the room you've been preparin'!"

She smiled, but he saw the uncertainty on her pretty face and the uncommon tears that had formed in her blue eyes and began to spill down her cheeks.

He placed his hands on her shoulders and gazed down into her serious eyes. "Tis you I love, Alainn O'Brien. You more than anythin', more than my chieftainship, more than kin or clan, more than this castle or this land, or in truth more than Ireland. Never doubt that you are first and most important in my life, you and our son, for, without you, nothin' else really truly matters to me. Tell me you know this without a doubt, Lainna!"

"Of course I know it, Killian, for 'tis how I feel as well. But you are a man of growing importance."

"No buts, Lainna! Now my sweet and beautiful wife, show me this chamber."

⌘

ALAINN LED HIM through their bedchamber and into the adjoining room. She pulled her nightdress close to her as the hearth had not been lighted and the chill in the large chamber caused her to shiver. Killian had wrapped a heavy quilt around his unclothed, muscular frame and he held it open so she could join him encircled within the warmth of the blanket.

"You should light the hearth and the candles as well!" He suggested.

When she attempted to move to seek the flint and do as he'd requested, he pulled her back to him.

"I could have lighted them myself, if I'd thought to see them lit in that fashion. I wanted to see you work you magic, for it delights me to see you create fire so effortlessly."

She smiled up at him at his insistence of using her magical powers. She waved toward the fireplace and soon a hearty fire blazed in the hearth. The many candles throughout the chamber flamed as well.

When Killian looked upon the walls in the room, he gasped. "You did this, Alainn? I didn't know you were so talented in your abilities to create such elaborate paintings."

"Well, I'm not really, nothing like Rory. If he'd been here I would have asked him to assist me."

"No, Alainn, 'tis truly beautiful and enchanting."

Killian looked upon the many pictures painted upon the wall. There was a large detailed painting of the fairy glade that was located near Castle O'Brien, and many of the lovely fairies they had seen when they'd visited there after their wedding. There were pictures of the bubbling spring and the waterfall and of the lovely rolling hills so prevalent in Ireland and several dry-stone walls as well. Another painting clearly depicted a round tower and still another, the enormous dolmen that they had spent much time upon as youngsters and then again as adults. It had been beside the dolmen where they had first made love.

"Perhaps we won't tell our son 'twas that location where he was conceived." She jested.

Killian chuckled. "No maybe that might be one detail we might omit!"

There were also paintings of the four dragons, the thirteen hellhounds, and other mystical creatures, Alainn had seen during her time in the realm of the Celtic gods as well as some other mythical creatures of Celtic lore. There were pictures of Lugh and Aine, two legendary gods they had met also when they were in the glade.

"Where did you get the paint mixtures, Alainn?" Killian questioned in awe of the magnificence of the paintings she'd produced.

"I created many with herbal mixtures, plants, roots and flower petals for color variance, but some I got from Conner MacLain."

"The Scot who is a groom at your grandfather's stables?"

"Aye!"

"He paints, then?" he asked doubtfully.

"Aye, he paints lovely images of scenery, seascapes and landscapes, and sprawling castles in Scotland. He possesses a rare talent indeed."

"You know he's a dangerous man, Alainn!"

"Aye, well I know he could be if he was pushed. I sense he is mostly a gentle man and his aura is not dark, Killian. I think it has been circumstances in his life that have led him to live dangerously."

"Are you aware he spent many years in prison?"

"Aye, I've heard it said!"

"And do you know why?"

"Aye, I heard he murdered a chieftain!"

"And did you know that chieftain was his brother?"

Alainn looked seriously at Killian, before she responded. "Aye, I am aware of that, but I also know it was because his brother took Conner's wife to his bed."

"Aye, I was told of that, as well. But after he was released he made his livin' killin' men for coin; did you know that, Alainn?"

"I wasn't certain that was true. I thought perhaps it was simply gossip or rumor! Are you askin' that I stay clear of him, then?"

Killian seemed to consider this question for a moment. "I would not ask you to stay away from him. I believe you are a good judge of character, but be cautious, Alainn. Will you do that?"

"Aye, I will, my love. And now I am most weary and sure you must be exhausted as well, after your long journey. Come to bed with me, husband, for I feel the need to fall asleep in these strong arms. I have missed the sensation of your arms around me as I sleep. And our bed is so large and cold without you in it. The heated stones might warm my cold feet well enough, but they do nothin' for keepin' the rest of me warm."

Killian's deep green eyes filled with warmth and love as she spoke so sincerely of her love and need for him. It pleased her to know he had felt entirely the same while they'd been parted.

"Aye, well, I can keep you warm, all of you, my sweet Lainna."

As he lifted her into his arms and carried her across the room, she saw him stare at the large wolfhound curled up on the braided rug beside the bed. Alainn smiled at Killian's reaction to the dog in the bedchamber for it was not preferred when he was present. Alainn clucked her tongue and gestured to the door.

"Outside the door with you, Wolf. Milord is home this night and he will keep watch over me. You must sleep outside our chambers."

The old dog nudged her hand affectionately, wagged his tail, and obeyed without question as she opened the door with her magic and then closed it in the same manner.

Killian lifted her in his arms and carried her to the bed where she curled up against his warmth. She sensed him gazing down at her. Her heavy eyes opened to meet his and soon they both fell into a contended sleep.

Chapter Eight

ALAINN STIRRED EARLY, though the morning sun still had not yet risen in the sky. The child within her had been moving for some time and at the moment was extremely active and presently causing great discomfort for she felt an urgent need to pass water. She had hoped to disentangle herself from Killian's arms without waking him, but that had proven to be unsuccessful. He smiled down at her through the limited light pouring in through the castle window. He chuckled as he gently laid his hand against her belly and felt the many movements.

"He feels as though he's doin' somersaults, Lainna."

"Aye, and if I don't make it to the chamber pot soon, I'll be sorry and, come to it, so will you!"

"And weren't you up a few times in the night as well?"

"I was, indeed. I made several trips to the privy, and another to the kitchen. Sure I am famished half the time."

Killian gently kissed her cheek as she moved from him. He sighed deeply and she realized how tired he remained. When she returned from the small closet that contained the chamber pot, she saw he had fallen back to sleep. She gently pulled the quilts around him, found her shawl, and left him to his sleep.

⌘

SOME TIME LATER as Alainn stood in the kitchen and affectionately placed her arms around Cookson's neck in response to a kind compliment he'd given her, she heard the deep male voice behind her.

"Now if Maire O'Donnel had seen my wife in this fond embrace with another man maybe then she'd have cause to question her behavior."

They both smiled at Killian and Alainn went to her husband, pleased that he was jesting about her encounter with his cousin's wife, after she had related the event to him. She also remembered how loudly he'd laughed in amusement when she told him she thought she, herself, was evil. She recalled their conversation the evening before.

"Whatever did you do to make you feel you've done something evil?" He'd questioned with humor in his voice.

"I told her she should write me a list of how to behave as a chieftain's wife when I knew without a doubt she was unable to read or write. I wanted to take her down a peg or two for she always judges me so severely. But, it was very wrong of me and I feel horrid about it."

"Then perhaps we might ride over to their land immediately and apologize straightaway to the dear sweet woman?" Killian had jested.

"You're incorrigible, Killian O'Brien. I was being serious."

"As was I!" he'd said barely able to speak he was laughing so hard.

Now he was laughing once more and Alainn smiled at how happy he appeared to be. Perhaps Riley had been correct in assuming he needed the company of a woman in his bed to assure he maintained his good mood, for this morning he seemed joyful after the night spent together. Their lovemaking had most assuredly restored his usual good disposition and he clearly wanted to share his jubilance.

"I'm after planning a grand celebration, Alainn. I'm thinkin' we should invite the neighboring lords and chieftains and their ladies; host a great feast, some games and challenges and a hunt. A great hunt! 'Tis time we entertained our kin, our clan, and our neighbors as we've not held such a formal event in all the time we've been here. Before I am called off to another gatherin' of the Council of the Clans we will have a grand banquet and celebration. By week's end, it will be so. Would you be in agreement, Alainn?"

Alainn smiled at her husband's exuberance. His green eyes shone with excitement and anticipation.

"Aye, that would be a fine notion, Killian. Will you be capable of inviting everyone you want to attend by week's end? Will you be capable of creatin' such a grand feast with limited time and notice, Cookson?"

Both men nodded excitedly and Alainn became caught

up in their merriment.

"Then tell me what I can do to assist the two of you in accomplishing this great celebratory event."

"Well, you can assist me in inking the messages of invitation, and I'll see them delivered on the morrow. But, for now, I've something to show you. I've brought you a gift I procured in Dublin. Come with me and I'll present it to you."

Her excitement grew as Killian escorted her out the door. Even his touch on her arm seemed to create a heat within her and, when she looked up into his eyes, she noticed his own desire was also present. She found herself drawn to him so unquestionably and soon their lips were together once more on the castle steps with the guards nearby.

"My God, Killian, I cannot keep my thoughts from you for but a moment. I think 'tis you who has some type of magical power over me. And when our son is born and my body healed from the birthin' then we'll share the torrid, primal, passion we once did. We'll continue with the reckless abandonment we once shared in our physical love."

She knew many men would be insulted to know she spoke of a time when they would share a greater level of passion since they had made love many times the previous night, but she sensed he knew precisely what she meant and he was not offended. In actuality, she was aware he was aroused in knowing they both longed to be together in a wild, reckless and uninhibited manner.

"Aye, well, if you speak of such things so openly, I'll be driven to take you here and now, Alainn, and I am uncertain I can rein in my passion for much longer, if you keep lookin' at me with that lustful expression in those unusual blue eyes."

"I could freeze time, Killian. Make everything and everyone around us immobile so we can be together here or anywhere else you would desire it!" she whispered as his hands had gone from her back to her hips.

"I think I can restrain myself long enough to show you what I've promised, and to make it back to our bedchamber."

"But perhaps I cannot!" She sensually cooed.

The sound of a cart approaching distracted them and, when Killian looked toward the cart, he smiled and glanced at her once more.

"It would appear I've two gifts for you."

As Killian led her down the steps to the cobblestone street, he introduced her to the man driving the cart.

"This is my carpenter, William McCree."

"Tis good to meet you, William!" She extended her hand to him and he shook it heartily. "I am most appreciative of the wooden bath you created. Your work is perfectly crafted."

"Milady!" He beamed proudly at her praise.

Killian looked at the article in the back of the cart now draped with bed sheets. "Tis ready, Will? I'd thought it would take you longer."

"No, I finished it as quickly as I could, Milord, for I knew you wanted to present it to your lady."

Alainn was growing exceedingly impatient as the two men discussed what lie beneath the coverings. Killian surely sensed her impatience for he nodded to the man to reveal the surprise, and Alainn squealed and fought the urge to bounce up and down as she looked down at the beautifully crafted object. Tears spilled down her cheeks as she ran her hand along the smoothly carved wood. Killian lifted it from the cart and she stared down at the lovely cradle.

She still had not spoken a word and the tears still flowed in earnest. Killian took her in his arms and held her tight, and the other man appeared concerned.

"Is it not to your liking, then, milady? Would you like me to fashion another? If you tell me what design you would prefer, sure I can create whatever type might be more to your pleasure!"

"No, Will, she likes it most well! My lovely wife sheds tears of joy as often as of sorrow, and sure these are tears of joy."

"Aye, 'tis beautiful, William! You must have worked tirelessly for a lengthy time to produce such a fine and lovely cradle."

"Aye, well, your husband asked me to begin it as soon as you came here to Castle O'Donnel those weeks ago. And he has paid me more than fairly for the work I've done. In truth, he has called no rent due for the remainder of the time my family and I live in our cottage. Milord is an uncommonly generous man."

"Aye, he is most generous! I thank you, Killian, and you, William, as well."

Killian shook the young man's hand. He sat back in the cart and was about to drive away when Killian called after him.

"Will, we're to host a celebration here at week's end. You must attend, you and your wife, and there's to be a grand hunt as well. Would you be interested in accompanying me?"

"Aye, certainly, it would be a great honor, milord."

"It's settled then." Killian smiled and waved to the man as he set off.

⌘

IT WAS OFTEN customary for a chieftain to invite a servant to attend a feast or take part in a hunt with the nobles if they were pleased with the work a man had done for him. And Killian was well pleased with the wee cradle that he placed within the room next to his and Alainn's bedchamber.

As he glanced at the many lovely paintings upon the wall, the quilts and blankets Alainn had created for their child, and now the beautifully made cradle, he thought the room looked nearly ready for the child they would welcome in only weeks. His heart felt as though it would burst with pride and excitement at knowing the woman he loved would soon give birth to their son. He felt a certain amount of fearfulness and anxiety at knowing many women died in childbed. In truth, he was only too aware that nearly one in three women died during the birthing, and many others from complications after the birth. But he would not allow himself to dwell on that horrid possibility. Alainn was a strong woman and a magical healer, sure she would remain well and survive the birthing, though the knowledge the child was surely large did cause him to worry for her, and he prayed it was unnecessary.

Alainn glanced at him and must have seen the concern in his eyes.

"I will be well, Killian. I will live to love you and our child."

"Aye, it must be so, Alainn, for I could not bear to be parted from you, or to be the cause of your end."

⌘

ALAINN WANTED TO able to take away the fear he held in his eyes although something regarding the birth of their child had her undeniably fearful as well. Despite the fact she was a seer and often possessed the ability to know what the future held, when it came to her own future, she was often as uninformed as any other human. She changed the subject to distract their fretful thoughts.

"Come break fast with me now, and I believe you've promised me another bestowment?"

"A wee bit greedy you are, wife."

"Only when it comes to gifts from my husband," she whispered as she then proceeded to unfasten his belt, and tug on his trews.

"My God, you're a wanton woman, and greatly demanding."

"And that is not likely to change, my love." She softly spoke as she pulled his lips down to her own.

⌘

AS THEY LAY upon the rug on the floor in the room that would soon be their child's, their many articles of clothing scattered about the room, Killian looked down at her lovely blossomed body.

"Tis clearly improper to bed my lady here upon the floor when she is with child."

"Aye, well, you had little choice in the matter, I'd say, for I fairly accosted you and had my way with you. Maire O'Donnel would not think it proper by any stretch of the imagination, but she believes I should be hidden away to hide my shameful condition, so perhaps as long as I don't leave the concealment of hidden rooms, this would be acceptable to her."

"She's an unpleasant woman, at best, Alainn. Don't be grievously affected by her cutting words; she has always been difficult. I remember my mother finding her unkind and disagreeable even all those years ago."

"I do attempt to hold my tongue; I don't intend to speak rudely to her, but I seem unable to stop myself when she is so forthcoming with her unwanted advice and opinions. How did your mother contend with the woman then?

"I don't actually recall how she dealt with her, for my mother was a more demure woman."

"Less of a bitch, then?"

"Less spirited, I would suggest." He chuckled.

She smiled at his diplomacy in dealing with her and her willful ways.

They heard a muffled noise coming from the corridor and then a loud knocking upon the door in their adjoining bedchamber.

"Milord, the servants have brought you the item you've requested. Should we leave it here in the corridor, or would you like us to come inside your chambers?"

It was the voice of his steward, Fergus Flannery, and Killian could hear his wife Eireen out there as well.

"No, have them bring it in then, Fergus."

"Killian O'Brien, are you mad?"

Chapter Nine

S HE HASTENED TO grab her clothes and began to dress, but upon realizing it would not be accomplished before the men were in the room, she employed her magic to don her garments. As Killian remained lying there entirely unclothed, she urged him to get dressed or at the very least to cover himself before the servants and Eireen were allowed to view his appealing physique.

"Get yourself dressed, Killian O'Brien, before Eireen has a clear view of you in your entirety!"

"I'm feelin' too lazy and content just now. My wife kept me up half the night in a state of lustful arousal."

"And that condition seems to have returned!" She glanced down at his impressive proportions and aroused condition, and he simply smiled and made no effort to cover himself as the door to the chamber was about to be opened. She hurriedly glanced at his garments upon the floor and then at him. She waved her hands and in an instant he was dressed as well. She was certain her eyes flashed with obvious anger and jealousy.

"I knew you'd not allow another woman to see me unclothed. I've missed bein' entertained by your magical feats and, despite what you say, I know how much you adore workin' your magic. Besides, some things are achieved so much more simply by way of magic," he whispered in her ear.

"Emasculation may well be one of them," she whispered back as she glowered at him, but then smiled as he pulled her into his arms for a kiss even in full view of the many servants, the steward, and his wife. When the kiss was ended, Alainn allowed herself to look at the immense article being hauled into the room with great care. It was the largest, grandest, most beautiful harp Alainn thought she had ever seen.

As she walked toward it and looked back at her husband, her tears rolled down her cheeks once more, and he passed her his handkerchief. She dabbed her eyes and then threw her arms around his neck. The servants appeared embarrassed and the steward was clearly uncomfortable. Eireen seemed to recognize the great emotion Alainn was feeling.

"You see, Fergus, 'tis not only I who weeps when the emotion is strong, and not only at displeased emotions. Lady Alainn is given to weeping as well."

"Lady Alainn carries a child and therefore her tears are understandably justified."

Alainn had finally left Killian's arms and she sat down upon the stool that accompanied the immense harp. She pulled her hands across the strings and smiled up at her husband, eyes still blurred with tears. She played a lovely and complicated piece Killian had often heard his aunt play. Then she began a sweet lullaby often sung to babes by their mothers. Alainn jumped as the babe within her signaled his delight at her playing.

"Killian, you must come feel your son's sturdy kicks."

The servants, who had all been enjoying the music, left them alone as Killian went to Alainn's side and placed his large hands to her belly and she continued to play.

"He's sure to be musically inclined as his mother."

"And his father as well," she added, for Killian had been practicing his fiddling these past months and had become much improved as to when he had once serenaded her on the evening he'd proposed.

"I love you, so, Alainn. I am the luckiest, most blessed man in the country and, if I were to die today, I swear I would die a contented man."

Alainn stopped the playing and stood by his side, placing her head on his chest she inhaled the familiar, wonderful masculine scent.

"If I spent a hundred years with you on this earth, joined in complete love, and utter enchantment, it would still be not enough, Killian. I think our souls shall be joined for all eternity. We are soul connections, you and I, so even death will not part us; I feel it in my bones."

He squeezed her to him tightly and she knew he felt a needling within his soul at this talk of death and being parted and was aware they both welcomed the knock upon the door. It was Pierce MacCarther, the captain's son. Alainn hadn't seen him since the day they had met in Glynnis's cottage. She was relieved he seemed as eager to forget that day as she was.

"Alainn, Killian! Good morning to you both. You requested to be alerted to when Lady Mary returned, and her coach has arrived this morning. I can take you to see her, if you wish it?"

Pierce had known Alainn all her life. Killian had known him a long while as well. Pierce found it entirely foreign to refer to them by the titles of milady and milord and they had long ago told him it was not a requirement.

Alainn smiled in learning her friend, Mary, had returned to Castle O'Rorke. She was thankful for Pierce's friendship as well. Although he was now betrothed to her best friend Molly, and they were to wed in the spring, at one time he had set his eyes on Alainn. For years, he had been quite smitten with her and even written her poems of his great love. Killian knew of Pierce's affection toward Alainn and he had often taunted her about the boy's infatuation. Pierce was now a loyal servant to Killian and a valuable asset to Killian's army, as well as a friend.

"I thank you, Pierce, for the news of Mary's homecoming. I am much obliged, but Killian will take me to Castle O'Rorke for he has business there. Thank you for your kind offer, though."

"Aye, Alainn."

Killian's eyes filled with question as he looked at Alainn after Pierce had left them alone. "And what pressing business have I at Castle O'Rorke?"

She smiled back at him and her blue eyes filled with a mischievous quality. "You must speak to your cousin on taking his marriage vows more seriously, or indeed I will be driven to use magic to change the man."

"And why, when you are displeased with him, do you refer to him as my cousin? I think Riley and I have little in common as of late."

"You have an uncommon ability to change a man's mind to your way of thinking. And if I deal with him in that regard, he'll be no use to his wife or any other woman, for he'll be dead or a gelding at the very least, I should think!"

"Aye, well, I'll talk to the man then, but I can't promise you anything, Alainn. He's boar-headed and does not take kindly to bein' told what to do and, in that regard, I suppose he is your cousin." He taunted.

Alainn good-naturedly tossed the nearby cushion at her husband, but it hit the door he'd closed behind him.

Chapter Ten

ALAINN STOOD UPON the lowest fence rail glancing up at the magnificent white stallion within the pen at Castle O'Rorke. It was a giant of an animal, as large as Killian's horse, Storm, and then some. It was pure white with a golden mane and tail and only a tiny gold marking on his forehead shaped much like a lightening bolt. The animal was a wild sort, completely unbroken and her cousin, Riley, had declared it untamable.

Alainn glanced over at the discussion now taking place between Killian and Riley, the one she had prompted Killian to initiate and, by the displeased look on both their faces, she concluded it was not going well. Perhaps it was none of her concern that Riley had been unfaithful to his wife, but Mary was a valued friend and Alainn longed to see her happy. Lately, she had sensed Mary's displeasure and Alainn believed in truth homesickness was not the only reason Mary had journeyed back to Scotland.

As she looked up at the huge horse, she tried to calm him for she sensed something most unusual and perhaps even magical about him, but she also detected a fury within the beast's soul. She talked to him soothingly and she noticed him quieting. She stepped down from the fence and met the dark brown eyes of Connor MacLain.

"He's a beauty, isn't he, Lady O'Brien?"

"Aye, that he is."

Killian had drawn closer as soon as Connor had approached Alainn, and Alainn thought he acted undeniably protective and uneasy whenever she was near the large Scot.

"Your grandfather and your cousin seem to think there is little hope of him ever being tamed. They think it would be best to end his life or to let him go into the wild."

"That's entirely horse shite; I could most certainly tame him!" She declared indignantly.

The man glanced at her with doubt in his dark brown eyes but, obviously a sensible man, he kept his mouth shut.

"Truly, I could tame him, not this day, mind you, but one day I will!" she added.

The man tried to keep his opinion to himself, but a snort escaped his lips. He was a large man, as tall as Killian, which was rare, and as brawny and powerful as well. His thick copper hair was wild and clearly unmanageable, and his brown eyes held a stubborn quality.

"You shouldn't doubt her, or question her ability, Connor, for she'll be spurred to mount the damn beast here and now just to prove you wrong." Killian reasoned.

"Well, I didn't suggest I'd do it today, the horse would surely object to it and so would our son, but one day, after the child is born, I will manage it. Mark my words, the both of you!"

Alainn haughtily tossed her head in the air and her long blonde hair, now bound, began to work its way loose from its ties as she walked toward the stables and away from the men.

⌘

KILLIAN SMILED AT her determination, but Riley who had caught the tail end of the conversation appeared less pleased.

"My God, she's a vixen. You should not concern yourself with matters between Mary and me when you clearly have no rule over your own wife. As her husband, it is up to you to control her and you should tame her, Killian. She needs to be less spirited, I'd wager, or she'll cause you great concern through all your life!"

Killian was about to answer, but the Scot did so for him.

"And would either the beast here or the woman be as beautiful or as desirable if their spirits were broken? Sometimes the spirited ones may cause us the most consternation and uncertainty, but it is that very reckless spirit that appeals most to us. Don't tame her entirely, O'Brien, for you'd be the sorrier for it."

Killian was uncertain how to respond to that comment regarding his wife by a man little more than a stranger, when he caught the sight of something else that disturbed him even more. He saw Alainn smile warmly at a tall, blonde young man and something in that seemingly innocent smile evoked a great jealousy within his soul. He went to her side as he heard her speak to the man.

⌘

"Danhoul, 'tis most wonderful to see you. In our recent telepathic conversation you did not indicate we would see each other soon. I did not know the bonnachts or any members of the kern, the Irish army, were here in this area; are the English nearby as well, then?"

"No, in truth, I have been summoned by your grandfather. I am to be in his employ, to be in his private army."

Alainn was filled with uncertainty for she'd not heard her grandfather mention enlisting new men to the clan or his army. She knew very little regarding Danhoul Calhoun's history, but she did know he was a druid, that he possessed unusual abilities, some of the same abilities she did. He had been at Castle O'Brien and he'd bravely assisted her and Killian in dealing with a dark entity. He'd also attempted to heal her when she'd been struck with the poisoned dart for he did claim healing powers as well.

Danhoul was younger than she was, but had grown taller and physically matured much in the months since last she'd seen him. His dark, honey-blonde hair and smoky blue-grey eyes were unusually appealing to her. And the tiny cleft in his chin and his stubble-covered jaw drew her gaze. She could not for all her dwelling on the subject discern why this young man was so undeniably attractive to her. Killian approached and she felt something akin to guilt as he stood beside her.

"Danhoul!" He nodded in greeting the young man.

"Killian O'Brien! You are a man spoken of often in both the circles of armies and clans. You have achieved notoriety in a short time, and I am honored to call you an acquaintance, if not yet truly a friend!"

"And you, Danhoul Calhoun, have built quite a reputation for yourself, as well. Barely more than a boy of six and ten, yet I'm told you have become a fearsome warrior and a learned soldier. And Niall has persuaded you to train and instruct his army then?"

"Aye, though I'm certain a man of greater experience or more advanced age would be better suited for the position!"

"Cleary Niall believes you are the man for the position and he is a seer as well, though I might suggest it is your druid connections that have him thoroughly convinced!"

"You knew Danhoul was to be in Grandfather's employ, Killian?" Alainn questioned.

"Aye, he spoke of such during our time at the meeting of the clans."

The two men looked at each other with an unspoken challenge in their eyes and Alainn knew there would be surely many times these two would lock horns, and her intuition told her she would most likely be the cause of their discord.

Her grandfather approached and he and the young soldier seemed intent on speaking. Riley had once more engaged Killian in conversation and she decided to go search for Mary. She'd been told by a servant Mary would be available for a visit, but that had been some time earlier. When she entered the stables she witnessed a most unexpected sight. She found her good friend, Mary, in the arms of the groom, Connor MacLain. It was clearly a passionate embrace. Her eyes widened in disbelief and as she saw Riley approaching, she threw them a warning look as she began to reprimand them soundly.

"My God, Mary! What are you thinking? Riley could have you hanged for treason if he saw you like this. You know it is unlawful for a woman to be unfaithful to her husband, and most especially the wife of a chieftain. And Connor, are you so eager to return to prison or to swing from a rope? This will surely not end well for either of you if you should pursue this further."

They quickly pulled apart as Alainn spoke, and she noticed the fury in Mary's dark brown eyes, but the passion as well. The Scot's eyes were also filled with deep longing as he gazed at Mary even though they had distanced themselves from one another. Alainn hurried to Mary's side and threw her arms around her as she realized Riley was fast approaching with Killian close behind.

"I have missed you much, Mary? How was your visit with your family? Sure, you must have been most pleased to return to your husband?" Alainn baited the woman and waited for her reply.

"Aye, I was pleased to return to Castle O'Rorke!" she replied and she boldly glanced after the groom who had once again gone to tend to the castle's horses.

Alainn couldn't wait to be alone with Mary so she could speak with her regarding the heated embrace she had just found her in, but Mary seemed less than eager to have that conversation, for she claimed tiredness due to her long journey. She politely excused herself to return to the castle. Alainn knew by the stubborn look in her friend's eyes, it would be best to wait a time to speak further on the subject.

While Killian and Riley stayed within the stables and discussed a matter regarding what horses would be best suited if they needed them during a battle with the English, Alainn felt drawn to go back to view the large white stallion. Once again, she stood on the fence and talked soothingly to the snorting, rearing animal.

"Hello, you mighty beast, perhaps a magical beast, you are a most impressive sight! Sure we can get to know each other better one day soon. What do you think of that notion, Lightning?" She purred.

She saw that both Killian and Connor were looking at her with concern on their faces, so she soon stepped back from the rail as they approached. And, out of the corner of her eye, she saw Danhoul Calhoun, who was furthest away from her, beginning to draw nearer as well. She heard his voice call out in alarm and in warning.

"Killian, get to your wife!"

Chapter Eleven

KILLIAN DID NOT hesitate, but raced toward her as the large Scottish man did so as well. Alainn turned to see the immense white horse charging toward the fence and directly at her. Killian grabbed her and pulled her away as the animal hit the fence rails and shattered the thick planks. Connor MacLain was also directly in line of the roaring, angry horse and Alainn saw the enormous animal bring his front hooves down upon the other man. She watched in horror as the man's shoulder and arm were nearly ripped from his body and, as Killian pulled her away, she noticed a broken shard of the wooden fence had pierced his forearm. He groaned in pain, but was mostly concerned about his wife's safety. She hurriedly assured him she was well, but then hastened toward the other man who was lying in a crumpled heap upon the ground, writhing in agony. Danhoul Calhoun, the young soldier went to him as well.

Alainn tore strips of her skirts and placed them upon the bloody wound, and applied pressure while the man called out in pain. She imagined the many vials of potions in her chambers that would assist with the pain, and she summoned them to her. They appeared in her hand straightaway, and she opened the lids and poured a hearty amount down the man's throat. Killian had knelt beside her, having pulled the wooden stake from his own arm and wound it up with a strip of his tunic.

"Are you well, Killian? Is the pain great?"

"No, 'tis most certainly bearable, and sure it's a far cry from this man's serious injuries."

"Aye, well I will tend to your wound as well, Killian, but first I must see to these injuries or Connor may well lose his arm."

She laid her hands upon the man's torn flesh, skin and bone, employing her powers to heal him and she noticed he was startled to feel the wound grow much less painful. She also noticed how much calmer he felt and could sense him wondering what was in the elixir he had been given. He soon fell into a deep sleep, which was the best remedy for him at the moment. Without worrying what Killian, Riley, or Danhoul would think, she reached inside her frock and pulled out her charmed dagger. She slit her palm and allowed her own blood to seep onto the wound of the other man. She then bound the wound tightly once more and wrapped her own hand.

"He must be taken to our castle, Killian, for I must attend to him closely."

"Aye, I'll have a cart sent for him."

Alainn next went to examine Killian's wound and though

it was a manageable wound, it would need to be closed by manner of stitching. She also noticed his amulet glowing brightly.

"Your amulet prevented serious injury, Killian!"

"And it was Danhoul's warning that surely saved your life, Alainn."

"And yours and Connor's quick actions."

She only then noticed the magnificent white horse lying upon the ground, clearly wounded as well. She looked toward it in concern, but Riley called out to her.

"Stay away from the hellish beast, Alainn! I will end his life, before he harms anyone else."

"No, Riley, you must not!"

"Alainn, he nearly killed you. He is a danger to all around him and to himself," Killian agreed.

Alainn used her powers to sense what the animal was feeling. She shook her head as she spoke.

"No, Killian, the animal has been charmed with a dark spell. He was driven to charge me, not by mistake or by accident, but by design, someone has employed the animal to do their bidding. Someone with strong magical abilities wishes me harm and, by God Almighty, I mean to find out whom."

Riley had continued toward the horse with sword un-sheathed and Alainn prevented it.

"Killian, I ask that the horse be taken to our stables, for I am certain I can undo the spell against me. Please tell me you'll allow it!"

Though a look of doubt crossed his handsome face, he looked down at her as she pleaded to him and he finally relented. As the cart arrived and Connor MacLain was carefully loaded upon it, Alainn rode alongside the ailing man and Killian went to speak with Danhoul.

"How did you know the horse would charge my wife?"

"Well, you're possibly aware I experience visions as she does. I saw her dead when the horse's hooves struck her head and caused her death. I am thankful you heeded my warning."

"And I am thankful to you for saving Alainn's life."

The two men shook hands with respect for each other as it seemed they would be required to rally their forces; once again their partnership would be required.

ALAINN DOZED AS she sat at the bedside of the injured man. He'd been in extreme pain, she'd needed to relocate the joint, set the bone, mend the torn skin which had taken hours, and much magical healing as well. She'd issued him an herbal remedy many times in the night, in truth, probably too often and in quantities too great, therefore she sat by him vigilantly watching his condition. She had needed to keep him in a restful state lest he waken and thrash about in his great agony, surely causing further harm, and disturb the probably more than one hundred stitches. She didn't suspect his wound was becoming purulent, but it was still too early to determine whether it might.

She heard a sound by the door and watched as Killian came to check on her again as he'd done several times through the night.

"He's not about to murder me any time soon, Killian O'Brien. He's hardly capable and not liable to do so at any rate. You needn't be fearful for me." She knew her tone sounded less than amicable and realized her lack of sleep was making her prickly.

"I didn't suspect he'd murder you, Alainn. I was just comin' to check on his condition and on yours. You must be dead tired and that can't be good for you or the babe."

She smiled up at his concerned and tired face. She stood and grasped the small of her back and gestured for him to come to her. He complied. She put her arms around his neck, and he drew her closer. She was nearly asleep on her feet as she leaned her head against his strong, broad chest and felt his warmth surrounding her. She glanced down at the wound on his forearm as well.

"Is it terribly painful?" she asked with deep sincerity as she tenderly touched her hand to his injury.

"No, 'tis nothin', Alainn."

"Hardly nothing, Killian, it took more than two dozen stitches to close it and some magical healing as well."

"But it could have been much worse. I could have fared as badly as the Scot. Sure, it's a miracle that he still lives much less still has his arm attached to the rest of his body. That was a horrid injury. He's you to thank for his life and his arm, I'd suggest."

"And he is to be thanked for saving my life, and you and Danhoul as well."

"You've never felt compelled to spill your blood for anyone other than me, Alainn."

"It was by impulse and necessity I shed my blood to save him. And gratitude for he saved me from the horse's fury. I have used my powers often this night in attempt to discover who charmed the animal against me. I cannot seem to begin to conjure that information."

"Danhoul knows of magic, and has unusual druid capabilities.......

"Danhoul would never hurt me!" She interrupted before he had completed his thoughts.

"I did not imply he would, Alainn. He helped us back at Castle O'Brien and was clearly responsible for savin' your life; I'd hardly believe he was the cause of your near death. But why are you so damn defensive when it comes to him. You really don't know the boy so very well, and still I sense there is somethin' more between you, somethin' I don't care for in the slightest. What power does he have over you, and what connection do you have to him?"

There was both jealousy and concern in his tone and she looked up into his green eyes that were now consumed with both.

"I've no connection to him beyond our shared abilities and gratitude for all that Danhoul did to assist us back at Castle O'Brien!" She assured him, but she turned from him as she spoke.

He took her arm and turned her to him so that he could look deeply into her startling blue eyes.

"And though you may have on occasion kept information from me, you've never actually lied to me in your life, Alainn? What about the boy makes you feel the need to do so now?"

She stared at him, uncertain how to respond, but she finally found the words that he wasn't' certain gave him any consolation.

"Aye, I've never lied to you, Killian, and I won't speak falsehoods to you now. But, I swear, I don't know why I feel a deep connection to Danhoul. I feel as though I know him, that I know him well from another life or another time and, aye, there is a force that pulls me to him. I don't understand it and I certainly don't welcome it. 'Tis you I love, Killian O'Brien, and only you I shall always love, so doubt me not, not for a second, husband!"

"If you'd allowed me to finish my statement, I was actually wonderin', with his many supernatural abilities, if he might be able to learn the origin of the magic spell that has been used against you."

He kissed her then and, before she could respond to his thoughts, they heard the stirring from the man lying on the bed.

"So I've been healed by a witch, then, is that the whole of it?" the Scot asked in a pain-filled voice. He had obviously heard the conversation that had just taken place.

"Aye, you have!" she admitted as she went to the man and began to remove the bandages that covered his massive wound.

He moaned loudly and called out, and then cussed furiously.

"Why the blasted hell don't you just leave it be? It doesna hurt nearly as badly when you just let it lie as it is!"

"And if it is not cleansed thoroughly and often, it will fester and rot and I will be forced to sever it entirely to save your life."

The man groaned loudly again.

"Your wife has a rare talent for telling it like it is and not holding back anything. How do you put up with it?"

Killian smiled at the other man as he watched his wife diligently work at easing the other man's pain and affliction.

"You, yourself said the spirited ones are the most beautiful, and she's both beauty and spirit to rave of, and both in vast quantities."

"And you know if she presented these powers in England or France or even in the country of my birth she'd be taken to trial and surely burned at the stake for her gifts."

"Aye, I'm aware of the superstitious nonsense and the barbaric practices."

"There were suspected witches in the prison where I was held. And I watched many an innocent woman hauled off to be given an unfair trial and to meet a painful death. Some of them were surely only healers, and others with no more powers than me."

Alainn shivered at the thought of dying by flame and she carefully wound the fresh clean bandages around the man's shoulder and down his arm. She was aware Killian was more than perturbed at the man for his comments.

"I'll thank you not to frighten my wife, Connor MacLain!"

"It wasn't my intention to frighten her, but to purposely warn her, I suppose."

"I am standin' right here beside the two of you and you needn't treat me like a child. I am well aware of what fate befalls many a woman in other countries, and I am most fortunate to live here in this country. Though open displays of magic are not advisable or most intelligent actions, even in Ireland, I know of no women who have met their death by so doing."

They were then interrupted by the door to the chamber being thrown open and an obviously very angry Mary O'Brien bursting into the room.

"Why was my husband's groom brought here for healing, we have a healer at our castle and my husband's grandfather is notably capable in that regard as well?"

Killian and Alainn and exchanged startled glances, in noticing the other woman's displeasure.

It was Killian who responded. "Mary, you know as well as anyone, Alainn is a gifted healer, and she's not only ensured Connor lives, she's most likely saved his arm. Why are you so enraged about this?"

Mary had yet to meet Alainn's eyes and Alainn sensed her unhappiness, but her jealousy as well.

"As soon as he is well, he can be returned to Castle O'Rorke!" Killian assured her.

"I think that is not a wise consideration, Killian! I believe it would be beneficial to have Connor remain here at Castle O'Brien for a time, for the wound will need to be closely watched and we will need assistance in taming the stallion." Alainn suggested in a firm tone.

Killian watched as the pretty, young Scottish woman's face turned a rosy red in her fury. He wondered what had transpired between the two women to cause such discord for they had become fast friends from the first time they'd seen each other. Initially, it was not a relationship that was likely to form a friendship for Mary had been betrothed to Killian. They had very nearly married though Killian and Alainn had been desperately in love, even then. He could not wrap his mind around what was forcing such a wedge between the two when he heard the other woman's spiteful words.

"How many men would be sufficient for you, Alainn O'Brien?"

"Mary, I know you don't mean those hurtful words, and

you know as sure as I'm standin' here, that Killian is the only man I love."

"Perhaps... but apparently that doesn't stop you from bewitching and charming every other man you come in contact with. Are you just naturally beguiling to them or do you truly put a spell on them so each one of them falls hopelessly in love with you?"

"Mary, you are one of my dearest friends and very important to me. How can you think I would be that immoral or so completely without conscience?"

The man lying on the bed was as noticeably uncomfortable by the exchange between the two women as Killian.

"Mary, I don't know what you think Alainn has done to wrong you, but I will speak to the goodness of her character. She does not entice other men, not purposefully or willingly!" Killian offered.

"Killian, do you think you could actually see any flaw in her character, you are so bewitched by her yourself. I think if she should decide to take any number of men to her bed you'd be even then unwilling to see it as a fault."

"Mary, that is a dreadfully untruthful thing to say, and not only are you Alainn's friend, I consider you to be my friend as well. But, if you keep talkin' to her and about her in that manner, I'll ask you to be gone from our castle indefinitely!"

"Aye, well then, Connor will accompany me to Castle O'Rorke!"

"No, Mary, I shall stay put, I believe it is best if I stay here to ensure I will be healed entirely."

"You see, it has already begun!" She hissed and left the room with tears in her dark eyes.

Alainn would not meet Killian's eyes and, as she headed for the door, he caught her arm and saw that many tears flowed down her own cheeks and a sob escaped her lips.

"What in hell is goin' on, Alainn; you'd best tell me now?"

"Aye, Killian, we'll speak on this directly, but I must have a word with Mary first."

Killian nodded, knowing it was unlikely he could dissuade her even though he thought further discussion between the two women was not necessarily a wise consideration.

Alainn hastened down the long corridor, but Mary was already halfway down the castle steps before she finally caught up with her. She touched her arm, but Mary pulled away in a temper.

"Mary, what has you so very angry with me?

Chapter Twelve

"MARY, TRULY I am entirely in the dark regarding your unpleasantness. If it is because I caught you in the arms of another man, 'tis true I don't pretend to like it for I am most fearful for you, but we must discuss it. I know you have been unhappy recently and I thought perhaps you and Riley had quarreled when you left to Scotland so suddenly."

"Aye, well, I've no desire to speak with you regarding Connor or Riley, so just allow me to be on my way!"

"Mary, I consider you to be one of my dearest friends. You must tell me what has caused this terrible rage you seem to feel toward me."

"You want the truth of it then, do you? You might not care to hear what I have to say on the matter, for I've no kind words for you at the moment!"

"Tell me what's on your mind, Mary, for we've no hope of reconciliation if you won't even tell me how you feel I have wronged you."

"It wasn't enough that you wed Killian when he was to be my husband. I know within my heart he and I could have been happy for I was well pleased to be his intended after we met. Then I recognized the two of you were in love, and I liked you, so I was willing to end our betrothal for I sensed he would never feel anything for me. And when I turned my sights on Riley, and he seemed to care for me as well, I was thankful and relieved to find a husband I was compatible with, and for the first few weeks of our marriage, I thought we would remain so."

Alainn saw the woman's brown eyes had begun to fill with tears once more, and she fought the urge to embrace her and offer her empathetic consolation, but she recognized the woman would not desire Alainn near her. She waited for her to continue.

"It was after you and Killian came to live at Castle O'Donnel that things began to change. Riley scarcely seemed to want to be near me, he barely spoke to me and almost never came to my bed. I was uncertain why he had changed so drastically. I thought maybe he was unhappy being here and far distanced from his family and his childhood home. When I tried to speak with him, he became angry and defensive, and soon after I found him with a servant girl, and then another, and another. When I became outraged at his blatant infidelity, he simply told me to get used to the notion for he wasn't about to change his ways because he was a married man, that his desires had not lessened because he'd spoken a few empty, worthless vows, I believe was how he phrased it."

When she stopped speaking, Alainn's tears began falling down her face.

"Sorry, I am, Mary. Genuinely sorry, I am that my cousin is such a dishonorable and unfeeling arse! But, you must tell me why you are so displeased with me."

"Are you not the all-knowing seer; the woman endowed with so many magical powers? Surely you know why I feel such contempt for you?"

"I don't Mary; truly I don't."

"So you dinna ken how Riley feels toward you?"

Alainn's heart sank at what the other woman was alluding to, for once, a long while ago, Riley had admitted having feelings for her. It had been before she'd learned of her true parentage and they'd never spoken of it again.

"Oh, so you do ken how he feels? You must or you'd not wear such a grim expression at the moment?"

"He spoke of such only once and it was many months ago. I thought he was over whatever he believed he once felt for me."

"Aye, well he's not over it as you say. And he told me plain how he feels for you. The night before I fled to Scotland, he told me straight out for I forced him to tell me why he had distanced himself from me. He told me he had, and would only ever truly love one woman, that he could take a thousand women to his bed, but that he would still lust for only one. He told me he would have wed you even knowing you were his cousin if you had not been so entirely in love with Killian. He said he wished with all his heart it was him you were married to, his baby you carried, that it was his bed you shared each night."

Alainn glanced around to make certain no one else heard the exchange between them for if Killian suspected any of this he would surely be driven to challenge, Riley to a battle of swords, a battle that Riley could not win for Killian was unsurpassed in his ability with a sword and she knew of no one who could best him.

"Och, you needn't fear I'll tell Killian about it, for now you have a secret of mine that must be concealed as well. I knew Conner back in Scotland; he'd come to be groom for my father. We were attracted to one another immediately, though we mostly fought the attraction. And he is past nine and twenty, and I only eight and ten years. I knew my father would force me into an arranged marriage to a noble and that the longer we were together the more difficult it would be to be parted. Therefore I asked to be allowed to live with my cousins, the McConnels in Ireland. It was the most difficult decision I have ever made, to leave him behind."

"And he followed you here?" Alainn questioned, feeling the other woman's pain.

"No, he says it was by sheer coincidence that he came to Castle O'Rorke, for I wasn't to be living at Castle O'Rorke. He had no notion I would be here when he came looking for employment, and he still thinks it was coincidence. I think it was our destiny!

But, now, he seems to believe it's an impossible consideration to think we could ever have any future together and unwise for us to be thinking about it, and I say to hell with that. If my husband can lust for you and sate his lust with spending time with most every woman he sees, then I think I shall find some happiness where I am able. But now, all Connor talks about is you, and your common interest of painting, and your love of horses and on and on and on. And he has even risked his own life to save yours. So, clearly, he is falling for you as well as every other man who is in your presence. There's already your husband's captain and his son, Pierce, not to mention that soldier who is now at our castle, and Riley. My God, do you bewitch every man you meet just to see if you're able?"

"I bewitch no one, Mary. I swear to you on my very life, I truly have never bewitched anyone by use of my powers or otherwise. And the only man I ever want to desire me is Killian."

"So you say, but that does little to calm my fears or keep me appeased."

"What can I do to appease you then, Mary; what might I do to make amends for I want no quarrel with you. I want only for our friendship to be renewed."

"That is surely not possible, Alainn, for what I want is never to see you again. I want you gone from my life entirely!"

Alainn felt the color drain from her face and she slowly

lowered herself to the steps as she softly whispered to herself. "You want me dead!"

"I didna say that."

"But you thought it; I heard the words as clearly in my mind as if you'd spoken them aloud to me. You wished I had died those months ago."

Mary looked up to see Killian approaching and Alainn sensed her anger and her rage turn into a deep and profound sadness, for she was aware she had loved her like a sister, but now saw no solution to the impasse.

"I didna say that!" She repeated, but her words fell on deaf ears.

Alainn was overwhelmed with deep melancholia. She wanted to be gone from this moment and without further thought she disappeared before the disbelieving eyes of the other woman and the worried eyes of her husband.

"Christ, Mary, what did you say to her?"

"It was not what I said, but what I thought. I can scarcely control what I think and it is not as if I actually wanted her to hear my thoughts!"

"I know, it's not an easy feat bein' a friend or a husband to someone who can hear your thoughts, especially when you're in the middle of a disagreement, and thankfully she can only hear my thoughts on rare occasions. But tell me then, what were your thoughts; what did Alainn hear?"

The young dark-haired woman hung her head in shame despite her fury, and whispered. "I wished her dead! I wished she'd died from the poison back at Castle O'Brien."

"Christ, Mary, you didn't! I think it best you leave immediately, before I say somethin' I'll regret, and I think it's a damn good thing you can't hear my thoughts at the moment!"

As the woman mounted her horse and galloped off, Killian looked up at the blackened sky and heard the roar of the thunder overhead. Before he'd made it to the top of the castle's steps the sky opened up and he knew Mary O'Brien would have a most unpleasant ride back to Castle O'Rorke. He also knew without question who was responsible for the sudden bout of unfavorable weather.

Chapter Thirteen

WHEN KILLIAN DIDN'T find Alainn in the chamber with the injured Scot, he presumed she must have gone to their bedchamber. Their chambers consisted of many adjoining rooms and when he heard the sounds of items being smashed against the wall of her dressing room, he'd most certainly discovered her location. He slowly opened the door and cautiously stuck his head in to witness several different objects being hurled through the air magically. If any of them ventured anywhere near his location they came to an abrupt halt mere inches from him and he was thankful of the fact he was not affected by her magic. As the pitcher and basin on the stand before her smashed against the wall into perhaps a hundred pieces or more, he looked at her and saw the fury in her blazing eyes.

Killian O'Brien knew his wife well and once, when they were children, she had confided in him. She had admitted when she was saddened and distraught beyond what she felt she could endure, she would force herself to turn the sadness into anger for that was an emotion she could manage with her magical abilities. He recognized the sadness that still lay somewhere deep within her lovely blue eyes, but the rage overruled the melancholia at the moment.

He stood there, saying nothing for several moments, just watching the many items being tossed and hurled and smashed against the stone walls, only to be lifted up once more and smashed until there were only the tiniest of shards left. He noticed the pretty turquoise combs he had once given her remained on the dressing table as well as the brush that had once been his mother's treasured possession. Obviously, even in her furious state, she held those articles dear to her and would not risk their destruction by way of her powers.

He saw the fire roared wildly in the hearth and he heard the thunderclaps remained close overhead. The flashes of lightning lit up the angry, dark sky, and he finally dared to speak when he thought she seemed to be tiring after pitching her great fit.

"'Tis hopeful I am that Mary made it home safe without bein' struck by lightning."

She threw him a furious glance and picked up a fragment of glass in her hand and aimed it at him. He ducked and lunged at her and grabbed her in his arms.

"Are you tryin' to injure me because you're displeased with your wee Scottish friend?"

"She is not my friend, nor shall she ever be considered my friend again!"

"That would be a pity, Alainn, for I know the two of you

seemed as close as two women can be."

"Aye, well there's naught to be done about it, for I'll not grovel or apologize when I have wronged her in no way!"

He noticed she still shook with the anger and emotion she felt, and she pulled from his arms and he saw the wooden stand thrown against the wall as well, and it, too, smashed. The brush and her combs gently sailed to her hand and she tucked them in the pocket of her gown.

"We'll soon have no furniture left if you continue you with your wee tantrum."

"Don't mock me, Killian O'Brien. If I was a man I would surely be issuing a challenge or beheading her. I am not a damnable man, thank the lord!"

"Oh, so now I'm to be the brunt of your rage, then? And how is it I have earned that great honor?" He jested and taunted her further as she glowered at him.

"If you weren't so damn handsome and so entirely appealing to me, I might wish the entire male gender in this whole county to become emasculated or at the very least impotent for a long while!"

"That might be a bit rash, at that." His expression had become serious as he approached her again. "You must tell me what has happened, Alainn? I know somehow it involves Riley and Connor MacLain, but what exactly has transpired that has Mary so damn fashed? Is she involved with the Scot in an unacceptable fashion?"

"They're not lovers if that's what you're questioning.

But, I believe it may only be a matter of time," she admitted honestly.

"Christ, Riley would kill her, the both of them I'm sure, and now that the man can hardly hold a sword, it would not be a fair match."

"Aye, well, he'd surely have him hanged if he suspects they've been together."

"Aye, he might! But why is she so angered at you?"

"She thinks the man is attracted to me, and I think she's lost her ability to see reason entirely, for I've never noticed a hint of anything but friendship and courteousness from Connor MacLain."

"So he's never attempted anythin' of a carnal nature with you?"

"Never, Killian, I swear it to you."

"And what of Riley?"

Alainn glanced at him with uncertainty in her eyes, unclear how to answer and exactly what question he was posing to her.

"What of Riley?" she spoke the same question he had issued her.

"Does she think you have been with him?"

"Are you asking me if she believes I have shared a bed with her husband?"

"Aye, I suppose that's what I'm asking."

She swallowed hard and avoided his eyes.

"No, she knows we have never shared a bed, of course

she knows that."

"But she knows it's not because he doesn't desire it to be so?"

Alainn's face revealed her complete disbelief in learning that Killian seemed aware that Riley had feelings for her. She nodded, but did not speak.

"I am not a stupid man, Alainn, nor unintuitive. I would have to be entirely daft to not know Riley has burned for you for some time. And I don't pretend to like it, but I can hardly flay him for it, when I have felt such a deep yearning for you for nearly half my life. And as long as he never acts upon his desires, never attempts anything dishonorable or inappropriate toward you, he won't find my sword through his heart, but should he ever..."

"He won't!" Alainn assured him.

"So, he has spoken to you of these feelings he has for you?"

"Aye, once a long while ago, but he has never ever been anything but proper with me, Killian."

"Aye, because he knows I'd kill him without a second's hesitation.'

"And because he loves you well and he has a deep respect for you, too, Killian. You are like a brother to him."

"But he cannot conceal the fact he is displeased that you and I are happy together. I sense his obvious discontent."

"I sense it as well, and I held such hope that he and Mary would be happy together, now it sounds as if their marriage is anything but happy and, in truth, I think it is in a shambles. I am fearful for her should she act upon her feelings toward Connor. I think Connor attempts to keep his desires in check, but sure it will only be a matter of time, should Mary continue to pursue him. That is the reason why I thought it best he remain here so the opportunity will be less likely that they become close."

"Aye, sure you're correct in tryin' to keep them apart, but 'tis unlikely it'll be managed if they truly long for it. She should not be entertainin' notions of goin' to another man's bed when she has vowed to stay true to her husband."

Alainn seemed displeased with his opinion and of course was not able to keep her thoughts to herself.

"And he can take perhaps a hundred women to his bed, fornicate with the servants, the peasants and any number of whores and that is simply acceptable because he is a man. And she wants to take one lover, a man she truly has deep feelings for, and that is considered wrong?"

"'Tis adultery no matter what the circumstance; and I'm not sayin' what Riley does isn't wrong, but 'tis mostly accepted."

"Not by me!"

"Then 'tis most fortunate he is not your husband!"

"Aye, extremely fortunate for he would most certainly find himself dead with his ballocks ripped from his body."

The complete fury and anger on her face had returned and the many broken pieces of wood and glass began to swirl through the air again.

"Calm you down, Alainn, for your temper cannot be good for you or for our son!"

"How am I to calm down when I feel so entirely angry, hurt, and displeased I should like to commit murder?"

"I can maybe think of a way to calm you, Lainna!" he whispered in her ear as he pulled back her hair and began kissing her neck.

"I've no desire to do any such thing, Killian O'Brien! I am furious and having you bed me' is not what I need."

"Oh, I think a proper beddin' might be just what you need!"

"Then think again!" She pulled away from him, but he quickly pulled her back to him and placed his lips on hers in a thorough kiss.

Her blood hummed as hot as her temper at the moment, but she refused to be persuaded.

"I must go see to Connor's condition!" She reasoned as he pulled her to him yet again.

"Aye, well, firstly you must see to your husband's condition and he to yours."

"I have no condition, I assure you!" She hissed as his strong hands caressed her breasts over her frock.

"Oh, I beg to differ, Lainna!" he whispered as his warm hands slipped beneath her chemise and her nipples peaked. He skillfully untied her fastenings and soon her breasts were bared and his mouth upon them each in turn.

"You are a damn barbarian!" She seethed and then gasped as her body responded unquestionably.

Her hands held tight to his thick, dark brown hair and he looked up at her with his passion-filled emerald eyes and her heart soared with love and with longing. He carried her to the settee and gently laid her down. He lifted her skirts and she felt his hands upon her, caressing her long smooth legs, touching all of her. She moaned in appreciation of his actions, and her temper finally gave away entirely to passion. She felt his hot kisses on her legs, on her inner thighs and then she arched her body as his mouth touched upon her in a most intimate and pleasurable manner.

"Killian, you must not continue, not when I am so well into my term," she whispered in ragged breaths.

"Is it unsafe for the child?" he briefly terminated his present actions and questioned.

"No, there is no risk to the babe," she shook her head.

"Uncomfortable, unacceptable, or unpleasant for you, is it?" he said with an arched eyebrow as his hand gently found her womanhood and continued pleasuring her.

"No, not any of those," She gasped loudly with no hope and no desire to dissuade him.

Once more she felt his mouth upon her and she writhed to meet his every movement. She moaned and panted with the intensity of the gratification she was feeling, and when she felt the overpowering ripples of dizzying sensations flowing from her sex to every other part of body and her entire being, she called out his name.

"Killian, My God, Killian! You create a fire within me that will never be tamed or quenched completely. I need you within me now; I need you to fill me entirely! You must take me now!"

Her trembling hands assisted him with the fastenings on his trews and she smiled at him sensually as she removed his impressive manhood and fondled it with great need. And when he entered her and their eyes met, she felt every ounce of anger and tension and unhappiness leave her for he had done as he'd promised, bedded her properly and taken away her temper, and filled her only with love and lust and completeness.

"You needn't look so completely smug about it!"

"Needn't I?" he whispered, the smile evident in his alluring eyes as well as on his full, sensual lips.

They lay together on the settee his long legs sprawled uncomfortably over the end of the narrow piece of furniture. His hands still caressed her breasts and he was compelled to ask her what was on his mind.

"Do they contain milk even now, or is that only formed after the child is born? They've grown and blossomed in a lovely manner, but I know they are tender now."

"It only comes later after the babe is born and, aye, they are tender, but I adore your touch, Killian. You always know exactly how to touch me and to treat me, during lovemaking and in all aspects of our lives. And I thank you for that! And I thank God for you and what we share, for I have come to know how rare a love it is we share!"

"And I know what a treasure I have in you, Lainna, and I also recognize our love is uncommon. How horrid it must be to have an unrequited love!"

"I do believe Mary loves Riley, but the love diminishes with each wrongdoing he commits, each woman he takes to his bed, and each harsh and unkind word he speaks to her. I know it is wrong, but I cannot fault her if she finds comfort or pleasure in another man's arms."

"You know I can't condone that, Alainn. I understand it but, even still, I cannot condone it. And she'll be in grave danger if Riley suspects anything goin' on between her and the Scot."

She had no time to respond to his comment for they heard a knock upon the door. She glanced down at the many broken and shattered objects on the floor and closed her eyes tightly. Within seconds the entire lot of the items was restored to its original state.

"My God, your powers have grown even without using them so frequently!"

"Aye!" she agreed with a mixture of delight and despair for a part of Alainn feared using her powers while another part of her reveled in it. He also knew there was something about her powers she felt compelled to conceal from him. That troubled him more than he cared to admit, but he did not push her on speaking on the issue.

As he stood and donned his trews and fastened the ties, he smiled down at her, victoriously, and she beamed back at him despite herself. She straightened her skirts and he looked at her breasts still uncovered. He placed a soft kiss on each one as another knock came to the door. He assisted her with the fastenings and then retrieved his sword from where he'd laid it on the floor.

"You may enter!" he finally called out.

They were both startled to find a thoroughly soaked, bedraggled and woeful looking Mary O'Brien standing at the door. The tears flowed down her cheeks as readily as the water from the recent rainfall pooled on the floor from her drenched skirts. She shivered and shook and sobbed, all in earnest.

"I am gravely apologetic, Alainn." She whimpered. "I had to come back to tell you that, I could not leave things so horrid between us, and I need you to know I would never ever wish you dead. You are as dear to me as anyone in my life, and certainly the only one I can confide in. Please tell me you'll accept my apology for I shall be distraught forever if you canna see it in you to forgive me. I know not what I shall do if that be truth, truly I do not!"

Alainn hurried to her side and embraced her tightly, her own clothes now soaked as well, and her own eyes filled with tears. She smiled up at Killian through her tears and he touched her shoulder as he headed toward the door.

"I'll have the servants bring up some heated stones, warm blankets and some hot herbal cider, for I suspect the two of you have a wee bit of talkin' to do!"

Chapter Fourteen

THE WEEK PRECEDING the celebrations at Castle O'Donnel was filled with many activities in preparation of the banquet, the games, and the hunt. The entire castle, its nobility, and servants were kept busy with unending chores and responsibilities. Killian and many of his men and army had readied the playing field. The great hall had been cleaned and fairly shone from top to bottom, which was no small feat considering the expansive proportions of the room.

Alainn had spent a good deal of time in the kitchen, assisting Cookson and the many servants in his employ. And now the morning of the great hunt was upon them. Alainn knew how excited Killian had been this morning as he prepared to ready his horse and his weapons.

Eireen's husband, Fergus, had called her to assist him, but she had also been enlisted to watch Fergus's grandson Kale. The child was an active wee lad and Eireen was clearly uncertain what to do with the boy for she could surely not mind him and carry through with her husband's request. Alainn offered to watch the boy until Eireen was done and as she hurried after him down the long corridor, she giggled at his unsure steps. Killian was just coming to say farewell to her when he saw the heartwarming sight.

"You couldn't wait 'til our own wee son was born, you felt the need to abduct another wee lad to fill your days?"

Alainn beamed widely as she scooped up the squirming child who had nearly made her breathless in chasing after him.

"Tis Fergus's grandson. Eireen needed to assist Fergus and she was to watch the boy for the day!"

"So you're carin' for servant's children, then?" Killian did not seem entirely pleased with the notion though Alainn could not discern why. "Where is his own mother?" he asked.

Although she had still not made acquaintance with the small boy's mother, Ciara, Alainn had found her husband Will to be a likeable man, therefore she was pleased to watch his son and to help out Eireen.

Alainn had not related the disturbing encounter she'd had with Glynnis, but she had made good on her promise to have the guards keep close watch on the woman and her granddaughter, Ciara. They reported back daily to Alainn, and claimed no animals had been found since Alainn's meeting with Glynnis. Alainn had been relieved to hear it and so she had seen no reason to divulge the incident to Killian. She finally answered his query regarding Ciara's whereabouts.

"From the horridly unpleasant smells coming from the

herb chamber I'd say Ciara and her Glynnis must be creating some type of powerful concoction. It is truly a pungent scent. Perhaps they might need a truly knowledgeable healer to assist them?" She jested.

"Aye, well, you look as though you have your hands full already!"

"I think it will only be for a short while. He's a delightful wee child, just learned to walk only recently for he's not more than five and ten months."

Killian glanced at the boy and smiled. He watched as Alainn looked up at the stone walls and smiled herself.

"What do you see or hear, Alainn?"

"Echoes!" she answered. "There are echoes throughout nearly all the walls of this castle. Echoes in time are how I refer to them. I hear them often, but sometimes I see images as well. Structures made of wood seldom hold the echoes, for wood is porous, but stone is thick and nearly eternal and holds the memories. You lived a happy childhood, Killian. I see and hear you and your brother and sister often, and your parents as well. But, I also hear far-off distant echoes from centuries ago; some from over a thousand years ago, to the first Irish king who lived here, a druid king. He was a most passionate man."

"Passionate, in what regard, in ruling his kingdom?"

"Aye, in that as well, but he was a masterful lover!"

"You've heard that?"

"Aye, and seen it as well at times, mostly in our bedchamber for that was where he slept and loved as well! He was a fine form of a man and seemed most knowledgeable in his techniques. I've seen him lyin' by the hearth atop many luxurious animal pelts and the woman most certainly didn't seem to object to his lovemaking."

"That must be somewhat disturbing for you to see and to hear?"

"Not entirely, sometimes I find it most arousing!"

"You don't, Alainn!" He sounded troubled at the suggestion and her bold talk.

"And would you not find it arousing, Killian O'Brien, to hear and see others making love?"

"I am a man, Alainn, 'tis different entirely!"

"So you think!" she suggestively smiled.

"Are you tryin' to make me jealous of some damn king that's been dead for hundreds of years?"

"Over thirteen centuries in actuality, and he may be dead but the echoes and his spirit are most certainly alive."

"You lovely wee vixen, would you like me to take me to our bedchamber and create some wee echoes of our own?" He playfully grabbed her in his arms and held her tight.

"I suspect we already have, my love. Centuries down the road, some young witch, perhaps even one of our descendants will stand in our bedchamber and be driven to blush at the heated passion exchanged between you and me. And if she's as hot-blooded as I, then she'll think you a gifted lover as well, and sure she'll not object to the sensual echoes."

He leaned down and gave her a passionate kiss and she thought he'd perhaps sooner be carrying her off to their bedchamber than to be off to the woods for a hunt.

"What was that for?" She smiled at his display of open affection.

"Can I not bid my wife farewell in grand fashion?"

"Aye, I insist upon it!" She smiled again as she followed the small child who'd begged to be let loose again to explore the long and winding corridor. "And young Kale's father will be headin' out on the hunt with you along with many of your guards and your kin and clan?"

"Aye, he's waitin' outside most impatiently. I just needed to see you before we left, for you know how I despise bein' parted from you!"

"Oh, Killian, you adore goin' out on the hunts and you are an expert hunter. You were the envy of all the other men back in Castle O'Brien for your rare expertise and ability to never come home empty-handed."

"Well I'm hopin' William will be fortunate enough to hunt a stag for 'tis always a grand feelin' to take down one of those huge beasts, and they offer a good many meals for a family. He used to be a fairly able lad with a bow!"

"You knew him when the two of you were younger?"

"Aye, we're reasonably close in age and his father was carpenter for mine."

Alainn saw the main doors of the castle open and the child she had picked up once more for he'd tumbled over and needed comforting, shrieked in joy as the man entered. Alainn saw it was his father, William, and the boy nearly jumped out of Alainn's arms and ran to the man.

"Wee Kale, why is Lady Alainn needin' to watch over you; where is that mother of yours at the moment?"

"With Glynnis in the healing chamber, I believe, William and I'm not opposed to watchin' the lad, he's a darlin' wee boy."

"Aye, he is. 'Tis blessed I am to have such a sweet, healthy lad, but he's got a good deal of zest in him, and he'll surely tire you in your delicate state. Take him to his mother if you should feel your strength waning, for 'tis after-all her duty to care for our son!"

Alainn sensed there was a strained tension in the man's voice when he spoke of his wife. Since the man seemed such a charismatic fellow and knowing Eireen's dislike for her stepdaughter as well, and what the woman had surely done to the defenseless animals, once more Alainn developed an ever-growing dislike for the woman she'd yet to encounter.

William took his son and began following him down the lengthy corridor and Killian held Alainn once more. She was overcome with a sudden pain inside her head and she grew dizzy and unsteady on her feet. Killian noticed how pale her face had become and he lifted her into his arms.

"What is it, Alainn? You've just had a vision, aye?"

"Aye, but it was a blurry vision, as though something or someone does not want me to see it."

"And what is it that you saw?"

"I saw the woods to the north of the castle, and an animal, an angry, snorting animal, with tusks. And I saw blood, an unusual amount of blood. The ground was red with blood."

Chapter Fifteen

"CHRIST, PERHAPS WE should postpone the hunt or cancel it all together!"

"I'm not certain, Killian. I could see no faces. Are there wild boar in these woods?"

"At one time they were common, 'tis less common now to see them, but not unheard of."

"Well be cautious, Killian! You and all of your men will have horses and weapons; sure you'll be safe enough. But the animals are acting entirely peculiar lately. First the stallion charged me and, yesterday, when I went to the stables even Storm seemed unusually wild and restless. My mare nipped me, also"

"Caileag is the gentlest mare I know; she bit you?" he asked in a concerned tone.

"Aye!"

"And why did you not tell me about this?" His voice depicted his displeasure.

"Because I knew you'd tell me to stay away from the stables and I wanted to see the stallion and all of the horses for I adore them. And I miss riding very much!"

"Let me view the bite!" he ordered.

She hesitantly lifted the sleeve of her gown and revealed the large round bruise and the torn skin.

"By Christ, Alainn, you should have told me, and I forbid you to go near the stables until we discover what dark magic has caused these animals to act so unruly."

"Killian, I would be heartsick if I had to distance myself from animals entirely; you know how I feel… what deep love and connection I feel for them."

"Aye, and I love you, and I am wrought with concern for you. What of Wolf?"

Killian knew how Alainn doted on the large wolfhound. The dog had been healed by Alainn when it was younger and since then it had been completely loyal and devoted to her, which was why they had brought the old dog with them from Castle O'Brien. She turned from his gaze and he noticed the disturbed look she now wore.

"Tell me, Alainn; what of Wolf?"

"He growled at me last night, when I tried to put him outside our door, he snarled at me and bared his teeth. He has never ever acted in such a manner toward me. I must find out what spell has been used upon these animals so it can be undone!"

"Aye, well, until then you keep your distance from him and any other animal you might see, wild and domesticated alike!"

The large arched door opened once more, and Riley,

Mac, and Pierce entered the chamber. Alainn was reluctant to meet Riley's eyes after what Mary had told her regarding his feelings toward her. It was the first time she'd felt so completely uncomfortable in his presence.

"What has your wife in such a dismal disposition this day, Killian? Are the two of you quarreling?"

Killian did not answer the man for he was deep in thought at the moment regarding the hunt.

"Are we soon to be off then, cousin, for the men are anxious to begin the hunt? 'Tis a grand day, and promises to be a bountiful hunt!"

"I am not certain the hunt will take place this day, Riley!" Killian offered.

"What are you talkin' about Killian?"

Killian glanced at Alainn and was uncertain how much to disclose to the other man.

"Oh, I suppose she's dictatin' your life so entirely, controllin' you so completely that she'll not even allow you this time away from her now? Doesn't she know it's the man who is to determine what's done in his own castle? I would have thought you'd have tamed her some by now, especially since she carries your child. Women tend to be somewhat more docile when they've a child in their belly!"

"And you know this from your vast experience with women who are with child?" Killian angrily retorted.

"Ah, it's one of those moods you're in then, is it? Has your bed been a bit cold these last nights then; is that the reason for your ill temper? Has the beddin' been less than satifyin' to you because of her condition or has Alainn been refusin' to share your bed, entirely?"

"At the moment, you are the reason for my ill temper, cousin, and I swear if you ever mention a bed and Alainn in the same breath, you'll not live to draw another."

He had put his hand to the hilt of his sword and Alainn touched his arm to dispel his uneasiness and displeasure.

"I have had a vision, Riley, and it involves the hunt somehow and an animal and a good deal of blood!" Alainn explained.

"Aye, well, when an animal is killed there is usually a good deal of blood; surely you know that, though I know you have always refused to attend a hunt!"

"Aye!" She pondered his words, though wondered why she would have a vision if it only was an animal's blood that would be spilled.

A large number of men had gathered in the immense open chamber and they all appeared to be excited and eager to get on with the hunt. Killian looked at Alainn once more and she shrugged for she was uncertain what to tell him. Riley decided for them for he uttered a loud whooping cheer, which surely meant the event was soon to begin. Killian wore a look of hesitancy.

"Be cautious, the lot of you, be exceedingly mindful this day!" Killian's loud authoritative voice called out to all the men surrounding him.

"Especially if you should see a wild boar!" Alainn added.

The men all nodded to her, but she wasn't certain that any truly heeded hers or her husband's words, so eager were they to begin their sport and camaraderie. Killian quickly kissed her before he left and his hand lingered ever so long on her belly before he headed out the door.

⌘

THE REMAINDER OF the morning Alainn felt uneasy and after Eireen had come to collect Kale, Alainn was undecided as to how to fill her morning so her worries would diminish. She'd had no further visions, but the uneasiness nagged at her well into the afternoon. She'd checked on Connor MacLain several times, but he was doing much better, his wound improving and she thought his temperament was becoming irritable, which often indicated a man was beginning to grow impatient with keeping to a bed. She felt certain it would be soon he could be up and about.

When she heard the sound of horses' hooves outside the castle, she sensed urgency in the speed they approached. A gnawing dread within her had her heading out the main doors with a swiftness she thought herself unable, considering her roundness. She was relieved at first glance to see Killian was atop his horse and surely not injured, but at closer inspection she saw his tunic was soaked with blood and then she noticed the figure slung over the back of his horse. He jumped down from his mount and hurriedly pulled the man down. He glanced at Alainn with panic on his face and fear in his heart. She hastened to them as Killian carefully laid the man upon the steps. She stared down into the pale, lifeless face of William McCree. His eyes were closed and she noticed the deep and gaping wound on his stomach. She placed her hand to his chest and could find no heartbeat.

"What can you do for him, Alainn?" her husband asked in a ragged voice.

"He's gone to the beyond, Killian, there is no amount of healing that can aid him now."

"But you must try, Alainn. I remember once when we were younger, back at Castle O'Brien, there was the tiny boy that was pulled from the pond. He did not breathe. You healed him, brought him back from death. You saved his life when no one believed it was possible."

A crowd of concerned and despairing men hung back waiting to see what the chieftain's wife could do by way of her healing for many had heard what she was capable of, and a few had even witnessed her unusual healing abilities.

Alainn looked up into Killian's anguished face and wanted greatly to take away his obvious pain, but she knew the injured man was long since beyond help.

"If I could, Killian, for you I would, I swear it, but 'tis not possible. His skin grows cold, his heart does not beat, and his blood has begun to congeal. See for yourself, no more does it flow from the wound."

"But could you bring him back, by way of your magic, is it possible?"

"Back from the dead? It would be unthinkable to even consider it Killian, perhaps even evil! I would not dare attempt it, for his soul has already left his sorely damaged body!"

As she glanced down at the open wound she felt her stomach grow queasy at the sight, for many of his internal parts were visible through the gaping hole. Killian sat down upon the steps and appeared to be in filled with great grief and much guilt. Alainn placed her hand on his shoulder and tried to console him.

"This is not your doing, Killian."

"Aye, but it is, Alainn, your vision was surely an ill omen. I should have listened to you and to my own bad feelings regarding the hunt!"

Glynnis, the old healer had obviously been called for she hurried to where her granddaughter's husband now lay dead upon the steps. Her thin, haggard face appeared much older than her six decades for it was creased with many lines and her wild, long gray hair, her missing teeth and unusual appearance caused many to fear her. Her lips were tightly pursed and her dark eyes held a hint of accusation as she looked from Killian to Alainn.

"Why was he not brought to me straightaway? I might have healed him!"

"His life was ended back in the woods, Glynnis!" Alainn

declared.

The woman touched her hand to the man's chest and then to his neck. She looked upon the mortal wound.

"Aye, perhaps you are correct!" she whispered in a hollow tone. Her eyes stared off toward her cottage, and Killian looked at the old woman with dread in his eyes.

"She is in the herb chamber?" he questioned.

"Aye!" the old woman simply answered. "I will go inform her!"

"No, you must allow me to do it, Glynnis! As chieftain it is my duty!"

Something in the old woman's eyes left Alainn curious for she looked at Killian with an odd expression, but then nodded.

"Would you like me to go with you, Killian?" Alainn offered, hoping to give him the support he would surely need to deliver the news of the tragedy.

"No, there's no need, Alainn. In your condition, you should not be made to be party to such sadness and despair."

Alainn attempted a half-smile for him, and he gently touched her arm as he started off walking slowly and his dread was evident even in his gait. He motioned to the men around him to remove the body and asked that he be taken to the crypt to be washed and prepared for burial. Glynnis followed behind him.

Riley had now approached with his hunting party and he slowly dismounted and shook his head as he walked toward

Alainn.

"My God, I have never seen anythin' like that. First the wretched horse threw him for no good reason and then out of the brush charged this fierce and raging boar, the wildest I've ever seen and I swear he charged toward the man as if that was his sole intent and purpose. No one could prevent it, though Killian's arrow went through the heart of the beast in mere seconds, the damage had already been done. The man was gored right through the gut. I knew well enough nothin' could be done for the man, but Killian insisted he must try!"

Alainn clearly recalled Killian's disheartened expression when she told him she could do nothing, and it filled her with an unwelcome emptiness inside. She glanced up at the noticeably disturbed look on Riley's face as well. She began to feel dizzy and most unwell, and when a woman's tortured scream rang out through the cool, autumn afternoon, Alainn sat down upon the steps and began to weep. She could hear the mournful wails coming from the area where Killian had just gone. The young widow surely must be devastated and as much as she had already formed an unfavorable opinion of the young woman, she realized that was somewhat unfair for she'd not yet even laid eyes upon her. Although the woman's unusual practices with the animals was not to be condoned, and her cruelty most objectionable, many other healers did employ animals' hearts and such to create remedies.

Alainn empathetically imagined how she would be reacting if someone had just alerted her to Killian's death. She felt light-headed and nauseous and her head began to reel. She was about to lose consciousness, she felt herself falling. She must have moaned or appeared unusually pale for she felt Riley picking her up and carrying her into the castle.

Chapter Sixteen

I T HAD BEEN months since she'd felt so ill, and months, also, since she had felt the urgent need to spew. And this had been going on for some time now. Though there was nothing left in her stomach, still she retched. As she hung her head over the basin while Eireen held it for her, Alainn's stomach heaved, yet again. It must have been the horror of hearing the other woman's grief, the sight of the huge amount of blood or the gruesomeness of the entire scene that had caused her reaction. But never in her life had she had a violent reaction to such sights. There were many horrific occurrences she had witnessed as a healer and they'd not evoked such an adverse result, but then she had not been seven months into her term either.

Riley stood outside the open door of the bedchamber and she saw the concern written upon his face. And Eireen looked distressed herself.

"Eireen, you should go to your stepdaughter, sure she needs you more than me. I can hold my own basin. I'm not even certain why I feel ill, though I admit to being heartsick for Ciara and wee Kale."

"Aye, it will be a terrible loss, for Will was a good, decent man, and he was a kind and patient man with Ciara, and a loving father to Kale. But, I think my presence will not be welcome or necessary. Glynnis is there, and my husband as well. And your husband was to accompany her to her cottage, also, for she was understandably distraught and she actually fainted I'm told. However, milord decided she should remain at her grandmother's cottage for it was thought she should not be alone so far off into the country. Sure, I'm not certain where she'll live now for no woman should live alone without a man when so far distanced from others."

Alainn watched as Riley gingerly walked into the room.

"Are you well, Alainn? You gave me a fright! You got so pasty white, and if I'd not been there you might have cracked your head open upon the stone steps."

"I do thank you for assisting me, Riley! I appreciate the gesture, for I think an injured head would not go well with my queasy stomach."

Just then she saw Connor MacLain lean his head in the door as well.

"I heard you were ailing. I ken something must have bin amiss for you've not missed wrapping my wounds even once in all the days I have been here."

Alainn glanced from one man to the other, but clearly Riley suspected nothing, for he smiled warmly at the other man and spoke.

"Aye, you'll never find a more dedicated or experienced healer than my cousin. And Killian tells me you're jumpin' ship and goin' to be the groom here at Castle O'Donnel. I suspect you'll be missed for you have a way with the horses. No wonder Killian and Alainn are so fond of you for they like the horses as well, as does my Mary!"

Alainn looked up at Connor and noticed his eyes held a dreamy quality with the mention of Mary O'Brien. She doubted Riley would pick up on that. She had little time to dwell on that for Danhoul Calhoun entered her bedchamber without having asked permission. He headed to the bedside and touched her hand. She pulled it away shocked at the familiarity he seemed to feel he could show toward her. He took her hand once more and closed his eyes, clearly intent on something, though she didn't know precisely what. Riley was not pleased with this and was about to tell the young soldier to get his hands off of her when Killian came into the room and found it filled with a goodly number of people. He glanced toward Alainn in concern.

"Are you well, Alainn? Has somethin' happened with you or the babe? Should the midwife be summoned?" He looked at the young man who still sat with his hand clasped through hers.

"No, Killian, I assure you, I am well enough. I simply have a putrid stomach."

"She collapsed on the steps is what she did, and has been spewin' nearly constantly ever since! Aye, I think the healer should be called, and maybe the midwife as well!" Riley explained.

"I am not so very concerned about the wretched stomach. But, she is unwell somehow and in danger, in grave danger. She'll not need a midwife, but a guard outside her chamber," Danhoul commented.

"And I suppose you're offerin' your services for that; are you then?" Killian sarcastically spoke as he went to Alainn's side.

"No, anyone will do, I suppose, but keep her clear of any animals for I've had another vision. Is there a dog anywhere near your chambers?"

Killian's face registered alarm at this, and he questioned Alainn.

"Where is Wolf, Alainn? Did you put him outside this morning as I asked?"

"Aye! I did, Killian; I told you I would!"

"And what of the bite on your arm?" Her husband questioned further.

"I'm certain it is well enough, I put a potent healing ointment on it, though I have not checked it since this morning."

Killian went to pull up her sleeve, but Danhoul beat him to it without having been told where the injury was located. All present were noticeably startled to see the inflamed and oozing wound on her arm. The entire arm was now swollen and when the young man touched his hand to it, he cussed.

"Shite, 'tis on fire! When did the mare bite you?"

"Yesterday, but you'll remember Killian, this very morning it was only a bit bruised and barely open. Sure 'tis because the animals have been charmed with a dark spell that it has caused such a reaction."

When the man pressed on the wound it began to weep further and Alainn screamed out in pain.

"Get the healer!" Killian ordered Eireen who was standing there with a fearful expression on her pale face.

"No, Killian, I don't want Glynnis to attend to me, she has no fondness for me and she's enough to deal with this night in consoling her granddaughter."

"In truth, I don't actually give a tinker's damn what you want at the moment, Alainn. I only want you well, and by the look of your pallor and the condition of your arm, you are most definitely not well!"

"What of the healer at Castle O'Rorke, Riley? Could you bring her here?" Alainn further questioned in hopes of not being made to deal with Glynnis.

"Aye, I would if I could, but she's oddly disappeared. She's apparently been at the castle for a number of years now and has been known to be most reliable, but it has been two days now that no one has seen her and her cottage is empty. Her possessions remain, yet she is nowhere to be found!"

"Get Glynnis!" Killian repeated in an even louder tone.

Alainn looked up at Killian and saw he still wore the blood-stained leine he had worn today during the hunt. He had not even time to change his clothes, wash or eat his evening meal, and she looked at how tired he appeared, and very worried as well."

"Perhaps you might summon my grandfather. He possesses some healing ways."

"I can heal your wife if you allow it!" Danhoul declared.

"You're a healer as well then, it's not so often a male possesses healin' qualities?" Riley interrupted.

"Aye, once male healers were far more prevelant than their female counterparts, now it is more uncommon, I admit. But I do have some healin' abilities like your cousin. But I'd rather be left in private to attempt it!"

"I'll not leave you here alone in our bedchamber with my wife," Killian stated, "'Tis clearly inappropriate! I'll stay here as well and then you have my permission to do what you will for my wife, if she is in agreement as well."

"Aye! Do what you can, Danhoul!" she agreed.

"Are you certain this is wise, Killian? He's a young soldier and we don't know him so very well, sure he could end up doin' more harm than good!" Riley directed the question to Killian, but it was Alainn who answered.

"He is a druid and a healer, Riley. He assisted us at Castle O'Brien when I was ill. He's a better healer than Glynnis by a long stretch and perhaps as gifted in his healing qualities as I am." Alainn suggested. "And I believe Grandfather did not employ him to train his army as much as he did to watch over me!"

"Is that true?" Riley questioned the man.

"Aye, I suspect that might be the whole of it!" Danhoul admitted.

"By Christ!" Killian seemed completely displeased about this, but still sent the rest of the people from the room so the young man could work whatever magic he might conjure to heal his wife.

When the man began to unfasten his tunic and then removed it entirely, Killian could not still his tongue.

"What by God's bones do you think you're doin'?"

Then they both noticed the scars upon the man's chest, several narrow slices that were near the middle of his chest. When he pulled his dagger from its sheath, he slit another spot and then poured the blood on Alainn's open wound. She felt it grow warm, but the pain seemed to leave her almost instantly.

"Why did I feel no pain in this wound? All day I have noticed no discomfort!"

"Sure that is part of the nefarious spell as well. Whoever has decided to cause you harm is capable of strong magic!"

"And can you see who that is?" Killian asked in a voice both weary and anguished.

"Not yet, but I am hopin' the answer will soon come to me."

"And why do you cut your chest? I have used my blood to heal others before, but I always have only sliced my palm or my wrist!"

"Aye, well, use caution when you cut near the wrist for healers bleed unusually profusely from the wrist, 'tis how many take their own lives when they are compelled to do so. I find the blood nearest the heart contain the greatest healing powers. But, sure you'd not be wantin' to cut up your lovely chest!"

He smiled down at her and there was a mischievous twinkle in his eyes, Alainn blushed and turned from his gaze.

"I'm appreciative for what you've done for my wife, but I'd also thank you to remember she's a married woman, and to take your eyes and your thoughts off her chest. I think maybe you should find yourself a woman and spend a time with her in your bed, before I have to teach your some manners regardin' keepin' your eyes and your thoughts from my wife!"

The young man who was most appealing without benefit of his tunic and far more muscular than Alainn might have thought smiled suggestively at Alainn once more, before he spoke.

"When I find a woman as lovely or as appealin' as your wee wife, then maybe I might actually decide to take a woman to my bed!"

"You've never..." Killian began, but Alainn finished.

"Not ever?"

"Well I am just past ten and six, 'tis not as though I'm ancient!

"And why would that be of any interest or concern of

yours, Alainn?" Killian reprimanded her in a most displeased tone.

"I'm not interested, merely surprised!"

The young man dabbed at the fresh wound on his chest and Alainn tried to keep her eyes from that very chest, which of course Killian noticed.

"You can leave now!" Killian pointed toward the door.

Danhoul took her arm once more and Alainn noticed the wound was beginning to heal and the bruising and swelling were much improved as well. Killian looked at it with great relief and reluctantly patted the other man on the shoulder.

"I do thank you, most sincerely for attending to Alainn's maladies. What can I do to repay you, then?"

"You might allow me to stay here at your castle, for 'tis here that I would be most effective in watchin' over her or seein' visions if they pertain to her."

Killian noticed the look the young man wore whenever he looked in Alainn's direction, and he wanted to both embrace the man for healing her, and beat him soundly for the way he looked at her with such longing.

"I'll watch over my own wife, Danhoul, but should you see any other visions, I would welcome some warning."

"Aye, well suit yourself then, O'Brien!"

He winked at Alainn as he left and pulled his tunic over his chest as he headed out the door.

"Keep her away from all animals!" He offered the advice to Killian as he walked past him.

Alainn attempted to stand and was soon overcome with dizziness.

Killian went to her side and steadied her. "Christ, it's been a horrid day! But, I am thankful you seem to be on the mend. You had me sorely worried, Alainn! You usually heal so quickly. What unnatural power must be in that spell against you and all the animals?"

"Riley told me he believes the animal charged William in a purposeful manner!"

"He spoke to you of what happened then?"

"Aye, sorry I am about it, Killian. It was a terrible tragedy and I am regretful that you had to be there to witness it and that you feel accountable for it! 'Twas not because of you that it happened."

Killian had begun to remove his soiled garments and went to the stand that held a pitcher and basin. He wrung out a cloth and began washing the blood that was stained on his chest. Alainn slowly stood and went to him. She took the cloth from him, looked tenderly into his saddened eyes, and began to wash his broad chest.

"Alainn you needn't do that. You're ailing and wounded!"

"Aye, but my wound is on the mend, I think it will take much longer to ease the wound you feel within your heart."

"Aye, I do feel responsible, in truth I am ble. 'Twas me who called the hunt, and me who invited him to attend. I did not heed your warning even after you told me what you saw!"

"But, Killian, hunts are commonplace, and the man was thrilled to be asked to attend. You could hardly anticipate what the unruly animal might do, and, as for my vision, it was muddled and mostly unclear. And 'tis not as if all my visions have all been proven true. Over a decade previous I told you your father still lived and that has yet to be proven true. I have had visions for months of you and your cousins dying at the hands of the English and just last week you were all together and much closer proximity to the English than usual and no harm befell you. How can you have any faith in what visions I see?"

"But I do have faith in them and in you, Alainn. I still believe within my heart that my father is alive and because the English did not attack us when last we were together does not indicate it might not occur one day, for I am probably as fearful of that ominous vision as you are. I should have called off the hunt today. I would have if Riley had not been so damn eager and so obstinate about listening to you. But, I am the chieftain of this castle and he should not have influenced my decision in any manner!"

Alainn took a wrap from the stand and gently dried Killian's chest and then placed a tender kiss on his lips. He responded, but she realized how distracted he was. She leaned his sword and scabbard against the oak night table by the bed where he always kept it while they slept. She recognized the great guilt and torment Killian was feeling, and though she thought it was usual for Killian to take on the pain of his people, something nagged at her at how far he had taken this guilt.

"How fares Ciara?" She dared to ask.

His deep green eyes filled with a greater agony as she posed the question and she immediately regretted having quizzed him on the painful subject.

"She did not take the news well, as I'm sure you heard, and she remains mostly inconsolable. She was nearly fitful before I left. Her father and grandmother could scarcely control her, so great was her grief. Glynnis finally gave her a remedy to make her sleep. And she blames me for Will's death!"

"She blames you?" Alainn repeated his words. "How could she, Killian?"

"She said if it weren't for me her husband would have spent his day as he always did, creatin' lovely items and articles and perfectly content in so doing!"

"But surely the man hunted for his family's food?"

"No, apparently he seldom has through the years, I am told. He bartered with others with the articles he crafted. I suppose I had no business takin' him out on the hunt after all!"

"But, Killian, you said he was a fair shot with a bow, and he seemed so eager to go on the hunt! Please don't flay yourself or listen to her accusing words. She speaks with a bitter tongue influenced by grief!"

Killian sat down on the bed. He slumped forward and his entire body seemed consumed with his pain. Alainn went to him and pulled his head to her bosom and kissed the mass of thick chestnut brown hair. She felt his pain and his guilt and tried to take away what she could. She, too, soon felt overcome with maudlin woefulness.

"You're trying to heal my heart. I can feel it, Alainn. You are attemptin' to take away my despair and ease my sore conscience. You should not, for it will drain you and you're already ailing. And sure that can't be good for our son!"

"We're well enough!" she whispered as she headed for the door.

"But where are you off to?"

"You must eat, Killian, you've had no food since this morning, and sure tomorrow you'll have to meet with Ciara again and the priest, the sexton, and the gravediggers. The wake must be planned. You'll need your strength and if you're physically drained you'll have no reserve to fight your emotional despair."

"How did you acquire such wisdom in less than eight and ten years?" he asked with a warm smile on his face and the evidence of his deep love for her in his expressive green eyes.

She smiled but didn't respond as she opened the door. As the door closed behind her Killian remembered the words of the young soldier, Danhoul Calhoun, regarding Alainn needing a guard. He instinctively picked up his sword and went after her.

Chapter Seventeen

A s she came around a bend in the long hallway, she
heard a low menacing growl and out of the corner of
her eye in the darkened corridor she watched in horror as her
beloved wolfhound leapt at her. She tried to hold up her
hands to magically prevent the attack as she screamed in
terror and in pain as his teeth caught her shoulder and
narrowly missed her throat. Then she saw the animal drop to
the ground with Killian's sword still sheathed straight
through him.

Killian ran to her and caught her before she fell to the
floor. The blood was spilling from her wound and he noticed
her tear-filled eyes as she looked down on the cherished
animal that she had adored for many years. She began to sob
into Killian's shoulder.

"I had to do it, Lainna. Tell me you know that?"

"Aye, I know it well, Killian, as well as I know you just
saved my life and that of our son!"

She glanced toward the wolfhound and he briefly released her from his arms so she could go to the animal. She
softly touched his thick fur.

"Oh my dear old Wolf, sorry I am that you fell prey to such dark magic. I will see to it that whoever created the damnable spell will be justly punished!" She sobbed.

Eireen and Fergus Flannery must have heard the commotion for they came to investigate and soon the entire corridor was filled with other servants wanting to learn what had transpired.

"Eireen, we'll need some cloths to serve as bandages for Lady Alainn's wound. Fergus, see to it Danhoul Calhoun is sent for immediately. The chamber next to our bedchamber must be prepared for the man will not only need to heal her, he'll be staying with us from now on as he must be close at hand to help keep constant watch over her!"

THE DAY WILLIAM McCREE was laid to rest was a dismal dreary day; a day befitting such a mournful event. Alainn was standing in the graveyard next to Killian as the cold wind gusted and the driving rain pelted down miserably. Alainn noted how many people attended the service. Surely, all the servants, villagers, and many nobles of Clan O'Donnel, were in attendance. She stood, holding tight to Killian's arm, and she tried to keep her eyes from the location of where the family of William McCree stood. She could vaguely see Eireen holding the young boy, Kale, and a lump formed in her throat at knowing the boy would not remember his father. They had seemed so fond of each other. She thought that in itself was a tragedy.

Fergus Flannery and Glynnis, the healer, stood on either side of the young widow, holding tight to her arms as though to keep her from collapsing. She keened and wailed loudly in her great sorrow. Alainn could only see the long, black curly hair that hung down the woman's back. She thought it strangely curious that she had never met the woman when she had lived here for over two moons. When the priest spoke first in Latin, and then in Gaelic, which was customary in Ireland, Alainn listened to the profound words.

Father Sean was kind and caring and Alainn had grown to admire and respect the man. She thought of the priest that had been employed by Hugh O'Brien at Castle O'Brien and she shuddered, for that man had been the person responsible for her poisoning and causing her near death. He and the dark demon who had called the man to do his evil bidding had formed an unholy and deadly alliance. She'd not seen the demon since then but, lately, she thought she sensed his presence and that left her feeling a terror she had seldom felt in her life.

She pondered if the demon could be behind the animals' peculiar behavior and the attacks on her. She had tried to conjure his image to learn if he had been involved but, thus far, she had been unable. Every time she dwelled upon who was behind the dark charm placed upon the animals, her head begin to hurt but, more disturbingly, she had experienced a distinct pain and tightness across her belly. Clearly someone or something was purposely keeping her from learning the truth. She had even suspected Ciara may be behind the spell put on the animals, but Alainn doubted she was capable of that degree of dark magic, and given the fact she'd hideously abused so many animals she couldn't foresee her being capable of controlling animals.

She shivered once again and Killian took her hand and held tight to it, obviously thinking it was the cool, damp weather and the present mournfulness that had caused her chill.

When the solemnities were concluded, each person present walked past the graveside to respectfully toss their handful of soil upon the coffin that now rested within the grave. Killian waited till everyone else had left before he approached the grave with Alainn on his arm. She bent down to pick up a handful of earth and Killian did so as well. As they drew nearer to the family, Alainn felt another unpleasant chill as she glanced at the young woman for the first time.

Ciara lifted her swollen eyes to meet Alainn's. Her eyes were almond shaped and amber colored. Her complexion was dark and almost exotic looking. Her lips were full and her figure perfectly proportioned and appealing. The expression in her eyes held no kindness as she looked upon Killian and Alainn. Alainn tried to view the widow respectfully and nodded toward her. She was about to tell her how terribly aggrieved she was for her great loss when the woman spoke first.

"You should not have laid your hands upon my husband. It has been said you are a witch and surely your touch cursed him and perhaps even caused his death! He should have been taken to my grandmother, her healing powers are uncommon. She might have saved him if she'd been allowed the opportunity."

Alainn was startled by the harshness of the woman's accusations and by her furious gaze when she stared at her.

"My wife did nothing wrong, Ciara. It was I who took Will to her, and it was already too late, nothin' could be done. Even Glynnis agreed; nothing could have been done!"

"And you, the great and powerful Chieftain O'Brien, you are the reason my husband now lies cold in the ground. He had no business being out on a hunt. If not for you and your damnable hunt my child and I would not be left entirely alone!"

Killian went to the woman who was now sobbing openly and he gently touched her shoulder to console her. The woman flung herself into Killian's arms, clutched him tightly, and wept openly. Alainn's heart constricted and her breath caught in her throat. She met the eyes of Glynnis, the healer, and there was a strange expression within the dark eyes that were much like her granddaughter's.

Alainn glanced at Eireen as she held the sweet, wee boy and Alainn knew she must leave this graveyard straightaway. She felt her stomach grow queasy and it was not from her injured arm, for that had healed unquestionably quickly after Danhoul had aided her with his blood, as did the wound from the wolfhound.

Killian's back was to her, which allowed Alainn to slip away unnoticed as he remained holding the woman who was weeping and clinging to him in such desperation. As Alainn rounded the stone gate-post that lead to the graveyard, she saw Danhoul looking at her with a curious expression. She knew he had read her thoughts.

"You know you're not to be alone, Lady O'Brien!"

"Don't refer to me by that!" she snapped. "Call me, Alainn. I've told you I despise the title of lady."

"Then why did you marry a chieftain? Though I suppose at the moment you're askin' yourself that very question, or that particular chieftain at the very least!"

"Leave me alone, Danhoul. I am retiring to my bed-chamber. You needn't worry for my safety; you and Killian have made certain I am nearly a prisoner in the castle. I might as well be taken to the north tower."

"There's not even a window in that tower. 'Tis a dark and unappealing place."

"Aye, precisely."

"But your chambers are quite luxurious and your hus-band would offer you any pleasure or comfort you might ask for. He is only keepin' such close watch over you because he is vexed about you, as am I. And we've great cause to be fretful for the powers of you and I combined have not been able to discover who means you such harm."

They had walked alongside each other up the steep hillside toward the castle. The ground was damp and muddy from the recent rain and the slipperiness beneath their feet caused the chivalrous young man to take her elbow to ensure she did not fall. She was not entirely pleased to have him near her at the moment, for she wanted to distance herself from men in general, but he seemed determined. He stayed in her company till they reached her chambers.

When they stood before her bedchamber he opened the door with the key as had become customary since the dog had attacked her. As he went to leave her she held out her hand in order for him to pass her the key.

"I know by way of your powers you have already procured possession of your husband's key from the pocket of his overcoat. If I give you this key, then you shall possess both keys. You intend to lock him out of his own bedchambers."

"Ah, you are a most intelligent and intuitive lad."

"He'll be fiercely riled!"

"That will make two of us, Danhoul. And you can be sure to tell him he can find another bed to sleep in this night for he'll not be sleepin' here.

Since Danhoul had already capably heard her thoughts there was no reason to keep her voice silent on this infuriating subject.

"I knew Killian had a colorful past and that he'd bedded

a good many women. I knew well enough he'd been with both virtuous maidens and known whores, but it stuns me to learn he was entirely aware Ciara was married and belonged to another man and still he took her to his bed. It has left me questioning what other secrets he may have and how well I actually know my husband!"

"I understand you're most displeased and enraged by this discovery, but I think I'll leave it to you to alert your husband to the sleeping arrangements, for I've no desire to pass that bit of information on to him."

"As you wish." She seethed as the door closed and she was left alone in the chamber.

Chapter Eighteen

SOME TIME LATER Alainn heard the voices of Killian and Danhoul outside the chamber. She was feeling completely outraged and lamenting so entirely, she went to the chamber where her child would soon sleep. She sat at the stool by the large harp and played as loudly as possible in hope that she could keep the raised voices from coming to her. In truth, she wished she had war drums to play for the sound of something loud and thunderous and angry might appeal more to her at the moment. She felt hurt and enraged and betrayed. She'd been foolishly guileless. Always priding herself on her intuitiveness and her instinctual ability even beyond her magical abilities as a seer, how could she have missed what was right here before her eyes? She heard Killian's loud angry voice hollering through the door, but she paid no mind to the sound, though it continued on for some time.

When the sounds finally quieted, she angrily changed into her nightclothes and decided it would be best to simply put an end to this damnable day. She would go to sleep if she was able, and perhaps tomorrow she would feel less irate and more understanding or charitable. She sat upon the settee and untied the ribbons from her hair. She took to brushing her long golden tresses as she gazed into the looking glass upon the wall.

She was soon disturbed by a loud battering sound against the outside door. She closed her eyes to envision what was happening, when she heard the slamming against the door once more, this time even more forcefully. She envisioned the huge timber that was being hurled against the portal, and she was disbelieving that even Killian would go to this drastic measure to maintain access to his chambers.

She angrily drew closer to the door and screamed at him.

"Killian O'Brien, don't be such a damnable arse! You'll knock the door down entirely!"

"That's the general idea of a batterin' ram!" he replied with evident annoyance.

"Aye, well you can surely break the door, you can most certainly force your way inside, but you'll not be able to make me to talk to you and you sure as hell can't force me to share your bed or be anywhere near you!" She screeched in a furious tone.

"Well sure we shall see about that! But if you make me break down the damn door then we'll not have a hint of privacy, and I've a feelin' we've much to discuss."

Alainn was so enraged by now she thought opening the door was possibly not a wise notion, but she believed Killian was truly stubborn enough to go through with knocking down the door, so she finally relented. When she looked at the sight outside the door she grew even more perturbed. Six men stood holding the massive timber that had already caused the door to begin to bend and bow. She glowered furiously at each one of them. There stood Pierce and Mackenzie MacArthur, Connor McLain, Danhoul Calhoun, Cookson Kilkenny and at the very front, of course, Killian O'Brien.

"Have I no allies here in this castle, then?" she asked in a voice that though angry was nearly tearful as well. "Cookson, you are my dear friend, and Pierce and Mac, you have been my friends for so many years as well!"

"Aye, but Killian is your husband and our chieftain!" Mac admitted, and he and the men wore sheepish expressions.

"And, Connor MacLain, are you entirely daft, if you have ripped open that wound by liftin' that weighty timber, I swear you can bleed to death for all I care, for I'll not lift a hand to prevent you from losin' the damn arm." The huge Scot wore an expression something close to a grin and she hurled the large key at him, but he ducked in time to escape being hit.

"And you, Danhoul Calhoun, I think I am the most disappointed in you. You have read my thoughts, you know what causes me such discord and unhappiness this night and still you won't give me this time of peace to come to terms with what I know and what I'll do regarding the entire cursed situation."

She spoke telepathically to the man.

"You need your husband, to protect you and to keep you balanced. 'Tis in dark times when you are distanced from him, you'll be most tempted to turn to the dark side of your own powers! For always you will need a guardian, Alainn!" He answered her with his voice and not in the usual telepathic manner.

Both Killian and Alainn looked at the man with an odd expression for they'd heard Aine, her great grandmother and Celtic goddess, issue that very warning once before.

Alainn finally allowed herself to look up at Killian and by this time they had placed the large timber on the floor. She felt enraged and frustrated when she looked at him; she desperately wanted to assert her powers. So instead, in her temper, she turned and angrily, loudly slammed the door once more, in truth several times. Finally Killian stormed in and slammed the door himself.

"You can go straight to hell, Killian O'Brien! You can, for I don't give a shite if you do. If I have to look upon your face anytime soon, I swear I'll feckin' kill you!"

"And you can stop that damn cussin' for 'tis most unladylike and unbecomin' to you. I've never used that filthy language in your presence!"

"Aye, you have once before!"

The man strained to think of when she might be referring to and then seemed to recall. "Aye, well, I'd just been lashed and thrown into a dungeon by my uncle. I was feelin' more than a little pained and furious!"

"And you don't think I'm feelin' pain and fury at the moment? Do you think I truly well care if you find me unbecomin'? And if that's truth than you can simply go to your brazen, black-haired wench!"

"Alainn, you are bein' entirely unfair!"

"It's unfair, I'm bein', is it? Aye, well, now I find it a wee bit unfair that you didn't feel compelled to tell me there was a woman right here in this very village who had shared your bed!"

"Christ, Alainn, it was past two years ago; you and I weren't married, betrothed, or, in truth, the likelihood that we would ever be anythin' to each other was surely none."

"But you admitted you cared for me then?"

"Aye, of course I cared for you, I've told you I've cared for you for many years. But, tell me, how did you discover the truth of it?"

"Well, 'tis not a welcome ability to have powers such as I do, for you recall you questioned me on the reason why I did not choose to have our son's room readied in the chamber you'd slept when you were younger? Do you now maybe have an actual inkling why I didn't care to be present within those walls?"

"By Christ!" he shook his head as he sat down upon the bed.

"Aye, well, I certainly didn't notice Christ within the walls of that chamber, but I did see you, Killian O'Brien, and your accursed black-haired trollop, but I could not see her face for in my visions she was positioned atop you, at the time. But I did see your face and I did hear the echoes of your lustful coupling, and it repulsed me so entirely I can't even think of that chamber without becoming either overtaken by a putrid stomach or filled with enragement. It was not until today did I see your lover's face. If you had not embraced her this day, had not held her in your arms, I would surely not have come to the realization, that she was the one from the images."

"'Tis sorry I am that you had to witness whatever it is you've seen, though without your cursed powers you'd be none the wiser, so I am at a bit of a disadvantage in havin' a wife who's a damnable seer. But you think I owe you an apology for bein' with her, and I'm not entirely certain I agree with you!"

With that, she picked up the pitcher that stood on the stand and she hurled it at him in a fury. He narrowly missed being hit by the weighty object, and he glared back at her.

"How do you suppose that discussion might have gone, Alainn, if I'd confessed to you there was a woman here I once had bedded? 'Tis not as though I've not been made to suffer your jealous temper in the past. You'll recall how you reacted when you found I'd been with Mellane, the miller's daughter?"

"Found you'd been with her, if you recall I actually found you with her... mid-coitus Killian O'Brien, 'tis not the same by any measure. 'Twas good of you to bring up that sore subject this night." She sarcastically stated.

"You have never trusted me entirely, never been confident that I would remain true and faithful to you. Never in the time we've been wed have I ever given you even the slightest reason to doubt my fidelity. And now you flay me for somethin' that happened years ago. I want you to know my time with her meant nothing to me; it was entirely for pleasure and physical gratification."

"And that is supposed to give me solace and pacify me then, is it?"

"Aye! It is, for 'tis only you I have ever loved and you know it! She was here, I was lonely and lusting, and so it happened."

"And happened and happened and happened, apparently many times!"

"Christ, you can be damnably difficult!"

"And you can be a lecherous, unfeeling arse. So you think you don't owe me an apology because I was nothin' to you at the time, I was not anyone of importance to you and you did not lust for me when you were beddin' her?"

"I didn't say you meant nothin' to me, and I doubt it would make you feel any consolation to know I did lust for you when I had her! I think every woman I've ever had was because I lusted for you."

"Then you and Riley are apparently more alike than you care to know!" She seethed, trying to ably cut him with her words.

He drew nearer to her and grabbed her arms angrily. "You can be the most insensitive woman, the unkindest wee bitch, I've ever known!"

"Then go to your whore and have her, 'tis not as though you've her husband to consider, not that he was actually a consideration when you were with her before!"

She might well have physically slapped him, so taken aback was he by her uncommon cruelty. The look on Killian's face was one of disdain at her words, but of disbelief as well. She continued speaking her mind.

"You think you feel guilt because of William McCree's death, but it is because you bedded his wife, and on more than one occasion, that has you so completely consumed with guilt. And I know you are a man of strict Catholic upbringing; that she must have been undeniably appealing to take her when, even then, you knew she was wed to another man! And was it worth it, Killian? Was it worth a few minutes pleasure to have your soul in torment even now?"

His green eyes held a haunted quality. "No! I have regretted it much in these past years."

"And is the boy yours?" she pulled no punches in wounding him.

"Alainn, has your absurd jealously turned to utter madness? With the curse upon the O'Briens until only recently, how would I have possibly fathered a healthy, living child?"

Alainn's thoughts grew muddled and she was filled with

confusion. She slowly lowered herself to the bed as if to allow herself time to consider the words she had just spoken.

"I have the strongest sense that he might be your child." She whispered more to herself than to him.

"How could that possibly be?" Killian queried with much uncertainty.

"Does she possess magical abilities?"

"None that I am aware of."

"And was it only here in the castle the two of you… were together?" She hissed.

"What does that have to do with anything?" Killian was clearly not eager to discuss this further.

"Did it ever occur in a fairy glade or perhaps a magical cave, someplace filled with enchantment that the curse might not have been able to reach? But sure she would have had to deliver the child somewhere else as well." She continued to muse.

"It happened once in the woods near the castle."

"Enchanted woods?"

"How would I determine if they were enchanted?" He narrowed his eyes. "I noticed nothing unusual about them." He spoke lowly not actually wanting to relate any of the details of his time with Ciara.

"Aye, I suppose if you were so consumed with lustfulness you couldn't stop yourself from fornicating with a married woman, it is doubtful you would notice anything unusual about where you copulated with her." She caustically replied.

"Perhaps your damnable deep, unwarranted jealousy has simply caused you to imagine entirely ludicrous and unrea-slitic possibilities, Alainn!"

"Aye, sure that must be the truth of it, my jealousy has created a madness within me that has me believing your married lover carried your son. Clearly my powers fall short when it comes to matters regarding you, milord!"

It had been many months since she'd referred to him by his title. He did not attempt to reason with her, but threw his hands in the air, and responded only by walking out the door.

Chapter Nineteen

WHEN, BY THE middle of the night, Killian still had not returned, Alainn felt her anger and jealousy giving way to sadness and regret at her vexation, her temper, and her many unfeeling words. She closed her eyes and tried to envision where he was at the moment and was relieved to learn he was just outside the door to their bedchamber. She wrapped her shawl about her shoulders and carefully opened the door. He was apparently not asleep for he turned to look up into her face. She attempted a half-smile and with some difficulty lowered herself so that she was seated on the floor beside him.

"What is it you're doin', Alainn?"

"I'm spendin' the night with my husband, for 'tis what a wife is meant to do. And since my husband has not come to me, though for that I cannot blame him, I apparently will spend my night here with him."

He stood, stretched his back, now stiffened from his uncomfortable position and then held his hand out to her. She took it and he assisted her so that soon she stood with him.

"Come to bed, Killian! Our bed is so cold and lonely

without you in it! I understand you remain displeased with me for my horridly jealous temper, but we are wed. I don't want to unnecessarily spend this night or any other without you. And tell me you might begin to forgive me for my despicable outburst!"

"Aye, well, I suppose if you can forgive me for what led to the outburst, I can forgive your reaction!"

She smiled, placed a soft apologetic kiss on his lips, took his hand, and led him inside. Although they did not make love, he held her and that was at least a beginning to mending the unpleasant quarrel between them.

WITH THE MANY arrangements being made for the banquet Alainn and Killian had spent little time together. She found her thoughts often filled with the absurd possibility that Killian had fathered a child that wasn't affected by the curse. She could think of little else and as much as it tormented her, she needed to attempt to discover the truth. She tried to envision where in the woods Killian and Ciara may have been intimate. When she began to instinctually sense the location, she quickly procured her cloak and began walking toward the forest north of the castle. She found herself going deeper and deeper into the forested area where little sunlight found its way inside. She shivered and pulled her cloak tighter as the temperature grew cooler. If it was a magical location where the intimacy occurred, Alainn did not sense it to be here. It was certainly not enchantment she was feeling, but dread. She began to lose her ability to remain intent on the task at hand when an eerie sensation encompassed her and she heard several low disturbing growls. She had been so intent on what she was doing, she foolishly hadn't even considered the spell placed on the animals and that entering the forest would possibility put her in danger, she was reasonably certain these guttural snarls weren't being made by an animal.

She began to feel as though she was being watched and momentarily wondered whether the demon might be nearby. She began to imagine he might found behind each and every tree, and that he would soon spring forth from his conceal-ment and pounce upon her. She placed her hands beneath her heavy belly and began to move faster and faster until she was nearly running. She turned to look behind her sensing she was being followed, and nearly tripped on a large tree root. She grew chilled at the thought she had recklessly placed her unborn child in danger to investigate the ridicu-lous notion she might discover the location where Killian and Ciara had coupled to learn whether they had possibly created a child together. When she finally found her way out of the forest and saw the castle in sight, she heaved a deep sigh and tears of relief filled her eyes. Perhaps Killian was correct afterall; surely her jealous nature had altered her clear thought and caused her to imagine outlandish possiblilites. She decided from that moment forward she would put the outrageous notion out of her mind and simply ensure her own babe was kept safe and well.

Still weary and shaken by her experience, she had retired that night before Killian had come to bed. And the following morning when she arose to find him already gone from their bed, she believed he remained displeased with her and was undesirous of dealing with her and her jealousy. They would be made to speak further on the subject of Ciara McCree, and her child, but they were both avoiding it. She did not foresee how soon she would be made to deal with the objectionable subject, but it happened that very morning.

When Fergus and Eireen Flannery asked formally to have audience with her, she was uncertain why they would want to speak with only her. She realized how nervous and jittery they both appeared as she sat across from them at a table in the drawing room. Fergus cleared his throat and began in a slow, uncertain voice.

"You'll know of course, my daughter, Ciara is a widow now and with a wee son to care for. Her cottage is deep within the woods and I believe it is not safe or reasonable for them to live there alone. They have been staying with my first wife's mother, Glynnis. Her cottage is small and her habits unusual. She is often up half the night mixing strange concoctions and I feel it is unwise to leave the child there with the woman. In truth, she has always seemed somewhat frightening even to me, a grown man. The cottage is drafty and the peat logs barely seem to heat the earthen floor.

Eireen and I have large ample servant's quarters with an extra room. Ciara must work for her keep now and Glynnis tells us she is becoming most astute at healing. We were, well, I was wonderin' if Ciara and wee Kale might come live with us here in the castle?"

Alainn wanted nothing to do with Ciara McCree or even her innocent, young son at the moment. She wanted to be as far distanced from them as possible, but she didn't want to appear entirely rude or unfeeling for the woman was without a husband and the child without a father. That thought left her feeling even less charitable regarding the situation for, in truth, the child might, indeed, have a father, and a noble chieftain at that, although, she could scarcely wrap her mind around how that could be possible.

Alainn finally, with much difficulty, summoned the ability to speak to the man who sat before her expecting an answer. The thought of the wee boy spending his days and nights with Glynnis or anywhere in the vicinity of the nearby chamber where she had witnessed the pitiful tortured animals, left Alainn feeling heartsick. She attempted to simply harden her heart to and distance herself from the entire situation.

"Sure, 'tis my husband you must speak to, regarding this, Fergus. He is chieftain; I have no say in such matters. It is clearly his decision to make!"

"Aye, milady, I realize that is the usual way of it, but milord has already informed us he will leave the decision up to you entirely. He will not speak on it one way or the other!"

If she hadn't wanted to strangle Killian before and, in truth, she had many times in the past days, she most certainly did now. If she told Fergus she did not want the woman and her child here in the castle she would seem like a cold, unfeeling, selfish woman. And she didn't believe she was any of those things, not usually! And this would be a test of her faith in Killian. He was asking her to decide whether she truly trusted him or believed he would remain faithful to her.

If she told Fergus she would not allow his daughter to live here, it would clearly tell Killian she did not trust him, or believe him capable of being faithful to her. If she allowed Ciara to live here, it would speak volumes as to how she believed in him, in his character and in his wedding vows. And it would mean the woman lived here in the castle under the same roof. Ciara was beautiful and beguiling and possibly possessed magical abilities. Alainn felt certain the woman still had feelings for Killian. She would be a constant temptation!

She found herself growing ever angry at Killian for putting her in this position, yet if he had made the decision, she would have been furious if he'd simply allowed Ciara to live and work in the castle. And if he hadn't allowed her to, she would be led to believe he still burned for her and didn't trust himself to be around the woman.

Both Fergus and Eireen sat curiously waiting for Alainn to answer and she was no more close to a decision than she had been moments earlier. She glanced at Eireen and she was certain the poor woman was no more eager to have her stepdaughter living with them than Alainn, but she knew the woman adored the small boy.

Alainn was growing impatient with herself at how ludicrous this was that she couldn't make a damnable decision. She was supposed to be a wife of a chieftain though her childish tantrum she'd displayed the other night in dealing with Killian could hardly be considered the behavior of a lady. She finally inhaled deeply and looked into the serious eyes of Fergus Flannery.

"Aye, they may live here with you, Fergus. Your daughter may work here in the castle as is the present arrangement, but I must let it be known with no uncertainty, I do not desire her to be anywhere near me!"

"Aye, it shall be as you wish, milady!" he quickly agreed, and though the man threw her a curious look, he bowed to her respectfully and graciously thanked her. Eireen bowed to her as well, and then gave her a hint of a smile as they left her to her troubled thoughts.

AFTER DEALING WITH the unwanted decision, Alainn went to the kitchen as was her usual morning routine. She spotted Cookson and he lowered his eyes when he saw her heading his way. She smiled to reassure him she harbored no hard feelings for his part in aiding Killian the other evening. She went to the nearby pitcher and filled her cup then added several spoonfuls of honey, stirred it quickly and then, glancing at Cookson with a look of displeasure, swallowed it. She sputtered and spat and tried to keep the liquid down. She heard the chuckle behind her and turned to look up into the amused face of her husband.

"What exactly is that concoction that tastes so entirely displeasing to you and why would you choose to drink it then, Alainn?" Killian asked with mirth in his eyes.

She was still making a humorous face and her nose was wrinkled as was usual when she was displeased with something. Cookson answered for her.

"She does it without fail twice a day, and 'tis milk with a good portion of honey to make it less repulsive to her for she's greatly disliked milk since she was a wee child!"

"I didn't know that about you, Alainn. Why do you force it down then, if it is so unpleasant for you?"

"'Tis for the babe. Cookson's mother, Margaret, once told me it will help our son to grow strong and healthy and it will ensure I've enough milk to see him well nourished."

His face glowed with pride and love at the thought, and he took her in his arms. It was the first time he'd shown such an open display of affection since she'd lost her temper with him. He put his lips to hers in a soft and loving kiss, when they were interrupted by a closing door. Alainn turned to see Ciara McCree had entered the kitchen.

"What is 'she' doing here?" Alainn hadn't meant to sound so harsh or bitter, but her sharpness clearly took everyone off guard. Cookson stared at her with apparent disbelief and Killian would not meet her eyes. Finally Cookson answered for the other young woman had not spoken.

"She comes in to claim milk for her wee boy."

"And why does she not simply go to the dairy shed as do most others?" Alainn struggled to keep her voice controlled.

By this time her young son had followed her inside the kitchen and Alainn was beginning to feel embarrassed at the many eyes that were upon her.

"'Twas I who thought to simply save her the long walk to the shed. And Ciara has been helpin' me here in the kitchen, as well. If that is not to your liking, milady, you need only say the word!"

Cookson had never called her by her title for they'd been dear friends all their lives. By now all the kitchen servants were all looking at her as though she was a shrew. To make matters worse, the young widow scurried over to Killian and dropped to her knees before him.

"Milord, you must forgive me for my unkind words earlier this week!"

Though Killian surely did not wish to have such close contact with the woman knowing how strained it was between he and Alainn, he must appear amiable toward the recently widowed woman.

"Ciara, there is no need to apologize. You were clearly overcome with grief."

Alainn felt her blood beginning to boil and she slowly turned to leave the entire undesirable scene when she felt a small hand on her skirts. It was the wee child come to see the kind lady who had played with him and been most affectionate toward him just days earlier. She crouched down to look into his sweet face.

"Wee Kale, 'tis good to see you. Would you care for a honey-cake; if 'tis permitted?" she stood and glanced at the other woman who had finally risen. She was further embarrassed to see Ciara fall to her knees once more, this time at her feet. She clutched Alainn's legs tightly and dramatically wept.

"Oh, milady, you, too, must accept my heartfelt apologies in the wrongful accusations I hurled at you. They were spoken in haste, for my heart was nearly broken and my mind clearly affected, and I take back those unkind words, most assuredly. My father tells me 'tis you I have to thank for my son and I being graciously allowed to stay here in Castle O'Donnel. I thank you most sincerely for bein' so uncommonly kind and generous to my wee boy!"

Chapter Twenty

ALAINN WANTED TO be anywhere but here in her present location or predicament. She dared a sideways glance at Killian, and noticed that now he and the entire kitchen staff were waiting to hear her response.

"Stand, Ciara. You needn't kneel before me; I would not demand anyone ever kneel or bow to me. And I did not take to heart your words spoken at the churchyard. I recognize your sorrow and bear you no ill-will because of that incident!"

"Thank you, milady!" the woman said as she rose and she held tight and then kissed Alainn's hand.

She wanted to tear it from Ciara as she did so, but Alainn forced herself to smile politely then watched as the woman collected the milk, and her small child before heading out of the kitchen toward the herb chamber. When what seemed an insufferably long moment had passed and everyone had apparently returned to their own duties, Alainn nodded respectfully to Killian, and then started out the door toward the courtyard. She heard Killian's footsteps beside her.

"What has you so upset now, Alainn? You had to know

when you agreed to Ciara stayin' here in the castle, that you would happen upon her on occasion."

"Of course, I knew, Killian. I just didn't expect it to be so soon, and when the thoughts and images are still so fresh in my mind. And seeing her on her knees before you brought to mind another deplorable image that I witnessed and I was tryin' most desperately to forget. You are apparently not aware I am privy to *all* the many intimacies the two of you shared during your time together!"

Killian's handsome face colored at her words.

"And how would you like me to respond to that, Alainn? Clearly there is no way to undo what's been done, but 'twas years ago, no matter how fresh it may seem to you. I feel nothing for her, bar sympathy in the loss of her husband."

She did not acknowledge his words, but simply kept walking.

"I've business to attend to in the great hall today so that it will be cleared for the banquet on the morrow."

"Aye, go on then to your many duties, Killian. I will see you this night."

She was trying desperately to not sound like a spoiled, callow, unreasonable child, or a wretched old crone. He turned to look at her and noticed her lip quivering as was common when she was hoping to still her tears. He relented and took her in his strong arms.

"It was not my intention to hurt you, Lainna, to make you feel awkward, nor put in an uncomfortable position."

"I realize that, Killian, and you speak the truth, most men who have taken lovers do not have wives with the curse of second sight, for believe me when I say it is no gift!"

"Oh, I most sincerely believe you, Alainn, for 'tis not somethin' many would choose to possess, I am certain."

⌘

AFTER THEY'D PARTED ways and Alainn began walking toward the small herb garden she'd planted near the east solar, she found Danhoul heading toward her, an expression of deep concern on his face. Out of the corner of her eye she saw a black streak diving toward her. She instinctively threw out her hands and her magical abilities took over. The bird that was only mere feet from her fell to the ground, dead! Danhoul got to her in time to strike down a second crow with his sword. When an entire flock seemed intent on attacking her, Alainn felt her powers and her temper take on a new life. The lot of them simply burst into flames. There was a pungent scent of burnt meat and singed feathers in the air, and nearly fifty dead birds on the grass at their feet.

"My God, Alainn! A dark soul maintains control over the animals and still means you great harm!"

"And I have had quite enough! I have adored animals all my life. I have already lost my cherished Wolf because of this despicably horrid spell. I will not live in fear of animals, forced to keep them at bay. I will take back my kinship with the beasts and I will do it now!"

The young man beside her looked uncertain, but he recognized the determination on her pretty face, and by hearing her thoughts he realized she'd already had a difficult morning. He nodded his head and smiled at her, encouraging her to continue on.

She looked up toward the sky as she held her hands out before her.

"No more shall the birds or the beasts seek to harm me,
From the power that has held them, they will henceforth be
    set free
And should another such attempt dare come to be
The doer of the spell shall be so cursed ten-fold, plus three!"

Danoul stared openly at her as he spoke.

"You would dare curse them by the power of thirteen?" he asked with doubtful eyes as large as shields.

"Aye, I will and have, for I am done toying with whoever it is who wishes me harm. To protect my child, I would resort to that and much, much more!"

"'Tis a most disenchanting number to be cursed by. Only the strongest of witches would dare utter the curse of three and ten!"

"You think it was not warranted, Danhoul?"

"Now I did not say that. I am only uncertain if it was wise to use such powerful magic. It could be directed back to you, if the evil-doer is capable of strong magic. The dark ones will surely be alerted to the usage of such a strong curse!"

"And perhaps it is the dark ones that have called upon the animals to harm me, or have employed an evil human to do their bidding for them. I have seen it before!"

"And if you and your man are at odds, you will be open to their temptations and to their threat."

"Killian and I are not at odds!"

The handsome young man pushed his wavy, honey-blonde hair from his eyes as was a common habit. He smiled a half-smile and his smoky-blue eyes now held a playfully taunting quality.

"If you say so, but I doubt you'd be lookin' so entirely displeased if you felt all was well between you."

"I've just been attacked by a cursed flock of crows and they'd surely had a dark spell put on them to be so vicious about it! You think I should be dancin' for joy, then, do you?"

"No, I s'pose not, but I've seen you deal with worse and with a smile if all is well between your husband and yourself. And I've not seen a smile on your lovely face since you learned about the healer's granddaughter's time with him. And you're right to be suspicious of the woman. I sense she is not nearly as sincere as she would have you or your husband believe. Yet I find her aura completely unusual, it appears to change often!"

"I have noticed that as well, Danhoul. Sometimes it seems mildly clouded and other times dark as pitch."

"Aye, the woman is surely not easily understood even with our supernatural powers of perception, but I do feel she's not to be trusted."

Alainn felt such an overwhelming sense of relief in having someone confirm her suspicions without making her seem entirely irrational and unreasonable, she approached the young man, embraced him tightly and then placed a hurried kiss upon his cheek. She saw his cheeks color slightly, but he only smiled once more, and did not need to ask her why she'd felt compelled to show him affection.

Chapter Twenty-One

I T WAS THE night of the feast at Castle O'Donnel. Killian had thought it might be respectfully appropriate to cancel the event due to William's death during the hunt, but most everyone disagreed. Perhaps it might even be considered a slight to the man who had been killed, for sometimes it was a sign a man was thought of highly, to celebrate after a death. And the Irish were noted for their love of drink and celebration to honor a life. And, so, although the sporting events set for the week had been cancelled, the banquet and the entertainment were to be held this evening.

Alainn felt no more like celebrating than jumping off the highest turret in the castle and, in truth, that might actually seem more appealing to her. There was awkwardness when she and Killian were together and they had yet to make love. She felt lonely at night sharing his bed, but not holding one another and scarcely daring to touch. She despised the fact he had shared Ciara's bed even though it had been some time ago and she and Killian had not yet been bound. Killian was a man of reasonable conscience and, in truth, she believed he had moral fiber to spare, but he had uncharacteristically bedded another man's wife and possibly fathered the woman's child, though she had yet to come up with a reasonable explanation on how that might have occurred when the curse had been in place. As she experienced the child kick inside her own belly, she felt as though Killian had betrayed him as well, even as unreasonable as that sounded.

As Alainn brushed and pulled her hair to the side, tying it with ribbon to make it look regally presentable, she looked down at the dress she wore and felt the tears come to her eyes as they had so many times in the past days. Killian had selected and purchased this dress for her before they were married. She'd worn it the night he proposed. It had needed to be altered to fit her expanding body, but the tailor had capably managed by adding side panels. He made it appear as lovely as it had all those months ago. The dress was varying shades of blue and consisted of both velvet and silk fabrics. The skirt was full and now that it had been refitted it drew more attention to her bosom and then hung softly so that her belly was not clearly visible, but her cleavage surely was.

She placed the turquoise combs in her hair and looked up as she saw Killian enter the room. He glanced at her and then appraisingly looked at her once more, but still did not break the silence. He went to the enormous armoire chest and began searching through his many garments.

She finally dared to speak. "Would you prefer if I stay out of sight in my chamber this night? As chieftain, you must of course be readily available to greet your guests and entertain them. My presence is not truly necessary. Sure you might feel less on edge if I remain concealed in this chamber. Certainly Maire O'Donnel would think it more fitting and less shameful!"

"In truth, it would be shameful to hide you away, so beautiful you look this night! But, sure 'tis to be your choice, Alainn. Certainly, I want you by my side, as always, but I'll not force it if you'd rather remain parted from me."

"'Tis not me who keeps such distance!" she dared to whisper.

"By your uncommon coldness toward me, I don't get the sense you long to be near me so very much. Are you tellin' me you actually want me here with you; that you'll want to share my bed in an intimate manner?"

"And would it be another's bed *you'd* rather be in?"

"By God's nails, I knew there was little use in attemptin' to talk to you. I'll don my garments and be off then. It might be a wee bit awkward at the feast tonight if you can't speak with me without hurlin' insults, nasty expressions, and accusations in my direction."

"Then I'll remain here if that is truly what you wish!"

"By, Christ, woman!" He voiced his exasperation. "That is not my wish and you well know it, and maybe'tis you who'd like to stay here so you can be nearer to the boy then for you've ever *so* much more in common with him."

"Now who's being entirely unreasonable? I hope to come

back as a man in my next life, for I could use my sword to handle all unpleasantness, I could simply lop off my enemies heads and be well praised for it, demand fidelity, but not be required to remain true to my spouse, be demanding and cantankerous and have no one think poorly toward me if my mood was less than congenial! Cuss and belch and break wind and never care if my behavior is rude or unattractive or unbecoming…"

Killian looked over at her and a smile crossed his broad lips and mirth filled his eyes. She glanced up and saw the sight and soon found herself smiling as well.

"Are you quite through, then?" he asked as he drew closer to her and bent down to place a kiss upon her lips.

"Aye, for now, I suppose I am," she admitted, now feeling much less irritable.

He lifted her into his arms and carried her to the bed as he began disrobing her.

"Killian, I've only just finished dressing, and 'tis nearly time for the guests to arrive."

"And I've gone without lovin' my wife for far too long and I'll assist you with re-donning your lovely dress, though I'd be a bit more pleased with it if it actually covered even half of your beautiful breasts. And as far as the guests arrivin', I suspect they'll obligingly drink their mead wine and wait a few moments if they must."

"A few moments?" she asked feigning displeasure.

"Well several moments, then, Lainna!" She smiled and

kissed him passionately.

⌘

THE EVENING WAS going well, in Alainn's opinion; in truth, it was most untypical. Maire O'Donnel had not been rude to her, the many other chieftains, lords, and ladies had been courteous, and she had not felt out of place in their conversations or their company as she'd feared she might. As always, Killian never failed to impress her with his eloquence and charm. His smooth and charismatic manner of dealing with men and women alike left little doubt as to why he was such a popular man with the ladies, and a knowledgeable and respected chieftain. Sometimes he awed even her, and she had known him most of her life and was surely his greatest supporter and the first to boast about his many talents and attributes. As she glanced at him speaking with Maire O'Donnel, she believed he had even managed to melt the icy heart of the usually abrasive woman.

He must have felt Alainn's eyes upon him from across the room, for he turned toward her and smiled as he continued to speak with the matronly woman. As she made her way toward her husband, Alainn looked out into the sea of people and spotted Ciara McCree. She had hoped the woman would not make an appearance this night, but Eireen had explained her stepdaughter thought it would be accepted for her to attend even though her grief was so new, as her husband had been greatly anticipating the event and so she was there in his stead.

Although the woman did not dance or outwardly make merry, she seemed to have a goblet of ale in her hand each time Alainn noticed her, and she spent nearly the entirety of the evening in the company of several different men. Alainn tried, without success, not to be critical and suspicious of the woman. Yet she felt everything about her reeked of insincerity, including her grief. She hoped it was her powers of perception alerting her to these truths and not simply her own bitterness and jealousy that ruled her thoughts entirely.

Mary and Riley appeared to be on better terms this night. Riley seemed to be on good behavior and he danced nearly every dance with his wife and did not openly ogle any of the servant girls. Connor MacLain was not present and Alainn surmised he and Mary had not seen each other in some time. Perhaps Mary and Riley would still stand a chance at happiness. Alainn prayed it would be so, and if Mary harbored any ill-feelings toward her because of Riley's confession, she had concealed it well.

When Alainn made it to Killian's side, he lovingly placed his arm about her shoulders and drew her to him. They noticed the distasteful look Maire O'Donnel now wore for she clearly disapproved of their open display of affection. Killian apparently wanted to set Alainn at ease and so he taunted the older woman.

"Does my wife not look enchantingly beautiful this night, Maire?"

The woman appeared as though she did not wish to reply to the direct question, but as she looked up into Killian's handsome face, even she seemed charmed by him.

"Aye, 'tis a lovely garment she dons this night!"

"And hasn't she the loveliest hair you've ever seen?"

"Killian, don't put Maire on the spot so; she has six daughters with lovely red hair I've been told, sure she prefers hair of that shade."

The woman threw a look of near gratitude at Alainn, but then was further dismayed by the young chieftain's next move.

"You must excuse us, Maire, for I'm after takin' my lovely wee wife for a dance for I've not yet had the pleasure this night!"

"You can't mean to dance with the lass; she's great with child!"

Killian smiled broadly at this. "Aye, well, I do indeed intend to dance with her and, aye, I'm aware she carries a child!" He leaned closer to the woman and whispered as he spoke the next bit, "I'm the man who planted the seed!"

"Och!" The woman's ruddy colored cheeks darkened further and she huffed aloud, her continued disapproval evident, so Killian baited her and pushed the issue further still.

"And were all your six daughters a product of immaculate conception, then, Maire, or were they created in the usual way?"

"'Tis hardly proper to openly discuss such subjects with a lady, Killian O'Brien!"

"Well, I only wanted to ensure that you'll not make my lovely wife feel shameful because she carries my child or shares my bed, for we are married so 'tis biblically acceptable, legal, moral, and entirely enjoyable!"

"Killian O'Brien! Enough of that talk!" Alainn scolded him harshly. "Maire, you look as though you could use a drink, come with me and we'll find some cider."

"I think whiskey might be preferential, Alainn!" the woman admitted as she fanned her rosy cheeks.

Alainn was torn between smiling and glowering at Killian as she took the stunned woman's arm. But, even as they walked away from Killian, who wore a broad grin and a devilish glint in his eyes, she noticed Maire O'Donnel couldn't keep her eyes from him.

"I swear the man could seduce the holy mother!" Maire spoke in a low tone more to herself than Alainn.

Alainn presumed the woman's husband, Cormac, would be surprised to find his wife in an unusually amorous mood this night.

When Alainn returned to her husband's side he chuckled again and took her in his arms. He placed a thorough kiss on her full lips and then did as he'd promised and danced every dance with his noticeably pregnant wife.

THE FEAST HAD been delicious and the many male entertainers were undoubtedly talented. When Alainn espied her harp being carried to the center of the great hall, she questioned Killian with her eyes. He grinned a sly grin, but he did not answer. She noticed Danhoul heading toward her and he had his fiddle in hand. He took her arm and led her to where the harp now stood.

"Your husband insists we must play and sing for the guests. He didn't tell you earlier for he knew you would fret about it and somehow find a way to decline. As it is, he knows you have little option."

"But 'tis seldom women perform in the presence of nobility."

"I believe your husband wants to show the nobles his wife is not only beautiful, intelligent, and educated, but unusually talented as well."

"Aye, well, it would appear we are set to sing and play then. It's been some time since the last time we sang together."

"Then it was thought you were a peasant, now you are the grandest and loveliest of ladies, Alainn O'Brien."

"Don't make me more flustered than I already am for, in my heart, I will always feel like a commoner no matter that I live in a castle and I'm married to a chieftain, Danhoul."

"Then you must imagine yourself back at the gatherin' that night, singin' for common-folk with no expectations but to hear the great natural gift of your voice."

Alainn sat down upon the stool and gently strummed the harp while Danhoul expertly pulled the bow across the strings. The poignant Celtic melody filled the air and soon the two voices blended in a lovely rendition of an ancient Celtic song. A hush fell over the entire room as enormous and overflowing with people as it was.

Killian looked on and his eyes locked with Alainn's. She smiled as though she sang only to him. When the song was completed, Danhoul bowed and Alainn nodded her head. When the crowd applauded and cheered in appreciation of the talent, Alainn smiled as the child within her kicked steadily in response. Killian came to take her hand and led her away from the center of the room to the seat beside him at the head table.

"You were remarkable, Alainn! You've the most angelic voice. And soon I will listen to you sing our son to sleep at night and I'll have the good fortunate to listen to your lovely voice all my life, God willing."

Soon the guests had begun to dwindle for the night grew late. Alainn found herself growing ever weary and in urgent need of slumber. Killian assured her it would not seem discourteous or improper if she made her way to their bedchamber. He claimed he would bid the few stragglers farewell, and he would soon join her.

When she had readied herself for bed and donned her nightdress, her stomach rumbled noisily in pangs of hunger, yet again. She would not be capable of sleep at any rate, not with the rumbling and the child squirming and kicking, clearly voicing his disapproval of her hungry state.

"I just ate mere hours ago, you wee imp." She playfully scolded her unborn child, but reasoned if she went down the back stairs to the kitchen she would only see the few servants who might still be present in the kitchen, and surely even they would be gone soon for 'twas nearly the middle of night. As she pulled the shawl tightly around the nightdress knowing, how cool and drafty the corridors and stairwells of the castle were, most especially at night, she lighted a candle to take with her. She believed since she had recently uttered the spell of thirteen she would now be perfectly safe setting out alone.

As she made her way down the many winding steps, she heard voices coming from a small, nearly hidden alcove off the stairwell. She knew it was a man and woman speaking, but could not make out the voices or what they were saying. Although she had not actually intended on listening in on the conversation, when she finally discovered who the voices belonged to, she listened most astutely.

"You must go to your bed for clearly you're filled with all too much drink!"

"Aye, I've had a good deal to drink, but 'tis not drink I would be filled with this night, if t'was my choice!"

"I will have a servant see you safely to your chambers for you're liable to do harm to yourself for sure you can barely walk."

"Tis no servant I want in my bed, but our chieftain!"

Chapter Twenty-Two

"CIARA, ENOUGH OF that improper talk; I am a married man!"

"And I was married when last we were intimate. I see no difference, or no reason why we cannot resume what we once shared."

"Ciara, I truly love my wife and intend to remain ever faithful to her. Sorry I am that you are alone and have suffered a tragic loss, but I'll not be offerin' you comfort in that manner, this night or any other!"

"You'll soon her tire of her. And now that she is great with child, sure she can't pleasure you as often or capably as you are accustomed."

"Ciara, we are through speakin' on this! Wait here while I send for a servant to take you to your chambers."

"No, milord! You must not go, for I ache for you still. In these years that we have been parted there has not been a night that I did not burn for you and think of the most passionate times we shared together!"

Alainn could no longer contain her jealousy or her rage and when she stepped into the alcove, she saw the other woman attempting to kiss Killian though he kept her at arm's length.

"If you do not distance yourself from my husband this instant, I swear your son shall be orphaned this very night!"

Killian turned and surely noticed the unmistakable jealous fury on Alainn's face.

When Ciara made no attempt to move, Alainn held out her hand and the woman screamed in surprised outrage when a loud and forceful slap was heard and a raised red handprint formed on her cheek though Alainn had not stepped any closer to her. The woman's eyes filled with disbelief, and her hand went to her cheek, but instead of showing fear, it was anger that encompassed her face and her cat-like eyes.

"You cursed witch!" Ciara shrieked.

Danhoul arrived in time to see Ciara lunge angrily toward Alainn. The candle Alainn held in her hand was knocked to the ground and the flames caught her nightdress. Killian went to Alainn and hastily extinguished the flames, while Danhoul held back the other woman who apparently remained intent on getting to Alainn. When Killian successfully put out the flames with little damage done to Alainn's skin, his relief was short-lived for he saw her fly furiously at Ciara and she raked her neck with her nails. Ciara screamed, clutched Alainn's shawl and clawed at her nightdress. The garment was soon torn along with the skin on her arm, when Alainn grabbed a hearty handful of Ciara's dark hair and pulled hard. The men managed with some difficulty to separate the two ill-tempered women.

Killian held tight to Alainn, and Dahoul did the same with Ciara. It was at that precise moment all present began to feel the ground shaking, and rumbling beneath them. Both men looked at Alainn for they were aware it was her causing the unusual and dangerous occurrence. Alainn seemed nearly oblivious of the shaking as she threatened the other woman.

"Should you ever attempt to take my husband to your bed again, you will be the sorriest wench in the land, for you'll be made to deal with me! And though I sense you may claim some form of magical abilities, they fall drastically short of those which I possess. I promise you that! If you do not abide my words, I shall gladly reveal the extent of my powers."

"Alainn, settle you down; you needn't be so enraged, she's filled with drink and doesn't even know what she's doin', I'd wager!" Killian reasoned.

"That's utter horse shite! She knows well enough, and she's simply unscrupulous, untrustworthy, and promiscuous!"

"Danhoul, see Ciara to her chamber, for she's clearly not fit to walk so consumed with drink is she at the moment!" Killian ordered.

"Aye, I'll accompany her."

"Be cautious, Danhoul, she is not to be trusted!" Alainn

E I G H A N N E D W A R D S

fumed as she spoke.

"And, in truth, you would not be so very eager to see him in my bed either." Ciara slurred as she glowered at the chieftain's wife.

"Well sure he's one of the few men here in the entire county that hasn't yet had you!" Alainn cattily retorted.

The dark-haired woman sneered at Alainn once more and it took a good deal of strength from both the large men to keep the two women from getting at one another again. When the ground began to shake yet again, Danhoul called out to Killian.

"Calm your wife, Killian, or she may bring the entire castle down upon our heads!"

Finally the younger man picked up the drunken woman and threw her over his shoulder. Her rude comments and furious protests could be heard for sometime as she was carried away.

Alainn remained so angry she shook from head to toe. She felt Killian's hand on her arm and the tears streaming down her cheeks as a result of her hot temper.

"I want her gone from this castle straightaway!" she vehemently raged.

"Alainn, she is filled with drink, and both hurt and angry. She is trying to come to terms with her loss!"

"By taking my husband to her bed?"

"I don't believe she really even knows what she's doing entirely. And tomorrow she'll surely be regretful if she should actually remember any of this!"

"Killian, if you attempt to make another excuse for her, I will see her not only gone from this castle, but from this realm!"

"I understand you are displeased and I'm not sayin' you don't have a right to be upset, but I ask you to please let this incident pass. Sure, she's not accustomed to consumin' so very much drink!"

"And the fact she attempted to harm me with fire; how do you explain that?"

"I don't believe that was purposeful, Alainn."

"And if someone attempted to harm you, the great chieftain, they would be tossed in the dungeon without question!"

"Ah, so now you don't just want her gone from the castle, but thrown in the dungeon as well. And how would that look, do you suppose, if I had a widow with a young child, her husband barely cold in his grave, placed in the dungeon? Do you suppose I would earn the respect of the other servants or the villagers by so doing? I s'pose if you had your way she'd receive a lashing as well!"

"No, I don't want to see her lashed unless 'tis I who can wield the whip! And if the flames had done damage to more than my nightdress would you feel even some of the fury I now feel?"

"Alainn, try to calm down. Come to our bed and let me hold you!"

He attempted to take her in his arms, but she would have

no part of it.

"Lainna, 'tis you I want and no amount of persuasion by Ciara or any other woman will make me stray from you. If anythin' this incident should make you more confident of that."

They were interrupted when Danhoul cleared his throat to alert them to his return. They both noticed the many scratches upon his cheek.

"I have seen her safe to her chamber, not without a worthy battle," He announced as he wiped away the trickle of blood from the fresh wounds. "Now you must calm your wife before her powers put the castle and its occupants in grave danger!"

"Don't talk of me as if I am a child in need of disciplining!" She spewed.

"Alainn, be reasonable, Danhoul speaks the truth, your wee temper if you allow it to run rampant could be the death of the entire lot of us."

She glared at her husband as she spoke. "Do you believe I want to feel this jealous rage; or that I welcome these damnable powers? Do you know what I would give to have them gone forever, to be allowed a life of normalcy?"

"Lainna?" Killian tried to take her in his arms once more, but she simply pulled away and headed up the narrow winding steps to their bedchamber.

The two men looked at each other with equal expressions of concern and frustration.

"You'd best find a way to dissipate her insecurities and appease her. Sure, you're the only one who can do that now. I believe she is correct in assuming Ciara is not to be trusted. I sense there will be much discord between the two of them in the future. And the widow may have an unpredictable dark side to her you may not recognize or be allowed to see, for she is not without powers herself. 'Tis true they are nowhere near as immeasurable as those of your wife, but then I know of no one whose powers are like Alainn's. Whether she wants them or not, she has them and in multitudes you or I and even the gods have not witnessed before!"

"Are you attemptin' to cause me more fear and trepidation, Danhoul?"

"No, Killian, as a seer I am simply forewarnin' you to be prepared for much unrest as long as the two of them remain anywhere in close proximity of each other!"

"I will take that under great consideration then, Danhoul! And now, I s'pose I'd best go to her and see what can be done to calm the woman."

"Which one?" he sarcastically queried.

"My wife, you arse!"

"Good, see to you keep your distance from Ciara, you may be immune to Alainn's magic, but the rest of us are not!"

Chapter Twenty-Three

AFTER ALAINN DONNED her garments the next morning, she gently rubbed a healing balm on her ankles. The burns were barely visible, only a few tiny reddened marks remained, but they stung fiercely. If she was just a woman and not a witch with fairy lineage, she was certain there would be little pain, but because she was a witch she was unnaturally susceptible to wounds caused by flame. And her temper still burned as fiercely as the reddened marks on her legs.

Killian was already gone from their bedchamber and she knew he was in a rare unruly disposition this morning as well. She had denied him the previous night; the only time since they'd become intimate, she had refused his advances entirely and stubbornly kept to her side of their bed. It was the first time she'd allowed her anger and jealousy to rule her emotions and her desires so completely. Killian was a man accustomed to getting his way, in his life and in his bed. And this morning he had worn a look of frustration and displeasure.

Now, some might think he was overly demanding to expect his wife to partake in carnal activities in her advancing term, but they were both aware her desires remained nearly insatiable even though she carried a child. They had always shared a passion uncommon to most, she believed. Therefore, Killian knew well enough she had denied him physical love and pleasure only to punish him for defending Ciara. She knew how he felt regarding women who used their bodies as a way to either punish or reward their husband, and his disappointment was not so much in that he'd not been pleasured, but that she'd stooped to a measure he disagreed with.

When she made her way toward the kitchen, she stopped short realizing Ciara McCree was most certainly within the room. She used her powers of perception to confirm it. She hoped the troublesome woman had a throbbing headache and a putrid stomach from ingesting such quantities of ale. It rankled her to think she now felt uncomfortable entering the kitchen and she would not be likely to partake in her usual companionable morning conversation with her friend, Cookson. And she needed to procure her milk and honey mixture. As Eireen headed down the corridor toward the drawing room, Alainn stopped her.

"Eireen, might I ask a favor of you?"

"Certainly, milady, what is it you require?"

"Would you ask Cookson to come to me; I must speak with him?"

"Aye, milady!" The woman gave Alainn a questioning

look, surely wondering why she had changed her morning routine and wouldn't simply speak to the man behind the nearby door, but she did as she'd been instructed.

When Cookson came out only a moment later, he appeared mildly perturbed to be taken from his many duties.

"Alainn, what is it you need?" he asked in a hurried tone. She thought he still seemed sore with her for her harsh way of speaking with Ciara the previous morning, but she was thankful he did refer to her by her given name and not her title as he'd done then.

"Sorry I am to pester you, for I know how busy you are and what long hours you must keep in order to run your kitchen as efficiently as you do, but I must ask a small favor."

"Aye, name it then, Alainn."

"I need a servant, specifically a servant-girl that you trust completely to bring me my milk both morning and night."

"You don't care to simply come for it yourself as you've done these past months?"

"No, I think that is not possible any longer."

"Because of the Widow McCree, you'll no longer come visit me in the kitchen?"

"Aye,'tis because of her I no longer feel comfortable being there."

"I don't see what you have against the woman, Alainn. She seems amicable enough and I quite like the woman. She's been dealt a hard blow, havin' her husband taken from her with a wee son to raise, and I'm told she and her grand-

A CHIEFTAIN'S WIFE

mother have had some type of fallin' out, so the healer no longer wants her in her chambers so very much. Now she has no choice but to help out in the kitchen to make certain she has food enough to feed the two of them."

"I'm sure they'd hardly starve, Cookson! Killian allows none of his servants or villagers to go without food. He has drastically reduced the rents and allowed his subjects to thrive more readily than any chieftain I am aware of."

"But she feels she must work for her keep, she's a proud woman and does not expect charity."

"But who cares for her wee son while she spends her days there?"

"Eireen has him some, but he is with his mother a good deal of time in the kitchen. Thus far it has not proven to be detrimental to any of the duties."

"A busy kitchen is no place for a small child; there are many harmful and dangerous objects within. He could be burned or scalded. The many open hearths are a great peril to a wee one and what of the vast quantity of knives and cleavers?"

"Alainn, you spent most of your childhood in a kitchen or a healer's chamber and both are dangerous places. You survived well enough. You seem to have a clouded opinion of the woman and I am uncertain why, but I have much to do for even your husband has not yet broke fast and I am told he is off to visit your grandfather this morn, so I must soon get back to my duties. There is a young woman, Nellie

223

O'Shea, who seems most trustworthy. Do you know her?"

"Aye, I know of her, she seems a reliable young girl."

"I'll have her bring you the mixture you require with your morning and evening meal, if that is acceptable to you."

"Aye, it is much appreciated, I am grateful to you, Cookson."

"Aye!" He smiled as he left, but Alainn did not find herself prone to smiling this day.

As SHE ENTERED the great hall, she saw most of the many tables from the celebration had been cleared away. The enormous head table had been readied for the morning meal and Alainn felt herself wishing she was back at Castle O'Brien. It was the first time she'd felt this way since she'd arrived at Killian's castle. She longed to be back there, preparing herbal concoctions for the many patrons who appreciated her talents and knowledge. She longed to speak with Cook and Margaret and Molly, to her Aunt Siobhan or Rory, and to take her breakfast in the kitchen where she'd taken her meals nearly all her life. And she desperately longed to go to the magical fairy glade where she'd always gone when life felt difficult.

She was overwhelmed with loneliness and homesickness and soon tears were brimming in her eyes. She had no desire to have Killian see her teary eyes or her dismal mood, so she hurried up the winding back steps toward the castle's closest tower. As she stood at the top of the east solar looking down and watching the sun rise over the nearby lake, she touched her belly and felt her son move. She inhaled a deep breath and tried to calm her unsettled feeling, but even the beauty of the morning and the knowledge she would soon birth their son, didn't seem to aptly cheer her this day.

She fought the tears, but they rolled softly down her cheeks and fell upon her gown. She swiped at the tears angrily and pushed her unbound hair back behind her shoulders. She saw the bright sky begin to turn darker and fill with grey clouds. She inhaled several times and held out her hands toward the sky. She watched the clouds begin to scatter and the sun peeked through once more. She smiled at that, but still a soft sob escaped her lips.

"You would trade this life as a fine noble lady and a chieftain's wife, to go back to being a commoner?"

She heard the male voice behind her and looked into the concerned face of Danhoul Calhoun who so perceptively read her thoughts.

"I have never held a great desire to be a lady of position, 'tis true, but I would not wish myself away from Killian. I only would ask to be free of some of the uncertainties I now face. The entire castle thinks of me as an unreasonable shrew. I am uncomfortable around most everyone for Ciara has capably managed to turn half the servants against me. They think she is a grieving widow who has been treated unfairly for no apparent reason by a bitter woman of noble birth. Killian believes my jealousy is completely unwarranted. And I feel an overpowering sensation of gloom around me. Surely whoever placed the curse upon the animals will attempt to cause further harm to me. Is there a dark power near us, Danhoul? Do you sense it?"

"Aye, there is something most definitely amiss. I cannot define it, not entirely either, but something evil is at work."

"And is Ciara part of it?"

"Maybe, although not outwardly. Perhaps she may be cunning or skilled enough to hide her powers or her allegiance with the dark one. Sure I do not trust the woman entirely, yet I can't aptly discern her powers. I do believe you are correct to be suspicious in regards to her."

Alainn shivered and the tears fell once more.

"Ah, lass, don't cry so. Sure between you and me and your husband, we'll find a way to overcome whatever threatens the peace here."

She looked up at his blue-grey eyes so filled with compassion and empathy and she was only driven to further fits of weeping. He hesitantly took her in his arms and softly patted her back trying to keep the embrace as innocent as possible, though he sensed on his part what he felt for her had never or never would be purely dispassionate. He did not distance himself from her even though he heard the boots on the steps behind them.

Chapter Twenty-Four

"YOU SHOULD BOTH be warned if any of the servants or guards found the two of you like this you could spend time in the dungeon for injustices toward your chieftain!"

His tone infuriated Alainn and, though she moved from Danhoul, she glowered at Killian.

Alainn looked up at the blazing green eyes that bore into her soul. She wanted to cry again, perhaps even needed to weep until enough tears fell that she could rid herself of the uneasiness she felt. But as was typical with her, she chose sarcasm and anger over melancholia in dealing with Killian.

"Aye, send me to the dungeon if you like. Sure sending your wife and the mother of your unborn child to the pit would be more openly accepted than a recently widowed woman!"

"You seek comfort in the arms of another man, and I am not to flay you for it, then?"

"If I should seek comfort in his bed, then you can flay me for it!"

"The two of you might leave me out of your constant

bickering! And Killian, Alainn is only hopin' to make you feel some of the jealousy she now feels and, in truth, there's no way you could ever feel what she feels, for she has only ever been in your bed! But you might try to put yourself in her position, Killian O'Brien and, if you don't, you're maybe not quite the man I thought you to be."

"And what makes you believe I truly give a shite what you think, Danhoul Calhoun?"

"Because I know you are a man of conscience, of integrity and honor. You are burdened by what others think of you. It's important to you to be respected, and the fact you shared a bed with a married woman is the one flaw that has haunted your Catholic conscience ever since. Perhaps you might dwell on why you were tempted to Ciara's bed; why you could not resist her, even knowing she was wed. Consider the fact you may have had a spell put upon you, and maybe then you'll see why your wife loathes the woman as she does, considerably more so than the many other women you've had through the years."

"You think Ciara cast a love spell upon me?'Tis not true, for I tell you plain, I never felt even a shard of love for the woman."

"There are spells of lust as well, Killian. In truth, I have found they are far more difficult for a man to resist for 'tis more common for a man to feel lust than love at any rate," Alainn explained.

"You've created such spells?" Killian questioned.

"Aye, not for me, but for those who sought a husband I have done so on occasion."

Now the look in her husband's eyes had gone from furious to displeased, but he was clearly considering all he'd been told.

"You think Ciara truly has powers?"

"Aye," Danhoul said, and Alainn nodded.

"Christ, 'tis all we need to have two witches under one roof!"

"'Tis a situation easily enough remedied!" Alainn sniped.

"I can't turn her out, Alainn! What of the boy?"

"I didn't say turn her out to be fodder for the wild animals. Send her to another village, there are many in the area. Find her a comfortable cottage if you must so I needn't see her every day."

"Would you be suggesting this, Alainn, if I'd not shared her bed? Would you be as suspicious about her if we'd not been together? Or is it your cursed jealousy that makes you mistrustful of Ciara?"

"Aye, perhaps it does color my opinion of her and I am unable to be impartial. But I do feel she is a troublemaker and she does possess some magical abililities. I am somehow unable to decipher her abilities as I usually can. You have always trusted in me and my abilities before, Killian. Why do you fail to believe me now when I tell you she is surely not to be trusted?"

He stared at her as he spoke. "I don't believe your jealousy allows you to see Ciara clearly or fairly."

She turned from him and inhaled deeply attempting to calm her unease.

"Do you sense her to be dangerous, Danhoul?" Killian posed.

"Not entirely, for I agree with Alainn there is something unusually difficult to determine about Ciara."

"Can either of you tell me for certain Ciara is responsible for the spell placed on the animals?"

They both shook their heads.

"Do you believe she is evil or that she is allied with the demon?"

Alainn was clearly displeased, but she shook her head. "I don't know for certain."

"Danhoul?"

"I believe she is not trustworthy and that there is a level of darkness to her abilities?"

"And is there not a darkness to your abilities, Alainn? At times of unrest and turmoil do your powers not take on a dark side?"

"You dare compare her to me! Well, if you won't see her gone, perhaps I might spend a time at my grandfather's castle till you make the decision, Killian. The woman you claim to love and whom you know carries your child, or the woman who most probably placed a spell of lust upon you to lure you to bed, and whose son could be the child of any number of men?"

"So am I to banish each and every woman you might feel a hint of jealousy toward? You should not force this, Alainn! And why are you so certain there have been many men?"

"Because recently her husband's spirit has come to me in my dreams. I have spoken to him at length of her many adulterous affairs!"

"You speak to the spirit of Will McCree?" Killian's face had grown ashen at the consideration.

"Aye, in my dreams I do. He tells me there were many men."

"But why would he stay with the woman, then, if she continued to behave so like a whore?"

"Because, in the beginning, he wasn't willing to believe or accept her adultery and then, he, too, was not certain of the paternity of the child and he loved the wee lad dearly."

"Then we'll keep them here, Alainn, for a time. Perhaps you and Danhoul can learn the truth of it. If, by some turn of fate, the boy is mine, I can't simply be done with him. Will you at least agree to that, Alainn? If you tell me he is not mine, I'll find some other place for them to stay."

"I could tell you now that you did not father her child!" She lifted her chin and her eyes filled with stubbornness.

"But you would not, for you have not spoken falsehoods to me before, and I trust in your word and in your abilities. One day it is to be hoped you can learn the truth."

"And until then how will it be between you and me, Killian?"

Killian nodded his head to Danhoul and gestured that he and Alainn be given time alone to speak privately. When they'd heard his footsteps grow faint on the stone steps, Killian pulled her into his arms in a possessive embrace. His lips came down hard upon hers.

"This is how it will be between us, Alainn, it will be as it has always been for us!"

He lifted her gently yet capably against the stone wall and impatiently pulled open the lacings of her gown and her chemise. Her breasts were exposed entirely and he fondled and kissed them with a tender, but persistent passion. She felt his hand beneath her skirts, he held her against the turret. He capably one-handedly unlaced his trews and in little time he possessively thrust himself within her. She wanted to fight him, to remain angry at him, but he controlled her so entirely when he loved her. Her skin tingled and her body welcomed him as always. She felt herself gasping as his lips caressed her neck. As they reached their culmination together, she passionately called out his name and was certain even the people on the ground below who appeared barely larger than insects, would surely hear her being pleasured. As she felt his warmth spill within her, she heard his own jealousy in his voice.

"You will not seek comfort in the boy's arms, and you will not deny me this intimacy that we share! I am your husband, for better or for worse, and you will not dictate when I can have you, woman. I have sworn to remain faithful to you and, by Christ Almighty, I promise you I will." His voice came in ragged gasps as he kissed her neck, her shoulders, and his tongue found her breasts once more.

"You brutish savage, put me down! You will not order me about or order me to your bed!"

Her words only seemed to further arouse him for she felt him harden further. And what infuriated her more than his actions was the fact her blood still boiled with the need for him to take her once more.

As she glanced down at the great distance to the ground below, she whispered in his ear, "You have obviously taken the heights of passion to an entirely new level, Killian O'Brien!"

He lifted her pointed chin to face him and he looked deeply and fervidly into her eyes before he claimed her lips and her body yet again.

Chapter Twenty-Five

A S THEY RODE in the carriage on the pathway to her grandfather's castle, she saw Killian smile at her for the first time that morning.

"So it's entirely self-satisfied about beddin' your own wife you are feeling then, is it?"

"'Tis not about the beddin', but about the fact you wanted it as much as me."

"You're impossible, Killian O'Brien!"

"Impossible for you to resist!" He goaded her.

"And unnecessarily arrogant about it as well."

He only smiled a devilish grin and kissed her once more.

"Why did you insist I accompany you to my grandfather's castle? Are you afraid I'll scratch out the trollop's eyes or share another embrace with the boy as you refer to him? I assure you, he's no boy!"

Killian's smile faded, but he spoke with only a mild irritation in his voice. "Don't make light of either, Alainn. Please avoid Ciara when you can, and don't tempt another man or it will make you appear no better than she is."

"I am nothing like her, Killian!" she emphatically declared.

He chose to ignore her comment, but spoke once more. "I believe you seemed in need of speakin' with a friend, and now that you and Mary appear to be on good terms once more, I thought it would be beneficial for you. I have sensed your maudlin temperament and I know how you miss Molly, and Cook and Margaret."

"I do, and Rory and Aunt Siobhan as well."

He noticed the loneliness in her tone and it worried him, especially knowing the topic he needed to discuss with Niall and Riley.

AS SOON AS Mary came down the stairwell to the main entrance way of the castle, Alainn knew she had something on her mind. Alainn suggested they go for a walk for the sun was shining brightly and the morning was pleasant. They started out toward the south meadow where many late wildflowers still bloomed. Alainn was considerably shorter than Mary, for Mary was tall for a woman and her strides were long, yet even in her increasing term, Alainn enjoyed a brisk walk. Since she could not gallop freely on horseback, she longed for the exhilarating feeling of the wind blowing through her hair. She called to the wind and it responded immediately. As the warm wind blew, she untied her hair and felt it being tossed and blown.

The two young women talked companionably for a time,

and Alainn was grateful Mary had put aside her displeasure with her. She thought the young Scottish lass might be a better person than herself for she doubted she could find it in her to act friendly toward a woman she knew her husband had feelings for. When Mary grew quiet, Alainn sensed she wanted to speak to her, but her often reserved manner made her uncomfortable speaking of certain topics.

"Tell me what's on your mind, Mary. Whatever you need to say, I'll listen and not be affronted."

The woman's cheeks colored and she still remained quiet.

"It has to do with physical intimacy; whatever you must speak to me of is in regards to that subject?"

"Aye!"

"What of it, then?" Alainn pushed further.

Alainn considered reading the woman's mind to discover what troubled her, but she reasoned it might be better to allow her friend to voice her concerns aloud. Mary finally began to open up to her.

"You'll ken my mother told me it was improper for a woman to experience pleasure from physical joining. While I do not find the act repulsive as she led me to believe it would be, I do not actually find it pleasurable. When I think I might actually begin to feel something akin to excitement, it is simply done with."

Alainn realized how difficult it must have been for the woman to summon enough courage to speak of the private matter. She'd barely even begun to think of a response when Mary continued speaking.

"I don't suppose even your magical abilities can help me in that area, but I've another matter I need to discuss with you as well. I ken you are able to create potions, concoctions of herbs that ensure a woman will not conceive a child."

"Aye, I created such potions for many women back at Castle O'Brien. They are reasonably effective, but not foolproof by any measure. But, I must ask what man's baby are you not wishin' to carry, is it Riley's or Connor's?"

The woman threw her a cautious glance, but after some time she responded. "I have never been with Connor in such a manner, and I do not plan to be, not now, at least… not yet. It's not that I haven't thought about it, for I have, and I know how horridly vulgar that must sound to you, but I do fight the urges I feel when it comes to him. We have scarcely seen each other since he has been living at your castle. And it isn't that I don't care for Riley. I do! In truth, I believe I do love him, but I love Connor as well."

Alainn knew Mary waited for reaction to her confession, but she made no comment for she was attempting to respond in a manner that would not appear judgmental, so Mary spoke on.

"I ken you love Killian so entirely you can't believe a woman could love two men at the same time, but they can for I tell you plain, I do!"

"And if you don't plan on acting on your feelings for

Connor, why do you not wish to carry Riley's baby?"

"It isn't that I don't want that either, it's that I don't want it just yet. I need to know he does actually care for me in some capacity before I carry his child."

"'Tis considered a crime to prevent a pregnancy in the Catholic religion and to attempt to prevent a child of a man who desires an heir, especially a chieftain, is punishable by strict laws."

"I am much aware of that, but how would he know for certain? Although sometimes I believe the only reason he comes to my bed is in hopes I will soon carry his child."

"And perhaps carrying his child might improve the relationship you and Riley share. He would surely think of you with high regard when you carry his child, it may be all you need to become closer."

"And if it isn't, Alainn, then a child would be created when our future is so uncertain."

"I do not wish to steer you wrong, Mary. It would be no great kindness for me to suggest you must stay with a man or bear his child if he disrespects you. But I must tell you no one's future is entirely certain. I feel I must ask you, Mary, do you entertain serious notions of leaving Riley, for I believe that would be a perilous consideration; that he could be a dangerous man if crossed. I'm certain he'll never grant you an end to your marriage. He loathes the very notion of a woman leaving her husband. You must think it through and give it much serious consideration."

"I do recognize that, Alainn, and I truly dinna ken what will come of our marriage. I suppose I will end up like my mother, bitter and lonely, knowing her husband takes mistresses and whores. And she was with child more than not for most of their early years of marriage. Eleven children in thirteen years, and then when my youngest brother was born she was damaged so severely, the midwife warned my father not to go to my mother's bed ever again unless he wanted her dead in childbed."

A concerned look crossed Alainn's face and she touched her belly and Mary noticed.

"Forgive me, Alainn; that was inconsiderate of me, I did not intend to cause you undue concern."

"No, Mary, I have assisted midwives before, I know well enough of the perils associated with childbirth."

They were quiet for a time, but Mary finally asked once more.

"Will you give me the potion, Alainn? Tell me you'll do that for me, only until I see whether Riley and I might mend things between us."

"Aye, I'll do it, but if either Riley or Killian learn of it, neither will be pleased with either one of us. And, again, I must tell you it is by no way entirely reliable. You well might become with child."

"I ken it well, Alainn. And I don't want to cause discord between you and Killian. The two of you remain happy and so entirely in love."

"Aye, we're deeply in love but, even at that, it doesn't come without strife, Mary. 'Tis unrealistic to think anyone can be happy all the time, I suppose."

"And what of the potion? Is it ingested or used to wash out the seed?" Mary questioned her face turning dark scarlet as she spoke of the personal subject.

"There are both types; and to use both in conjunction with the other is best in preventing conception. The latter is more difficult to conceal from a man, for it needs to be done immediately following the beddin', if your husband is the type who likes to hold you and show affection following the intimacy it will not be easily accomplished."

"That will nay be a concern, then," the woman regrettably admitted, and Alainn felt saddened about that as well.

⌘

WHEN THEY'D BEEN walking for some time, Mary suggested it might be wise to return to Castle O'Rorke and Alainn felt certain Mary was simply concerned about her strolling for such a lengthy time in her condition. She was about to argue and tell he she felt as well as before she carried a child, but it occurred to her, Mary seemed tired herself. She reasoned if the woman was in love with two men that would be enough to cause any woman to have sleepless nights and be overly tired, for Alainn thought loving one man was sometimes a definite source of fretfulness and unrest.

As they turned to start back, Alainn noticed a tall structure she'd not seen before. It caught her interest immediately and she began striding toward it to get a better look. She realized it was the ruins of an ancient castle. The enormous rocks were scattered in disarray and few of the greenish-grey walls remained standing. But one tower seemed entirely intact. She pondered why she'd never noticed it before, but reasoned she'd never strayed this far from the grounds of Castle O'Rorke, and the trees had recently shed many of their leaves which surely left a clearer view of the ruins.

She felt undeniably drawn to the location even though Mary warned it might be dangerous to approach for the walls may not be stable. Alainn insisted upon getting a closer look and, when she glanced up at the tall tower, she noticed a female apparition in the uppermost window. Such a sensation of sadness seemed to encompass the woman, Alainn felt her heart own constrict in empathizing the spirit woman's lamenting. Yet Alainn recognized an undeniable connection to the spirit as well. Mary tapped her shoulder and she jumped for she'd been so intent on experiencing the other female's pain, and trying to decipher why she was so drawn to the specter she had nearly forgotten Mary was there.

"Alainn, we really must return, you look unusually pale and we still have the long walk back. The menfolk might worry, especially Killian, for he's very protective of you."

"Aye, we'll start back then!" she regrettably agreed as she looked up at the window once more.

The spirit woman gazed down at her and their eyes met.

The sorrowful grey eyes were filled with such utter desolation, Alainn wanted to immediately climb the steps to the tower and learn what maudlin event had happened to the woman to make her grieve after so long.

Alainn surmised in life this spirit woman must have claimed magical powers, for Alainn had been capably blocking her ability to see spirits for some time now. It was often much too disheartening or sorrowful to see these restless spirits that were for one reason or another bound to this earth instead of going to the beyond. Because she was able to see this woman's spirit with such clarity led Alainn to believe she must have been capable of doing great magic when she lived. She felt such an uncommon connection to the spectral woman she yearned to go converse with her.

Yet when Alainn looked toward the northernmost wall, she noticed a dark shadow, and she knew something sinister lurked in the shadows of that wall. Something unimaginably terrible had happened here very long ago, Alainn sensed. And when that thought crossed her mind she saw a vision of the woman in the tower and the king who had once lived in Castle O'Donnel. She longed to learn more, a part of her wanted to investigate further even knowing the evil presence was near, but when the child moved within her, her thoughts were once more brought back to this time. She smiled at Mary to reassure her she was well for Mary was looking at her as though she thought she might collapse.

"Are you certain you're well, Alainn. The color has gone

from your face entirely!"

"No, I assure you, Mary, I am well enough. Come now, we'll go see what our men have been discussing this day. It appeared to be important for they clearly didn't want us around while they were speakin'!"

"Aye, I got that impression as well. Riley and Grandfather have been speaking lowly and acting secretive since the celebration last evening. I heard something to do with a messenger that brought word of news from Castle O'Brien, but I did not push the issue of learning what news was brought for Riley does not care to share such details with me. He reminds me of his father in that regard!"

"Aye, I suppose he is like his father in many ways," Alainn regretfully agreed.

They'd barely made it halfway back to the castle when Alainn saw Danhoul atop his horse and approaching her with a concerned look on his face.

"You are not to be without the company of me or your husband; you know that well enough, Alainn O'Brien!"

Alainn did not care for his commanding tone or his unusual gruffness. She most assuredly longed to tell him so, but there was little they could openly discuss while in Mary's presence. She signaled for him to get off the horse so they might have a word in private and they stood on the other side of his horse distanced from the curious Scottish woman who had to wonder what they were speaking of.

"My spell of thirteen is still in place, no one can harm me

by way of magic, not for at least another fortnight. And, in truth, the spell will probably hold longer than that since it was spoken during the full moon."

"Aye, well, 'tis better to be cautious than regretful, and you should be warned to stay away from the castle ruins, a mighty battle between good and evil was fought there many centuries ago. I sense the echoes of evil still remain. And if your enemies are unable to get to you by way of magic because of your spell of thirteen they may still choose other methods of harming you."

"I understand your concern, Danhoul, but I am a seer, sure I'd be able to see impending danger."

"But perhaps not when 'tis you in peril, and maybe not in time to actually do anything about it. You'll recall you did not foresee being struck with a poison dart back at Castle O'Brien!"

"I shall be more cautious next time, but I do not take kindly to being ordered out by one man, much less two, or to being made to feel like a prisoner. And I doubt you would care to accompany me every waking moment and listen to Mary and I speak of womanly discussions. Though u might learn some valuable information that might aid you one day when you are wed, I suppose!" She softened her tone and smiled at the young man.

"I can't even imagine bein' wed and feelin' so completely responsible for someone. I am not always in favor of tryin' to keep you safe and I only do that as I am in the employ of your grandfather. The gods forbid I ever marry anyone half as difficult as you!"

"And I adore you entirely, as well, Danhoul Calhoun," she whispered in a caustically sarcastic tone and threw him a nasty glare that made Mary glance at them in further curiosity.

Danhoul mounted his horse again and rode far enough ahead of the two women that he could not hear their voices. Mary sent Alainn an impish grin and she dared to declare her suspicions.

"You may not know what it is to be in love with two men, but I'll tell you plain there are at least two that are in love with you, and I'm not including my husband in the lot!"

"You're not suggestin' Danhoul loves me?"

"Aye, he's falling hopelessly in love with you; that's exactly what I'm suggesting."

"That's absurd, Mary! I would know if he felt anything more than friendship and responsibility toward me.

"And you think yourself a perceptive seer; I would suggest you are lacking when it comes to matters that pertain to you!" Mary seemed almost pleased that hers was not the only life without complications.

Chapter Twenty-Six

KILLIAN HAD BEEN quiet on the ride back home. When they reached the castle, he accompanied her to the door, but then begged leave for a time as he had pressing business to discuss with his captain and his steward.

Alainn reasoned if she was to create the potion she had promised Mary, she would need to walk to the lake for it was along lakeshores and river banks an herb grew that was known to be beneficial to women who did not wish to carry a child. A small dose seemed to ensure a woman did not conceive, a larger dose was sometimes known to terminate a pregnancy, but Alainn had always refused to create a potion with that potency and ability.

When she reached the shores of the lake, she stood for a moment, simply reveling in the beauty of the land. She adored Ireland, the rolling hills, the emerald valleys, and the rocky terrain, as well as the open glens, sparkling lakes, and magnificent seascapes. Their Ireland was a land of vast diversity and she well knew it was the great beauty that appealed to anyone who landed on its shores. But so many marauders throughout history had attempted to conquer and change the people, and Alainn felt saddened the English meant to do just that once again.

As she searched through the many plants that grew along the mossy banks, she noticed, with resentment, she was not alone. She saw the outline of Ciara McCree walking along the shore as well. She planned to swiftly procure the herbs and be gone from the area before Ciara drew any closer to her location. The woman apparently had other plans for when Alainn was bent using her dagger to dig deeply and remove the plant's roots as well, the woman hurried toward her and oddly, by Alainn's estimation, she wore a smile upon her face.

Alainn briefly used this undesired closeness in proximity to assess the other woman's appearance, for Alainn reasoned if Ciara had been even partially responsible for the spell placed on the animals, it would be likely she might possess bites or scratches since Alainn had reversed the spell and directed it back to the issuer. It would surely stand to reason whoever was actually responsible would be in peril by way of vicious and frequent animal attacks. Alainn looked as closely as she cared to at the woman and was nearly disappointed to find she did not appear to have outward wounds, although she deemed they might simply be hidden by her garments.

As she lingered on that thought Alainn was immediately presented with the oddest vision. She saw a young spirit girl perhaps on the verge of womanhood. She appeared strangely familiar. In truth, she bore a striking resemblance to herself at that age though her hair was paler and her eyes were darker, an entirely different shade of blue. As Alainn stared on at the spirit attempting to determine her identity, she was startled when the spirit touched her arm. Never in her visions had she had direct contact with anyone. Always before, when she was presented with a vision, it was as though she was watching the happenings from a distance or from above, looking upon those in the vision, but not actually a part of it. In the vision, they were standing at the lakeshore where Alainn now was, but the spirit seemed insistent on having Alainn accompany her and when she touched her arm again they were both taken to another location.

THEY WERE NOW standing within Glynnis's horrific chamber, but as it appeared when she'd first happened upon it. The stench filled her senses completely and the pathetic animals all looked at her with fear and desperation in their eyes. She strained to see inside the darkened chamber when her spirit companion began to emit a bright glow which capably showed the way.

She was urgently motioning to Alain to follow her as she pulled open the partially concealed door Alainn had seen when she had been there before. Behind that door was indeed an earthen tunnel, as Alainn had suspected. The scent of damp earth filled her nostrils. She proceeded to follow the spirit and the glow that encircled her continued to light up their dismal surroundings.

They seemed to walk for an endless time through the long and winding tunnel and Alainn curiously pondered why the spirit might not have saved them the long walk and simply transported them to wherever the intended location might be. The spirit eventually floated through a portal that led out into the night air. She continued on to a clearing and by the light of the full moon, the spirit pointed eerily toward a rock formation. There were several such circles of stones in the area, believed to be burial chambers or locations where druids had once performed rituals and even human sacrifice. But as they approached, the young spirit woman put her fingers to her lips as if to warn Alainn she must remain silent and concealed.

Alainn stayed hidden behind one of the large pointed stones and peered around it. There were half a dozen women all dressed in long black gowns. They were chanting loudly and in the center Alainn was affrighted to see the dark demon in human form. She shivered and slowly moved back behind the stone, her heart thumping and her skin crawling. The spirit girl drew nearer to her and she could see her eyes were filled with fear as well.

"You must look on further, Alainn!" the girl whispered.

Alainn shook her head in fervent disagreement and began to start back toward the tunnel.

"He took my life and my powers and he longs to take yours

as well!" The spirit girl revealed through telepathy.

"Who are you?" Alainn replied in the same manner.

"My name is of no importance at the moment." The spirit lifted her chin and flared her nostrils as Alainn had seen her Aunt Siobhan do so many times when she did not desire to speak on a topic! This spirit was surely her sister, who had been murdered, found strangled in the woods, when she was only three and ten.

"You are Shylie, my aunt Siobhan's younger sister? You are my father's sister?"

"Aye, it is truth, Siobhan is my dear sister, and your father Teige is my brother, but now, Alainn you must listen and you must observe."

Alainn remembered longing to have this vision come to an end and she shook her head in attempt to do so, but Shylie took her arm and held tight. *"Do not be distanced yet, for you must learn more."*

Then the voices grew louder and when she dared to peek around the stone once more, she saw that the women's gowns had been discarded and they were all entirely un-clothed. The dark demon was at present mating with one of the women in the circle while the others watched on, and soon he made his way to the next and the next.

Alainn had no desire to watch such intimate relations, much less be witness to this unnatural coupling and depravi-ty, so she looked away, but the young spirit insisted she must not leave yet. Alainn occasionally allowed herself a quick glance. When the demon made his way to the last woman, she watched in disbelief as the other five magically shape-shifted into varying animals from wolves to falcons. Only the one with the long dark curly hair remained in human form and Alainn felt an even stronger repulsion as she watched the demon wildly claim her. She turned away and hid once more. While she listened to the guttural grunts and moans of the fornication, she heard an especially disturbing sound, and when she dared to look once more she watched in horror as the man turned into the hellish incomprehensibly ugly beast she had seen in the dungeon at Castle O'Brien. And his maniacal laughter as he copulated with the woman chilled her heart. As he finally moved from the woman he stared up directly into Alainn's eyes, and the woman who still lie upon the ground stared at her as well.

Alainn was confused and her mind struggled to comprehend what she was seeing for the woman was surely Ciara, and yet she was obviously much older, with many steaks of white through her dark hair and numerous scratches, bites, and scars upon her sickly colored skin. She stood and began to walk directly toward Alainn who was now frozen where she stood. When the woman who so uncannily resembled Ciara snapped her fingers the five women who had recently become animals, soon turned back to human form again, and they all cackled eerily and leered at Alainn, and began walking toward her.

Alainn gasped aloud and the woman stared deeply into

her eyes, as she spoke.

"Did you truly believe yours was the only line of power-ful witches?" She sneered wickedly and pointed straight toward Alainn's belly and shook her head. "You were sorely wrong, foolish woman!"

Then the spirit girl, Shylie, forcefully grabbed her arm, shook her abruptly and she was once more back at the lakeshore.

⌘

STANDING ON THE shore of the lake, Alainn tried to come up with a reasonable interpretation of the vision she'd been shown by the spirit, Shylie. The menacingly disturbing woman looked as though it surely must be Ciara, but she was considerably a woman of more advanced years. She was surely nearly two decades older than Ciara was now. Her dark hair had many coarse white streaks throughout, and her middle possessed a thickness and her breasts a heaviness that often accompanies age. Her face was a sickly shade and when Alainn dwelled more upon the vision it became clearer, Alainn recalled the many bites and scratches on the woman's hands and face as well as open wounds and scars. She had an unusual pallor as though she might actually be a corpse. Alainn shook her head to rid herself of the displeasing image.

She tried to decipher why she would be shown this vision at this precise time when she had been curious to learn if Ciara possessed wounds caused by animals. Was this how

Ciara would appear in the future? Would Ciara, when she was older and wiser, more accomplished in dark spells or more powerful magic possibly claim the ability to travel about in time as Alainn had once done herself? Could she have come to this time to place the spell on the animals, and then have returned to her time? When Alainn had placed the spell of thirteen on whoever had created the spell, had the evildoer been affected by the spell of thirteen even if she'd returned to another time? The spell of thirteen was unusually potent and far-reaching, but could it span two decades?

As Alainn dwelled intently upon the unusual and perplexing vision, she was startled at the voice of the actual woman beside her.

"Are you quite well, milady? You appear distressed."

Alainn shook her head and steadied herself once more. "No, I am well enough."

Ciara nodded and continued speaking to her. "Milady, so you do maintain your interest in bein' a healer? I have heard through many that you were a respected herbalist and healer at Castle O'Brien. I would appreciate it much if I might learn from you. I sense my grandmother is envious of your ability and is not always congenial toward you."

Alainn remained shaken by the unusual vision and now uncertain how to respond to Ciara. Surely Alainn's harbingering vision was from somewhere far in the future. She must simply concentrate on her present unpleasantness in contending with this woman who seemed intent on appearing to be cordial.

Had Ciara actually not remembered the vexing incident between the two of them on the night of the celebration, as Killian had suggested she might not? Or was she tactfully avoiding the subject and hoping to grovel and be friendly toward her so Alainn would harbor fewer ill feelings toward the woman? She could not deny Ciara could be outwardly charming, and her aura seemed ever changeable. It was still dark, but not nearly as black as when last they met.

Perhaps Ciara did not realize Alainn was well aware she and Killian had been lovers. Alainn narrowed her eyes at the woman and found herself scarcely able to bear being anywhere near her when she dwelled on that sore subject. She chose to respond in hopes the woman would soon take leave.

"Aye, I make herbal remedies on occasion when they are required or it is asked of me. And, 'tis not uncommon for healers to feel resentment toward others of that lot, but I assure you I have no intention of interfering with yours or your grandmother's healing. And I am not interested in revealing my own recipes for herbal remedies, to you or to anyone else." Alainn tried unsuccessfully to keep her mind from the many maimed animals that had been found within Glynnis' chamber and the unsavory potions Ciara surely had created from the unfortunate animals.

Ciara seemed to ignore what Alainn had said entirely for she continued on with her questioning. "What potion do you intend to create with that item? I am not so very learned in the area of all herbs for my grandmother seems unwilling to apprentice me entirely. I know the plant is oft used for womanly concerns, but I am somewhat uncertain what its true purpose is. I believe my grandmother feels threatened by me learning all that she knows. She seems to need the reassurance that the villagers and servants will come only to her for their potions and remedies. But she is an old woman and I have told her she is selfish and bitter if she will not pass on the abundance of knowledge she carries within her mind!"

Alainn wanted to tell the woman, Glynnis was probably as suspicious of her as Alainn was herself, and perhaps even fearful since the woman had been so callous and cruel with the tortured animals, but she bit her tongue and continued on with her task not wanting to continue conversing with the woman. But Ciara remained, watching Alainn's every move and seemed disinclined to end the conversation.

"So tell me, milady, what potion will you mix with the herbs you now seek? Is it to create a remedy or elixir for your own use or for another?"

"A healer seldom divulges such personal information, Ciara. Surely, Glynnis has cautioned you on the need for privacy and secretiveness when dealing with remedies?"

"Aye, well, she is a peculiar old woman, some say her mind is not as it should be. She is closed mouthed a good deal of the time, but how am I to learn if neither of you who seem so capable will instruct me? Do you intend to become healer for Castle O'Donnel, then, when my grandmother passes?"

"No, I have absolutely no aspirations to become a healer in such capacity, Ciara. And, in truth, you should not eagerly await your grandmother's passing simply so that you may take over her duties. No one ever knows how lengthy their life may be. Your grandmother may live a goodly long life, perhaps three more decades."

Ciara looked down her nose at her in obvious disbelief and scoffed, so Alainn elaborated.

"Morag, the old wise woman, who was healer at Castle O'Brien and taught me nearly all that I know, lived to be over five and ninety. Glynnis may outlive the both of us, Ciara, for often if a woman lives past childbearing years she may well live a lengthy life."

"Aye, for tis not uncommon for young women to meet their dismal end in childbed, or soon thereafter!" Ciara dared to allude to the unfortunate truth and she stared at Alainn's belly as she spoke.

Alainn noticed, but chose to address the comment with hopefulness. "Sure, you'll marry again and have many other children, Ciara, and I pray to carry this child and many other children as well, but 'tis hoped neither of us shall bear ill in bringing children into the world."

"You've clearly not labored and birthed a child before or you'd maybe not be so eager to declare you'd be inclined to do it many more times. The birthin' of my Kale was not a pleasant time, for the labor was long and he was a large babe, but I suffered no long-lasting ill effects. The midwife, Eibhein said I was well built for childbearing, that any man would be fortunate to have me as their wife for I could surely present them with many healthy sons. She tells me I healed remarkably well considering the grand size of the boy."

Alainn did not care to consider that the woman's son had been of great size when he was born for that may be another indication Killian had fathered the child. And the boy was tall for his age, even now. William McCree had not been a large man, but of average stature. But who was to know the proportions of the other men she had apparently been with around the time of Kale's conception might have been.

"Has Eibhein been seein' to you and your condition? Has she mentioned whether she believes the child is expected early or might be delayed?"

"I believe the child will come when he is expected due."

"I have some experience with midwifery for I have accompanied Eibhein on occasion and by the look of you, I would suggest the child will be early. You carry low and are larger than most by this period of term for I understand your wedding took place in early summer, so unless the child is unusually large it will come before nine months past the date of your nuptials. I suppose even women of your station and with your title do not always wait for the vows to be spoken to give themselves to men."

"I hardly think that is of any concern to you, Ciara. My

marriage took place in late spring in actuality and, aye, nine months will not have passed from then till the time my son is born."

"So 'twas the babe that was the inducement for your marriage then, was it?"

Alainn found herself becoming completely infuriated at this blatantly intrusive line of questioning by the bold and abrasive woman. "Again, I warn you, Ciara, none of what has happened between my husband and myself is of concern to you. If you are as tactless with Glynnis as you have been with me this day, I see most assuredly why she does not care to share her herb chamber or her secrets with you!"

"It was not my intention to affront you, milady. I was curious is all, for I've not had occasion to speak with women often, for I have few female acquaintances."

"Aye, well you'll remember, Ciara, it was curiosity killed the cat!" She stared into the woman's own cat-like eyes and she once more thought of the wretched animals, including the pitiful dead cat in the cage as she haughtily spoke once more, "And 'tis perhaps because you've been bedded by a good number of both the villagers' and the servants' husbands that they care to have little to do with you. That does tend to put a bit of a damper on relationships with other women!"

Alainn could contain her temper or control her tongue no longer and she noticed the fury in the amber eyes that glared back at her.

"Since it is clear you were not virtuous on your wedding day how does your husband trust you when you apparently gave yourself to him without benefit of nuptials? A man can never trust a woman entirely when she gives herself to him in such a manner when they are unwed!" Ciara dared to declare. "And you have a slight build, perhaps not beneficial for birthing a child without duress or ill fate. And if you are forever afflicted by the birthing and cannot give milord more children, will he desire to stay in your marriage or your bed?'

"I am done speakin' to you, Ciara. In truth, I forbid you to speak to me ever again. I find your company objectionable and your conversation inappropriate. I will henceforth be pleased to end all association with you!"

"Aye, well, you can distance yourself from my son then as well, though I'm certain Killian does not wish to be excluded from Kale's life entirely!"

"And I would ask you to never again refer to my husband with such familiarity! Because you shared a bed with him some years ago does not give you that right. And if you actually had proof he was your son's father, or if you truly had any notion whatsoever whose seed was responsible, you would have long since asked my husband to claim him!"

"And one day it may come to that and what discord that would cause for you, for he would be heir to the chieftainship."

"Not on your life, Ciara! For should Killian actually accept the boy as his own he would still be an illegitimate child, and that would cause a great insult to the memory of your own husband, to take away a boy believed to be his son. He was a good man, Ciara!"

"Aye, William was not unpleasant, mostly tolerable, I suppose, but no chieftain, or no man of any amount of importance or appeal, not like milord!" The woman's lips curled into a distasteful smile and then she actually licked her lips and her eyes filled with sensuality as she spoke of Killian.

The skies darkened and a cold wind began to blow. Alainn sensed a great need to be distanced from the meddlesome and oppositional woman. Although she did not welcome the use of her magical abilities in Ciara's presence, she deduced if the woman remembered any of what had happened the night of the celebration, she was already aware she possessed supernatural capabilities. She reasoned using them to leave hastily would be preferential to using them to harm the woman, and in her raging temper she believed the harm might be deadly or irreversible.

Alainn held tight to her amulet and the herbs she had collected, she closed her eyes and imagined herself in her bedchamber and she disappeared, leaving Ciara to deal with the bitter and fast approaching storm.

⌘

KILLIAN HAD REMAINED nearly silent all evening and Alainn knew him well enough not to prod him to speak of what was troubling him. He would tell her in his own time, she believed, and she did not mention any of what had occurred between her and Ciara.

She had briefly discussed it with Danhoul. Though he'd thought it unwise to wage battle with the woman or use her powers, he believed in light of her temper and the level of her supernatural abilities, it was fortunate Alainn hadn't struck the woman down with a lightning bolt!

Alainn's thoughts filled with discord regarding Ciara and all she'd spoken of. The disturbing vision and what it could possibly indicate kept her mind occupied far more than she cared for as well. Although she did not wish to dwell on the unpleasantness, she could not fall asleep, especially since Killian had not yet retired for the evening. It was not until he had come to bed much later than his usual time that Alainn finally could still her curiosity and concern no longer regarding his obviously disparaging mood. As his large warm form drew near to her and he put his arms around her, she noticed the tension in his taut muscles.

"What's on your mind, Killian? Tell me what makes your heart heavy this night!"

"I thought perhaps you'd be asleep by now, Lainna!"

"Thought or hoped?" She quizzed.

"You're more than a wee bit suspicious, my love."

She turned to face him though the bedchamber was dark, save the peat logs that had burned low in the hearth.

"I know you well and somethin' has you grieved this night. I can only surmise if you're not willin' to discuss it with me, it must be something that will leave me troubled as well!"

"Aye, I'm apologetic to say so, Alainn. I must leave again and journey to Galway. I hope to not be gone so long as before, but I am loath to leave you when Danhoul is so concerned someone means you harm… and with the wee babe only weeks away from arrivin'!"

Even though she felt saddened they would be parted again, she needed to set his mind at ease.

"Danhoul worries overly much; the both of you do. I will be well enough. But you must tell me, what takes you to the Galway then for 'tis not the usual meeting place, another meeting of the Council of Clans?"

"Aye, there is to be another vote. The clans who are in allegiance with the English have raided two more castles along the southeast shores, the last one not a day's ride from Castle O'Brien so we are avoiding Dublin at the moment. We are to vote on whether to take action to prevent further attacks and whether to stand together as one army or for each clan to remain in position to protect their own land and castles. The other option is to strike out against them before they can attack once more. And I cannot see how an agreement will ever be reached, for 'tis an enormous decision to make."

"What will your vote be, Killian?"

"Well I'll not stand by and watch my castle raided or my kin and clan murdered, but I am not so eager to start an unprovoked battle with them for they have weapons and numbers that far exceed what we lay claim to. And I am of the opinion if we were to meet with the king perhaps an agreement can be reached before there is more blood spilled on both sides."

"You would meet with King Henry of England? Surely that is a most dangerous consideration, Killian, for clearly the man is not to be trusted. He creates much havoc in his own country. He has commanded the death of many of his own subjects, had his own wife beheaded, ordered the destruction of many churches and abbeys, and I have heard it said half his court and advisors either fear or despise him."

"Aye, it's not certain he would agree to meet with us and there'd be no assurance he'd be trustworthy enough to follow through with what he said anyway. His own personal life seems to be in a shambles most of the time. I doubt his head is where it should be on the runnin' of his country or his life! But, still, I wonder if lookin' him in the eye, talkin' to him face-to-face, man to man might make his following assaults less severe."

She disliked pondering a time or a possibility of Killian going to England much less speaking with the unscrupulous and infamous King Henry VIII. She dismissed the notion and posed a query.

"When do you leave for Galway then, Killian?"

He seemed hesitant to answer.

"Killian, you leave on the morrow?" she asked in a voice filled with dread.

"Aye, I was not eager to reveal that to you, for I know

the uneasiness you feel already with all that has transpired as of late. I am much chagrined to leave you again, Alainn!"

Alainn felt her lip trembling and her tears threatening to fall, but she attempted to put on a brave front for she realized Killian had enough on his mind without having to deal with her melancholy tears. Clearly, any discussion of her encounter with Ciara, or her confusing and disturbingly irksome vision would only fuel his worries. His arms tightened around her for surely he felt the same despair in knowing by the next night they would not be together.

"Sorry I am, Killian, that I am terribly difficult much of the time. I need you to know I trust you and I do have immeasurable faith in you, as a man, as a chieftain, and as my husband. I remember Aine warning me I would one day pay for my great jealousy. I cannot for all my attempts seem to prevent the emotion, but I must be less uncharitable toward you because of it. I want no wedge between us, Killian. It was unforgivable of me to be so unreasonable when we are often parted much more than I would desire. And I must apologize for denying you a physical love last night. I was furious at that woman and I made you suffer because of it, and myself as well for I despise being parted from you in any manner."

"'Tis important, Alainn, that you know I will only be your man, I have spoken the vows and told you many times, and I assure you it will always remain so!"

"I do, of course I do, Killian, but I still need to hear you say it on occasion."

"I am yours, Alainn, and I always will be only yours. Will that suffice for now, then, Lainna?"

"Aye!" she whispered, as their bodies lie together in the fashion of spoons, his chin resting upon her head.

He placed his large hand on her belly and chuckled as was usual when he felt the strong movements within her.

"And I must thank you, Killian, for how you are to me; for being a tolerant and patient husband, an affectionate man, and a generous lover, for many women are not so fortunate in having men love them as you love me."

"Well though you may be a bit strong willed at times, Lainna, I recognize what a great gift I have in you, as well. I know of no other woman who I can tell my heart to or who knows my heart as you do, and who wants to be loved as frequently as you. But, how is it you know not all men are generous lovers? Do womenfolk actually discuss such matters on such an intimate level?"

"Occasionally," she murmured.

Alainn was unable to divulge Mary's discussion to Killian, but she suspected he knew well enough who she was referring to. He didn't inquire any further so it was simply left at that.

As he continued to hold his hand on her belly he spoke of something that both pleased and frightened her. "Before I set out on my journey on the morrow, I want to name our son."

Chapter Twenty-Seven

"KILLIAN IS THERE something you're not tellin' me, is there a possibility of battle in Galway or on your journey?"

"That is always a possibility, Alainn. You know that well enough, even when times are not as uncertain as they are now with the English, there has been dangerous unrest and brutal battles waged between Irish clans for centuries. I only thought it would be a good time to think on a name, since we've not discussed it at length."

She shivered for though she did not sense any immediate danger the reoccurrence of her vision of the O'Brien clan dying on a battlefield was ever present in her mind and her fears.

"Will Rory be at this meeting in Galway, and Riley as well?"

"I've been tryin' to tell Riley to stay back, to send Niall to vote for the O'Rorke clan, if your grandfather is improved enough by then, and maybe my Uncle Sean will represent Castle O'Brien this time for word has it Uncle Hugh remains unwell. Sean and Rory share joint chieftainship for the time being. I even attempted to convince Cormac to cast my vote, but he insists the council elected me for a reason, and it is apparently law, anyone who sits on council must attend."

"Aye. 'Tis surely important for you to attend, Killian. I'm certain Riley will be boar-headed and not stay back regardless of whether Grandfather makes the journey."

"Don't be fretful about it, Alainn. There was clearly more chance of attack near Dublin for there are more English guards there nearer to The Pale, and more Irishmen who are English supporters. We all managed to make it home safe and well from there! Did you not indicate in your drawing it was surely closer to Dublin? Sure, we'll be safe. Now, enough of this dreary dismal talk. Tell me; what names do you fancy for our son?"

"Sure 'tis often the father who names the male children, Killian. You must choose a name to your liking."

"Aye, well I've thought on it for some time now. He could be named for my father or my brother, or your father."

"Or you, Killian. But, we will surely have many sons therefore many names will be needed at any rate. Whatever name you choose will be to my likin' for I am honored to carry your child."

"Then I'll think on it more this night."

"And is thinkin' all you want to do this night, husband? If we are to be soon parted again then best we make this time together memorable."

As she softly put her hands on his stubbled cheeks, and

kissed him he pulled her close to him in a passionate gesture and hoped she was still unable to read his thoughts and know his fears.

⌘

SOME TIME HAD passed and, as they both lie awake, each with many concerns on their minds, Killian nudged her gently and whispered.

"Come dance with me, Lainna!"

She turned to face him and could make out his face by the low, soft firelight.

There was mirth in her voice. "Dance with you Killian; 'tis the middle of the night."

"Aye, I'm much aware of that, but you're awake and so am I. Let us distance our fretfulness and our disquieting thoughts for a time and dance, my lady."

Killian took her hand as she left the bed to stand beside him. She was donned in her nightdress, but he was entirely unclothed.

"And will you not be chilled to the bone then, my love?"

She smiled at his impressively strong and muscular form. By way of her powers she held her hands toward the hearth and it blazed brightly soon filling the chamber with glowing warmth.

"And shall we dance without benefit of music, husband?" She beamed up at his handsomeness, and his chestnut hair as it fell appealing around his face nearly to his shoulders.

He smiled back at her as his arms tightened around her. "Well if you can so aptly create fire, I suspect you can magically create music as well."

The door to the adjoining chamber which held the grand harp, opened effortlessly and the immense instrument magically slid through the doorway. Killian's fiddle which had hung upon the wall sailed through the air as well. Soon the harp's strings moved of their own accord, and the fiddle immediately joined in. A lovely Celtic ballad filled the chamber and Killian grinned in appreciation of his wife's enchanting magic.

They held each other lovingly and danced together and before long their cares lessened and their hearts grew lighter.

"You are so very beautiful to me, my sweet Lainna."

"And you to me as well, my Killian!"

He stared down upon her with seriousness in his eyes as he spoke. "No matter what the future may hold for us, Lainna, we shall always have this night, this magical time together… the music, the fire, our unparalleled love, just the two of us so unquestionably happy, filled with much hope and anticipation of the joy our wee son shall bring to us. Whether I should die in battle as a young warrior, or in my sleep as an aged old man with thinning silver hair and a frail broken body, I shall always hold in my memory this night with you, this enchanting time with my captivatingly lovely and magical wife."

Alainn questioned him briefly with her eyes as though he

might suspect something ominous soon to befall them. But she simply returned his smile and his love, and his words of adoration.

"Aye, we shall always call to mind the wondrous memories of this night to draw elation and contentment on darker days, Killian, my handsome husband, my stalwart champion… my only love."

They shared a tender kiss and he grazed her full lips with his fingertips and stared into her eyes. He untied the fastenings of her gown and it slipped to the floor. They continued to move together to the music for a lengthy time, skin touching skin, hearts beating together. He gazed down into her sparkling, pale blue eyes and saw his passion was mirrored within those eyes that held his heart so completely. He lifted her in his arms and carried her to their bed and loved her once more.

AS ALAINN SAT at the table in the great hall, she waited for Killian to finish his meeting with Fergus. They were going over details Killian must see to before he left on his journey. Alainn had not been feeling entirely well this morning. She'd felt a nagging pain across her back, and occasionally a slight discomfort encircled her midsection as well. She was hesitant to think their lovemaking might have caused the worrisome sensation for Killian had been gentle, gentler than she might have wanted, but she reasoned perhaps soon they would be forced to terminate their physical love until after the child was born.

She also thought of the strange vision she'd experienced by the lakeshore the previous day. She recalled so vividly the peculiar and somewhat gruesome appearance of the woman who surely must be Ciara when she grew older, and at how the woman had threateningly pointed at her rounded belly. Did she mean harm to her unborn child? Could she harm him through way of a vision?

Chapter Twenty-Eight

A LAINN WAS SEATED at the long table surrounded by many others, but still she shivered at the memory of the vision and, as much as she despised thinking about it or dwelling on it, she was quite certain that it held great meaning and a strict warning. As she waited for Killian to come to her so they could break fast together, she felt another ache across her belly, nothing severe, but nothing to ignore either. She remembered the vile woman from her vision who had purposely pointed displeasingly at her belly. Could an unpleasant happening or a frightening encounter in a vision cause pain or harm to the person who had experienced it? She placed her hand to her stomach and sent a healing sensation throughout her body. The discomfort dissipated and she breathed a sigh of relief. Perhaps it was simply a form of warning that Ciara might wish her son harm some time in the future. Alainn did not care to dwell on that unpleasant possibility either.

Alainn tried to calm her fretful thoughts by using her knowledge as a healer. She was certainly aware women often times experienced a false labor sometimes weeks before their time, so she attempted to ignore her fretfulness. She believed remaining calm would be most beneficial at this time. She allowed herself to dwell on her night with Killian, her perfectly romantic time, dancing with her love. It took away some of her trepidation of which she was much relieved.

When Killian finally came to join her he kissed her before he sat, but she noticed the creases in his brow. He seemed notably distracted and Fergus came to him once more to have him sign a decree before he had an opportunity to begin his meal.

"Your tasks are many, Killian, and your worries not a few!"

He nodded as he spoke. "There have been reports of horse-thievery nearby. Clan Gallagher had their stables raided. Over half the horses were stolen and several others killed when the stables were set fire. And 'tis believed the culprits are in allegiance with the English and are selling the horses to the English army. I've had to sign a decree that any man found guilty of that crime here at Castle O'Donnel will be hanged.

There's not been such a grievous punishment issued since I've been chieftain and, in truth, I believe there were few hangings here in all the time my father was chieftain. I truly hope it does not come to that. I've enlisted more guards and more men to our clan's army, but 'tis a worry. And if they can get to the horses, then they can get to the village, and perhaps to the castle and to you! And just knowin' I must leave you now makes me question where my full concern should be… most especially when you are nearing your term. My place should be here with you to keep you protected!"

"But you are needed in Galway, Killian. And, in truth, your vote may protect many. You are a wise man and I trust you. Others can protect our castle, but not so many men can rally the clans as you seem able. So go to Galway and do what you must and what you can!"

His expression was one of mixed emotion, relief at her words of comfort to him, but deep concern as well. He seemed nearly disinterested in eating his meal which was unusual in itself for Killian always possessed a hearty appetite. They were sitting there together when the young servant girl brought Alainn her cup of milk, and Alainn thanked the girl. She smiled sweetly at Alainn and handed her the drink, barely glancing at Killian, though she bowed respectfully to both of them. When she left, Killian questioned her.

"You have a servant girl bring you the milk now?"

"Aye, 'tis a convenience."

"And is it tasted first then, if you don't prepare it yourself, as all the food we eat is to ensure there is no poison present?"

"I hadn't thought of that, but either Cookson or Nellie will surely have prepared it and they are trustworthy. And if it were poisoned I would surely know for I'd be hard-pressed to find a poison I don't know well, by scent alone."

"Aye, but be cautious, Lainna. There are unscrupulous sorts who wish ill to nobles at any time, but now most especially, and you are apparently a target of someone who wishes you great harm. Have someone taste it first from now on Alainn; it will ease my mind."

"Aye, I'll do it then," she said smiling reassuringly as he stood and donned his overcoat and then his woolen cloak. The weather had grown cooler and the ride to Galway would take the better part of the day. Some of the trip was near the coastline so the wind from the sea could be most bitter and unpleasant.

"If you could manage a bit warmer weather to make the journey more agreeable, I'd be appreciative." Killian smiled as he took her in his arms.

"I'll see what I can do. Who will be traveling with you, Killian?"

"Several of the army's guards will accompany us, as well as a hearty amount of my clansmen. Pierce has decided he wishes to come with us. Unfortunately, your grandfather remains feelin' most weary as you'll know, so Riley will be travelin' with us and many of the O'Rorke and O'Donnel clans as well."

"And have you had word of Rory?" She felt compelled to ask.

"We've had no further correspondence, but I promise we'll be cautious, Alainn. Danhoul will be stayin' here and Mac, as well as a good portion of the guard and the soldiers.

The castle will be well protected. And heed the boy, but keep him at bay!"

"Killian, fret not about me, just do what you must and come back to me safely; Godspeed, my love."

He kissed her, a long and tender kiss. Ordinarily, she would have escorted him out of the castle and down the steps, walked with him until he mounted his horse and watched him ride off until she could see him no longer. However, she sensed his urgency to begin the journey, and given the pain she'd been experiencing, she thought it best to move as little as possible. She stood on her tiptoes and kissed him again resolute that she would shed no tears until he was gone.

He placed a kiss on her belly as had become a certainty each time he left her. When he opened the huge door of the main entrance, she attempted a surely unconvincing smile and a hasty wave then turned from him so he would not see the tears she could not prevent from falling. She headed straight for their bedchamber and was only halfway up the winding stairwell when she was startled to see Killian beside her again.

"I think we should name him Cian, for my brother, for 'tis hoped both my father and yours may one day be found, and we'll name the babes that follow after them. But, in honor of my beloved brother, who did not live to wed or know the joy I have shared with you, if it pleases you, I want to have him named Cian!"

"Aye, it well pleases me, Killian." She wept as he took her in his arms again. "I promised myself I would not have you see my tears, that just this one time I would behave as a lady, to be regal and poised and not act the part of a emotional girl-child, but it saddens me so when we are to be parted, Killian!"

"And if you did not weep when I was leavin' I'd worry more so, Lainna, for 'tis how you are and though I'd not choose to see you melancholy, I know 'tis only because you love me well that causes your tears. And that is all a man can truly ask for, to be loved well by a woman he loves equally well. And I do, Lainna, I love you entirely, completely, unendingly! Now, I must go, for the sooner I'm off, the sooner I'll be back here with you."

"Aye, fare thee well, hurry back to me, my love… to us!" She held her hand to her belly and he placed his over hers, kissed her quickly once more and was gone.

⌘

ALAINN SPENT NEARLY the entire day in her bedchamber, she read and slept and scarcely moved from the bed. When she'd woken from her sleep midafternoon, she was dismayed to find she had begun to experience discomfort again. She went to the enclosed privy and was relieved to find there was no bleeding, but she couldn't dismiss the fact she was troubled. She had little appetite for her evening meal and when the servant came to collect the tray, Danhoul stepped inside the room as well.

"Are you unwell Alainn?" he asked immediately concerned by her paler than normal complexion. "Are you ill?"

She waited until the servant had left them to reply.

"Not ill, not entirely, but I have noticed a slight pain in my belly that causes me some consternation, for the babe is not to arrive for at least a moon and a fortnight. I am aware a child can arrive early, and all can be well, but I fear 'tis too soon."

He walked into the chamber leaving the door ajar so no rumors of indiscretion or infidelity could be started. He placed his hand on her middle and he couldn't conceal the concern when his eyes met hers. He kept his hand there and she immediately felt some relief. When the young servant-girl Nellie O'Shea rapped on the door, she seemed startled to find another man with his hands on the chieftain's wife's blossomed belly. She barely looked at Danhoul and acted shy toward him as she had with Killian in the morn.

"You may set the milk on the table, Nellie, thank you!"

"And has it been tasted?" Danhoul asked the very same inquiry Killian had issued that morning.

"Aye, the castle's taster checked it nearly an hour ago. He remains well, and has declared it fit."

Alainn took the mixture and drank it making the usual disagreeable face when drinking milk.

When Danhoul was satisfied that he'd healed her to the best of his capabilities, he insisted Alainn enlist her own many healing abilities as well, and then he ordered her to go to sleep and not to move from the bed until morning.

"And if I should need to pass water, which only occurs perhaps half a dozen times each night?" She jested, trying to ease the young man's mind.

"Call me and I'll carry you to the chamber pot!" He returned the humor.

"And how would I summon you for the charming deed?"

"You can throw your thoughts to me from many miles away, in truth I suspect you can throw your thoughts to me wherever you might be. I think even you are unaware of the capabilities you possess!"

"Aye, well, if I'm throwin' my thoughts to you, I'll make certain it is of greater importance than my bodily functions."

He smiled at her as he left, but if she heard his present thoughts, he knew she'd realize he was gravely worried about her and her unborn child.

⌘

FOR THREE DAYS, Alainn went through the same discomfort and uneasiness. The midwife was called and confirmed that there was a possibility the child would come early, but she assured Alainn no seeping had happened yet, which was surely a fortunate omen. She told her to keep to her bed and to keep rested and nourished.

Eireen had been most fretful about her and fussed about constantly. Danhoul hung about her nervously as though he was the father of the child. Even Connor MacLain and MacKenzie MacArthur had been to her bedchamber. Cookson had insisted on bringing her the milk-mixture himself the past two times. He even revealed that he, personally, had tasted her food and the milk to make certain no one had been trying to harm her.

Mary had also come to visit and though she hadn't been aware of Alainn's condition, she was sorely vexed when she learned of the development as well. Alainn thought as a healer she should be able to decipher why the pain would come and go. It was most mysterious to her.

When she fell asleep on the third night after Killian had left, she was awakened by severe cramping in her belly. She cried out and Danhoul was beside her almost immediately. She insisted on him helping her to the privy closet and when she came out he knew by the look on her face, the news was not of a positive nature.

"Danhoul you must summon the midwife, but in the chamber next door where I keep my potions, you must get the vial next to the heal-alls. It is a honeysuckle mixture, a remedy to assist women with discomfort during their monthlies, but it has been known to stop a child from coming before it's time. I tried to summon it to me, but when I am in pain it is much more difficult for me to clearly direct my powers."

She was startled to see him close his eyes and it appeared in his hand. She reached for it as she felt another pain grip her belly. He administered the dosage and then placed his hand to her belly again. Alainn was trying to keep herself from becoming panic-stricken. She'd not felt the child move often in the last hours which was not a fortuitous sign for often when a babe was about to be born they grew quiet.

Finally, even before the midwife arrived, she felt the pain subside and she fell asleep with Danhoul still holding her hand. The midwife observed her condition and once more told her to keep to her bed and perhaps the progression of the labor would not advance further.

⌘

THAT NIGHT, ALAINN had a most telling dream. The spirit woman she had seen within the round tower came to her in great clarity. She was encircled in a glowing light and though she spoke not a word, she clearly revealed to Alainn why she'd felt pain in her belly. In the dream Alainn had calmly nodded in understanding to the spirit woman, and trusted her without question. When she awoke in the morning, she was not only fearful, but furious.

Alainn called out to Danhoul in her mind and he came to her as surely as if she'd screamed his name. She told him of her suspicions and when the servant girl brought her the milk, she did not drink it. She had one of the other servants send for a worker from the dairy shed. When the chieftain's wife asked to have the extremely ornery female cat now heavy with kittens brought to her bedchamber, the servant

thought she'd possibly lost her mind, but he did as instructed.

After Alainn allowed the cat to drink the milk intended
for her, they waited. And sure enough not long after the cat
ingested the milk she began to show signs of distress, and
soon after that she'd already given birth to her litter.

"How could I have been so foolish? I am a healer and an
herbalist; I was certain I knew herbs as well as anyone. I have
been well schooled in their uses since I was a young child.
How could I have missed the fact that the milk contained
lesser skullcap, an herb known to induce birth? And it is
often most bitter; how did I not notice it?"

"But placed in the sweet honey mixture and in the milk,
which you admittedly dislike, it may have made it undetect-
able, Alainn, and it is odorless." Danhoul tried to set her at
ease and take away her feelings of guilt.

"Who would want to harm you and your child?" Eireen
asked with great distress in her voice.

"Having a taster clearly did not help in this situation!"
Mary, who'd be visiting daily, reasoned.

"Aye, well, I never thought to employ a woman with
child as a taster, for it would only have been such a person
that would have had any ill effects, and I would not put
another woman with child at similar risk at any rate."

"We must learn who has attempted this great injustice to
you, Lady O'Brien!" It was Mackenzie MacArthur whose
riled expression clearly revealed his anger at the situation.

"And your husband should be alerted straightaway. I will have a messenger send for him, and advise him to return home at once!"

"No, Mac, there is little benefit in that. I believe all will be well now. The midwife assures me no further advances have been made toward the birthing and as long as I don't consume any more of the concoction and I rest, all will be well, I'm certain. Killian would only worry unnecessarily and be taken from important matters he must attend to."

"Aye, well, if you're entirely certain, we'll not send for him just yet, but I will be questioning everyone who has been in the kitchen and the dairy shed in the past few days. Anyone who has touched the honey or the milk will be under great suspicion. The servant girl and even young Joseph will be made to explain much!"

Alainn wanted to inform Mac she was certain who might have had something to do with the nefarious deed, but she had absolutely no proof whatsoever that the Ciara McCree of the present or in the future would attempt anything as despicable as trying to cause her to miscarry. The woman had only acted violently toward her the once and that was when she was in a drunken state, and Alainn thought she'd not been without fault that night either.

The meeting by the lake had not been friendly and had irked Alainn without question, but Ciara hadn't seemed dangerous. The vision had no concise certainties simply more mysterious questions. But who else would benefit from her losing the child, she wondered? Why had her intuitive powers not alerted her to the herbal concoction placed in her milk? Perhaps it was a person with supernatural powers of their own who had created the mixture or somehow veiled the truth.

Her mind once more went to the unpleasant and disparaging image of the woman from her vision that so closely resembled Ciara, or perhaps was Ciara in the future. Was it simply a vision, a warning, something untoward may happen perhaps two decades in the future when Ciara was older? Was the woman in a pact with the demon as the vision implied? Did it indicate that Ciara would try to harm her son when he was a man? Thinking of all of this simply made Alainn wearier, and no more close to learning the answers. She decided to leave it to Mac to discern what had happened, for she wanted nothing more than to go to sleep and forget all this unpleasantness.

She was undoubtedly much relieved the spirit woman from the tower with whom she felt such a deep connection seemed inclined to want to assist her. In her dream, she had pointed to both the containers that held the honey and the milk. She had shaken her head in stark warning and then knocked over the contents spilling them entirely. As the liquid had fallen to the floor it had soon turned to blood. The spirit woman had simply vanished once she was aware Alainn had understood the ominous warning.

Alainn now drifted off and she placed her hand to her

belly, felt the beloved movement in response and went to sleep in peace, hoping this night held nothing but restful slumber.

⌘

WHEN THE MORNING sun filled the bedchamber, Alainn yawned and stretched and was relieved to find she felt almost entirely improved. She rose and had a bath prepared for her. After she'd bathed and dressed and brushed and knotted her hair, she started downstairs for she felt nearly famished, which had to be a good omen. She'd barely had an appetite the last few days, and now she felt undeniably hungry.

When she sat down at the long table in the gigantic chamber, she thought it was a ridiculous notion to be seated here at this immense table when she would be dining entirely alone. She envisioned the kitchen and to her delight she learned through her powers Ciara McCree was not in the kitchen this day. She opened the door and found the entire lot of servants staring at her when she entered. They all grew noticeably quiet and some bowed to her nervously, others nodded respectfully, but no one spoke. She walked toward Cookson and she noticed even he wore a grim expression.

"What is it, Cookson? Why is everyone acting so oddly toward me?"

Cookson placed his hand on her arm and attempted a smile. "Ah, well, sorry I am about what nearly transpired, Alainn. I don't know how it could have happened. We've all been careful here in the kitchen. I trust all the servants, and I kept the honey supply in a cupboard few had access to. Only Nellie and I added the mixture. Mac has been in a temper and on an uncommon rampage this morning. He's been grillin' anyone who has ever set foot in this kitchen since the day you arrived, I'd wager.

Everyone is worried they'll be placed under suspicion. He has threatened to have the entire staff turned out and have a whole new lot of servants brought in if the culprit can't be found straightaway. He was even lookin' at me with a hint of ill-temper. I told the man I've known you since you were born, that if I'd ever wanted to harm you, it would surely have been when you told my father I'd swatted the fly and it landed in the pot of soup back when I was still a young lad!"

"Aye, well, it was the chieftain's soup, and if he'd spotted it, sure your father would have found himself in a more severe predicament than you were."

"Aye! That's what my da said, then, too."

"I'm certain Mac will get to the bottom of this, Cookson. Sorry I am that it has to be unpleasant for you and all the kitchen staff until it's sorted out."

"Aye, well, I'd like it settled too, Alainn, for you know how dear you are to me. Sure you're like a sister to me, and I would want no harm to befall you or the babe. But, here, sit you down and have some ham and eggs. I've freshly baked scones, as well, and I'll make certain to show you no milk or honey for a day or two, I promise you that."

Cookson pulled up a chair and took the time to sit down beside her. For the first time in a long while, she felt like she was free to enjoy a conversation with her good friend.

⌘

UPON RETURNING TO the sitting room in her chambers, Danhoul soon came to locate her and he appeared relieved that she was noticeably improved and in brighter spirits.

"You've taken this position my grandfather has assigned you very seriously, Danhoul. Sure you'd like a reprieve from the great consternation I have become?"

"I do not dislike my present task. 'Tis true you can be a most difficult woman at times, magical beings almost always are," He smiled as he spoke. "But I prefer watchin' over even the likes of you and sleepin' in a castle to fightin' the English and sleepin' on the ground every night... never certain I'd live to see tomorrow."

"That must have been a difficult life, Danhoul, especially for a man so young."

"Well at least you didn't refer to me as *the boy*!"

"You are able to hear my husband's thoughts then, are you? His thoughts seldom come to me."

"Aye, I hear them and I am aware he resents me and he appears to claim an aversion to my age, though he is not so very old himself. Not many men at two and twenty are highly regarded chieftains and elected to the council of the clans. I'm certain there are men at council who might refer to him as the boy."

"If he actually thought of you as a boy, he'd not think of you as a source of temptation, so do not take his thoughts so personally, Danhoul! And he clearly does not truly think of you as a boy or he'd not leave me in your guard. I know he does appreciate your abilities and your visions that have proven invaluable in seeing no great harm come to me thus far. But he resents them as well for 'tis something you and I share that he can't be a part of."

"But I did not foresee you nearly losing the child! I had no inclination whatsoever there would be such uncertainty."

"Nor did I; no seer can see all, Danhoul. It is presumed I am a woman with unusually strong magical abilities and I am not capable of seeing everything, especially when it pertains to matters regarding me. Sometimes I suppose it is best we don't see everything. 'Tis difficult enough to see all that we do!"

"You should not turn from your abilities as you've done, Alainn. I understand your reasons, but I disagree. They are an intricate part of you. You have rarely used your magic except in a temper, not gone to a fairy glade or conversed with any magical creatures in all the time you have been here at Castle O'Donnel."

"I've talked to you and you are magical. Well, you have magical abilities at any rate. I saw the spirit woman by Castle O'Rorke and thankfully she was the one who came to me in my dream and warned me of the potion in the honey and milk mixture. I feel a strong connection to her. She seems to dwell within the round tower by the old castle ruins. You spoke of the place, of a great battle between good and evil? How do you know of this and who is the woman?"

"I do feel a deep connection to the place, and to the woman, as well, but I tell you plain, you must not go there, not yet."

"What is it you know and do not speak of, Danhoul? Is it something you have been informed of by the gods?"

He immediately felt he had misspoken. "When the time is right, I suspect we will both know more of the happenings there and the reason for our connection to the location."

"But there is a fairy realm near that location, I sensed that as well. I hope to go to a fairy glade during Samhain for 'tis a most magical time. 'Tis only a little over a moon away."

"Aye, but I would suggest you avoid that area entirely for even the dolmen near the round tower was once a dark place. Many barbaric druid rituals took place there. I have witnessed the dark memories there. It was a morose time. One you would not wish to see." Danhoul's eyes filled with a far-off expression as though he was reliving what may have taken place there. Alainn cleared her throat and he continued speaking once more.

"There is another glade nearby as well; go there if you must! It lies near the oak grove that borders your grandfather's and your husband's land. It, too, was a place where ancient druid rituals were held that predate history, but more celebratory and less somber happenings."

She was well aware of the seriousness in his tone and she felt inclined to listen to his wisdom and not question him further, which she surmised completely surprised him. She simply spoke on of other magical locations.

"I have sensed there is a fairy glade and portal to other realms in the caves near the coast. I have walked there often, but never entered for 'tis only accessible when the tide is out. It would be dangerous to go there during high tide. The spirit woman in the tower is somehow connected to that location as well."

"Her name is Deidra."

"So you know much of the woman?"

"I know some, but what puzzles me is why she came to you in a dream to warn you? Why would she not come to you in daylight then, during waking hours for you have the ability to see spirits at all times? Sure you'd more readily believe her and know it was not simply a disagreeable dream."

She turned from his eyes and sheepishly admitted. "I have blocked the ability to see most spirits, but I seem unable to control them from coming to me in my dreams. 'Tis why I believe the spirit woman must have possessed strong magic in life for I saw her again this morning in daylight while awake. She was in the chamber when I gave the cat the milk mixture. She appeared most pleased I had listened to her warnings."

"Alainn, you should most definitely not have blocked that important ability, for often spirits have portent messages for us that will benefit or aid us."

Her hackles rose at his words. "Do you know what it is to be surrounded by so many spirits every day of your life? I am able to see the spirits of people who have passed only hours ago and those who have been gone for hundreds, sometimes thousands of years. It is most unsettling to see so very many specters standing amongst the living, existing here with us. Some are most agreeable and simply wish to remain near those they loved in life, but others are not so cordial, and quite vexing and unpleasant. If it were only a few spirits now and again I was witness to, then I would be accepting of that. Are you not capable of seeing the dead then, Danhoul?"

"I do see them but, no, not in the great numbers you speak of. I suppose it would be unnerving. But, for now, Alainn, until we learn if Deidra's spirit or any other has news and warning of other threat or perhaps knowledge of the dark demon, you must allow yourself to see them once more."

Alainn rolled her eyes and shook her head. "Danhoul, I am attempting to live the life of a woman, just a woman, not a witch, not a magical being, not someone from the line of a Celtic god or fairy princess."

"And if these abilities are capable of saving your life or

the lives of those you most care for?"

She sighed deeply. "So be it, I will allow myself to see spirits again for a time.

"Do it now, Alainn, I insist it be done now."

She threw him a displeased look, but closed her eyes and appeared deep in thought. She moved her lips and then touched her hands to her eyes. She slowly opened them and looked all around her obviously seeing what he did not.

"Samhain is drawing near. Have you any notion the number of spirits that walk the earth during that time?"

"I would suppose it is many." He empathized. "Why did you not tell me you blocked this ability?"

"Well 'tis not as though I tell you every single thing, Danhoul Calhoun. I also did not inform you of my recent vision, a vision where I was guided and accompanied by the spirit of Shylie O'Rorke, my very own aunt. In this disenchanting vision was a woman who looks much like Ciara but was perhaps Ciara maybe many years in the future, and sure she was even less pleasant than she is now."

Danhoul's eyes grew wide at the information she had kept concealed. "How am I to protect you if you keep such subjects from me? We must speak on all of these topics now. Tell me straightaway all you know of the spirit girl and of the woman who may be Ciara in the future."

Their discussion was interrupted when the Mac came into the chamber, indeed in a rare temper regarding the dangerous herbs Alainn had been given. He told them he knew from experience back at Castle O'Brien, Danhoul, the young druid, claimed some magical abilities, and he wished to enlist his assistance in questioning some of the servants. He had apparently heard of the man's ability to sometimes read others thoughts, and believed he might be able to discern who was being truthful.

He was certain Alainn could possibly help out as well, but he thought it wise to shelter her from any further displeasure or connection with the incident. Alainn assured Danhoul she would be spending the remainder of the day in her bedchamber for she was still feeling tired and in need of rest.

"Aye, you make certain you take it easy. We will discuss this matter at length at another time, and you must alert me if you intend to leave the castle."

"I've no intention to do anything of the sort, Danhoul!" she said with assurance as he left her.

He glanced back at her once more and something unsettled him though even his powers of perception couldn't decipher what caused the nagging uneasiness he now felt. He started down the corridor, but hurriedly returned and placed a protective charm upon the doorway of her chambers so that no one with harmful intentions, hopefully even the dark demon, could enter or harm her when she was within. He desired to be capable of placing a charm upon Alainn herself to ensure she remained safe, but unfortunately charming a location was much more easily managed than charming a person, especially a witch.

Chapter Twenty-Nine

ALAINN AWOKE IN a cold sweat, her nightdress soaked through with perspiration and her heart filled with dread. Again, she'd experienced a most disturbing dream. She did not dream of Deidra, nor did she see Ciara in the present or the future, but she dreamt of something decidedly more grievous than any of that. She'd dreamt of Killian's death. It was not a vision, for visions only occurred when she was awake, but it was so similar to her reoccurring vision, it left her more than fearful. And the dream revealed more details.

The vision had always only shown Killian and her cousins lying dead upon the ground alongside half of Clan O'Brien. There had been English forces present as well, and the ground had been soaked in blood. But this dream had revealed a different location and it had showed her the true lay of the land. It was much hillier than in her previous visions. And she was reasonably certain she knew the exact location. If she'd not once made the trip from Castle O'Brien to Galway, she would not have recognized the land formations.

She got out of bed quickly and hastened to get dressed. She wasn't certain what she planned to do or hoped to accomplish, but she knew something must be done. She'd barely gotten her slippers on her feet when she was struck by a blinding pain in her head and an overwhelming sense of nausea. She thought she might faint so intense were both! And the vision she now had was clearer than ever before.

Alainn was certain the reason she was seeing it now in such precise clarity was because it was actually happening at this very moment. Killian and his men were in battle with the English even now, and they would meet with death in little time. She must somehow get to Killian, but wasn't certain she could manage it, and what she could actually do, if and when she accomplished that feat. She wanted to alert Danhoul, maybe even to enlist him in aiding her.

She frantically attempted to telepathically call to Danhoul as she had done often before, but in doing so the sharp excruciating pain within her head returned. She placed her hands to her head and willed the throbbing to terminate. Time was perilously short. She inhaled several deep breaths and concentrated on Killian, on being taken there to Killian, and closed her eyes tightly.

When she opened them again, she smelled smoke all around her, and she recognized the pungent scent of blood. She was standing behind one of the few trees in the area. She saw English soldiers wearing their typical scarlet uniforms and many of them were mounted on horses. Several others stood by large weapons that spouted fire. Although Alainn had never seen such weapons before, she had heard they existed.

She saw a sea of English soldiers, almost as far as the eye could see and they were surrounding the Irish soldiers. The clans were trapped within a deep valley and hedged in on all sides. Alainn realized with great fear and disdain that very few Irishmen remained alive. The first man she recognized was Pierce MacCarther. She'd not seen Pierce in any of her previous visions, but she barely had time to form that thought when she saw him fall to the ground, struck by the object that spewed at an unimaginable speed from the weapon of fire.

She threw out her arms and with all her strength and ability concentrated on freezing time. It had been a very long time since she'd attempted that deed, but she saw she had most certainly accomplished it, for everyone now stood completely silent and still as bronze statues.

She lifted up her skirts and moved as quickly as she was able toward the valley now strewn with dead bodies. She recognized several. Many were O'Brien's. She saw Hugh and Sean, Killian's uncles and the new captain to Castle O Brien, all dead, their bodies torn and bleeding. Her eyes fell upon Riley, and then Rory only a few feet from him, as well. Rory was dead, Riley had his eyes closed and his face was twisted by the tormented pain. The peculiar thought occurred to her, as twins they had been born together and now they had would die together, also.

Her heart ached as she went to Rory's side. She had always loved Rory like a brother and thought of him as one of her dearest friends. He was a kind and gentle man. The tears ran down her cheeks as she touched his head. She felt heartsick at seeing Riley near death as well. There would be nothing she could do for him for his stomach was splayed open and bleeding profusely. Her thoughts went to her beloved grandfather for his only two grandsons would now be gone.

She had to find Killian; she'd possibly made it there before he'd been killed. Perhaps as some of the details had been altered with Pierce being there and the English weapons being so unusual, perhaps the order of the O'Brien men's death would also be altered. She prayed it would be so as she frantically searched for Killian.

She stepped over bodies of English and Irish alike. Though only armed with swords and bow and arrows, the Irish had always been fierce and skillful warriors and they'd clearly taken out many Englishmen. If they'd not been so hugely outnumbered and the English hadn't claimed unusual and advanced weaponry, the fight would have been more evenly matched.

Alainn felt the tears still running down her cheeks and heard the sobs, but barely realized they were her own. And then she spotted him. He lay upon the ground, his sword still run through an Englishman, and there was a sword in his chest as she'd seen in her visions, but he was also hit by one of the fire weapons. She strangely found herself trying to remember the name of these weapons for she'd heard Killian and Mac speaking of them.

She knelt on the ground beside Killian and looked into his deep green eyes, for they remained wide open, but there was no life left within them. She screamed; she heard herself screaming over and over again as she pulled his head to her lap. Her entire dress was soaked with his blood and she rocked him as she would a child. She felt the child moving within her and was tormented further knowing he would never know his father.

She had not been able to stop any of this horror for all of her damnable powers. Why had she been shown the cursed vision if she wasn't meant to prevent the tragedy? She felt the rumble of thunder overhead as much as heard it. The cold rain began to fall and she could not hold time at a standstill for much longer. There were many English soldiers still standing, sure her life would be in danger if she did not soon seek safety.

A thought occurred to Alainn even in her intense unbearable grief, she could not simply still time; she could reverse it. She could go back in time. She'd only ever done it once before, the day she had seen the evil demon in the dungeon of Castle O'Brien. And that was the day she had nearly lost their child. Although she'd also been struck that day by the poisoned dart, she had never revealed to anyone, but she suspected it might have been her traveling through time that had contributed to the near miscarriage as much as the poison.

She had to make a decision. If she attempted to save Killian she could lose their unborn child. As she looked down at the man she now held in her arms, she felt her heart breaking into a thousand shattered pieces. If she didn't make a move soon, she and their unborn child would soon be dead as well. And for an instant that was precisely what she wanted. She wanted to be dead, to simply be joined in death to her Killian.

As her hand touched his, still warm for he'd surely only been gone for a short while, she knew she had to save him. But, if she died trying, then she would take the life of her child as well. How could she dare risk losing her precious unborn son? Perhaps she would lose them both. The seconds passed and she felt herself unable to move, as petrified as all the others surrounding her, and it hurt intensely to breathe. She recalled Killian's words when they thought they would lose the child those months ago, he'd said they would have many children. She couldn't even be entirely certain this journey would cause harm to her unborn child. And so she instinctively chose.

Chapter Thirty

S HE WILLED HERSELF to go back in time. She didn't know
how far to go back or even how far she was capable of
going back. Because she wasn't aware of the specific events
that had occurred earlier in the morning, she commanded
herself to go back to when there was little light, for even now
it was just past dawn. She thought of Storm, Killian's horse,
and imagined him upon the horse. Nothing happened. She
looked down upon the amulet she wore. It bore the mark of
the triquetra, a druid symbol. It surely offered her some
magical protection. But, it also seemed to limit her powers
and Alainn knew she needed whatever powers she could call
upon, so she pulled the amulet from her neck and shoved it
in the pocket of her gown.

Once again she concentrated intently and she felt herself
becoming dazed and disoriented, but when she opened her
eyes she saw Killian off in the distance, he was alive and
riding Storm as she'd imagined, but the English already had
the Irish surrounded. She heard the thundering sound that
came from the harquebus. She had finally remembered the
name of the weapon. They were many large weapons and

they were being fired from atop a wooden support for they appeared to be very heavy. She tried to call out to Killian, but the noise all around her was deafening and she heard a movement from behind her.

An English soldier was standing, looking at her with great interest and she remembered Killian once telling her if a woman was present on a battlefield she seldom met with a quick death, for she was often made to suffer rape as well. She doubted even an Englishman with little conscience would rape her when she was so obviously with child, but she wasn't certain.

She felt the anelace, the small dagger she kept within her pocket fly from its location by way of her magic and straight into the heart of the English soldier. As she pulled it out with use of powers as well, she tried to make her way to Killian or at least close enough that she could be heard. She was about to move closer using her magic, as she tried to magically urge him to draw nearer to her as well, but as she looked toward him she saw him pulled from his horse by a foot soldier. He ran the man through with his sword, and she saw him bravely take out at least half a dozen more of the enemy before she saw the object being hurled at him from the harquebus at unbelievable speed. She threw out her hands and tried to prevent it from hitting him. At the same time she threw her anger and fury at the man standing behind the weapon. She saw the man and the weapon burst into flames and there was an enormous explosion from the location.

As she looked back at Killian she saw him upon the ground. She stopped time again, and ran to his side. He was still alive. She breathed a huge sigh of relief, but it was short-lived for although the sword seemed to have caused only minimal damage to his shoulder, she saw the large open wound that had been caused by the fire weapon. She'd not been capable of stopping it. It had gone straight through him and it was dangerously close to his heart, so close she despaired at being capable of viewing his beating heart. The damage was massive and she knew within her own heart it was surely a mortal wound. The blood gushed uncontrollably from the wound. As it spurted and sprayed disturbing each time his heart beat, she dropped to the ground and firmly placed her hands to his chest in attempt to stop the bleeding. She called upon her magical healing powers. She saw his eyes open and he looked at her with such torment, she wanted to cry out in protest. She felt his hand upon hers. His voice was weak as he spoke.

"Alainn, you must go back. You must save yourself and our son for sure there'll not be an Irishman left alive this day. No amount of healin'can save me now. Even your magic cannot heal this wound. You know that to be truth. So do as I've asked you, my Lainna, go back now, save yourself and our son, and remember to name him Cian!"

Alainn bent over and pulled him to her. She softly kissed him and his lips formed a smile as he died in her arms.

Chapter Thirty-One

S HE HELD HIM to her tightly as she screamed out again and she wailed so overwrought was she at the injustice of it. She no longer seemed conscious of the ability to make choices; she simply knew she had to go back further still. For the briefest of seconds she considered doing as he'd told her and going back to their castle. But she couldn't manage it. She envisioned the road she'd seen leading to the valley. She thought of the stars in the dark night sky and imaged the darkness of midnight. She attempted to calculate where the clans might have been at that time. She closed her eyes and felt herself being taken back once more and she then noticed the pain across her belly as well. She would lose them both, she thought as she felt herself flying and her world spun and tilted. The dizziness and loud humming filled her head. She felt as though she might lose consciousness entirely.

When she finally regained clear thought, it was completely dark. She looked around and could see no one. Had she gone to the wrong location, to the wrong time of night? She remembered being told once that some witches had the power to span centuries. In her pain and grief could she have misjudged so poorly she'd been sent back to another time entirely? She was beginning to feel panicked when she heard voices.

Beyond the trees was an encampment. She looked out to see many blanketed enclosures and several campfires burning. She couldn't make out the faces of any of the men who sat around the fires, but she believed they were Irish, at least.

She was peering closer trying to ignore the dull pain in her belly when she felt a hand on her shoulder. A man she did not recognize then grabbed her by the arm roughly and pulled her into the clearing.

"Are you a spy for the English!"

"No!" She insisted.

"Then why is a woman, clearly with child, here in the middle of nowhere if not to spy on the clans?"

"I am looking for my husband!"

"And what clan does he belong to?"

"What clan are you?" she answered with another question for Killian had spoken of some clans who were in alliance with the English.

"We are the O'Neills!"

"Thank the Lord!" she whispered, but the man heard.

"Who is your husband?"

"Killian O'Brien!"

"Clan O'Brien is surely hours from here. We are to meet up with them at Gentle Valley on the morrow just before dawn."

"Don't go there! Stay clear of that valley!" She warned with deep conviction.

"What the hell are you talkin' about woman?"

She heard a loud commanding voice from behind her.

"This man is the O'Neill, woman; you'd better explain yourself straightaway!"

Alainn looked up into the face of a dark haired man, who wore a long and shaggy beard. She realized it was surely Collum O'Neill, the great Irish Chieftain.

"You should not go near the dell you speak of for it will be a massacre!"

The guard who held tight to her arm seemed to be gauging how the other man would react to the woman's warning.

"And how do you know of this?"

"I am a seer. I possess the gift of prophecy, and I have seen well over a hundred men from many clans dead! And I must find my husband to warn him as well."

"He is in Clan O'Brien." She heard the guard tell the chieftain.

"Well, that is not entirely true!" Alainn explained.

"You just told me that, woman!" The guard accused.

"Aye, well, I did tell you he is an O'Brien, but he is chieftain for Clan O'Donnel. Surely you have heard of Killian O'Brien, for he sits on the council of the clans."

"Aye, I know him well, for I sit on the council as well!" the chieftain elaborated.

"Clan O'Donnel is at the camp nearest ours. I can take

you to him if you desire it. Sure he'll want to see you for if my wife was out traipsin' about in the middle of the night when she looks as though she's about to birth my child, I'd be entertain' thoughts of beatin' her soundly, I'd wager!"

"Please just take me to him, milord!" she whispered as she felt another pain wrack her midsection.

"I've no other way of getting' you to him other than on foot or by horse. It'll only take a matter of minutes if we go by horse. So are you willin' to go then?"

"Aye, I need to get to him. And you must warn any of the clans you can get word to that it will be an impossible battle."

"I can take her if you like, milord!" The guard offered.

"No, I'll take her myself, for I'll want to see O'Brien then and ask him what his opinion is on this pertinent information his wife seems to possess."

She nodded for him to lift her upon the horse when he looked at her as though he wasn't even certain how to attempt to lift her without harming her in her condition, but he managed it and he mounted the horse and sat behind her. The ride was not smooth and by the time they came upon the lights of the campfires ahead, Alainn was soon experiencing another sharp pain.

She heard the many guards come to find out who was approaching and they were all relieved and startled to see who it was. She recognized one man from Castle O'Donnel and he called out in disbelief.

"Milady! How... What... I'll get milord!" he finally managed.

When she saw Killian striding toward her, alive and well, she burst into tears, and fell to sobbing again.

"What the hell is going on here, Collum? Alainn how did you get..." He stopped speaking for as he held up his lantern he'd obviously seen the front of her gown and cloak. He carefully lifted her off the horse and took her into his arms trying to calm her before he attempted to ask any further questions.

"Are you injured?" he finally asked when he thought she'd be capable of speaking.

"No!" She managed in a sob.

"Then whose blood is upon you in such great quantity?"

"Yours, Killian. 'Tis your blood!" she whispered and began weeping again in earnest as she continued to wipe the fresh blood from her hands on her garment.

"Alainn, you must settle yourself down so I can make sense of this and we can speak on this at length."

The other chieftain, Collum O'Neill, glanced at her with a harrowed expression on his face while Killian held his inconsolable wife in his arms.

"She says she's a seer! And she tells us we should not meet the other clans as we had planned. She speaks of great loss of life and destruction in the valley."

"Alainn, is it your vision, the one you've had for months now?"

"Aye, 'tis where I've only just come from!"

"What nonsense is this she speaks of?" O'Neill raised his voice as he spoke.

"I have been there and I have seen it happen, witnessed it all in its gruesome entirety and seen you dead! And you as well!" she said as she looked up at the man and remembered stepping over his corpse earlier for she'd seen his dark beard, red with blood that had poured from his mouth. "And this is your blood, Killian, for I held you in my arms while you died, the second time!" she said between sobs.

"Is she afflicted, man? Have you an entirely addle-minded wife, then?"

"No, she's as clear minded as anyone, Collum, and if she says she saw us dead then, aye, she did for she's seen it in a vision. But how did you get covered in blood, then, Alainn. I don't understand it and I'm much acquainted with your ways."

"It was not seen in a vision, not this time, Killian. I saw it before my very eyes as surely as I now stand with you. I used my powers to try to save you, but I saw you dead upon the ground, and so I went back in time, but I was still too late for that time I witnessed you being shot and then held you while you breathed your last breath. So, yet again, I went back to an earlier time and now I am here with you. And I implore you; you must not go near that valley! I will not see you dead again!"

With that she collapsed in a faint in his arms, he fearfully picked her up and carried her to a location near the fire.

"Do you believe what she just told you?" Collum O'Neill asked for he'd followed Killian and as he tried to grasp the absurdity of what the woman spoke of.

"Aye, I believe her, Collum!" And look at her gown, sure there's so much blood upon her, it would have been a mortal wound.

"I think she'll be birthin' the child before another day is done. I sense she is in pain beyond her melancholia!"

"By God's bones, no, 'tis too soon; and I doubt there's another woman anywhere near here to aid her, much less a midwife."

"Well, I tell you my wife has given birth eight times; our firstborn took the better part of a day and a half to arrive, so clearly we've no choice but to address the battle first. What do you intend to do? Will you march in to meet the other clans as planned? If not, we must alert them, as well. And how many English were there? Did she say she saw you shot? By an arrow, is that what she was indicatin'?"

Alainn began to regain consciousness although her head was spinning again. She heard the man's voice barking questions at Killian. She replied to his inquirires.

"There were three times as many English as with all clans combined, half were on horse. Another quarter on foot also had swords, but several possessed a harquebus."

"By Christ!" She heard Killian say.

"Are you certain?" the other chieftain asked.

309

"Aye, entirely certain, for the air reeked of the smoke that poured from them."

"I'll send out guards to alert the other clans positioned in the area, but some will not be reachable by the time we were to meet." Killian spoke to the other man.

Alainn heard other men approaching and she looked up into the disbelieving face of her cousin Riley.

"Alainn, what's goin' on? What are you doin here? How did you get here?"

Killian swiftly enlisted several of his men to forewarn the neighboring clans, and then told Riley what he knew.

"But we can't just leave Clan O'Brien to be slaughtered by the cursed English. They'll be expectin' us to meet up with them to make it a fair battle, and 'tis doubtful we can reach them in time to make them aware it is a trap or that they'll have no assistance from the rest of us!"

"But it won't be fair at any rate, Riley!" Alainn declared. "The English are so many and their fire weapons capable of striking from an unbelievable distance."

"Well, I'll not sit by and do nothin' while my father, my brother, and the rest of my kin of Clan O'Brien meet with certain death. I'm goin' to warn them."

"I believed your father was ailing and unable to make the journey?" Killian questioned.

"Aye, well, I wish he'd remained so, for I've had recent word he's journeyin' with them as well. I have to try to get to them, sure if I ride all night I'll make it in time."

"It is not a certainty, Riley!" Killian voiced his dubiousness.

"What other choice have I?" Riley asked his voice filled with despair.

"What if the rest of the clans march on even now and surround the English. They'll not be expectin' us and we'll have them at a disadvantage. And if we're not trapped in the valley the fight will be more evenly slated." Killian suggested.

"Aye, it could work!" Collum agreed.

"No, there are still far too many, Killian! Aye, you wouldn't be trapped, and surrounded, but what of the fire weapons?"

"We'll have to do what we can, Alainn, for as Riley has said we can't just allow all the men of Clan O'Brien to be slaughtered!"

She had gotten up from her place upon the ground and she recognized the determination in his eyes and the stubborn set to his jaw.

"If we leave now and all of us surround them as they had thought to do to us, it will make the fight nearly fair. If they are taken by surprise they won't have time to place their weapons upon the stands. I'm told the weapons are remarkably heavy and it would take at least three or four men to lift each one. It would keep many men occupied, and if they don't get them to a place where they can be propped, having to use so many men to lift one weapon won't seem such a great advantage, and possibly cause many injuries to the men. Sure we'd get there before Clan O'Brien arrives and then maybe your vision will not come to pass."

Alainn knew there was no sense arguing, yet she thought the day would surely have no different end than in her vision. As another pain ripped across her belly, she tried to keep that from Killian, but she felt the cold sweat on her face and forehead. She looked up to see Killian staring at her with great concern on his face.

"Are you near your time as Collum has said?"

"Please don't go, Killian?" She ignored his query. "I ask you this as your wife, remain with me. Don't leave me this day!"

"But what kind of a man would I be, Alainn, if I didn't do what I can for the good of kin and clan, and all of Ireland? For sure they'll not stop here; sure they're intent on invadin' each castle and killin' every man in every clan, perhaps every woman and child as well!"

She looked up to see nearly all the men had gotten their horses and Pierce was leading Storm to Killian.

"Don't go!" She repeated with tears in her voice as well as her eyes.

He took her in his arms and held her tightly and kissed the top of her head.

"You know I must, Lainna. I would not be the man you fell in love with nor the man you'd care to be married to if I act without honor and behave as a deplorable coward!"

As she wrapped her arms around him, she searched for the knife he kept hidden within his tunic.

Chapter Thirty-Two

S HE PULLED THE knife from its sheath and was prepared to use it on him when he quickly grabbed it from her hand and thwarted her feeble attempt.

"You forget, my sweet Lainna, t'was me who taught you that strategy!"

"Your wife attempts to murder you?" Collum O'Neill suggested in a voice laced with deep disbelief.

"She would not kill me but, aye, she would wound me to save my life, I'd wager!"

The tears fell from her eyes so profusely she could no longer see. Killian sheathed the knife once more and then gently wiped the tears from her cheeks.

He whispered in her ear. "It may not turn out as you've seen. Perhaps you've changed events enough to alter the outcome!"

She felt his warm, strong arms tighten around her and she squeezed him desperately in return. She heard the piper's calling the men to be assembled. She'd always loved the Irish pipes, but now they echoed eerily and their mournful wails chilled her soul. She would never again think of them with complete fondness for now they called her man away from her, lured him to his end. She heard Killian's voice now as if in a distant fog.

"I've had two of my men go in search of a woman who can assist you. Stay here safely hidden, be still and attempt to remain calm and maybe the child won't make an appearance this day, Alainn! Pray it will be so, and if he does come early, sure he'll be strong and able to survive. And you must call him Cian!" he called to her as he mounted his steed.

"Aye, you've already informed me of that, this day!" she whispered as she watched him ride off with the men of many clans.

SHE WAITED THERE for some time. For what seemed like a dreadfully long time, she had quietly, obediently waited at the eerily silent location. She intended to remain there and do exactly what Killian had instructed her to do, but she remembered how the weapons had sounded, how the air had smelled of smoke and blood, and she also clearly recalled how the weapon had exploded when she'd set it to fire. With her supernatural abilities, she could assist in this battle, and then, and perhaps only then, would it truly be a fair fight. She envisioned the battle not as she'd seen it, but how it would be fought in the near future. She closed her eyes and wished herself there.

IT WAS DIFFERENT this time. The Irish were not surrounded and the English not so much at an advantage. There had already been fighting, but she saw few bodies upon the ground. She looked out across the men and she spotted Killian. He was atop a distant hill and in conversation with Collum O'Neill. She had already used magic so many times this day she thought another couldn't hurt. She soon found herself standing between the two horses. Both men were startled to see her appear and Collum's horse reared at the unusual occurrence.

"Alainn, I told you to stay put, and I meant it!"

"Listen to me now for time is short. Tell your men to only be concerned with the soldiers on the ground, and only the men with swords. I will control the others."

With that she disappeared and reappeared beside a tree where she was once more nearly out of sight. She first called the attention of the horses of the English. Each one reared and snorted and threw their riders to the ground in so rough a manner many were injured and not a few dead. Killian led his men toward the foot soldiers and did exactly as Alainn had instructed.

She concentrated on looking at each harquebus and she envisioned each one of them catching fire and bursting into flames. Surely twenty-five explosions happened simultaneously and soon the smell of burning flesh filled the air. The acrid and repulsive scent burned Alainn's nostrils and she was stricken when another fierce pain crossed her belly. She felt her skirts and was sickened to know they were soaked, for the fluid from within her womb had obviously begun to leak and flow heavily. She lowered herself to the ground beside the tree and clutched her knees to her chest.

The sound of surely hundreds of swords clashing and clanging rang out in the air and joined with the crackling of flames and the screaming of wounded and dying men. She thought of Killian fighting for his life on the battlefield and she glanced out and saw that Clan O'Brien had joined the fight. She saw even now Rory was battling an English soldier. Now the vision could be proven true after all, some of the details might have simply been altered, but the outcome not changed. She grew ever fainter and undeniably weak. Each pain seemed to go on and on now with little break in between. Their son would be born on a battlefield, was the last clear thought she formed before her world went dark.

WHEN ALAINN BECAME conscious of her surroundings again, she was once more consumed with agony. She felt a blanket covering her and Killian was by her side. She sensed Rory had survived as well. She said a prayer of thanks that they had lived through the battle, and as she glanced out upon the moor, she realized many had not. But clearly the majority of the men killed appeared to be English.

A pain so vicious gripped her body she tightly grasped Killian's hand.

"We spotted a cottage not far from here; Rory and Pierce have gone to see if there is a woman there who might assist you."

The forced smile on his face could not conceal the fretfulness in his tone or the deep concern in his enchanting green eyes.

Her heart nearly broke as she spoke, but she knew what needed to be done.

"Tis not a woman or a midwife required, Killian, for our child will come without assistance. You must send someone to a church or an abbey, for you must fetch a priest straight-away!"

"Alainn, what is it you know?" Killian's voice trembled as he spoke.

"Please do as I ask, Killian!"

She noticed Riley stood close enough that she might call to him.

"You must locate a priest, and make haste!" she ordered and she saw her cousin's eyes flash with fear, but he did as she said and wasted no time mounting his horse and riding off.

"He is surely strong, Alainn, and you are the bravest, strongest woman I've ever met. Since you were a child you have possessed the fortitude and valiancy comparable to any warrior!"

Alainn clutched his hand tighter as she bit her lip and felt the heightening pressure in the lower part of her body.

Rory hurried toward her with an elderly woman at his side.

"This woman says she has assisted with many a birthing before, Killian."

His eyes were downcast and he would not look at Alainn. The old woman, whose gnarled hands surely suggested she was quite aged, knelt down with some difficulty, but it was managed with assistance from Rory. She appeared to be a meek sort, and Alainn found it reassuring the woman took her hand and kindly patted it a time or two before she began to attend to her laboring.

"The menfolk must be sent away from here," she insisted. "A birthing is no place for a man."

She had brought several cloths and warm blankets of various sizes and she covered Alainn. She felt immensely grateful for she was dreadfully cold at the moment she couldn't keep from shaking. When Killian remained seated beside his wife, the woman gestured for him to leave as well. Alainn's stuttered as her teeth chattered when she spoke.

"No, p-p-please, m-madam, allow-w-w-w my husband to s-s-s-st-t-t-tay with me."

The bent old woman leaned over and whispered in her ear.

"Tis a kindness to him, girl, to have him distanced from you during your ordeal, for if he cares for you as he appears to, he'll be disturbed to see you in pain during your time."

"Do you wish to be d-d-d-distanced from me for a time,

K-k-k-k-killian?" she rasped, "W-w-would it be easier for you?"

"By all that is holy, Alainn! That should not be a concern to you at the moment; what is easier for me should not be a consideration! Do you wish for me to remain here with you?"

"Aye, I do!" Her blue eyes revealed her fearfulness and it caused his heart to constrict.

"Then I'm not goin' anywhere!" He held tight to her hand as the woman shook her head in disagreement, but pulled Alainn's skirts to assess the progression of the labor.

The men had left them to allow them their privacy, but Rory stood with his back to them and held tight to a large blanket to shelter them from the cold wind.

By the typical calculation used of the sun's light being divided into twelve equal amounts each considered to be one hour, several hours had passed and Alainn felt the intense pain so fiercely, she thought she could bear it no longer. But she bit her lip and did not call out or scream or cuss as many women did when she'd witnessed babes being born. Killian had spoken to her lovingly and with such great compassion and caring throughout the entire time, she wanted to conceal the pain she was feeling so he would not bear any guilt for this. She finally made a strangled, moaning sound that must have frightened Killian for his eyes held a question as he looked at her.

"I feel a great need to bear down!" she insisted.

"Aye, soon enough, lass; just hold off another moment or two!" The old woman warned.

"Killian, I am most weary! I fear I can bear this no longer!"

"Aye, of course you can, my sweet, brave Lainna!"

She closed her eyes tightly and he saw the tears slowly slide down her cheeks. He drew nearer to her so his lips nearly touched her ear.

"My plight is greater!" he whispered with tears in his eyes as well.

She smiled through her obvious pain at that, for the very first day she had spoken to him, when they were only children, they'd played the game she had created. It had been something that bridged the gap of their vastly different stations in life, and they'd played it often times since then.

"Tell me how your plight is greater?" she whispered as the pain was clearly visible on her face and in her lovely blue eyes.

"I must simply sit by and watch you go through this torturous agony and if I could take away any of this pain and discomfort, I would gladly do so, Lainna, my only love!"

"Aye, but you do, Killian, by being here with me, by holding my hand and telling me you love me. You aptly take away my pain and comfort me, as always."

She groaned loudly again and the old woman finally permitted her to push.

After what seemed like an eternity by Killian's estimation

as he felt his hand being crushed with how tightly she was squeezing, he dared to allow himself to look between her parted thighs. He saw the small head was now visible as the child was finally beginning to be pushed from within her. He saw the light brown curls and he prayed all would be well, though deep within his heart he feared it would not.

His fears were further fueled by Alainn's words spoken between ragged breaths.

"Has the priest arrived, Killian? Have you any word on a priest?"

He tenderly wiped the sweat from her brow and kissed her forehead.

"Not yet, Lainna, but I'm certain Riley will discover one soon enough!"

He was alarmed at how much blood pooled on the blanket beneath her. He silently wished Danhoul Calhoun was here, for he had healed her before, and maybe he'd be capable of doing so again. He was startled when he looked up and saw Riley. And with him not only did he have a priest, but the very man he'd just wished to be here with them.

Chapter Thirty-Three

HAD HE WISHED it, he wondered? Had the young druid such powerful, magical abilities he was able to come to them by way of a wish? Could he then see to the safety of Alainn and the wee babe?

The old woman shooed them away and told them to give them the space required to bring the child into the world. Riley and the priest obeyed, the other man did not. He went and kneeled by Alainn's head and touched his hand to her middle.

"Don't attempt to heal me, Danhoul, 'tis the wee babe who is in grave danger. I feel it in my heart. Please do what you can for our son!"

At that moment, she moaned deeply and loudly cried out for the first time in all the hours she'd been laboring. It was nearly dusk when Killian saw his infant son born. He looked down at their wee babe who remained joined to Alainn's body. He was small; there was no disputing that, but not as small as some, Killian estimated. And he was not blue or lifeless as he'd feared he might be when Alainn seemed so distraught. He felt great relief and joy when he heard his wee son cry.

After the woman tended to the cutting and tying of the life cord, she passed the baby boy-child now wrapped in a blanket, to his mother. Alainn glanced at him with tears in her eyes and managed a weak smile. She kissed his head and his cheeks and touched his tiny fingers and with a deep and profound sadness, she passed him to Killian.

"No, you hold tight to him, Lainna! You've been longin' to hold him for all those many months!"

"Killian, you must hold your son now, you must look upon him now, I fear 'tis certain to be the only time you will have!" The ominous tone broke his heart and he dutifully took the child from his wife. He looked down at the tiny sweet face as he opened his deep blue eyes and looked up at him.

Alainn laid her hands to their son the entire time Killian held tight to him. He could see the determination on her face as she attempted to heal him or make health radiate through his small body. He saw her lovely face as it crumpled in complete despair and when Danhoul also attempted the healing and looked at Killian without a hint of hope in his eyes, he continued to pray. When the child's breathing became suddenly raspy, Alainn immediately called for the priest.

The baby was hastily blessed and baptized and then the tragic chain of events happened quickly. Killian couldn't bring himself to even attempt to come to terms with any of it. The gasps became shallower, considerably weaker, less and less frequent, and then stopped entirely. He felt the tears falling down his own cheeks, but when he looked at Alainn the expression in her eyes made his own grief seem trivial. For the complete and utter sadness and desolation was so evident, Killian had to turn away from her. But she did not weep, not one tear did she shed.

After what seemed an unbearably lengthy time had passed, Killian attempted to speak with Alainn, to tell her he must eventually take the child from her so that he could be readied to be laid to rest, but she clutched him tightly to her bosom, and he knew he must allow her this time with their child.

His heart broke further as he watched momentarily while she removed the blanket and looked upon all of him. She tenderly touched each one his perfectly formed tiny fingers and toes. She caressed his cheeks, his chin, and his soft curls, and then once more wrapped him lovingly in the blanket. She held him to her heart and softly rocked him and sang to him. It was then Killian needed to leave, had to be distanced from the bleak hopelessness and despair for a time. He walked to a nearby secluded grove and he fell to his knees overcome with insurmountable grief, painful sobs wracking his entire body.

He sensed someone behind him and he didn't care at the moment that he was not alone. When he saw it was Hugh O'Brien approaching, he looked away. At one time Killian had cared deeply for his uncle, before he'd attempted a great injustice toward Alainn, and tried to keep them from being together. Killian kept his eyes averted from the other man. But his uncle came to him, knelt beside him, firmly took him in his arms and held him securely in a strong embrace. Killian remembered back to when his Uncle Hugh had found him gravely injured on the battlefield the day his father's castle had been invaded. His uncle had held him just as tightly that day as well.

He knew Hugh and his wife had lost many newly born babies. He would recognize Killian's grief. Killian felt strangely comforted, though they spoke not a word.

⌘

WHEN KILLIAN RETURNED to where Alainn remained lying upon the ground, he saw the old woman still seemed intent on tending to his wife's maladies. Alainn held tight to the lifeless child in her arms. Killian slowly approached and knelt beside her.

He tenderly whispered to her. "You must let me take him and have him properly laid in the ground, Alainn."

"Not here, Killian. He must lie at your castle with your people, by your mother and brother and sister." Her voice sounded hollow and emotionless as she spoke the torturous words.

"Tis a goodly ride, Alainn! I'll go ahead then and take care of it. It will allow you to rest and recover. You can be taken to this good woman's cottage, for she has offered us that kindness."

"No, I will make the journey with you and our son. I, too, will see him properly laid to rest."

Killian did not want to argue with her, he did not want to push her on this, so he stood and called the old woman over to where they could speak privately.

"Is she well enough to make the journey?"

"The young man who claims to be a healer has touched her belly and tried to stop the bleeding, but still it persists. I would not suggest it is wise that your wife makes a long journey, but sure you must ask the young healer, he seems to be more learned than I."

Danhoul had barely left Alainn's side and, in truth, Killian believed his unusual powers and constant healing might be the only reason why Alainn had not died as well. He summoned him so that he could ask him his opinion.

"Will she make the journey; is she strong enough to manage it?"

"I can't say for certain, Killian. She has lost a great deal of blood, though I don't possess a wealth of experience in childbirth, by way of my abilities I know she's surely lost considerably more blood than most women when they birth a child. But if she isn't able to see your son laid to rest, I'm not sure she'll be able to accept it, if indeed she can accept it at all! If she is taken by cart at a deliberately gradual speed, and remains lying flat and as still as is possible, perhaps no further harm will befall her. It shall make the journey longer, but will be less perilous for her, by my estimation."

"Then we'll start out as soon as we're able, Danhoul."

"You bear me no ill will for not bein' able to save your wee boy?"

Killian's green eyes were filled with obvious pain, but he spoke with candor. "No, Danhoul, if you and Alainn were not able to save our wee child even with employing your magical healing abilities, then I suppose it was God's will to take him."

"I'd not speak those words to Alainn at the moment, Killian! I suspect she'll need a great deal of time to come to term with whose will it was that caused this tragedy."

"How did you know to come here to aid us?"

"I heard Alainn's summoning thoughts. I sensed her grief and felt her pain and though I have been known to journey by way of magic as does she, when I attempted it I was entirely unable. I started out on horseback as soon as I knew she needed assistance."

"Aye, well, 'tis grateful I am to you, Danhoul!"

"My sincerest and deepest sympathy to you, Killian, for I know how much the wee child meant to you, to the both of you. It is my hope you might seek a united solace, that you grieve this loss together!"

IT WAS THE longest, most difficult journey he'd ever made,

Killian concluded as he drove the cart that held his ailing wife and the body of their child. She held tight to him. Though he was wrapped in a blanket and his face hidden from view, Killian felt so severely sickened by his own loss and Alainn's great misery, he thought he could not bear the insufferable injustice of it all. And when he heard her humming tenderly to the child as though he still lived, he wanted to leap off that cart and be gone from the entire morbid scene, but he drove on, and they arrived at Castle O'Donnel at twilight.

He'd had Riley go ahead to inform Niall and Mary of the happenings. He also asked him to have the sexton and the castle priest ready when they arrived. He'd told him to find an able man to create a tiny casket for the babe, for since William McCree's death no actual carpenter had been located.

The moon was full when the cart stopped and Danhoul jumped out with more force than Killian could hope to muster. Riley took Killian's arm and helped him down from the seat for he felt as though his legs could barely hold him. He saw Rory had followed on his horse and his Uncle Hugh stood there as well. Killian went to Alainn and lifted her from the cart while she still held their son. It was not usual to have a service and burial at night, but Killian reasoned if it was not done now, he wasn't certain the child could ever be taken from her arms. When he lifted her from the cart he noticed the warm wetness beneath his hand, and he saw the blankets where she had been lying were thoroughly soaked with blood. He gravely feared for her and for himself should he lose her as well.

"Alainn, I must take you to our chambers where Eibhein can see to your healing."

"No, Killian," she said in barely more than a whisper. "Not yet, we must first go to the churchyard! I must see it done as well!"

He carried her the entire way though he felt as weary as he ever had in his life. And when they reached the location he found Connor MacLain standing near the open grave and he saw the wee casket waiting there. Alainn held her head tight against his chest and she appeared to notice nothing or no one. When Killian gently set her to standing, Mary placed her arms around Alainn and sobbed openly. Eireen touched her cheek and Niall tenderly patted her shoulder, but Alainn did not look at them, she did not speak or acknowledge their presence. When the sexton came to her with the intention of taking the child, she pulled the child closer to her, and would not permit it.

Killian once more felt his heart being shredded. He went to her, kissed her head, and gently took the child from her. He knew she would have allowed him and him alone to take the babe from her arms. And the sad look she gave him was so mournful he would have gladly changed the day's events and gone back to him being the one that died that day, if he could have given her back their child alive and well. But he took the body of the wee infant and placed him on the soft white blanket within the small coffin himself. He wrapped him carefully and lovingly in the soft fabric, and placed a kiss upon his fingers and then upon the blanketed body of the wee babe. Then he went back to Alainn and held tight to her while Cian Donnel O'Brien was laid to rest having lived on this earth for less than one hour.

But he had been baptized so he was allowed to lie on holy ground with Killian's mother's kin. And through the entire service while most everyone around them was openly weeping and many pitifully sobbing, Killian looked down at Alainn and saw her eyes now stared blankly straight ahead, with a vapid, emptiness about them that disturbed him as much as the loss of their baby. When the wee coffin was placed in the ground, the dirt placed upon it, and filled in entirely, only then would Alainn allow Killian to take her to their bedchamber.

Chapter Thirty-Four

"SHE'S LOST A perilous amount of blood, milord, and she's not through with the bleedin' yet."

He heard Eibhein, the midwife's dire words and he saw Danhoul sat with his hands upon her middle attempting to heal her, but he believed Alainn wanted no part of being healed or getting well. It had been three days. She'd not spoken, not eaten, barely permitted sips of water to be placed on her lips, and still she had not wept. And that bothered him more than each of the other truths. When Danhoul walked toward him, his face a mask of grave worry, Killian felt consumed with a sense of impending doom.

"She fights me on this, Killian. For every attempt I make at healin' her, I believe she resists and she thwarts it. She does not appear to want to recover. In truth, I doubt she desires to live through this!"

Killian had thought that very notion for the past day and a half. When, with every attempt he made to speak to her or console her, she seemed to withdraw further and further within herself. He believed if he she didn't slip away due to the considerable blood loss, he might lose her to madness!

On the fifth day, when she became filled with fever, and her eyes closed, he thought he would go mad himself with agonizing grief and worry. Mary sat with her and wept ceaselessly and he thought Danhoul looked like he might break down himself. He knew how close the boy had grown to Alainn and he thought it quite likely he was in love with her. He couldn't even make himself feel angry about that, for the young man had tried for hours on end each day to heal Alainn and assist in bringing her back to this world, for surely she was not here in mind.

Killian never left her side, he tried to talk to her though he was uncertain if his words got to whatever place her mind and heart were now. He'd had Rory ride to Castle O'Brien to fetch Alainn's mother, in hopes Mara might heal her and, in the event she couldn't be healed, to allow her to look upon her daughter once more.

When Mara arrived she looked weary and disheartened, but she readily embraced her son-in-law and then went to Alainn's side. She appeared distraught when she touched her skin.

"She's nearly on fire! Sure 'tis childbed fever, I must send everyone away momentarily so that I might assess her condition.

Even Killian left them alone and when Mara came out of the chamber, she wore an expression of hopelessness and gloom.

"It is childbed fever, as I suspected. Her body has become most purulent, the fever rages because of it, and the damage is most severe. If she survives this which I confess, I believe is perhaps doubtful at best…" Her words trailed off and Killian finished for her.

"She'll not carry a child again." He said in a pained tone.

"Aye, 'tis unlikely. And I believe if my daughter had the slightest will to survive it would be most helpful, for I believe not only does she not care to survive this, she does not intend to live through this! There are some herbal remedies I might employ to assist with the fever and the purulence, but I tell you plain, I cannot hope to heal her by way of my magic if the young druid healer isn't able, for his abilities now far surpass my own."

"What can be done then; what can I do, Mara? I have talked to her both before and after she fell unconscious. I have told her how much I need her to come back to me; that together we can survive this tragedy!"

"But have you told her you forgive her?"

"Forgive her, why ever would I need to forgive her?"

"She blames herself entirely for your son's death. I hear it even now in her muddled and desperate thoughts."

"You must come quickly!" It was Mary who beckoned them back into the room.

Alainn's body was twitching violently. Danhoul appeared to be attempting to calm her, but to no avail. Killian's heart ached, but his anger flared as well. He put his hand on her cheek and he pulled it away in great alarm.

"Christ, 'tis true, she's burnin' up! We must cool her down somehow."

He thought of the frozen ground outside. For ever since they'd arrived back to their castle an unusual coldspell had hit, and the ground had been covered with bitter frost each morning. The pond near the north solar had been covered with ice this morning. He startled everyone in the room when he took Alainn in his arms and started carrying her out of the bedchamber.

"What do you intend to do, Killian?" Mary asked.

Mara said nothing, but she followed close behind. Soon Danhoul was striding beside him as well.

"What are you doing, Killian?" He questioned with concern in his voice.

He answered no one, but continued on with determined steps. When he reached the pond, he saw the ice had melted, but it was surely still severely cold.

He startled everyone further when he walked to his knees within the frigid water and then immersed Alainn beneath the ice water and held her there. Danhoul attempted to dissuade him.

"The extreme temperature difference may very well stop your wife's heart!" He sternly warned. "You're liable to kill her!"

"Aye, well I suspect she's on death's door now, at any rate!" Killian raged.

Mary was crying fitfully. Mara stood by and waited, for

she knew well enough what he was doing might be necessary and perhaps even beneficial.

Killian's voice was filled with anger and exasperation as he began to speak to his young wife. "You want to be dead, then I'll appease you woman! You long to go to the beyond and leave me to mourn the death of both of you; so be it!" His voice came out in ragged sobs.

"Killian O'Brien, you horrid man; leave her alone, this is unforgivable and unthinkable!" Mary hollered as she stood on the edge of the pond.

He turned and blared at her. "This is unforgivable; if you recall it was only weeks ago you wished Alainn dead, Mary O'Brien!"

The words hit her as surely as if the man had slapped her in the face and she stepped back in dismay.

When Alainn started coughing and sputtering, Danhoul spoke next. "Killian, 'tis enough, remove her from the water now!" When Killian continued holding her in the icy water, Danhoul threateningly rebuked him. "Killian, you must discontinue your present actions or I swear I'll run you through with my sword, for strong as you might be, you'll surely not be able to hold Alainn under the water and offer me much battle."

"Well perhaps you'd be doin' me a kind favor at that, Danhoul!"

There was unhidden anguish in Killian's voice, but relief in his eyes when Alainn had finally started fighting him. She was slapping at his arms and although it was ineffectual in her weakened condition, it was enough to show him she still had some fight left in her, that somewhere deep within her, even in her despairing state and failing health, she maintained the will to survive.

He pulled her out of the frigid water as she shivered and shook, but continued to hit at him. And he felt so completely overcome with emotion he passed his drenched and shivering young wife to Danhoul, and headed toward the stables where he could be alone with his own sorrow.

He prayed she would truly survive this grave malady and fully recover. After all they had been through, he hoped that one day they would meet this unspeakable tragedy together and, in so doing, perhaps their once powerful and passionate love would be renewed once more.

Chapter Thirty-Five

"THIS IS REPREHENSIBLE, Mara!" Mary offered her empassioned opinion, "In truth, it is ludicrous! I dinna ken why Alainn insists on spending all her days and nights in that dreadful tower. There are no windows, the bed is small and hard, she may as well sleep upon the stone floor, and the hearth is surely of an ineffectual proportion to the chamber. The pitifully small fire does not offer any comfort."

"Aye, well, 'tis certain the chamber was only intended to hold prisoners or to be used by soldiers during rare times of invasions by opposing clans. There are no windows as it was meant to keep out the enemy, only the narrow slits that would allow arrows to be propelled at oncoming invading armies. The tower was not built for comfort."

"Why does Alainn not sleep in her own grand bedchamber, and why do Killian and Alainn barely speak to each other? They should be sharing their grief and comforting each other. It has been almost a moon since they lost the bairn and nearly a fortnight that she's spent in that damnable chamber. And why doesn't Killian simply insist she come out of there? She just sits staring into nothingness; she won't even speak to me."

"I am much aware, Mary, you are rightly concerned for her, for both of them, as am I. But grief is a lonely, desolate emotion and not everyone approaches it in the same manner. Alainn purposely chose the unpleasant tower chamber. I would suggest she is doing penance for the guilt she feels in losing the child. She blames herself, and Killian can't come to terms with it, for although he feels guilt as well, I believe a part of him does blame Alainn. And she knows that well enough. Until he can forgive her, I doubt they shall ever make it through this. And Alainn has in no way begun to accept her grief. Killian tells me she has not yet shed a tear for her lost wee son. And, until she does, her heart will not ever begin to heal."

Mary dabbed her swollen eyes with her handkerchief and listened as Mara spoke on.

"Alainn is also an empath which indicates she feels others pain. When in the presence of others who are saddened over the loss of the babe, she experiences their pain. When Killian is near her she endures his pain as well as her own, and it is an insufferable sorrow to bear. I believe she has begun to numb herself so she feels nothing. And you needn't take it personally that she will not see or speak with you for Alainn has scarcely uttered two words to me in these weeks I have been here."

"Killian tells me you soon intend to journey back to Castle O'Brien. How could you possibly think of leaving Alainn?

Do ye not think it would be best to stay until your daughter is healed?"

"If I thought my being here was assisting her even in the vaguest manner, I would stay for as long as I was needed, but Alainn and I have never been close, not really. I have loved her with all my heart throughout her life, but she has not yet forgiven me for giving her to others when she was only an infant. I did it to ensure she had a better life, but no matter the reason, she feels I abandoned her. I know she was anticipating motherhood with immense joy. It saddens my heart beyond measure to know that she may never be allowed that great pleasure now!"

"For certain, there'll never be other children if she and Killian are seldom in the same room together, they won't be sharing a bed any time soon. And they had such a grand passion for one another."

"In time, I'm certain it will be restored."

"You ladies appear deep in conversation!" It was Killian who had approached them in the great hall and Mary started at his deep voice.

"What do you have in your arms?" She questioned.

"Tis a dog... a setter. McEwan's bitch had a litter of puppies. I was wonderin' if Alainn might care to see one. I know wee animals often offer comfort, and Alainn has always had such a deep affection for animals. I know how she's missed havin' a dog around since she lost Wolf!"

"Since you stabbed it through the heart!" Mara stated in

an accusatory tone.

"Well it was goin' to kill my wife; I had little choice!" Killian bristled.

"Aye, so I'm told, but did my daughter forgive you for it then, for slaying her valued animal when she understood the reason for it?"

"Aye, of course she did. It hurt her, but she did!"

Realization dawned on his handsome face. "Are you comparin' the loss of an old dog to the loss of our wee son; for if you are then I'll not be wantin' to carry on with this conversation, Mara, by Christ?"

"I'm only talkin' about forgiveness, no matter what the reason. 'Tis a most powerful inducement to the healin' to be forgiven for what deeds a person feels entirely responsible for. What if you wife had caused you to feel guilty for slaying her cherished dog even knowing it couldn't be helped, even knowing that you did what you felt you must?"

"She had a choice, Mara. Alainn surely had a choice, and I'll not discuss this further."

"And if she'd chosen differently, lest it be in the beyond, you'd not be discussin' anything ever again, Killian O'Brien!"

Killian's rancor was evident on his face and he set the small animal down upon the floor as he marched angrily toward Mara.

"Mary, I would ask you to leave Mara and I alone for a time, for sure you'd rather not hear the remainder of this discussion!"

Mary's brown eyes grew wide, but she obeyed and left the hall in great haste. Killian waited until he was certain the other woman could hear no more of what was being said. He towered over Mara as he stood beside her.

"Do you think I'm not well aware Alainn saved my life; and the lives of a hundred men or more from many clans? Do you think I don't know she willfully made the choice because of her great love for me? And do you know the guilt I feel in realizing the pain she is sufferin' is actually because of me? And, in truth, I can't make myself feel glad she made the choice she did. You might think me a callous, unfeeling man but, no, I can't forgive her for it, not yet! For 'tis a man that is supposed to protect his woman, and sure 'tis up to a mother to keep her unborn child safe!"

"Back at Castle O'Brien when my daughter was poisoned and dying and I asked you if I should administer the antidote knowing it would surely kill the child, you had no qualms giving it to her. You obviously held her life in higher regard than the child!"

"'Tis not comparable in the least, Mara! The child would have died either way, in that instance. I would have lost both of them!"

"Aye, well, truth be told, I don't think Alainn intended to live though this. I believe she thought if she lost the child she, too, would die, and then she would not have been made to live with the guilt she feels now, or the guilt you inflict upon her!"

"I've never let her know I hold her responsible in any way. I've never even admitted it to myself, so I'm not sure why I'm declarin' it to you this day."

"Because you need to speak aloud of your grief and loss as does Alainn, and if you can't do so, if you aren't able to soon work through it together, to mend your hearts together, the greater the chance you never will. And that would be a travesty, for the two of you share a love few lay claim to."

Killian was silent for a time as he tried to take in all the woman words when she spoke once more.

"She speaks to your priest on occasion; I think she finds some solace in that! You might try the same, for I recall how your prayers aided you at Castle O'Brien when Alainn was near death."

"Aye, well, I don't feel so inclined to speak with the priest or with God at the moment!"

"So 'tis great anger you feel toward God and everyone, includin' Alainn! Well, 'tis something I suppose, for Alainn allows herself to feel nothing bar guilt. She will need to embrace her own hidden anger, and then her deeply buried sorrow and sure you will be the only one who can ensure she is made to feel both. My presence here is not necessary, Killian O'Brien, for I can do nothing to heal her heart; that is entirely up to you."

"Christ, I don't begin to know how to allow my own heart to heal, what help can I be to Alainn?"

"Just go to her and tell her you love her; that would be a

tremendous beginning toward her healing."

He did not answer, but appeared deep in thought.

"When was the last time you saw her, Killian?" Mara quizzed.

He seemed disinclined to respond.

"I'd suggest it has been days, and I'd wager it's been a good deal longer since you actually looked at her. You might do that, for I fear you'd find her condition most disturbing!"

"What do you indicate by that? Danhoul told me she was beginning to heal."

"Aye, her fever has gone, her bleeding has nearly stopped and the purulence seems to have lessened, to be certain. But you should actually let your eyes fall upon her and then decide for yourself if she is on the path to healing! And be warned, the fire must be kept constantly burning in the tower's chamber."

Killian bent to retrieve the whining puppy who now sat at his feet. He noticed the many wet messes upon the floor.

Mara observed them as well and commented. "Alainn is not yet ready or capable of caring for anyone or anything as she is not doin' an adequate job of carin' for herself at the moment, but it is hoped one day she will."

Killian was obviously deep in thought as he turned away from the woman.

"Have you heard that Thomas O'Donaugh, your uncle's physician, has proposed marriage to me?"

He looked back at her as he responded. "No, I didn't

know that, Mara. So have you accepted then?"

"No, I am thinkin' on it, but in my heart I still love Alainn's father and I still hold on to the far-off hope he might one day return. I know how foolhearted that must sound, when it has been past eighteen years he has been gone now. Part of me wants to have the presence of a man in my life, the warmth of a man in my bed, but I know within my heart, there is really only one man I'll ever love. And I'm not sure I can do that to Thomas, to join our fates when I can't love him entirely."

"Tis a difficult decision, I'm certain!" Killian's eyes held some warmth and understanding as he looked at his wife's mother.

"You know the druid and magical healer, young Danhoul, has deep feelings toward my daughter? Don't push her away and force her to seek comfort in his arms."

"She would not!" Killian sounded appalled at the very suggestion.

"Men seek comfort for broken hearts in the beds of other women most regularly. Don't take too long to forgive her, Killian, for you would be loath to lose her, and she you!"

"I'll take that into consideration, Mara!" he said as he carried the yelping puppy out the door.

⌘

THE REST OF that day, Killian's thoughts were filled almost entirely with the conversation he'd had with Mara. She'd been correct about one thing for certain. He was angry! So angry, he felt ready to break into an uncommon rage most of the time. His temper was harsh and quick and he could barely bring himself to be near Alainn for his anger was not only directed at God and the English, but at her as well. And he was ashamed to think he couldn't actually remember the last time he'd looked in on Alainn. Had it been days?

Eireen and Mara diligently cared for her, and Danhoul had healed her to the best of his ability. He was aware Mary visited daily. But it nagged at him when he recalled Mara speaking of Alainn's present physical state and finally, later that evening, he decided he would check in on her when he completed his ledgers. But, as he sat at his large table, as he worked at the many figures, drinking his whiskey, he found himself nodding off, and then he fell into an unusually deep sleep, the first time since their tragedy had occurred.

Somewhere in the distance, he was almost certain he heard several loud voices shouting and the urgent pounding of fists upon doors, but he couldn't seem to make himself wake up.

Chapter Thirty-Six

A S HIS HEAD rested upon his arms, Killian began to hear
a persistent tapping beside him. He felt some annoyance at this, for he simply longed to remain in this long
desired deep sleep. And then he felt his tunic being tugged
upon, his arm being repeatedly poked, and soon after his hair
being pulled. With great difficulty, he was riled when he
sleepily roused and was startled to see a spirit girl before him.

"Finally, you awaken from the spell placed upon you,
and the potion you have consumed. Surely the dead waken
with less effort. Your wife is in immediate peril and you must
go to her at once!" The wispy blonde spirit ordered as she
once more tugged upon his sleeve, and then took his large
hand in her own and attempted to pull him to a standing
position.

Killian felt as though he was suffering the undesirable
effects of entirely too much drink, when in recollection he
had only had one small drink of whiskey as he had sat
working on his ledgers. He was bleary-eyed and unstable
upon his feet as he stumbled after the spirit girl as she floated
ahead of him and started up the winding steps.

"You must walk faster, O'Brien, sure you moved swifter as a wee boy just learning to walk, back when I spent time with you so long ago."

Killian shook his head and attempted to make sense of the spirit's words. "Who are you?" he managed though his tongue was thick and his words slurred.

"I am Shylie."

"Shylie O'Rorke, but sure you died many years ago!"

"Aye, you were but one year of age when I met my misfortune in the woods that border your lands and my father's. It was an evil being who took my life and who attempts to harm your wife this night."

Killian felt some urgency within his mind but, in his muddled state, he wasn't certain he understood the spirit's meaning, and he certaintly couldn't will his body to move any faster as he made his way up the many winding steps. He felt his head reeling as his eyes closed, as he fought the need to return to sleep. He finally lowered himself to the stone steps, incapacitated by the dizziness and inability to capably lift his feet.

"A strong potion was placed in your drink this night, O'Brien, and a potent spell placed on the castle. Your wife's mother and the young druid have been locked within their chambers by a dark magical spell. No one hears their shouts or their pounding. The druid cannot even summon his own magical powers. He has injured his shoulder in a courageous attempt to break down the door and he has even contemplated jumping from the window in his chambers, only to learn there is a barrier keeping him sealed within.

The humans all sleep an unnatural slumber, 'tis only you I could rouse because your wife has made you somewhat immune to magic, it is hopeful you can save her this night. But you must waken fully and you must do it now!"

Killian heard the young spirit's words, but it was as though through a thick far-off fog, and they echoed unnaturally. He simply wished to lie down even there upon the cold, stone steps his desire for sleep was so overpowering. He shook his head and placed his hands on the stone steps, trying to steady himself and stop the disturbing dizziness, or perhaps resort to crawling up the steps, when he saw another specter materialize beside the other.

"And who might you be?" he asked once more in slurred tone.

"My name is Deidra, although that is of little consequence at the moment, for you've never known me. I've been gone from this earth for well over a thousand years. You must awaken, O'Brien. It is imperative you awaken now!"

"Why does the spirit of my mother not come to me to aid me?' he asked in a manner that was almost incomprehensible, but nonsensically typical of one who was too filled with drink.

The two spirits looked at one another uncertain how to improve the current situation.

"Your mother would surely avail you if it was a possibility. Young Shylie and I possessed magical abilities and druid gifts in life, which we have carried with us to the spirit world, so we are capable of opposing the dark spell on the castle and appearing before you."

"If you're both magical spirits why can't you get to Alainn straightaway and prevent her from harm?"

"The chamber was charmed by the young druid to ensure no one meaning harm to your wife could enter, but the dark one has altered the spell so that no one possessing magical abilities can enter."

Killian sensed the deep urgency in their voices and the thought of a dark being anywhere near Alainn caused his heart to fill with fear. He stood once more though he teetered dangerously and remained noticeably unsteady on his feet.

"He'll be of no assistance if he cracks his head on the stone steps or stumbles and breaks his neck!" The spirit Deidre spoke loudly to the emptiness around them.

Then a great glowing light formed at the top of the last winding stairwell which led to the tower chambers. In his muddled seemingly inebriated state, he rubbed his eyes, wondering if all that he was seeing was purely a disturbingly real dream. But then from within the glow of light he recognized the figure of the Celtic goddess Aine appear before him.

"Why did you not come before this? I have been summoning you for a time now?" Deidra scolded the goddess.

"There is little time for explanation. The realm of the gods is in chaotic uproar. All gods have been forbidden to enter the human realm at this time."

She glanced at the man who remained on his hands and knees on the steps, his eyes attempting to see her, but it was obvious he could not focus clearly.

"Go now, O'Brien, or it will be too late, for a dark being lures Alainn to him and she is at present incapable of fighting him."

Aine placed her hand to his forehead and he became coherent once more.

Killian stood, shook his head, made his way up to the top of the steps and continued on down the now dark corridor.

Both the spirit women seemed relieved at that. Shylie smiled at him and then all three of the females were simply gone.

Killian wondered if it had truly all been a dream or his imagination, for he could sense no urgency. As he stood outside the tower room he listened, but could hear nothing, it seemed almost unnaturally quiet even for the middle of the night. Yet, as he placed his ear to the door, he was nearly certain he heard a low whisper, an eerie unrecognizable voice. He pondered how he would be capable of opening the door if it had been magically sealed shut by someone with dark powers and even spirits and a goddess could not enter, but he met with no resistance. He swiftly threw open the door and charged within.

Chapter Thirty-Seven

A S HE OPENED the door he thought he caught the glimpse of an unusual shadow upon the wall, and a feeling of dread encompassed him. Without hesitation, he walked toward the location where he had seen the shadow. He heard a whoosh as if a gust of wind had icily blown through the chamber, and up through the hearth's chimney. He blinked his eyes several times for the shadow, and with it apparently the dark threat, seemed to have simply disappeared entirely.

Killian looked around the chamber feeling completely confused and uncertain what had just transpired. He seemed unable to recall why it had been so imperative he get to Alainn. As his thoughts went to Alainn, he felt further unrest for he could not immediately see her and as his eyes searched the area he assessed the dark chamber.

One candle burned on the stand. No window was present in this tower room and the air smelled dank and musty. A small unadorned bed sat in the room. When he drew nearer to the bed, he saw only one thin blanket, which surely would not keep Alainn warm at night for she was often cold and needed him to hold her and warm her to take away her chill. The guilt returned to him at knowing she spent her nights alone in this dismal place.

Only the tiny candle provided any light for the turf fire had burned out almost entirely, but for a few glowing embers. The room was reminiscent of the chamber she'd lived in all her life at Castle O'Brien, although larger in size. The small hearth offered little warmth and he noticed the deep, unearthly chill in the room. He finally spied Alainn huddled against the far wall. For an instant, the spirit woman Deidra materialized before Alainn and the spectral glow surrounded both of them. As he drew nearer, the spirit simply disappeared again.

When he approached Alainn, he noticed she did not turn to look at him, but remained looking straight ahead. How tiny and forlorn she appeared! Even as he crouched beside her she did not seem remotely aware of his presence.

"Alainn?" he softly called her name.

Still there was no response or barely any indication she was actually alive.

He took the nearby candle and held it to her face to look upon her as Mara had suggested he might.

He gasped at the sight of how thin and frail she'd become. Her hair, tightly pulled back from her face, looked drab and lacked the luster it always held. He gently clasped her small pointed chin and turned her face toward him. He saw how pallid her complexion was, and he realized her eyes

were dim as well and they held a vacant stare. That frightened him as much as the thought of losing her to death, or
perhaps even to the demon, for he'd heard of people who
were lost forever to all-consuming grief that ended in
madness.

He returned the candle to the stand and carefully lifted
her to him.

"By Christ!" He exclaimed as he felt how light she was in
his arms and he noticed how sharp her bones seemed to be.
How had he let this happen? It had barely been a moon, but
he couldn't estimate how much weight she'd lost in that
time. He knew Cookson had told him her trays were returned barely touched, but he'd had little appetite himself
since their child had died, so he had not fretted knowing she
did not eat heartily. He found himself growing angrier and
wanting to lay blame for her failing condition.

When he headed down the winding steps with Alainn in
his arms, he noticed how she shivered and shook. He held
her tighter and she emitted a gasp that sounded as though
she was in pain. He met Mara on the steps, she had frantically been on her way to see her daughter, he glared at the
woman even as she spoke.

"My door was mysteriously locked; magically locked, I
would presume. I could not get to her for all my attempts,
magical or otherwise. I was fearful for her and what would
happen if the fire was allowed to die out!" She cried.

"Aye, it would seem there was some form of malevolence

present this night."

Killian felt his emotions reaching dangerous levels and his body and head both felt as though he had been through a lengthy arduous battle. His mouth was filled with an acrid taste. His head throbbed, his arms ached, and his legs felt leaden. As he looked down at Alainn, who remained limp in his arms, her eyes open, but revealing no emotion, he felt his temper flaring once more.

"Why the hell did no one tell before this day that Alainn was in such a dismal state? She is the wife of a chieftain, how could she have been allowed her to slip into such utter desolation?"

Mara's own temper rose at his accusatory ranting as they made their way downward. "We all told you she fared poorly, Killian O'Brien. Every one of us. Mary, Eireen, Danhoul, even the young cook, but you choose to ignore us, and to be consumed in your own despair and bitter anger!"

"I understand she hasn't wanted to eat, but I didn't know she was starvin' herself into the grave... and what of her hair and her clothes? She has always adored bathing and taken pride in keeping herself clean and well-groomed. Why did no one see to these things if she was not capable herself?"

"She is doing penance, Killian. She seeks atonement for what she believes she's caused, and she will do nothing that offers her the slightest comfort or pleasure. Would you have us force her? Would you force food down her throat, force the bathing and grooming, when she cares so little about anything at the moment?"

"Aye, you're damn well correct I'd force it!"

Danhoul heard the raised voices as he finally burst forth from his chambers once his door was simply unlocked. He held tight to his injured shoulder and hurried to the others, soon finding himself in the middle of the bitter dispute and the brunt of Killian's rage as well.

"You were supposed to be healing her, man! Does she look healed in any way? In truth, she looks as though she's on death's door!"

"Considering all that has happened, the uncommonly dark magic that has overtaken the entire castle this night, you should be thankful Alainn still lives. For I couldn't get to her even when I employed my powers, and neither could her mother. I could not make my voice heard and no amount of calling to Alainn through telepathy seemed effective."

Killian knew he should be filled with relief, but when he continued to stare down at Alainn, he felt his emotions and his temper soar. Danhoul noticed and spoke on further in explanation.

"Although I am not much learned in herbal concoctions, I know some and I suspect you were given a potion to make you fall into a deep sleep. I can detect the scent of valerian root upon you. Alone in small quantities, it simply is known to make sleep come easier, but in greater quantities and mixed with other herbs, with whiskey or ale or the like, it becomes a powerful sedative. Many do not waken if too much is consumed. 'Tis often a competent way to commit murder or suicide."

Killian despaired in realizing how close he had come to losing Alainn again. "I suppose it is grateful I am then, that two spirits and a goddess were able to assist us this night."

"Aye, I envisioned the two female spirits here this night, both filled with the sole intent of keeping Alainn safe, and it is only because of them and the fact you are mostly immune to harmful magic that this night had a fortunate outcome." Danhoul revealed. "It was surely the spirits' insistence and Mara's and my pleas that summoned Aine. She is certain to suffer dire consequences for crossing the worlds to the human realm, when it was presently disallowed, but 'tis most fortunate she came to Alainn's aid."

Killian wanted to simply be exceedingly grateful, but as always, feeling entirely ineffectual in dealing with supernatural happenings and magic beings, Killian fully intended to put his efforts into dictating and handling what aspects of Alainn's life he was able to control. He could see to her well-being.

Killian looked down at Alainn's failing condition. His anger overtook his clear thought.

He snapped at Danhoul again. "How could she have gotten to this forlorn state, she appears to be near death?"

"That is precisely where she desires to be, Killian! In truth, perhaps she did hear my warnings this night and was simply beyond caring, for I doubt anything matters to her at the moment. And you've no one to blame save yourself for her present state!" Danhoul finally returned Killian's displeasure and harsh words, and Mara concurred.

"Aye, we'll share some of the blame for her present condition, but there's only so much we can do without your assistance, Killian. And if you're not willin' to do your part then you might well have allowed her to die from the fever, for it might have been a kinder death, then starvin' herself or wishin' herself dead! And better by far than falling prey to a demon."

Killian had taken her to their bedchamber and still held her in his arms though it was clear he wasn't entirely certain what should be done for her. When Eireen dizzily floundered into the chamber to find the source of the angry shouts and raised voices, she visibly appeared unable to fully waken as well.

Killian finally resorted to hollering loudly to everyone around him.

"Get the servants to fill the tub with very warm water for she likes to soak in a bath. And find some of the soaps and balms she uses for she was always insistent on bein' clean. Her hair is in need of washing and brushing. Mara, you and Eireen must tend to her cleanliness. And bring her some food. She surely needs to take sustenance. Find something she will eat."

He continued to hold her as the Eireen then capably delegated the tasks to the many bewildered servants who came when summoned in the middle of the night. Mara became most displeased with Killian's demands and once more offered her opinion without holding back.

"Sure you should revel in the fact your wife is not in the demon's grasp this night! And you can see to it that her body is cared for. Maybe that will ease your guilty conscious and despairing heart, Killian O'Brien, but the water and the soaps won't cleanse her soul, and the food won't allow her to find retribution for what sins she feels she has committed!" Mara spewed.

Killian's green eyes filled with uncertainty and he was startled to hear Alainn speak when she had appeared oblivious to everything around her. Her voice was quiet and gravely weakened, but he was further aggrieved to learn she was speaking in his defense.

"Don't flay him, Mara, nor you, Danhoul! No man should be laden with the responsibility of bein' wed to the likes of me. Do not dare judge him for truly you've no notion what a great encumbrance and burden I am with all the unnatural and possibly unholy abilities I possess."

For a brief moment, he thought he saw a spark of life within those lovely blue eyes, and it briefly made his heart soar, but ache as well. The room was soon filled with servants scurrying about tending to the tasks he had ordered in an uncommonly demanding fashion. No one commented on Alainn's words, and he gently sat her upon the bed, trying to ignore the sharpness of her bones and her uncontrollable shivering.

"I will return shortly!" he said as he, Danhoul, and the servants left her alone with Mara and Eireen.

⌘

THE HEARTH FIRE was roaring and the entire chamber unusually warm as Alainn sat in the bath. She was vaguely aware of Eireen washing her back and Mara soaping her hair. She could scarcely feel the water around her so numb had she allowed herself to become. And as they dried her and dressed her in a warm nightdress, she simply allowed it for she found it difficult to even hold up her head. She was so weary, so tired of this existence. She heard Eireen weeping and some distant part of her felt badly for the woman whom she'd once thought of as a friend. That seemed so long ago, as though it was in another life, in another time. Now she could feel little emotion, she could ill afford to feel anything, for if she did, she believed she could not possibly endure it. After Eireen left the room Mara sat upon the bed with Alainn.

"Did you sense the dark one with you this night?"

Alainn shook her head and shivered so severely, Mara discontinued speaking on the abhorrent topic.

A small platter of food had be brought to them, cheese and scones, sweet cakes that were surely placed there by Cookson. Alainn nibbled at the food at her mother's insistence. It felt heavy and tasteless in her mouth, and she gagged when she attempted to swallow. Mara passed her a goblet of water and she slowly sipped. She disliked the sensation of the food and water as it found its way to her stomach so long empty. She felt as though she might spew, and she attempted to still the need.

They sat together as Mara brushed out her long hair. It occurred to Alain it was the first time her mother had ever brushed her hair. In the nearly eight and ten years she'd lived on this earth, her mother had never brushed her hair.

"'Twas Killian's mother's brush!" She heard herself say and thought how meaningless the words were. Her voice felt irritated so long had she been silent.

"It's lovely!" her mother replied.

"Aye, she was a kind and gentle woman... and very beautiful in appearance as well. I have seen her spirit here often. Most recently I saw her holding our babe in the churchyard. I thought to tell Killian, but wasn't certain if it would bring him comfort or simply cause more uneasiness with these damnable abilities I possess!"

"I think it would comfort him, Alainn. He's never appeared to be unreasonable regarding your powers. In truth, he has seemed unusually accepting of them."

"Aye, well, that was before they were the cause of his son's death!"

Mara moved from the bed and stared down into her daughter's eyes as she spoke. "But you are not entirely certain it was the use of your powers that caused the tragedy, Alainn.

You have not yet told your husband of the skullcap you were given that might have been the actual reason for the loss of your child."

"Aye, but it was me who chose to use my powers even knowing there had already been bleeding, so perhaps it was not the powers, but only me, who caused the death our child. 'Tis of little use revealing these truths to Killian, or debating the actual cause; whether me or the powers I possess, for they are one and the same, I suppose"

"There are those who would believe the curse remains, and suggest that is what took your child's life," Mara admitted.

Alainn registered little emotion when she replied. "The curse is ended. I feel it in my bones." Alainn assured her.

"But 'tis understandable that people might draw that conclusion. No O'Brien child has been born since the curse was allegedly ended. There are those who have suffered gravely because of it, and it has been whispered among gossipmongers that perhaps justice has been served, that it was befitting my grandchild would be taken by the very curse that I placed upon the O'Brien line, that my kin should be the last victim of my damnable curse."

"It was not the curse that took my baby's life. I am most certain of that, so you needn't bear any guilt on the death of my babe. It was only me, and my abilities. And how evil a woman am I to have used my powers in a way that would endanger my unborn child, our own precious wee son!"

"You used them to save your man, and the lives of a more than a hundred other men. No one can flay you for that, Alainn! Anyone who knows you realizes what an uncommonly great love you and Killian share."

"Shared!" She corrected. "He feels little for me at the moment, bar resentment and blame. I sense that well enough. And maybe he'll not ever get past that! And, if that be truth, how can I continue to saddle him with me and this undesirable marriage for the rest of our lives. Sure it would be wise to find an end to it."

"You have considered taking your life, Alainn? I hear it in your thoughts."

"But being ever raised in the teachings of the priests and Christianity, I hesitate, for I am not certain I can risk eternal damnation. I cannot be parted from my wee child's soul, nor from Killian's soul in death."

"Otherwise, you would see it done?"

"Aye, I would!" she admitted in a voice so lacking emotion they might well be discussing the recent snowfall.

"And would you have willingly gone with the demon this night as well?"

"No, taking my own life would have been much preferential to eternally dwelling with that foul beast, though I suppose I'd be made to meet many such hideous beasts if the hell the priests speak of does exist," she admitted.

Mara bristled and angrily moved from the bed. "Do not dare to entertain those desperate thoughts again, Alainn

O'Brien, for I sacrificed all comforts and human contact to see you safe and ensure you were allowed a decent life. I lived out my own life without the man I loved, and I swear to you I loved him as dearly as you love your own husband. And I survived. And I lived without you, for I only ever held you for two days. How dare you consider ending the very life I gave to you?"

"I did not ask that you sacrifice anything for me." Alainn benignly stated not in argument or accusation.

Killian came into the bedchamber when he heard Mara's angry voice. "What has you so riled, Mara?" he demanded to be told.

"Ask your wife, why I am angry beyond any rage I have felt in decades?"

"Alainn?" he questioned, but she simply turned away from him.

"Take her dagger!" Mara ordered Killian.

"What?" He wasn't certain why the woman requested that of him.

When he looked down at Alainn, he saw the resolve in her eyes and he took the anelace from the nightstand with a complete look of horror upon his face.

"Why do you both appear so stunned?" she asked, again in a weak emotionless voice, "'Twould be less painful than many a death, and quicker by far than most."

Killian's face twisted in anger and he crouched beside her. "You must promise me you will never do yourself harm!

Tell me you'll not end your life by your own hand, for if you do, you are truly a spiteful selfish woman, to even consider leaving me here to grieve alone and twofold!"

She turned her eyes to meet him, but she noticed how he avoided meeting hers. That only proved to make her heart break even further knowing he couldn't even bear to look at her. She did not speak.

"Promise me, Alainn!" he insisted.

"I promise I will not be the cause of my own end." She appeased him.

Although he still did not look at her, he gently touched her hand, but he kept the dagger with him. He glanced down at her and noticed she did not wear her amulet.

"Where is the amulet?" he demanded to know.

"In the hearth fire in the tower room," she admitted once more in an empty voice.

"Christ, Alainn! Do you not recall Niall warned you, dark powers can get to you when you are without the charm of the amulet? 'Tis most fortunate gods and spirits were with us and have granted us great favor this night, but you must ensure you wear the amulet always."

"My grandfather is a kind man, a wise man, and perhaps much knowledgeable of many druid ways, but he thinks the amulet can protect me from the dark entities. The darkness I now feel within my own heart is blacker by far than any evil I've been witness to, blacker than any other evil I might encounter, I assure you. No amulet can shield me from that darkness."

"You'll wear the amulet, woman, by God you will!"

He stormed out of the room and Alainn sighed a deep sigh as she lay down upon the bed. Her mother covered her and placed a kiss upon her cheek as she left her to her slumber.

She was asleep when Killian placed the charred amulet around her neck and covered her shivering, slender form with extra quilts. He placed several more peat logs on the fire. Before he left, he glanced back at her as she slept and felt utter self-loathing, surely as deep as her own at knowing he could not lie with her or hold her. He could offer her no comfort. Not yet!

Chapter Thirty-Eight

FROM THAT NIGHT forward, Killian became overbearing in his diligence in checking on Alainn's condition. He made certain the fire in the heath was kept blazing day and night, to the point the entire chamber was filled with uncommon and often uncomfortable warmth. He monitored closely what Alainn ate and made certain Eireen saw to it she bathed and dressed daily.

He felt certain Alainn despised him treating her like a child, but she did not resist him in any manner, which only caused him greater despair for he realized her spirit was far from being mended. But he was relieved to watch her health slowly return. Her hair shone once more, and her skin began to glow, though her eyes still held a haunted quality and she would never allow her gaze to meet his. She was meek and quiet and submissive, qualities many men would find most appealing in a wife, but it brought him displeasure, knowing it was entirely out of character for Alainn to allow herself to be controlled in any manner.

Mara had returned to Castle O'Brien and Alainn had met their farewell with no obvious emotion as she evidently confronted all of life at present. She still had not wept over the loss of their babe, and it wore at Killian's heart to know one day she would surely be overcome with such devastation and heartache, he wasn't certain she could bear it. But, he also knew it was necessary if she was ever to return to the woman she once was.

He had been sleeping apart from her from the time they'd lost their son. Since the night he'd brought her back to their bedchamber, he had found a room directly above her and he felt himself aching for her at night, knowing she was there alone and in need of love and comfort, but he could not bring himself to go to her when he had still not come to terms with their loss and both their parts in it.

Danhoul remained sleeping in the chamber next to hers and he felt the young man probably harbored similar desires for her, but he remained honorable and, in truth, he believed Danhoul Calhoun had distanced himself from her so she did not become entirely reliant upon him. Killian was developing a deep respect for the man, and he had begun to think of him as his friend and most certainly his staunchest ally in seeing Alainn well.

Killian had heard reports of the English drawing back and of many returning to England. The loss of the great number of men that day in the valley surely hit them hard even knowing what numbers they boasted. He'd never discussed any of it with Alainn. And, in actuality, they barely spoke, save the conversations regarding her wellness.

He quizzed Eireen on what his wife did to fill her days. He asked the woman if she read or sang or played the harp. He wondered if she ever thought to venture outdoors to the herb garden or to the stables, even to the chamber where she mixed and prepared potions. Always the answer was the same. She sat by the window and looked out upon the graveyard, but she would not go to the graveside of their son, or even move from the one room in her expansive chambers.

She never read, except briefly from the scriptures, and he'd been sorrowed further to hear she desired contact with even fewer people now. She had not yet seen her grandfather or Riley since the night they'd buried their son, though Niall O'Rorke had come daily in hopes of spending time and comforting his only granddaughter.

Alainn had apparently requested that Mary and Cookson no longer be allowed within her chambers. She now only saw Eireen, and Danhoul, and himself. Though he suspected if she could deny him the right to be near her, she might. He felt he could possibly force her to take nourishment and care in matters of a personal nature, but he could hardly order her to have visitors if she wanted so little company at the moment.

Samhain was fast approaching and he'd hoped Alainn would be acting and feeling more herself by now for, at one time, she anticipated it with great joy and elation. She had spoken of taking him to a fairy glade and watching the magical happenings she claimed only happened in such multitudes and splendor on and near that day. She'd also talked of going to the druid ceremony her grandfather always held to honor that holiday, but he suspected none of it held any meaning to her any longer.

Once, a very long time ago, when she'd first taken him to the fairy glade near Castle O'Brien, she had sadly spoken of believing they would be parted by the time Samhain fell. And when he thought about it, he was overcome with sadness for he realized they were indeed parted. Though they lived under the same roof and were married, it was a marriage in name alone for they seldom spoke and never touched.

He was perhaps more to blame for that than her, but it had gone on for so long now, he wasn't even certain where to begin to make amends for his wrongdoings toward her or to bridge the insurmountable distance that had formed between them. He couldn't even determine how he actually felt toward her anymore, whether he still harbored resentment and blame. He felt all consuming guilt and heartache. Of course he still loved her. He would always love her till the end of his days. And he couldn't dispute he still burned for her but, beyond that, he felt an emptiness rivaled only by her own, he suspected.

As he looked out the window across his study, he shivered, for the air held a constant chill. The ground was white, even though it was autumn. Winter should not yet be upon them. They seldom had snow in this area so close to the sea, but it had fallen more than a few times recently, and the ground remained frozen which was another completely foreign happening. He believed Alainn was entirely responsible. For although she'd previously caused weather changes during times of her anger or her jubilance, he felt certain it was the icy emptiness she now felt that had brought about the unusually cold and early winter. He was startled by the voice that interrupted his thoughts.

"Aye, 'tis her doin', the bitter cold and the ice."

"By Christ, you hear my thoughts now, Danhoul?"

"Aye, and they mirror your wife's much as of late. One of you must end this dismal separation, and I believe it must be you. Until you speak of forgiveness, she'll not be liable to heal entirely."

"Why is she so cold all the time?" He chose to ask a question rather than respond to Danhoul's statement.

"Blood loss and weight loss are both known to cause a constant chill and she's had dangerous degrees of both."

"But her weight increases now."

"Some, 'tis true, but since you've surely not seen her without benefit of garments, I doubt you know how thin she actually is!"

"And you're suggestin' you have?"

"Aye, Killian, indeed your wife and I have been enjoyin' a fervid love affair these past months! Can't you tell by her great joy and mirth, she's a woman well loved and deeply satisfied?"

"I'll thank you not to make light or jest about matters of that nature, and your sarcasm is far more typical of Alainn, or once was common for her at any rate."

Danhoul nodded.

"Why did the magical protection spell you placed on the tower room not keep the dark being from entering the chamber?" Killian asked for it had been on his mind for a goodly time.

Danhoul shrugged. "I am not entirely certain. I charmed the door, the hearth, the narrow slats; no being with untoward intentions should have been able to enter. It is supposed the dark one possesses the ability to create portals with which to enter a location. I suspect he wishes to get to Alainn before Samhain for then her own abilities will be at their strongest. She will be capable of resisting him, perhaps banishing him at least for a time. Her powers will be perhaps uncontrollable even by her at that time."

Killian was not eager to dwell on that consideration and, as always, the thoughts of both the evil being and Alainn being incapable of controlling her supernatural abilities left him feeling as though he understood very little of the world of magic. He glanced at the other man for he stood there as though he had something of further importance on his mind.

"Is there something you're wantin' to discuss with me, Danhoul?"

"Aye, and it's sure to be something you may not wish to

hear, but I'll simply tell you plain what I believe to be truth; the dark witch will attempt to lure you to her bed, and it will happen soon!"

"The dark witch? What are you talkin' about, Danhoul?"

"Ciara, the healer's granddaughter, she knows well enough you and your wife are not on intimate terms and soon she will attempt to take advantage of this knowledge! Though I have no proof, I believe she was in part behind the spell placed upon the castle the night the demon attempted to get to Alainn. And perhaps it was Ciara who slipped the potent sleeping potion in your drink that night as well."

"You truly think she is a witch? I have never seen her present any powers, and I am still not so certain it was a spell she put on me when we were together those years ago! I don't believe Ciara was anywhere near me or my drink the night in which you speak of."

"Believe what you will, but heed my warning. Ciara will summon you to her bed by way of her powers or simply her feminine wiles, I cannot say. However, I do know with no uncertainty, though Alainn may seem incapable of jealousy or any emotion at the moment, she'll not take kindly to you sharin' a bed with that temptress!"

"I've no intention of going to any woman's bed at the moment. 'Tis clear you don't care for Ciara, I see that plain enough, and if you believe she is in allegiance with the demon, I can see certainly see why you would not trust her. I know you have a keen intuition so I'd be inclined to heed your warnings. Yet I sense there is more, something I am unaware of, what has she done to make you distrust you so completely?"

The young, blonde-haired man seemed deep in thought and he pushed the loose stands of hair from his eyes as he often did when he was concerned about something. Killian noticed and thought it odd he was spending so much time in his company he was beginning to know his habits.

"She takes many men to her bed on a whim or to enlist them in her wrongdoings. She has been with your cousin and the young cook as well. She's attempted to seduce your captain, his son, the Scottish groom, and me as well!"

"By God's nails, I suppose she truly is a whorish woman! The fact she's been with Riley... well that does not surprise me in the least, he beds women constantly with inducement or no, but Cookson, sure he's never ever been with a woman before that I know of. Mac is a man of deep conviction and has already suffered through the dire consequences of seduction by a woman once in his life, so I doubt he'd fall prey to the woman.

Pierce seems completely devoted to Molly his intended, and Connor has his mind on another woman, so 'tis sure to be why they resisted her advances, but what of you, Dan-houl, what kept you from her bed, when you clearly are a healthy young man and your desires must be great if they have never been sated by a woman's touch!"

"Sure 'tis not my desire to have my first intimate experience with a woman known to be a fallen woman with little morality, or a witch with a darkness within her. And both her dark intentions and previous injustices toward Alainn keep me from going anywhere near the woman, much less to her bed."

"You believe she has caused actual harm to Alainn? Why have I not been told of this? If this is truth, why in hell was I not alerted to it?"

"I was asked to keep it entirely secretive, for Alainn could not prove it and still has no proof to speak of. And she reasoned if you heard of her dubious beliefs you would think her simply unwarrantedly suspicious because of her deep jealousy toward the woman."

"So you tell me then, Danhoul, I demand to know what harm has Ciara possibly caused Alainn?"

"I believe she attempted to—"

Chapter Thirty-Nine

HIS WORDS WERE immediately cut short by the dark-haired woman in question mysteriously appearing in the doorway. "Milord, I have brought you hot cider. I noticed you work late this night on your figures and ledgers; perhaps a mixture would calm you and make you more ready for sleep!"

Killian's green eyes narrowed as the sultry woman approached the two men. "I've no desire for cider this night, Ciara! And, tell me, how am I to know it isn't laced with a potion sure to make me fall into a deep unnatural sleep or fall prey to a purposeful spell?" He spoke in a rude accusatory tone much more cutting than he'd intended.

"As you wish, milord, but I beg you; do not permit whatever falsehoods this man has surely related to you to wrongly color your opinion of me. He is deeply embittered with me since the night I spurned his advances toward me, the night you asked him to take me to my chambers. He thought to take advantage of me in my inebriated state. I was astonished to think he would attempt such blatant indiscretions when I was so recently widowed. Now he seems insistent on causing trouble for me! Though I know not what he has said to you, milord, I am certain it was a vicious falsehood!"

Killian looked from Danhoul to Ciara and he saw she wore an expression of wounded innocence. He could also see the anger on the young man's face, and he reasoned he'd seen him angry very seldom. Killian noticed Ciara was staring at him as though she hung on his every word, and with an exaggerated trembling lip. In that moment, he knew without question she could not be trusted, though he most certainly did not want her to suspect he had seen through her. He thought he would benefit greatly from her believing he was beguiled by her. If she had tried to harm Alainn, he thought it would be of greater good to him if he appeared to be Ciara's friend, or if he feigned interest in her once more. He glanced at Danhoul and hoped the man had heard his thoughts for he needed to set a plan in action.

"Danhoul, I am sorely disappointed in your roguish behavior. I thought you to be a man of greater moral character! If you were not so important to my wife, I would have you tossed out of this castle so that I might never be made to deal with you, again. But, I see you are an asset to my wife's healing, so for now, you may stay. Be warned, keep your distance from Widow McCree or you'll deal with me and my sword!"

Danhoul convincingly looked at him as though he would actually like to battle with him that very instant, but he backed away from Killian and Ciara.

"Aye, have it your way then, milord, but mark my word as a druid seer I tell you she is not to be trusted. If she comes near me or attempts to harm Alainn I will not be liable to treat her as a pitiable widow, but as a powerful witch!"

As he turned to leave, behind Ciara's back, he nodded ever so slightly to Killian and then left in an apparent rage.

"Milord, I had no notion he was so entirely untrustworthy. Of course, I knew what he attempted with me was unscrupulous, but now I see his temper is clearly violent as well. Are you certain you want him near your wife in her grievous condition? Sure he might harm her or perhaps attempt unsavory deeds toward her for even in her recent ill health she is not without beauty!"

Not knowing what nefarious crimes Ciara might have committed toward his wife, Killian was most displeased to have the woman dare to mention Alainn, but he reasoned he must keep up the façade so he could learn more about the woman and her misdeeds.

"For now, I'll watch him closely, you can wager much on that, Ciara. But, let us not speak on the boy any longer, and I've no need for cider this night. I'll be drinkin' whiskey; would you care to join me then?"

The woman's dark amber eyes lit up like a candle in a pitch black room. "Aye, milord, if you think it will not appear forward or inappropriate for me to take audience with you while no other is present!"

Bile rose in his throat as he continued on with the unwanted guise of being interested in the woman. "Tis not as if my wife will know for she has not yet left her chambers in so many weeks. And if any other servants might see us, sure they'll wisely know to keep it to themselves."

"My stepmother may not, for she seems in thick with your wife, and she's never taken to me since I was a young girl. I've tried to tell my father she is not the woman he thinks she is."

As she gazed at Killian's face, he had the sense she had obviously decided it would be best to speak of other subjects surely more advantageous to her than her stepmother. She sat down upon the chair he had pulled out for her and she took the goblet, noticeably delighted he was showing renewed interest in her when she'd thought he was completely devoted to his wife. But the calculating woman was surely aware how little time he and Alainn spent together and she would well know how men were often ruled by their desires. She had indubitably decided to make herself and her bed appealing to him.

Killian did not need to possess the ability of hearing the woman's lustful thoughts to realize she was now recalling the passion they shared when they been together. By the sensual way she was staring at him, how she'd purposely loosened her laces to allow her cleavage to be seen, he knew Danhoul was right on the mark, and Ciara hoped to become reacquainted with him in that manner as soon as it could be accomplished.

⌘

DANHOUL KNOCKED UPON the chamber door and waited for Alainn to answer and to call him inside. When she did not respond, he quietly turned the key. He and Killian each kept one and they'd had a new one crafted for Eireen, as well. He doubted Alainn even realized the door was kept locked day and night as she'd never attempted to go out.

He saw she was asleep on the bed atop the quilts and bedclothes. She was still clothed in her garments and he thought he should call for Eireen to see her settled more comfortably in bed for the night. But she looked almost peaceful at the moment and by the heavy dark circles beneath her eyes, he knew she seldom slept and if she did it was fitfully. He dared to gently touch his hand to her cheek and he heard a sound escape her lips akin to a whimper.

He felt his heart squeeze for whether he'd wanted it or not, he was falling deeply and irreversibly in love with the woman. Again, he thought to himself. For as he looked toward the sky and thought of the Celtic gods and their part in all of this, he wanted to curse them and flay them for the pain she now felt. Though, for the time being, they were apparently involved in a brutal war raging through the realm of the gods, they had always dictated in part what befell Alainn and Killian, and himself.

It was surely by design she'd lost the child and he could

never reveal that to her without telling her the whole of it. And if he did that she would be made to suffer even further to realize she was a part of a great elaborate plan to one day set things right in the world, past and present. She and the woman with the red hair and green eyes, and the other brown haired woman whom he'd met only briefly, but could not recall as vividly.

Alainn stirred beside him for he'd forgotten his hand still rested lovingly against her cheek. "Killian?" she whispered half asleep in a voice filled with unhidden hope.

"Shh, go back to sleep, Alainn!" he whispered, and he heard her sigh.

"Danhoul, you should not be here!"

"Aye, I know it well, Alainn, but I must speak with you awhile, for 'tis soon to be Samhain. You should converse with your husband. Perhaps you might make arrangements to take him to a fairy glade or to your grandfather's great Druid celebration. Sure one of you has to make the first move toward the other!"

Alainn wearily sighed once more, patted his hand appreciatively for his concern, but remained with her back to him as she spoke. "I cannot, Danhoul, for Killian still cannot face me, or be in close proximity to me, not yet, and perhaps never, I fear!"

"You don't know that, Alainn. I would suggest he is simply as unsure as you are as to where to begin to mend what's broken between you."

She did not respond to his words and the silence soon became awkward. "Will you make certain the window coverings are fastened tightly, Danhoul, and check the fire for 'tis unbearably cold in here?"

"Aye, I'll add another peat log to the fire!" He though the chamber felt quite warm enough to him. "Climb beneath the bedclothes, Alainn and cover up more securely. I shall send Eireen to assist you with donning your night clothes and to spend time with you if you'd like?"

"No, save the woman the trouble, she is oft saddled with me from dawn till nightfall, sure she's her husband and other tasks to tend to, but if you'd just throw the covers over my shoulders, and maybe sit here with me for a time, I'd be much obliged to you, Danhoul!"

When his clearly desirous thoughts came to her, she turned to face him in disbelief.

"Forgive me, Danhoul! Go now, I would ask you to leave straightaway!"

⌘

SHE'D HEARD HIS impassioned thoughts regarding her, and she felt responsible for them as well. She should have realized he was a young man with the typical strong desires men possessed, and he'd never had a woman so surely he must be lusting often. He'd spent considerable time with her in her bedchamber, and she'd just asked him to sit with her on her bed.

As she glanced at his appealing face and masculine form, she felt herself shiver, so perpetually cold was she, and for the briefest time she pondered how it might feel to have him lie down beside her, for him to hold her and warm her, to make her feel alive again.

Chapter Forty

CLEARLY, HE HEARD her thoughts as well, for he left the room immediately and she listened to him calling for Eireen in a voice that now sounded much more disturbed than aroused. She would now be riddled with guilt over this as well, and it would simply be more subject to add to her growing sum of many.

She heard the key being turned in the lock and then Eireen hurrying into the room.

"Milady, are you well, Danhoul made it sound most urgent, as though you needed something immediately. Tell me what I can do for you!"

"Just talk to me, Eireen and start the fire, for I cannot keep warm for all my attempts."

"Aye, milady, I can most certainly do that for you, but I suspect young Danhoul could have accomplished either of those tasks while he was here."

"Aye, I'm certain he could have!" she whispered as she shivered again, knowing Danhoul's presence in her bed-chamber was not questioned by Eireen or even by Killian any longer. She would need to distance herself from the young man before she might be driven to commit another sin she could not undo.

⌘

It was the day of Samhain and when Eireen came to her as she sat by the window, Alainn sensed the woman's untypical anxiousness as she looked at Alainn.

"What is it, Eireen? What causes your uneasiness?"

"I would ask you a favor, milady."

"If I'm able, I will attempt to grant it, Eireen, for you have been a kind friend and a doted much upon me."

"Your grandfather is here, milady, as he has been here most every single day in the past weeks. He wishes to see you most assuredly."

Alainn looked away from the other woman and, as she did so frequently, she cast her eyes to the castle's graveyard that she could see in the distance. She had not seen her grandfather since that fateful night… the night she could not permit herself to think on.

"I would ask that you allow him audience this day, milady, as a simple request from me."

Alainn's eyes questioned the reason for her request, but her voice remained silent so the other woman knelt down beside her and placed her hands on Alainn's knees and stared deeply into her eyes.

"He is sorely aggrieved for you, milady. You are his only granddaughter, the daughter of his son who has been missing since before you were born. I can sense he feels a great kinship with you; you are the last connection to his beloved son. His eyes reveal his deep sadness at being unable to see you for himself. Please do not make me go back down those steps and tell him, yet again, you will not see him this day."

Alainn had always felt the woman was undeniably empathetic towards her and she could see how deeply Eireen was affected by her grandfather's melancholia as well.

"Please, milady, see the man, he is aged and weary. He longs to see you, his only daughter lives far from here and his grandson, Riley O'Brien, begging your pardon, milady, for I know he's your kin, but he's somewhat of a stubborn and unfeeling arse."

Alainn stared at the other woman, but made no attempt to reply.

"Please, Alainn!"

Although Alainn had often told Eireen to refer to her by her given name, she had always refused, saying it would be improper. She had never ever referred to her by anything but her title, and something in that spoken word, in her actually referring to her by her given name, made her feel the woman's deep friendship and it moved her. She swallowed hard, for she had been allowing herself to feel nothing for so long.

Alainn then glanced up at the armoire in her chamber for she was startled to see the spirit of Shylie O'Rorke sitting upon the tall piece of furniture. She was staring at Alainn with notable impatience, waiting for her to answer the other woman's plea. She had crossed her arms stubbornly and Alainn recalled she'd often seen her cousin Rory do such when he had been in discussion usually with his brother, and he impatiently awaited his response. The young spirit eyed her with growing impatience.

"My father simply wishes to look upon you, Alainn! Do you truly mean to disallow him that one small courtesy? I alerted your husband to the dark demon when he attempted to take you, so it would seem you owe me a favor in return."

Something close to a scowl crossed Alainn's face and her brow furrowed at having this unwanted decision forced upon her, but she inhaled deeply and finally responded.

"Aye, I will agree to see my grandfather this day, Eireen."

The caring woman embraced her warmly with relief on her face, and then hurried out the door before Alainn had a chance to rethink her decision.

Alainn was startled when Shylie then moved from her previous location and floated down beside her, and she was further surprised when the young spirit spoke aloud and not through telepathy.

"My father has come to see of your wellness and invite you to attend his druid celebration this night. Although I am aware of the deep pain that fills your heart, and of your wish to stay here in this chamber indefinitely, one day you must actually step out of the doorway. When that first step is taken it will set you on the path to healing your heart and your conscience."

I took no joy in anything. I feared becoming with child after losing the first and, when it happened, and I carried the second and the third only to see them die in my arms as well, no matter that I had taken every remedy and method supposed to prevent conception, beyond complete celibacy, I became mad with grief.

You may think of me as a respectful woman of high station, a chieftain's wife, a chieftain's daughter, a noble for all my life, that I always conducted myself in such a befitting manner, but, I assure you, that is far distanced from the truth. I once believed I must maintain a stoic countenance expected of my class, my position as a lady, but what transpired in those dark times, what misdeeds and sins I committed are known to no one, bar me.

When I learned I carried the fourth child after the curse was uttered, after I'd already lost three babes, I became desperate and nearly deranged, I begged Morag to give me a potion to expel the child from within me for I couldn't bear to carry to term simply to lose another babe.

She reluctantly agreed and so I took the potion, many times, but to no avail. I still carried the child. I found a woman far from beyond our castle, with the sordid reputation of being known to perform physical atrocities to women, which capably ended their time with child. I employed and paid her handsomely to rid me of the child, it was bloody and excruciating and horrific and yet, for all of that, it seemed it could not be undone.

I believed that because of the curse it was clearly fated that I must suffer indefinitely. I wondered what I had perhaps done in another life to have deserved such pain and unfair treatment, such grievous hardships. I became consumed with being rid of the unborn child.

I threw myself down the uppermost steps of the south solar, not caring that I may end my life as well. Perhaps I hoped it would come to that. All that I received for my trouble was a broken arm and a severely bruised head. I pleaded with Morag to give me a potion so that my life would be ended and I would not lose another child. She refused. And so even with all my efforts to shield my heart and lessen my pain, the end of my term came and I lost the fourth baby as well.

I birthed my wee daughter, the only daughter I ever carried, and I had wished so long for a girl child. She was beautiful and entirely perfect, with soft blonde hair, and I immediately regretted being set upon ending her life, even though it ended so assuredly at any rate. I was then completely inconsolable for I became consumed with grief and loss, but now I had added a new layer of anguish, an added depth to my incomparable grief and unwelcome emotions. It was the first time I felt guilt in regard to the loss of a child, and I soon fell into a darkness that no one should ever know.

Even my two dear young lads, my darlin' twins, Rory and Riley, could bring me no joy, no relief from the endless agony of knowing my babes lay in the ground, never having lived, barely having breathed. It was all I could think about. It consumed my every waking moment.

I thought to take my life twice after that. Once I drank the entire contents of two bottles of wine, and I then threw myself in the raging waters of the River Shannon. I believe it may have been my sister, Shylie, who pulled me from the depths that day, although I cannot say for certain as I do not possess the ability to view spirits. But I did sense her near.

The second time I sat at my tower window with my dagger to my wrists, even as I watched my wee boys frolicking about in the meadow below. They seemed happy and carefree and I believed it would be a kindness to end my life, for I couldn't be the loving mother I should have been to them, so consumed in grief was I.

That day it was not Shylie who prevented me from taking my life, but 'twas you Alainn. You had not yet come to live with Morag, you were still residing with the farrier, though he was no more a parent to you at the time than I was to my own boys. He was constantly filled with drink and I was filled with dark melancholia.

As I sat with the dagger upon my wrist, summoning the courage to end the bitter and desolate existence my life had become, I tried to bring to mind how selfish my deed would be, how aggrieved my parents would be when I was gone for they had lost each and every one of their other children. I attempted to imagine what shame would be brought upon Hugh, or what it would be for my children to grow up motherless, and yet none of it mattered to me then, I was beyond caring about anyone or anything it would seem.

Yet as I stared out the window, you looked up at me in all your childish innocence, your long, golden hair falling down your back, your bright blue eyes meeting mine. You reminded me so of my dear, lost sister, Shylie, but it wasn't even that similarity in appearance that touched my heart. It was that you had no mother, had never known a mother's love, had no father to speak of, no one who truly loved you, you lived the life of a pauper, your clothes were rags, surely you barely had enough food to eat, and yet you found such obvious joy in life, joy in everything around you.

You smiled up at me with love in your eyes and you sent a most uncommon warmth to me that I couldn't explain if I lived to be a century. I now realize it was surely magic you sent to me that day, for you healed my heart to a degree. I'm not saying I didn't still long to have my babies in my life, that I don't still miss them to this day, for indeed I do, but something changed. I let you inside my icy heart. Maybe you even took away some of my pain for I know you're a gifted empath. From that day forward, I was changed, my attitude toward life and toward my two precious boys, even toward

Hugh, was changed.

When I learned I carried the fifth child, strangely, I relished every moment, took joy in every movement, found merriment in each kick, my heart gladdened as my belly grew for I held on to every treasured moment while my wee boy child grew within me. As my time grew near, I knew the outcome would be the same, but I was somehow still thankful for having had the honor of carrying that precious child within me and, when I labored with him and he was born, I reveled in his beauty and perfection and then held him in my arms as I watched him taken to the beyond with all the others.

I knew with certainty I would never share my husband's bed again and that I would never carry another child, but I was at peace with that. And it was so! I told Hugh in no uncertain terms we would no longer share an intimacy. He may not have approved, but he did accept it.

What Hugh and I shared was never a great love, never an undying passion, or a rare gift. Not such as what you and dear Killian share, sweet Alainn.

I suppose what I wish for you, during this time of surely incomprehensible sorrow, is that you grieve together, that you find it in your hearts to approach your time of mourning together, for if you cannot do so, then it will be so much more unbearable.

I also must warn you, do not attempt to turn from the grief, to distance yourself from the pain, for it will rear its ugly monstrous head when you least expect it. When you feel as though you are capable of withstanding the pain; that you have capably dealt with the loss, a wave of unimaginable grief will wash over you and swallow you whole, pulling you down to the deepest depths.

You must allow yourself to experience the grief, to feel the anger, the sadness, the pain, the complete and utter despair, but if you share the grief, share each emotion, each sorrowful time, it will lessen the load, it will deepen your love and strengthen your commitment.

Do not turn away from each other. Allow Killian to help you to heal and you him. Allow him to make you feel alive, for you are alive, Alainn. As much as you surely feel as though you are not, or perhaps at times wish you were not... you are alive.

Seek solace in each another, seek comfort in each another, and, one day, Alainn, you will again find joy in each other and in your undying love.

Always Your Loving Aunt,
Siobhan

Alainn had stopped reading so very many times for she felt on the verge of allowing her aunt's kind words and obvious deep understanding to penetrate her shield. Although a part of her was appreciative of her aunt's candor and honored that she would share her darkest moments with Alainn, she felt she simply would not, could not, allow herself to feel emotion, not yet. She would not permit herself to weep no matter how empty or maudlin she felt at this moment.

When she came to the passage in the letter advising her to lean on Killian for them to grieve together, she felt her heart breaking again, for Killian appeared to no longer desire being close to her and she wasn't certain what was broken between them could ever truly be mended. She had finally placed the letter back within the drawer and simply sighed deeply once more.

Chapter Forty-Two

LATER THAT DAY, the evening of the feast of Samhain, Alainn was startled to see Killian come to their bed-chamber. He usually made it a point to come to her when others were present, so their conversations would be trivialities or limited to topics regarding her well-being. This night, he came alone. He held one lone blue flower in his hand, and he awkwardly passed it to her. She stood and questioned him with her eyes.

"I know 'tis the date of your birth this day, Alainn. As I walked past your herb garden this afternoon, I spotted this one persistent wee flower growing amongst the rocks. Though it would appear to be delicate and fragile, and although it was well covered in frost, still it grew."

Alainn felt certain he was drawing a comparison to her present precarious state and to the flower. She swallowed hard and lowered her eyes.

"I recalled how you favor the color blue, and thought it fitting you have it this day, on your celebratory day."

She took it from him, and tried to ignore the warmth of his hand against hers as they touched for the first time in weeks. She attempted an unconvincing smile as she absent-mindedly placed the flower to her nose.

"I am much grateful for your thoughtfulness, Killian."

She remained standing and when he glanced at her she saw the regret in his eyes at her continued morose state.

"Have you considered going to your grandfather's celebration? I was well pleased you agreed to see him this day. I know it meant much to him, and I believe he would take added delight in your attendance."

She knew he watched her reaction closely to determine if she showed any sign of interest or longing to attend.

"Are you askin' me if I desire to attend, or if I might attend in your company?"

He seemed uncertain how to reply. He spoke slowly, tentatively testing her response.

"I had thought perhaps you would like Danhoul to accompany you for he is of druid origin and sure he has previous knowledge of the druid ways and celebrations."

She cast her eyes to the floor once more as she spoke. "I have no desire to attend the celebration with Danhoul." She sighed.

"And would you go with me?" His voice was uncommonly quiet and contained an unusual nervousness as he posed the question.

She allowed her gaze to meet his and she saw a sadness within them that surely mirrored and reflected her own sorrow. "I fear I remain unable to face others, Killian, but I appreciate your offer more than you could know."

She attempted another smile for his benefit. He cleared his throat awkwardly, and she apprehensively turned her eyes from his stare.

"I thought maybe it might do the both of us good to leave this castle for a time, most especially on this your special day."

She once more allowed herself to gaze upon him and remained standing not far from where he now stood.

"I am not certain who will be in attendance or what people lay claim to druidism for not everyone admits the association to the old ways. Many keep that information secretive for often those who practice openly are chastised by the priests!" He nervously spoke on trying to make conversation.

She nodded and smiled once more. He inhaled deeply and she stared back at him. It was evident they both despised how uneasy they felt in each other's company and how awkward it had become to be alone together. After another moment of silence passed, Killian cleared his throat once more.

"Aye, well, I'll be down in the study, should you decide differently." He finally spoke.

She nodded and part of her wanted to tell him she'd already reconsidered and that he was correct, they should get away. She believed spending time together was necessary if ever they were to begin to mend all that had been broken between them. But she'd be forced to be near the churchyard and, though she looked out upon the place daily, she thought she could not bear to pass by their baby's grave.

He must have sensed her unwillingness or noticed the ever-present pain within her pale blue eyes. He turned and began to walk toward the door. She wanted to run after him and tell him she needed him, that if ever she was to feel whole and well again, she would need him to hold her and to love her but, most of all, she would need him to forgive her. But, instead, she kept silent and when he closed the door she felt a sensation of overpowering panic within her for now she knew she wanted to weep in earnest... she needed to weep.

She'd sensed the icy frozen wall around her heart truly threatening to melt, and that frightened her beyond belief. But how long would Killian be willing to wait? Clearly, his invitation this night was his way of attempting to make some peace between them, to begin to close the enormous chasm that separated them.

She sat down upon the bed and stared around the bed-chamber, she dared to glance toward the adjoining chamber where their wee son should now rest in the cradle, and she quickly turned away. She looked at the hearth and vividly recalled the night she and Killian lovingly danced together so happy and content and hopeful of what the future held. She couldn't allow herself to remember those fond memories of what once was, of how happy they had once been.

She felt a warm presence fill the room, but could see no

one there. She was soon overcome once more with the distinct memory of the night she and Killian danced together. She heard his deep sensual voice, felt his lips upon her own. It was such a clear memory it was as though it was happening once more. She felt him take her in his arms, carry her to their bed. She could sense their great love, their undying passion and their blissfulness that should have spanned a lifetime. She caught a sob in her throat and was immediately infuriated for she was reasonably certain it was a magical spirit who had forced her to once more dwell upon the cherished memory.

"Shylie O'Rorke, show yourself this instant, for I would like to have a word with you, I would. I do not welcome nor desire your constant meddling."

She was taken aback when a spirit appeared, but it was not Shylie. It was the spirit woman from the tower near her grandfather's land.

"You are displeased, young Alainn. I see that clear enough. But you cannot turn from your memories; you *should not* turn from the memories, most especially those that fill your heart with joy."

"I know you are the spirit woman from the tower, but who are you and how is it you know me?"

"My name is Deirdra. As for as how I know you, well, I'll simply say spirits are aware of much, they are privy to a wealth of information regarding the living, most especially if they were capable of magic during life."

"So that is the only connection I share with you; we both possess magical abilities?"

"Aye, 'tis part of our connection and all you need know at the moment."

There was something undeniably familiar about the woman and Alainn strained to discover why she was so drawn to her, to learn if she had seen her somewhere other than the once in the tower window. She determined the woman would surely have met with death when she had not yet measured three decades upon this earth. As Alainn stared intently at the spirit, Alainn decided it was something about her blue-gray eyes that made her feel as though she knew her, or should remember her.

The spirit apparently did not desire for Alainn to learn anything further in regards to her for she soon capably presented Alainn with another memory that pulled at her heart. It was the dolmen back at Castle O'Brien. It was she and Killian together, intimately entwined the first time they passionately made love.

Alainn turned away and closed her eyes tightly. "Those memories are of a most private, intimate nature, for Killian and me alone. Do you possess perverse, unnatural depraved traits, in desiring to watch such personal happenings?" Alainn rebuked the other spirit, displeased that she was allowing herself to feel such deep emotion.

"There needn't be physical intimacy in the memories I reveal, if it disturbs you so."

She then capably showed Alainn the memory of her first meeting with Killian, when they were only children. She watched and fondly remembered the encounter when she had magically healed him, when they had first begun their friendship and once more was forced to turn away.

"You and your husband share a rare love, Alainn. You are bound... eternally bound, not only by your love and your marriage, you are bound by something much stronger, by fate, by destiny, by the gods, who can say. But you must not turn from that great love. Our time upon this earth is short, young Alainn. Do not fritter away the little time that may be allowed to you!"

Alainn felt her heart ache and her tears so near to the surface. "I wish for you to leave now," Alainn whispered.

"I've not yet entirely accomplished what I've come here to do."

"Would you have me send you away?" Alainn threatened.

"Ah, so you intend to employ your magic again then, do you? 'Tis most certainly time."

Alainn lifted her chin determinedly and felt her hands trembling and tingling with the need to create magic. Her powers surged within her. It was Samhain. She was filled with more powerful and undeniable magic than any other time.

The two women's eyes met and the spirit issued an unspoken challenge as she once more created a tender memory for Alainn to view. This time it was of Killian presenting Alainn with the turquoise combs so many months ago, and then the memory was soon replaced with the most recent memory of him handing her the blue flower this very night.

With each memory, she felt her shield failing, her iciness thawing, her fears soaring at what emotions lay trapped within her purposely hardened heart. She glanced once more toward the chamber she had so lovingly prepared for her child, at the bed where she and Killian had so often shared such great passion.

She wanted to lash out at the spirit woman for causing her to remember, for forcing her to feel emotion again. She turned in a fury, in time to see the woman's eyes knowingly meet her own with an understanding smile as she disappeared in a hazy mist.

Alainn inhaled deeply and tried to calm herself. She felt perilously unsettled. She paced the chamber like a caged animal, and then sat upon the settee and looked out into the night where her eyes immediately fell upon the graveyard. She gasped aloud, for now her emotions were raw and far too close to the surface, too many and too strong to be suppressed any longer.

Alainn no longer desired to be here alone in this chamber, with the memories now so fresh and vivid. She needed to be gone from here immediately. But where would she go?

Perhaps spending time with Killian this night, seeing her grandfather again, attending a celebration would be beneficial, and she couldn't deny finding a fairy glade during Samhain was a magical happening. It might be a necessary distraction from the deep emotion she was beginning to experience.

She looked toward the next adjoining chamber, knowing there were many trunks in the room. Somewhere, within one of them, was a white robe once donned by druids during pagan rituals, and now worn during celebratory feasts. She began searching through them and when she found the robe, she took several deep breaths trying to compel herself to finally step outside of these walls.

She thought of the wisdom in her aunt's letter, of Shylie's well-meaning advice, of Deidra pressing her to remember her treasured memories, and of Killian's eyes as he'd asked her to accompany him this night. For Killian, she would embolden herself and finally leave these chambers. For the deep love they once shared, she would step past this doorway and hopefully one day soon into his arms.

Chapter Forty-Three

KILLIAN SAT AT his large, wooden desk, pouring over his ledgers as was how he seemed to fill all his evenings lately. He was beginning to despise the lonely reality his life had become. When he'd summoned the courage to go to Alainn and ask her if they might leave the castle this night, he was uncertain if he felt relief or disappointment when she'd declined. For, if they spent time together, they would surely be made to converse and they'd spoken so little recently, he found it hard to imagine back to a time when they shared an uncommon closeness and an ability to reveal what was in their hearts.

He heard a sound behind him and turned hoping it might be her. But it was Danhoul. The young man had been acting peculiarly toward him. They'd had no occasion to speak since the night he had pretended to be so angry with him. Every time they attempted it, Ciara seemed to instinctively appear or something prevented them being alone.

"I must leave the castle for a time this night, Killian."

"Aye, well, you've been a loyal guard to Alainn, and a valued friend to both of us, and if you need leave, I am certain you have good reason or that you feel she is safe for the time being."

The sound of footsteps behind them interrupted their conversation once again.

"Milord! I was hoping to speak with you, but I'll not care to be in the company of this man, so if you would be so kind as to alert me when you might be free for audience, I would be greatly obliged." Ciara declared.

"I am taking leave now, so I needn't be a consideration." Danhoul assured the woman.

"Will you be returning this night?" Killian questioned.

"'Tis unlikely, for I have much to attend to, and it is imperative I speak with Niall O'Rorke."

"Is it wise to leave my wife unattended for so long?"

"I suspect you can attend to her yourself for one night, unless you foresee bein' otherwise occupied this night?" He glared at Ciara as he spoke the words.

"No, of course, I'll watch over Alainn then."

"I have thoroughly charmed her chambers with a potent protection spell. Although, I suppose, in truth, it would take the powers of half the demons in hell to see her harmed this night, for 'tis not only Samhain and the time when her powers are nearly limitless, but also the anniversary of her birth. Eight and ten years ago this night she came to be and, if she so desired, I expect she could manage nearly anythin' this night! So, I'd not attempt anything nefarious towards her, Ciara, or you're sure to be the brunt of her powerful magic!"

"What harm would I possibly see done to milady?" The woman feigned insult at the suggestion, but both Killian and Danhoul seemed to be aware of the woman's true nature.

Danhoul did not answer the untrustworthy woman and headed out, setting the stage set for what he knew well what would transpire soon enough.

⌘

ALAINN HESITANTLY MADE her way down the back stairwell for she had no desire to meet up with any of the servants and be forced to have them address her formally and feel compelled to inquire to her health. She could barely will herself to go through with going to Killian and telling him she had changed her mind and would like to accept his invitation. She hoped he would remain in agreement to accompany her.

When she drew nearer to the study, she felt an ominous sensation that raised her hackles and eerily ran down the full length of her spine. An awareness of darkness filled her so entirely, she looked around the dimly lit corridor nearly expecting to find the demon she had encountered many times lately. She'd felt his presence that day on the battlefield she'd believed if she could have taken the time to look at the faces of each of the English soldiers present, she would have seen him as she'd seen him when he transformed into human form, as she'd seen him in the disturbing dream when she'd first seen Shylie.

LEIGH ANN EDWARDS

Since then, she'd often felt his presence in the tower room, even when she'd been so numbed to all around her. The night Killian carried her from the tower she thought her soul felt so dark she might well have been incapable of warding off the demon and she might simply have gone with him that night, but she'd seen an unusual soft glow and she was nearly certain she'd seen the spirit woman Deidra encircling her in her light. She appeared to hold back the dark being until Killian's presence had prevented the demon from reaching her.

Now that it was Samhain, all portals were open. Alainn had always been under the impression that white magic would prevail during this time, but the dark powers could not be overlooked or underestimated. Her own powers hummed wildly, along with her emotions, and pulsed unusually strongly throughout her entire body as though they needed to be released. She briefly wondered if leaving the castle was a wise consideration. But she remembered Killian's face, there had been a thread of hope and a glimmer of warmth in his eyes, and she forced herself to dwell upon that and to hold on to that hope.

She could smell the pungent scent of whiskey. Her senses were always heightened during this time of the year along with her powers. She'd never cared for the taste of whiskey and the smell often left her feeling repulsed. The man whom she'd believed was her father had possessed a deep affliction for drink and she remembered when she was a small child

416

he'd often come home reeking of whiskey. Although the man had never caused her harm or abuse, he had been neglectful and she still harbored a dislike for drink for the man clearly chose to spend his nights with his whiskey while she stayed in the cottage, alone and frightened. And she'd been only three years of age when he had sent her off to live with Morag the healer, so these memories were obviously deeply rooted.

She inhaled the scent again. Killian drank whiskey on occasion, and often, she surmised, when things were precarious or conflict was left unresolved between them. Perhaps, it would be best if she did not go to him if he was drinking for it might be an indication he was displeased, and she was undoubtedly the reason, since she had turned down his invitation this night. She flayed herself for her procrastination and she walked ahead determined to simply go to him.

She stopped short when she heard the familiar and unwelcome female voice coming from Killian's study. As numb as she thought she'd become and as diligently as she'd held her feelings at a distance, with Deidra already evoking undesired emotions this night, she now felt a slow rage simmering from somewhere deep within her. She could not simply allow Ciara to have Killian, or him to have her; she fumed at the very consideration. And the longer she dwelled upon this vexing thought, on the possibility that it had already happened and perhaps had been happening for some time, the more outraged she became. Her face burned with furious indignation.

When she stepped into the doorway, she half expected to find them in a lover's embrace, and she plotted what her reaction and recourse would be. By the time she spotted Ciara standing by the enormous oaken desk and Killian seated on the chair beside it, she was beyond clear and reasonable thought. She saw the two of them, each with a goblet in their hand, speaking comfortably together. She heard the woman's smooth voice and noticed she stood not a foot from Killian. When the woman reached out with the intention of boldly placing her hand on his, Alainn heard doors being thrown open, shutters being slammed, tables and chairs being lifted and flung back down.

When she looked at the two of them now staring at her with disbelief on their faces, she saw the dagger whiz through the air and land wedged deep within the wood, between his and her hands. She saw Ciara hastily pull her hand away and cry out in fear and in pain. She saw the trickle of blood that flowed from the smallest finger on her right hand and she felt undeniably pleased at the sight.

"Christ, Alainn, what are you doing?"

"You think me a fool entirely! Sure it must seem so!"

The many articles of furniture continued to sail about the room and, when a heavy chair was hurled through the air directly at Ciara, Killian knocked it away and sent it crashing to the floor.

"Calm down, Alainn! Whatever you believe has happened to make you so infuriated can be explained, I assure you."

Ciara's almond-shaped eyes were wide and filled with unhidden fear, but Alainn thought somewhere within the amber pools there was a certain amount of smug satisfaction as well. When she noticed that, she glared at the other woman, held out her hands and the powerful magic visibly flowed from her fingertips. Ciara was now completely frozen where she stood. Soon the many items fell to the floor with loud thuds and Alainn remained standing halfway across the room from her husband.

She inhaled deeply and attempted to calm herself as she heard a wicked disturbing whisper within her mind. She had heard that voice before and was well aware it was the dark demon who had been attempting to get to her.

"Use your powers witch! You know you want to take her life. Do it now! It will sate your fury and finally set you on the path to following me in joining the dark one. If you simply succumb to one malevolent desire on this, the night of Samhain, you will fufill your intended purpose."

Alainn's powers pulsed and surged through her as though they had a life of their own. She held her hands before her and her growing enragement fueled her magic. A ball of fire formed in her hands though oddly it did not burn her own skin always unusually susceptible to burns. The demon's words ignited a darkness somewhere deep within her and she pointed the fireball toward Ciara, deviously envisioning what it would be to watch the woman suffer as she was set ablaze. Instead, she fought the urge and hurled the fire toward the hearth where it hissed loudly and sent scattered embers across the floor.

Uncertain of how long she could control her rage or her unpredictable powers, Alainn turned to leave though she left Ciara in a completely immovable state.

Killian came after her. "Alainn!"

He took her arm and turned her to face him, but her eyes were filled with deep jealously.

"I thought it was your heavy heart that kept you distanced from me, from my life and my bed, now I see the truth of it."

"The truth is I have wronged you in no way, Alainn!"

She did not answer him, but continued to walk away. He followed her.

"How in cursed hell did you get the dagger. I had it locked away in the weapons chamber with my many swords and weapons."

"It is charmed by me for me, so it would appear it acts on my accord!"

"You're tellin' me you didn't call it to you or aim it at her, that you didn't make the furniture fly through the air, effortlessly create fire or turn Ciara into a damnable statue?"

"I did not consciously call or throw the dagger nor control the many items of furniture. But, aye, I purposely created the fire and froze the whore. I would have done much worse, but I suppose a part of me does not want you to think me evil, or to see you denied pleasure or happiness entirely! I suspect by dawn's light my spell of stillness shall be broken and you'll be free to do what you will with her!"

"She is nothing to me, Alainn; only a woman who I shared a drink with, and nothing more!"

"And 'tis common then for you, a married man, to share a drink with a woman you've previously bedded?"

She could see his temper beginning to flare as well, and she felt herself in turmoil once more.

"If I'd known your seeing us here together would actually evoke a sliver of emotion from you, I might have arranged it earlier!"

He watched the bright spark of anger and jealousy flicker in her blue eyes.

"In truth, I might just be driven to bed her if only to see if you might feel strongly enough to appear as though you actually give a shite about anything at all!"

Sparks flew from her unusual, light blue eyes as she reached out and slapped him hard across the face. And, when he stood there with satisfaction on his ruggedly handsome face, she slapped him again. And then she flew at him in rage and fury, and beat on his broad chest ineffectually.

He finally took hold of her hands and held them tightly preventing her from moving. "She is nothing to me, Alainn!"

"Send her away from here, Killian!" She ordered in a furiously demanding and possessive tone.

He remembered Mara's words indicating Alainn would need to finally feel deep emotion again in order to deal with the loss of their baby. She'd said she would need to experience the deep anger and agonizing grief. She was now as angry as he'd seen her in a good long while. So he purposely baited her further and pushed the issue.

"I will not!"

"Because you want her?"

"And if I do; why would that possibly matter to you any longer?"

"I am still your wife! You might better have chosen a handfasting, Killian, for you would be nearly halfway through your time of suffering!"

"Aye, well, what either of us should have done is hardly the issue. I'll not send her away simply because of your unwarranted jealousy, for I've not committed any sin with the woman. Has she wronged you in some way I was not informed of?" He wondered if she would speak of what had been done to her, for Danhoul had insinuated Ciara had attempted to harm Alainn.

"She is not to be trusted, Killian! She will attempt to lure you to her bed and, soon, she will ask you to claim her son as your own. I am now the only person who stands in the way of her having you to herself!"

"And how would you stand in the way; do you not think I could have her and you as well, if I so desired it? I am a man of nobility, a chieftain; 'tis nearly expected of me. I would hardly be the first or last to have a wife and a mistress!"

Now the fury had returned in her eyes and with the fury was indisputable jealousy, but also a stubborn determination he'd not seen in weeks.

She glowered at Ciara from across the chamber with a distinct hatefulness, and for a moment he thought she might actually strike her down with another fireball or some other form of powerful magic. But she simply turned her head and stared at the dagger still deeply imbedded in the wooden desk. He saw it fly to her hand. She placed in within the pocket in her gown she wore beneath her cloak. He now noticed it was not actually a gown, but a long, white druid robe. In her hair she wore the blue flower he'd given her this night.

"Have her if you must, but know this, you'll not have me, not ever again, not that you appear to desire me in your life or in your bed any longer. But until she is gone from your castle mark my words, I shall not return."

He grew disheartened as he watched her head toward the door. "You cannot simply escape your troubles nor can you run or hide from the heartache; it shall simply follow you wherever you might flee, Alainn."

She turned to look at him when he'd spoken, but she narrowed her eyes and walked on without response.

"I'll see to it by my orders, the guards will not permit you to leave, nor will they lower the drawbridge!"

She glared back at him as she quickly started down the castle's many stone steps and he followed close behind. He saw her glance at the far off stables and immediately the doors flew open. The enormous, white steed burst forth from the stables as if he had wolves on its tail. It galloped toward her with such tremendous speed he thought it might charge her as it had previously. Only recently, Connor had told Killian he had made no progress with the spirited beast and he was beginning to form the same opinion as everyone else who had worked with the horse; it would remain untamable and entirely unmanageable.

Killian saw the horse stop before her and she and the beast stared into each other's eyes clearly communicating without a word spoken. He watched the animal kneel down on its two front legs. Alainn threw off her heavy cloak and he only then noticed how unusually warm the air had become. Everything around them grew steadily warmer. Even the wind had curiously changed and as it blew upon the frozen ground and frost covered trees, he heard them snapping, coming alive with the new magical warmth.

Alainn mounted the animal bareback and she clasped her hands in the golden mane. When it reared and lunged, he saw both the horse and the woman were entirely encircled in an ethereal glow. She'd pulled her own golden hair loose from its ties and let it hang free as he'd not seen it in an age. She looked at him with her eyes blazing and tugged the amulet from her neck and tossed it to him. He caught in his hand and listened to her warning.

"Keep this and wear it with your own amulet, Killian, and maybe then you'll be kept safe from the temptress's spells, for surely they'll glow bright in warning of you beginning to fall prey to her darkness or her wiles."

⌘

KILLIAN STARED UP at Alainn. She was enchantingly beautiful. He longed to call after her to say something… anything to make her stay with him, but he realized through her anger and furious emotion, she would surely one day gradually begin to return to the vivacious and impassioned woman she once had been. If Ciara was even half as untrustworthy and possibly evil as Alainn and Danhoul seemed to believe, and as hell-bent on seeing Alainn harmed, then maybe she would be safer away from Ciara and from him… for now. He would discover what he could to aptly confirm the suspicions regarding Ciara. If she was truly evil, capable of dark magic and he should order her sent her away, she might very well attempt further wrongdoings toward Alainn as a way to get back at him. Therefore, he would take advantage of this time with Alainn safely distanced from the woman, to learn the truth and then deal with Ciara accordingly once and for all.

He continued to stare, mesmerized by the powerful magic surrounding the two, woman and beast. It seemed to crackle upon the night air. He looked on in utter disbelief as large golden wings appeared upon the horse. He stared at her with regret in his eyes, of all that had transpired, and fear of what their future might hold.

He dared to question her, uncertain if he cared to know

the answers. "What will you do? Where do you intend to go, Alainn? Will you go to a fairy realm, the realm of the gods?" His face conveyed his dubiousness at the many uncertainties and he added, "Sure, you'd be wise to dwell with your grandfather, aye?"

As the winged-horse disbelievingly hovered above him in midair, he noticed the glimmer and sparkle of the magical light emanating from both of them. She called down to him in response.

"For now, I am uncertain where I might go but, wherever I go, know this, Killian. I will no longer turn from my magic; no longer rein in my powers and supernatural abilities or attempt to keep them hidden away. They are a magnanimous component of who I am. You may believe the tragedy that has befallen us came from me employing my powers, and perhaps that holds truth, but attempting to keep them concealed away, pretending they are not part of who I am, has also not benefitted us in any way."

Alainn sensed many guards would soon be upon them and she had no desire to put Killian in a position where he would need to explain the unusual supernatural happenings. She glanced at him with pain in her eyes.

"No matter what fate might befall us or what the future might hold for us, know this one certainty, I shall always, always love you, Killian O'Brien," she whispered softly on the wind as he watched as they magically flew off against the immense autumn moon, and into the star-filled sky.

"And I you, my Lainna!" he replied to the darkness.

⌘

IT WOUNDED HIM terribly to know this time they would be parted because Alainn had purposely chosen to leave. As he stooped to retrieve the blue flower that had fallen from her hair, Killian held on to the hope that one day she would return to him.

Killian despaired at the wretched thought of Alainn being gone indefinitely. He was already beginning to rue not finding the correct words to make her stay. Even now he longed to go after her to urge her to come back, but he believed he must allow her this time away. Alainn was correct, she must willingly accept and embrace her unusual magical abilities instead of turning from them or keeping them hidden away as she'd done in the past. Ultimately, she must take this time to learn the extent of her magic, to both hone and harness her powers.

As his eyes followed the bright magical glow in the distant sky, he prayed his heart could endure this separation, their love and marriage would one day benefit from it, and that their fates would soon be joined once more. But until then, for the first time in her life, Alainn would finally be permitted to live a witch's life.

THE END

Don't miss Leigh Ann Edwards' next book in…

THE IRISH WITCH SERIES

Available now at your favorite online retailer!

ABOUT THE AUTHOR

Since she was a child, Leigh Ann Edwards has always had a vivid imagination and lots of stories to tell. An enthusiastic traveler and author for over twenty years, her adventures in Massachusetts, Ireland, and the UK inspired The Farrier's Daughter and its sequel novels in the Irish Witch series. Edwards adores animals, history, genealogy, and magical places—and Ireland is filled with many magical places. She lives with her husband and two cats in the lovely city of Edmonton, Alberta.

Visit Leigh Ann at www.leighannedwards.com

Thank you for reading

THE CHIEFTAIN'S WIFE

If you enjoyed this book, you can find more from all our great authors at TulePublishing.com, or from your favorite online retailer.

TULE
PUBLISHING

Made in the USA
Columbia, SC
24 October 2017